7K   4631   Expires JULY

DETENTION IS SERVED

entitled to draw books from the
Public Library

and is responsible for all the books taken on this card,
which must be presented each time a book is taken or returned

Report Change of Address Promptly

DUE	RETURNED	DUE	RETURNED
NOV 4	NOV	SEPT 3	SEPT 2
DEC 5	DEC 5	SEPT 11	SEPT 11
DEC16	DEC17	OCT1	OCT 2
JAN	JAN	OCT6	---------
JAN 17	JAN 21	NOV	NOV2
JAN 30	JAN 30	NOV 18	NOV19
MAR	MAR 5	NOV19	
JUNE 12	JUNE 19	DEC 14	DEC 2
G 19		DEC 29	DEC 29

DO NOT LOSE THIS CARD.
BOOKS DRAWN ON IT EITHER WITH OR WITHOUT
YOUR CONSENT MUST BE AT YOUR RISK.
LOSS OF CARD DOES NOT RELEASE YOU
EVEN IF REPORTED

Annaliese Harper knows that one tiny mistake can jeopardize a career before it's even begun. Letting your boss find the extensive collection of porn on your personal laptop is one way. Sleeping with him is another. Liese manages to do both.

As the new librarian at a prestigious small-town private high school, Liese is drawn to her sexy, charismatic principal, Ryder Whitehall—an attraction she refuses to acknowledge given their relationship and her recent liberation from a delusional ex-boyfriend.

Liese is certain Ryder's flirtation is the product of her sex-deprived imagination—until he discovers her digital porn stash during working hours and demands a private meeting. Behind closed doors, their attraction explodes into a dangerous, passionate affair that not only threatens their jobs and reputations, but most of all, their hearts.

PRAISE FOR HELENA HUNTING'S NOVELS

"Characters that will touch your heart and a romance that will leave you breathless."

-*New York Times* bestselling author Tara Sue Me

"Gut wrenching, sexy, twisted, dark, incredibly erotic and a love story like no other. On my all-time favorites list."

-Alice Clayton, *New York Times* bestselling author of *Wallbanger* and The Redhead series

"A look into the world of tattoos and piercings, a dash of humor and a feel-good ending will delight fans and new readers alike."

-*Publishers Weekly* (on *Inked Armor*)

"A unique, deliciously hot, endearingly sweet, laugh out loud, fantastically good time romance!! . . . I loved every single page!!"

–*New York Times* Bestselling author Emma Chase on *PUCKED*

"Sigh inducing swoony and fanning myself sexy. All the stars!"

-*USA Today* bestselling author Daisy Prescott on The Pucked Series

"A hot rollercoaster of a ride!"

-Julia Kent, *New York Times* and *USA Today* bestselling author on *Pucked Over*

"*Pucked Over* is Helena Hunting's funniest and sexiest book yet. SCORCHING HOT with PEE INDUCING LAUGHS. All hail the Beaver Queen."

-T. M. Frazier, *USA Today* bestselling author

TITLES BY HELENA HUNTING

PUCKED SERIES
Pucked (Pucked #1)
Pucked Up (Pucked #2)
Pucked Over (Pucked #3)
Forever Pucked (Pucked Book #4)
Pucked Under (Pucked #5)
Pucked Off (Pucked #6)
Pucked Love (Pucked #7)
AREA 51: Deleted Scenes & Outtakes
Get Inked

THE CLIPPED WINGS SERIES
Cupcakes and Ink
Clipped Wings
Between the Cracks
Inked Armor
Cracks in the Armor
Fractures in Ink

SHACKING UP SERIES
Shacking Up
Getting Down (Novella)
Hooking Up
I Flipping Love You
Making Up
Handle with Care

STANDALONE NOVELS
The Librarian Principle
Felony Ever After

FOREVER ROMANCE STANDALONES
The Good Luck Charm
MEET CUTE
Kiss my Cupcake (August 2020)

All IN SERIES
A Lie for a Lie
A Favor for a Favor (January 2020)
A Secret for a Secret (May 2020)

THE *Librarian* PRINCIPLE

HELENA HUNTING

ACKNOWLEDGMENTS

Filets, you are the warmest hugs, the best cheerleaders and the most amazing friends. I'm so glad I have you.

Deb, you are made of win. I adore you. Nina, I still owe you a sequin cape. It'll be pink. Shannon, you design the best covers, squishy hugs.

Anne, Alex, Kris, Kathy and Danielle, this marked the first trip round the editing track. Yours will always be the voices I hear when I'm making changes!

Jessica, working with you has been amazing. Thank you for polishing up my words and putting the commas in all the right places. Midian, you are a doll, and I love you. Ryder is yours! Mayhem, you make the insides so pretty.

To my 101 girls, I never would have been able to navigate this whole process without you. I'm honored to be part of such a special group of women. Liv and Daisy, thank you for holding my hand, for helping me figure out what in the world I'm doing, and for being my friends. Marla, I'm so glad I got to work with you! To my HH Street Team and my Locker Room ladies, you're the best. I'm so glad I have such amazing readers.

As always, to my fandom friends, I'm blessed to have you and honored that you're coming along for this ride.

For my husband. You are the best.

1

Signs & Signals

ANNALIESE HARPER APPROACHED the threshold of the ornate library, a live wire of anxiety and anticipation. In mental preparation, she'd donned her mask of fake composure and steeled herself against the inevitable onslaught of awkward introductions. Still, nervous tension twisted her gut as she checked out the staff of Fullerton Academy of Higher Learning from the safety of the hall.

Before she could make her move, Liese's phone chimed in her purse, the volume loud enough to startle her. She whirled from where her colleagues were gathered, muttering a cleaned-up curse. The cavernous hallway had amazing acoustics, judging by the impressive echo of her heels on the marble floor. She glanced over her shoulder, but no one seemed to have noticed the noise.

She rooted around in her purse and located the device; palming the phone, she muted the volume before it could chime again. Too wound up to head back toward the library straight away, she keyed in her password and clicked on the message.

An image appeared on the tiny screen.

"Oh my God," Liese snorted. She slapped her palm over her mouth to stop from laughing aloud as she gawked at the photoshopped image. In a perverse gesture of camaraderie, her best friend had sent an *interesting* picture of Liese's new boss, the incredibly attractive principal at FAHL, Ryder Whitehall. The face, at least, was his, but based on the substantial endowment hanging a little to the left, the body belonged to a porn star. She couldn't wait to get home to view the full-screen version in her email.

"Ms. Harper?" The voice came from behind her.

She jumped and fumbled with her phone. In a protective, graceless move, she clutched it to her chest for a moment before frantically punching the off button. She shoved it back in her purse and turned to find the principal in question standing mere feet away.

Her eyes were level with his chest, and his brilliant red tie seemed to function as an arrow, pointing down to where she shouldn't be looking. Despite herself, Liese took a moment to appreciate the fit of his suit and the way it hugged the long, muscular lines of his body. His shirt had to be tailored with the way it pulled across his chest, highlighting broad shoulders that tapered into a narrow waist. She imagined he must be cut under all those clothes, a thought she knew she shouldn't ruminate on overly much.

She looked up; at five-foot-seven Liese wasn't particularly short, but her principal had a good six inches on her, forcing her to tilt her head back to make eye contact. She made a concerted effort to keep her eyes on his face, lest her gaze wander lower, her mind still stuck on the pornographic image she'd been ogling.

Not that looking at his face was a problem. His eyes were a vibrant, rather mesmerizing shade of aquamarine, sucking her in. His short, dark hair was neatly styled, and Liese had the inexcusable desire to run her fingers through and mess it up. The straight line of his nose contrasted sharply with the soft, full curve of his lips.

"Mr. Whitehall, hi, hello." Liese cringed internally at the high, edgy tenor of her voice.

Mr. Whitehall leaned in, close enough that she could feel the apocalyptic heat he emitted. "It's just Ryder unless there are students present, Ms. Harper." His amused smile should have helped relax her, but it flustered her more. As did his proximity.

"Right, of course, Ryder."

"Nervous?"

"Unbearably."

He gave her shoulder a gentle squeeze. "You have nothing to fear. You'll fit in perfectly here." He inclined his head in the direction of the library. "If you find it helpful, we can discuss any additional questions after orientation."

"That sounds great." Liese gave him a genuine smile as he guided her down the hall and through the door, his fingertips brushing the back of her arm. The unexpected contact sent a shiver down her spine. He motioned to the right, where a table had been set up. Liese signed the attendance sheet while Ryder bent next to her and located her orientation package.

Unfamiliar colleagues milled about, many finding a place to sit. Worried about the seating arrangements and not knowing anyone, Liese scanned the room for empty chairs while also scoping out her coworkers. Her unease must have been obvious because Ryder took pity on her and introduced her to several staff members. She tried to pay attention to her colleagues' names and disciplines rather than fixate on the number of times Ryder touched her arm. She was almost relieved when Harvey Little, the assistant principal, motioned him to the front of the room. Ryder flashed Liese an encouraging smile and joined his second-in-command.

Dry mouthed, she grabbed a refreshment and set her things down at an empty table. She didn't like the way Ryder's touch affected her ability to think straight. The raw attraction that accompanied such benign contact with him caused alarm bells to ring in her head. Having a good-looking boss was one thing; crushing on him was entirely another.

Liese pretended to be interested in her orientation packet to pass the time. She hated the initial discomfort that accompanied meeting new people. Her goal wasn't just making friends; she needed to suss out her colleagues. High school teachers, like high school students, could be cliquey. The last thing she wanted was to take up residence beside the chatty teacher who would talk through the entire meeting and made her look bad.

"Hey, mind if I sit here?"

Liese looked up to find a tall, lean, well-dressed man with sandy blond hair and brown eyes smiling down at her. He looked safe. "Sure. Go ahead." She returned the grin and motioned to the empty seats.

"You must be our new librarian." He dropped into the chair opposite her and leaned back, stretching his legs out.

"Um, yeah, that's me. How'd you know?" She held out her hand. "I'm Liese Harper."

"Blake Stone, lone drama teacher." He leaned forward and shook her hand before reclining in his chair once again. "There were only two new hires this year. The other guy teaches science, and I met him when I was grabbing a coffee," he said. "Oh right. Well, it's nice to know I'm not the only new person here." She glanced around the room. No one else looked as out of place as she felt at that particular moment. Nonetheless, Liese steered the conversation, asking questions about Blake's program and what it took to run a full production as the sole drama teacher. "It must be a huge time commitment for you," she prompted.

"Sure, but I love doing it, and so do the students, so it's worth it. If you want to help out with this year's play, let me know. No pressure, though." He winked and looked over her shoulder, waving enthusiastically.

Liese turned to see a tall slip of a woman slide into the seat beside her. Her short blond hair was cut into a straight-edged bob, and thick-framed, funky glasses perched on her nose. "Don't tell me he's already trying to recruit you to help him with one of his plays. Don't do it. Blake is a perfectionist pain in the ass. You'd think he was running Broadway or something with his diva attitude." Authenticity was absent in her warning. She gave Liese a warm smile. "I'm Emily Captain. I teach art and art history."

"Liese Harper, the new librarian." She took Emily's outstretched hand.

"Don't listen to anything this one says." Blake brushed off Emily's comment. She retaliated by flicking a paperclip at him. Theirs seemed to be a long-standing friendship.

Conversation turned to summer holidays and start-up plans for the fall, with more teachers joining the table as it drew closer to nine o'clock.

Emily flipped through her package and turned it around to Blake. "Have you seen this? They haven't tried to outlaw it, but they sure are making it a big deal."

Highlighted by bright yellow paper was a photocopied article on workplace harassment issues, including a bolded section on inter-collegial dating.

Blake scoffed. "I bet this is because of that principal in Berks County."

"What principal?" Liese asked.

"The one who got caught having an affair with a teacher," Emily explained.

"I'm pretty sure it wasn't an affair. Neither one of them was married, from what I read, so that makes it a relationship." Blake noted as he flipped through the pages of the orientation package.

He appeared uninterested in the topic, and Liese looked surreptitiously at Ryder. Her thoughts turned to the slew of images her best friend had been sending since Liese had accepted the position at FAHL. She'd gone on endlessly about Ryder's attributes, both physical and intellectual, and in return, Marissa had indulged her with ridiculously porno-riffic pictures. Liese hadn't thought it much of an issue until now. However, keeping a folder of doctored images featuring her principal might not be the most ethical practice.

"Whatever. Relationship, affair, it doesn't matter either way." Emily gave him a withering look and turned to Liese. "Can you even imagine?"

"Teachers date each other all time," Blake replied, gesturing to the yellow sheet in front of him.

"That's different," Emily said.

"Not really."

Emily ignored him and turned her attention to Liese. "I heard the principal was transferred to an inner-city school, and the teacher has gone on the substitute list and can't get a contract anywhere. It's all political."

"They're consenting adults," Blake countered. "Personally, I would never date a colleague because it's a recipe for disaster. But I don't care what anyone else does, just so long as I don't find them doing it in the staff room." He twirled a pen between his fingers. "I think the whole thing is ridiculous."

"Ridiculous or not, two careers have been ruined because of it." Emily lowered her voice further. "And I think you're full of crap. You would've dated that history sub last year if she'd shown some interest."

"Are you kidding me? Never. She wasn't my type." Blake wrinkled his nose. "Come on, Liese, you must have an opinion on this—"

Caught up in the sudden image of her and Ryder going at it on this very table, Liese sputtered. Before she'd recovered enough to comment, Ryder stepped to the front of the room.

His voice carried above the din, and conversation ceased as soon as he uttered a word. "Good morning and welcome." All eyes moved to where he stood, posture relaxed. But for all his approachability, Liese could see and feel the way his presence commanded the staff's attention.

He scanned the crowd while everyone waited silently for him to continue. When his eyes caught hers, she felt a flush of embarrassment reach her cheeks. The corner of his mouth lifted slightly before he cleared his throat and addressed the faculty. Liese leafed through her package as he spoke to avoid staring. Compelling and articulate, his charismatic presence made it nearly impossible to tear her eyes away from him. The smooth cadence of his voice made even the driest of school protocols seem riveting. She even stopped imagining him naked for a few minutes, she became so enraptured.

At the end of the meeting, the principal formally introduced both new staff members, which meant she had to stand up and address everyone. Though she spoke for just a moment, for Liese, wearing a wool thong to a marathon seemed comfortable in comparison. She was relieved when the staff began to disperse and chat amongst themselves, and the colleagues at her table invited her for a drink later in the afternoon. She readily accepted, eager for the security that came with a group of friendly peers.

Ryder approached her as she gathered her things. "Any questions?"

"Probably a million, but none I can think of right now." She smiled.

"If you think of anything, you know how to get in touch with me. In the meantime, I'll forward you the list of potential advisors, and we can discuss who would be an appropriate match."

"Thanks. That would be wonderful." Liese had no idea what he meant by potential advisors. She must have zoned out during that part. She made a mental note to review the package to ensure she hadn't missed other crucial points.

Over the weeks that followed, Liese found she meshed well with the staff at FAHL, as Ryder had been confident she would. She had only two issues: first, even after Blake finally explained the role of a teacher advisor, Liese still hadn't managed to settle on a candidate from the list the principal provided. There were plenty of seasoned colleagues to choose from, but her unique position made it difficult to find someone who fit her needs. By mid-October she still hadn't made a decision.

Well, perhaps she had, but the one person she felt would be perfect for the role was the one she couldn't ask. That person was also issue number two. Liese couldn't contain her growing infatuation with Ryder Whitehall. The more she learned about him, the more alluring he became. And he made himself freely available to her as she settled into her new position; he was always there to answer questions and provide reassurance. Combine that with his admirable background in education and his authoritative, no-nonsense demeanor, and she practically melted whenever he came near her.

Late in October, he stopped by the library while Liese was cataloging new resources. As she stretched up on her toes to return a book to the top shelf, Ryder plucked it from her hand, his chest touching her shoulder as he shelved it.

"Thanks." Her response sounded breathless.

"Any time."

"How can I help you?" She needlessly rearranged several books, determined to avoid eye contact for as long as possible.

"It's come to my attention that you still don't have an advisor."

"I've been meaning to talk to you about that." Of course, that wasn't even remotely true. She had been evading the topic altogether.

"So you've found someone suitable?"

Liese smiled at his phrasing. She found his formality charming. "Not exactly," she hedged.

"Have you spoken to the staff members on the list I provided? Are you having difficulty finding someone to fill the role?"

"It's not that. I mean, no, I'm not having difficulty. It's just that what I need in an advisor isn't quite . . ." Liese sighed and rubbed her forehead. "I know it's not traditional, but I'm wondering if you could advise me. Your background supports the initiatives I'm interested in pursuing, and I already ask you all the questions I would ask my advisor. It could be a very informal role." She stopped rambling and pursed her lips, unsure how to read his complete lack of response. "It was a bad idea, never mind."

Ryder remained expressionless for a long moment.

"Principals don't typically take on advisor roles."

"I know. I'm sorry. I didn't mean to put you in an awkward position, sir."

Something dark flashed in his eyes, and his jaw tightened imperceptibly. "I said *typically*. However, I believe in this case I'd be willing to make an exception."

"Seriously?"

"Mmm, seriously." Ryder nodded, apparently amused by her reaction.

In a moment of impulse, Liese threw her arms around him. His body went rigid as she came flush against him, the air around them humming with energy. Lurid images formed in her mind, and Liese let go immediately, irrationally afraid he would absorb her thoughts through osmosis. She swore she'd felt his fingertips at her waist as she stepped away—as if he'd thought to hug her back at the very last second.

"I'm sorry. I didn't mean to do that." Her face felt like it was on fire.

Ryder blinked twice, his chest rising and falling as he took a deep breath. "It's fine," he said, his voice low and rough. He cleared his throat and smoothed his tie. "However, for the sake of propriety, I'd suggest any further displays of gratitude be saved for times when there aren't witnesses."

Liese glanced down the aisle, expecting to see a group of students with mouths agape, only to discover they were entirely alone. But it wasn't hard to imagine the kind of rumors that would start if they were seen engaged in such a public display of affection, and between the stacks no less.

Ryder's eyes went wide with mock horror. "How would I ever maintain order if the students found out I'd gone soft?"

"There would be absolute chaos," she replied, expression somber. "Food fights in the cafeteria."

"Overdue library books," he whispered.

"Oh, the insanity!" Liese grinned, the tension dissipating.

"Come see me at the end of the day, and we can set up a first meeting." Ryder moved past her, the back of his hand skimming her hip as he departed down the aisle.

Liese watched him leave, both elated and troubled. She'd gotten what she wanted; he'd agreed to be her advisor. But the feelings he evoked were still problematic. She'd be spending more time with him now, alone. If there hadn't been reason to fret before, there certainly was now.

2

Meetings & Miscommunication

"I HAVE A meeting with the principal tomorrow after work, so I'll be late getting into the city," Liese told Marissa, over the phone. The apology was implied.

It had been a few weeks since their last visit, and she was beginning to experience withdrawal. Leaving later wasn't necessarily a bad thing, though; she wouldn't have to contend with the worst of rush-hour traffic in NYC.

Liese put Marissa on speakerphone as she rummaged in her underwear drawer. She picked up a lacy, white thong and debated the merits of wearing sexy lingerie under her clothes when Ryder would never see it. Something about wrapping her best assets in pretty things made her feel empowered. Confidence inspired by lace and satin, as it were.

"Didn't you just have one last week?" Marissa asked. Liese could practically hear her wheels of perversion turning.

"We meet weekly." She searched for the matching bra and held up the two pieces together. If her blouse weren't white, she would have opted for her navy pinstriped set, or maybe something black. She could wear a sweater vest to hide them, but then she'd be too warm, as being in his presence gave her hot flashes.

"Is that normal?"

"Um, I guess? I'm not really sure because I've never had an advisor before, but I've been doing a lot of research. I want to get this literacy project up and running before second semester. Based on the research studies, it will improve test scores on the state exams in the spring. He's completely supportive of the initiative, and he's the one who arranges the meetings, so I assume it's common practice. We'll probably meet less often once the logistics are worked out." Liese frowned at the thought. She rather enjoyed her frequent meetings with Ryder.

"Okay, whatever you say, most of that sounded like nerd gibberish to me. But I find it interesting that he plans these meetings for Friday afternoons."

"He has a busy schedule; the end of the week works for him." Liese moved to her closet and pulled out a navy skirt and freshly pressed blouse.

"Don't you find it suspect that this hot, sexy man has nothing better to do with his time than meet his advisee afterhours on a Friday?" Marissa pressed.

"Don't even start. He's not interested in me like that. It's strictly a professional relationship." Liese twirled a lock of hair around her fingers as she surveyed her shoe selection. "Red heels or navy pumps?"

"Red heels, obviously. And I call bullshit on the professional relationship. No man gives up his Friday for the welfare of the education system, no matter how devoted he is to the cause. Besides, you're so hot for this guy you're on fire, *and* you're asking me about footwear."

"Navy pumps it is. It's an hour of his Friday afternoon, not the evening. And it doesn't matter if I find him attractive; nothing is going to happen." The latter half of that statement had become her mantra. Liese rationalized that if she told herself often enough, eventually she would adopt it as truth.

"You keep saying that like you think I'm going to buy it, and don't you dare wear pumps. Why do you even have pumps? Those shouldn't be an option. Ever." Liese prepared to defend her footwear, but Marissa cut her off. "Just send me a message when you're done being bent over Ride-Me's desk tomorrow—or whatever the hell it is you two do during these so-called meetings."

"Marissa!" Liese didn't know what was more undignified, Marissa's new nickname for Ryder, or how much she personally appreciated the image of being bent over his desk.

"See you tomorrow!" A dial tone followed, leaving Liese shaking her head.

Since Ryder had agreed to be her advisor over a month ago, they'd been meeting regularly after school. It wasn't unusual for staff to stay well past the end of the school day for a variety of extracurriculars, so Liese hadn't thought much of it. Friday seemed like a logical option, as most school meetings took place between Monday and Thursday. Besides, as an administrator, Ryder often had late meetings beyond those, and Liese was only too willing to work with what his schedule demanded.

The problem was, what had started as a harmless attraction was turning into a full-on infatuation. After each meeting, Liese would psychoanalyze their conversation, dissecting every glance and scrutinizing every touch, looking for some verification that the connection she swore she felt was real. It was beginning to drive her batty. And Marissa wasn't much help with her constant flow of photoshopped images.

The following morning, Liese spent an unconscionable amount of time primping before she left for work. Despite her preparations the day before, she changed her underwear three times; berating herself all the while because she continued to indulge in the ridiculous fantasy that Ryder might have romantic inclinations toward her. Still, she finally settled on the white satin and lace, complete with thigh-high stockings and garters. She was such a masochist. Even if Principal Whitehall felt something beyond collegial friendship, he was far too in control to ever act on the impulse.

By the end of the day, Liese's state of being hovered somewhere between nauseated and anticipatory as the final bell rang and students vacated the building, chattering happily about their weekend plans. Her office line rang just as she was about to lock up the library, and she smiled when the principal's extension came up. Her stomach twisted as she reached for the receiver, and she chastised herself for getting worked up. He was probably checking to make sure she hadn't forgotten their meeting. As if she could.

It turned out he wanted to relocate the meeting to her office, as his secretary was staying late, and he didn't want any interruptions. That was fine with her; the more privacy the better.

She checked her appearance in the compact mirror she kept in her desk drawer and applied a fresh layer of lip gloss. Coincidentally, she'd started keeping makeup at work after Ryder had agreed to be her advisor. The concealer she put on helped hide her under-eye circles from lack of sleep—thanks to her edginess. Her excitement over the impending meeting was too pervasive to be healthy. She ran her fingers through her hair, embarrassed by the amount of time she'd spent on it this morning with a curling iron. Ryder had once commented that he liked it wavy. She felt pathetic about the way such offhand remarks stuck with her.

Liese was in the middle of adjusting her skirt when her phone chimed. She dug in her purse and found Marissa had sent her a message. Against her better judgment, she checked it. There was no text, only a photo, and it was too small in the message window to adequately discern the content. She clicked the image, and it expanded on the screen.

A noise that sounded vaguely like a cat dying escaped her. Marissa had done it again. Ryder's head was superimposed onto the body of yet another well-hung porn star, and this time the image also included a woman—superimposed with Liese's face—sprawled out over a desk, much like the one she stood in front of now.

"Hi there."

Liese screamed, caught completely unaware. She turned to find Ryder standing in her office doorway, leaning against the jamb, his coat thrown over his arm, briefcase in hand. His suit jacket was unbuttoned, giving him a more relaxed look than usual. And sexier. If that was possible.

"Sorry, I didn't mean to frighten you," he said. "You seemed rather invested in whatever you were reading just now." Liese hit the button on her phone, and the screen went blank.

"It was my girlfriend," she explained.

Ryder stared at her, unblinking.

At his lack of reaction, she elaborated. "My best friend— she's expecting me later this evening. She was just checking in."

"Oh." He sounded relieved. "Am I keeping you? We can reschedule for next week if you need to go."

"No, no, it's fine. I'm happy to meet with you, unless you have another engagement." Liese slid her phone back into her purse, turning off the volume as she did so.

"I have no prior engagements."

Their eyes locked on each other for a few interminable seconds before Liese realized they were on her territory, and she should invite him in. "Would you like to work in my office or out there?" Liese gestured to the empty library beyond.

He glanced over his shoulder and then surveyed their current surroundings. "I think your office would be more private."

"Sure. Right." Liese nodded, clutching the back of her chair.

"Unless you'd be more comfortable working out there," he supplied, watching her from his spot in the doorway.

"What? Oh, no. Not at all. I'm perfectly comfortable with you in me."

His shock formed a counterpoint to her horror.

"In my office! I'm perfectly comfortable working with you *in my office*." Heat crawled up her chest to find a home in her cheeks. "I need some water, can I get you anything?" she asked.

It was best to pretend she hadn't made that comment. Though she could have sworn she heard him chuckle as he hung up his coat and dropped his briefcase beside her desk . . . She opened one of the overhead cupboards, filled mostly with school supplies, and retrieved two glasses. Her hands shook as she held each of them beneath the spout on the water cooler.

"Liese." Ryder was right beside her, the smell of his cologne a heady intoxication as she inhaled deeply. She needed to get a handle on her emotions before she managed to embarrass herself further. Usually she could maintain better control of her mouth. "I'm sorry," she whispered.

He gently pried the glass from her hand and set it on the desk. "Don't be. I'm not offended."

"I didn't mean to . . . I shouldn't have . . . sometimes you make me nervous," she blurted. "Damnit. Why can't I just shut the hell up?"

Ryder burst out laughing.

"I'm so glad my humiliation amuses you," Liese said.

Ryder reached around her for the half-filled glass, his arm sliding against her back, completely disarming her. The physical contact was accidental—of course it was—but it still had an impact. She should be used to the way his presence affected her by now. But no matter how hard she tried to convince herself these were just meetings between professionals, her body and her mind seemed to exist on two separate planes, and neither conferred with the other. Hence she couldn't speak without it coming out all wrong.

"I apologize. Shall we start again?" he asked, fighting a smile.

Liese gave him a baleful glare.

Ryder ignored it and topped off the glass, handing it to Liese.

"How was your day, Ms. Harper?"

"Horrible," she said into the cup.

"Oh? Would you like to talk about it?"

"Not really. Thanks for asking."

"I see." He paused. When she said nothing, he nudged her with his elbow. "This would be a good time to ask me how my day was, since we're being cordial with each other."

"How was your day, Mr. Whitehall?"

"It's Ryder."

"You called me Ms. Harper," Liese pointed out.

"My mistake, Annaliese."

"Liese."

"Liese."

"Would you stop it!" Liese flicked the lapel of his suit jacket in exasperation, her embarrassment diffused. He was good at that: relieving the tension in an awkward moment. They'd certainly had enough of them during their meetings.

"That's better. I'll take you feisty over subdued any day. Shall we get down to business?" Ryder gestured to her desk, where she'd laid out her research prior to his arrival.

There was something in his comment . . . while not overt, Liese caught a subtle undertone of implication. Or maybe she was reading too much into things again.

"Sounds good." Liese crossed the room and sat in her chair while Ryder pulled one up beside her. He loosened his tie and undid the top button on his shirt. Sidling in close, he picked up the folder with her most recent research.

They spent the next two hours poring over documents. She found herself enraptured by the breadth of his knowledge and his passionate stance. She couldn't decide what she was attracted to more, his intellect or his exterior. The combination was lethal—the worst kind of aphrodisiac imaginable. She counted every instance in which his shoulder touched hers, every comment with an undercurrent of teasing, every moment of prolonged eye contact. She was sure she could plot a graph to demonstrate the rise in all three over the time they'd spent together. Then she could plot a second one to illustrate how her level of infatuation correlated with those findings.

Liese shifted in her chair and reached across her desk for the chart they were discussing at the same time Ryder did. They knocked shoulders, and his fingers brushed the back of her hand. Flustered, she rolled back in her chair, sending several sheets fluttering to the floor.

"Sorry." She bent to pick them up.

He pushed back his chair, too, ever the gentleman. "Nice shoes," he said as he retrieved several pieces of paper.

"Thanks." Liese couldn't believe he'd noticed them. Maybe Marissa had been right.

They nearly cracked heads as they sat up at the same time, both holding fragments of her research. Ryder's eyes dropped to her lap and stayed there. Liese looked down to find that her skirt had ridden up, leaving the lace band of her thigh highs peeking out from the hem. Shuffling the papers into one hand, she smoothed a palm over her thigh, pushing her skirt back down to cover the garters she should never have worn in the first place. She glanced up at Ryder, who continued to focus on her lap.

The sudden buzz of her phone as it rattled against her keys snapped him out of the trance.

"Would you like to check that?" he asked, clearing his throat as he yanked on his tie.

"It's probably my friend Marissa." She discarded the papers and plucked her purse from the floor beside her desk, sifting through the contents until she located her phone. Marissa had sent her a message and left her a voicemail. Liese had no intention of checking either with Ryder seated beside her.

He looked at his watch. "I've monopolized your time long enough."

It was nearing six, well beyond the initial length of their meetings. Each subsequent meeting seemed to stretch on a little longer. At first it had been an hour, then a bit more, and now tonight they'd spent well over two hours talking, and not always about her research. In fact, the conversation had deviated frequently to topics bearing no relevance to education.

After they'd settled on a date for their next meeting, Ryder and Liese gathered their things. He helped her into her jacket, which smelled vaguely of his cologne since his coat had been humping hers for the past couple of hours.

He waited as she turned out the lights and locked up the library. They traveled the darkened, empty halls of the school together, the click of her heels echoing loudly around them. Ryder held the door for her as they left the building, his hand at her elbow as they descended the stairs to the parking lot. The lot was well-lit, and Liese had parked beneath one of the lights, which now illuminated her modest vehicle. Ryder walked her to her car and stood with his hand in his pocket as she put the key in the lock.

Liese had the ridiculous urge to hug him, or make out with him, as if they'd been on some kind of date. She really needed to stop indulging in her customized porn album right before bed; the dreams the images inspired didn't help keep reality separated from fantasy. "Have a nice weekend."

"You as well." Ryder held her door open as she slipped into the driver's seat. He hesitated and leaned in as she turned the key in the ignition. Liese turned her head in his direction and waited. For a moment she had the irrational notion he might kiss her.

"One last thing," he said with quiet seriousness. "Just so you're aware, sometimes you make me nervous, too. See you Monday." He retreated and closed the door. More confused than ever, all she could do was gape after him as he crossed the parking lot. How the hell was she *not* supposed to read into a comment like *that*?

3

Porn at Work is Bad

LIESE HADN'T BEEN able to get the principal's parting comment on Friday out of her head. All weekend she kept imagining what could've happened if she'd had the guts to make some kind of move. Maybe she should've grabbed him by the tie and yanked him into the car. Each fantasy became more and more explicit, until she'd concocted an entire scene, which ended with them in the back seat of her sedan, windows fogged.

On Monday, Liese couldn't wait to show Ryder the research she'd come up with over the weekend. She figured it was a good excuse to see him for a few minutes under the guise of professional business. But she was such a wreck in the morning she misplaced her thumb drive and ended up bringing her whole laptop to work instead.

Nevertheless, luck was on her side; the principal popped by the library during lunch, giving her the opportunity she'd been looking for. It might not have been a private meeting, but she'd take what she could get.

Liese stood behind the checkout desk with her laptop propped open in front of her. Ryder drove her to distraction as she tried to locate the right folder. He stood behind her, so close she could hear him breathe. Liese felt like a nuclear plant ready to combust. In the midst of all this, she was thankful for the good sense to stay put, otherwise she would have succumbed to the impulse to step back into him. Fortunately, her brain seemed to function independently of her hormones for the time being—sort of. Mostly. Not really.

Electric lust permeated the air around her as the images she'd conjured over the weekend resurfaced. Liese shut them down, though, because taming her physical, emotional, intellectual, and sexual response to Ryder in the presence of others had become her second job. Also, there were students present, and making a pass at him in front of them breeched the realm of inappropriate. Not that she hadn't contemplated the idea anyway.

Though she'd been successful thus far in managing the impulse, it was becoming increasingly difficult to control. During the privacy of their meetings, his mask of professionalism dropped. He was passionate, well spoken, funny, attentive, and encouraging—none of which should have been an issue. They were all traits she wanted in an advisor.

Unfortunately, those same traits were what she sought in a boyfriend, and disentangling the two prospective roles proved a challenge. Not that she wanted to date Ryder. She only wanted to re-enact every single one of the photoshopped scenarios Marissa had sent her over the past months. Some of which were incredibly debauched.

Initially she discounted the sly glances and inadvertent touches she and Ryder had shared. As individual episodes, she hadn't misconstrued them as improper, but cumulatively—well, that was something else. When he let his guard down and teased her, Liese tried to convince herself it meant nothing. It wasn't flirting. But it was difficult when he followed up with comments about how she made him nervous, too. With so many conflicting emotions, Liese worried she would crack soon, which could have a catastrophic effect on their professional relationship.

"It'll just take a second." She glanced over her shoulder, fretfully clicking through folders.

Ryder rocked back on his heels, his hands shoved into the pockets of his pants, smiling patiently. "Take your time." His voice was luscious caramel, wrapped in dark chocolate and rolled in sugar. She had the unconscionable craving to lick him and find out if he tasted as good as he sounded.

Liese found herself caught in the vivid teal of his eyes until they opened wide and his jaw dropped. One hand came up to pull at the collar of his shirt, and he coughed in a way that sounded much like a groan.

Liese's head whipped around as the laptop screen flashed with bold red letters spelling out the word *LUBE*, followed by the encouraging tag line: "Ease into ecstasy." In the ensuing video, the "easing" was anything but gentle. The figures slapped harshly against each other, making Liese thankful for the lack of sound. And, of course, the graphic scene was completed by Liese and Ryder's heads photoshopped onto the fornicating bodies.

Her own stupidity smacked her in the face. She could lose her job over something like this and end up banned from working in a school. Shame rushed through her as she slammed the laptop shut; a futile apology spilled forth. "Oh my God! That wasn't what I meant to show you. I'm so sorry, Mr. Whitehall."

She spun to face him, checking the library to be sure no students had witnessed the show. Ryder looked positively irate.

Although losing her job scared her, Liese also feared how this would taint his opinion of her.

His nostrils flared as he breathed, unmoving except for his mouth when his lips parted in preparation to speak. "That's quite obvious, Ms. Harper." His voice was a heavy rasp.

Liese opened her mouth, closed it, and opened it again, only to find no words would come out as the tension between them morphed from embarrassment and shock to something magnetic and dangerous.

Ryder addressed the students seated around the study tables. "Ladies and gentleman, the library is closed for the remainder of the period." Completely in control, he embodied the cool authority that so enamored Liese. Currently, it also terrified her.

The students sitting at the computer banks and tables fell silent. They looked up in unison, regarded their principal with a mix of fear and awe, and hurriedly packed their books, stealing curious glances on the way out. Ryder followed behind them, a forced smile plastered on his face. He ushered the stragglers into the hall, closed the door behind them, and turned to face Liese.

She'd seen him angry with students before. Hell, she'd seen him angry with other staff members, but this was something new altogether. Fury seethed below the surface, fused with a foreign emotion. Her mouth went dry as he returned. Her unspoken desire—the fragile thing she'd worked so hard to quell—merged with a sense of dread. Her heart raced and her palms felt damp.

"You have no idea how much trouble you're in." His tone held none of the subversive humor that typically colored their private exchanges.

She swallowed as he stopped in front of her. The way he loomed over her now made her weak in the knees. The notion their relationship could be anything more than professional should never have entered her mind, no matter the temptation.

"I can explain." Her eyes darted around the room in search of an escape she knew didn't exist.

"Your office. Now," he ordered, grabbing her laptop in one hand and her wrist with the other.

Though she was horrified, his warm fingers wrapped around her wrist thrilled her. The pull she fought ignited, flashing across her skin like fire. And then she remembered this might be the end of her career. He propelled her into the library office and dropped the laptop on her desk. He released her wrist and shut the door, turning the lock.

"Do you have any idea—" His eyes blazed, the words cut short as he tugged at his tie. Liese watched apprehensively as he paced the room, his head down, fingers gripping the back of his neck, jaw working as he ground his teeth together. She couldn't begin to imagine what he would do if he saw some of the other images she'd saved.

He gestured to the laptop. "What the hell was that!?"

Liese jumped, a squeaky sound came out of her, and she clapped a hand over her mouth. Ryder rarely raised his voice.

It would be in her best interest not to reveal that her best friend had created a whole series of photoshopped pictures of the two of them. She also thought it wise not to say anything about the folder she'd created to store them, or how they fed her unhealthy infatuation with him. Or how they functioned as her primary source of masturbatory material.

"It was mostly a joke," she mumbled.

"Do you think this is *funny*?" He looked incredulous as he towered over her, but his voice was smooth silk. Livid though he was, the tension between them pulsed like shock waves through the air.

"Not particularly, no," Liese replied, refusing to look away for fear of appearing weak, or guilty. If she could maintain a façade of self-righteous indignation, maybe he wouldn't touch her laptop again. In her peripheral vision, Liese noted the way his hands continued to clench and unclench at his sides. "Where did that picture come from? Are there more?" Much to her dismay, his palm settled on the laptop.

"I really wouldn't—"

Ryder ignored her half-made request and flipped it open. It only took a few seconds for the screen to flicker to life and the advertisement to pop up. The gif played in a loop, the vigorous pumping continuing endlessly.

Liese sighed. "I don't think there's a way to explain this without it sounding incredibly bad."

She buried her face in her hands and wished she could disappear as Ryder began to inspect the advertisement. Liese peeked through her fingers to watch him lean forward, hands splayed on either side of the laptop. He squinted at the image, and then looked her over. His eyes moved down her body and back up, tracking her with an expression that bordered on predatory. Satisfied fascination knotted Liese's stomach as the change took place: the undeniable draw she'd kept in check all this time echoed in his eyes. Some invisible line had been crossed, and Liese doubted she'd be able to return to the safety of the other side—the side where she pretended the attraction was all in her head.

"Please tell me that's not you." A note of aggression lent a sharp and bitter tang to the words. His fingers flexed against the desk, the tips turning white with pressure.

"It's not my body," Liese whispered, shaking her head.

"You're quite sure about that?"

"It's photoshopped."

"Is that so?" He quirked an eyebrow, relief relaxed the tense line of his jaw. He inspected the scene again, apparently no longer fazed by the naked, gyrating bodies now that he knew she hadn't made a porno and pasted his head on her previous partner. Ryder minimized the picture, allowing a series of folders to pop up on the screen.

"Do you have any idea how fortunate you are?" he asked as he moved the cursor over the page. "I don't think you understand the gravity of this situation. If anyone other than me had seen this, you would have been terminated immediately, regardless of how well you do your job."

"I'm really so—" Liese stopped mid-apology, her eyes drawn to the moving cursor. "Don't open that!" she screeched, lunging forward to cover the flood of thumbnails. He caught her hand mid-air, and her collection of Ryder-inspired porn became a glaring beacon on the screen.

"Jesus," he choked, his fingers gripping hers, keeping her close as he processed the images. And there were a hell of a lot of them. "What the . . ."

There were more than thirty thumbnails, so it was difficult to figure out which photo held his attention until he slid his finger across the mouse and clicked on an image.

It exploded onto the screen like a porn-tastic grenade. Of all the pictures available in her "RW" file, he had to choose this one. Liese had never taken the time to fully appreciate the lengths to which Marissa had gone to make the photos realistic, but this particular image showcased her talent well. Her knowledge of Liese's pornographic predilections might have been embarrassing, but Ryder bearing witness to them was a humiliation too severe to endure.

Liese saw herself perched on all fours on the bed, her long hair wrapped around "Ryder's" hand as he took her doggy style. The fingers of his free hand were anchored in the black satin laces holding her leather corset together. A blindfold covered her eyes. Black garters and ripped hose completed the look. The action shot had caught the penetration mid-thrust, lending it an erotic charge some of the other pictures lacked. That and the red handprint on her ass.

"Sweet mother of all things holy. Am I . . . Are you . . . Is that?" He released her hand and used the table for support to get a better look at the image. Ryder exhaled a labored breath, and his fingers went to his mouth, tapping at his lip in agitation.

Liese couldn't recall a previous occasion when he'd been anything less than composed and articulate. And she had no justifiable defense for the image. But part of her wanted him to react to it, wanted the wanting to stop so they could just give in already.

"They're photoshopped," she repeated.

His gaze lifted, and the heaviness of it made her squirm. "Yes, you've mentioned that already. My question is where the hell did the photos come from?"

"Um, well . . ." Liese hesitated, trying to think of a way to word it without making the situation worse. "It's . . . it's difficult to explain."

"Explain anyway," he ordered.

"It's embarrassing," she warned. For a fleeting moment she considered elbowing him out of the way and smashing the laptop. Then there would be no more proof the pictures existed. However, she doubted she was fast enough, or strong enough, to get it from him. Also, replacing it would be costly, and if she was out of a job that would be even more difficult.

Ryder's index finger made a continual circuit around the perimeter of the machine. "I imagine it is. However, I still want to know where the photos came from and whether I should be concerned about finding them posted all over the Internet."

"Oh, God no. Marissa—my friend made them. She meant to be funny, although she didn't really succeed. I mean, obviously I'm not laughing at those photos." Liese motioned to the screen, her face reddening. Ryder continued to glare at her in silence. "She knew I thought you were . . . she wanted to . . . I—I—"

"You thought I was what?"

Liese ducked her head, focusing on his tie, which seemed the safest place to keep her eyes. "It's really not appropriate."

"And this is?"

Liese wanted to rewind her day and go back to the moment she'd misplaced her thumb drive. If she'd taken another minute to look around, or had the foresight to email the damn document to Ryder instead, she wouldn't be in this position.

"No, sir." Liese's focus remained on the dark blue and silver pinstripes against a backdrop of white. A stray image of her fist wrapped around a similar tie popped into her head. In it, she was pulling his mouth down to hers, their lips a hair's breadth apart. "Look at me."

She wanted to feel some sort of ire, but couldn't. And though his words sounded like a command, a hint of yearning below their surface seemed to parallel her own. Liese held her breath, catching the movement of his hand out of the corner of her eye. Warm, soft fingers slid under her chin and tilted her head up, compelling her. And in that moment, the world inverted itself.

He was close, so close, too close—yet not close enough. She could see the flecks of blue in his eyes, fanning out into a vibrant green threaded with gold until they merged, creating the vivid aquamarine she wanted to drown in.

"I want to know . . ." His seductive whisper floated on the air around them, the thought never finished. His thumb swept back and forth along the edge of her jaw, a hypnotizing sensation, soothing and exhilarating, making her body buzz.

Liese raised a tentative hand, her fingers trembling as they grazed the fabric of his suit jacket. She couldn't find her voice. No longer able to maintain the veneer of professional distance, she swayed forward; thankful Ryder appeared to struggle just as she did.

"I shouldn't," he murmured, inclining his head, his mouth only an inch from hers.

He wet the plush curve of his bottom lip with his tongue. She noted a pale, thin scar—an imperfection in an otherwise flawless face. Liese raised her gaze to his, the dark edge of desire mirrored there. The softest sound left her, somewhere between a sigh and a whimper. Ryder closed his eyes, cutting off her view of the emotional storm that raged behind them.

His fingers curled into her hair, tightening at the nape of her neck as his free arm wrapped around her waist. He stepped in, his body pressed against hers. This was nothing like the uncomfortable hug they'd shared weeks prior, nor the fleeting touches since then.

Liese's eyes fluttered shut, lips parting in expectation. Just as she felt the warmth of his breath against her mouth, the school-wide public announcement system clicked on, an abrasive beep filtering into the room.

Liese became acutely aware of his erection against her stomach. Ryder's mouth, so temptingly close, hovered above her own. Uncertainty paralyzed her.

"Mr. Whitehall, call for you on line four," Betty, the office secretary, announced over the PA. A four-second pause ensued, wherein neither of them moved, followed by a repeat of the same message.

"Fuck," Ryder exhaled, his breath warm against her cheek.

"Okay."

"Pardon?" He seemed to snap back into reality. His hand dropped from her hair, and he took a step away, putting some much-needed, but unpleasant space between them.

"Nothing." Liese scanned the room, disoriented and un-nerved.

In a particularly graceful move, he reached around her and grabbed the laptop. "I think I'll take this with me. I expect to see you at the end of the day so you can explain why exactly you have pornographic images of the two of us together on your laptop." He waited a beat and gave her a curt nod. "Have a good afternoon, Ms. Harper."

And with that he walked out of her office, leaving her wondering if the almost-kiss had been a figment of her imagination.

4

University Degree Does Not Always Equal Smart

"OH MY GOD. Oh my God. *Oh my God.*" Liese leaned against her desk and tried to calm her racing heart.

Ryder had her laptop. He had access to all of her saved porn. All of it. And there was a lot. Like, more than there reasonably should be. Beyond the doctored images of the man himself, she had a small collection of videos she definitely didn't want him to see. She should never have brought her personal computer to work.

Even if he did seem to share her mutual attraction, once Ryder browsed the contents of the folder, he would probably fire her anyway. If he reported her to the board, she'd be forced to stand before a committee and talk about her porn problem. The potential consequences made her skin crawl with shame.

Liese spent the rest of the day in a haze of restlessness, petrified of the meeting to come. Yet while she worried about her impending termination, a small part of her fixated on what had almost transpired between them. Unless she was mistaken, Ryder had almost kissed her. Knowing she affected him that way lent her a dangerous sense of power. If the opportunity arose again she wouldn't have the restraint to deny him. The evidence of his arousal pressed against her stomach had felt like a victory.

Level-headed and driven, Liese had always given her career precedence over her sex drive. In college she'd refused a serious relationship for fear it might interfere with her academic standing. As a result, her father hadn't worried about her future profession. But, her mother's concerns during her undergraduate years had centered on her love life.

She cringed to think how they'd react if she lost her job over porn. As a sex therapist, her mother had always encouraged Liese to try what "felt natural." But Liese doubted her mom meant she should entertain a taboo relationship with her principal and allow Marissa to create photoshopped fetish porn to spur on the infatuation. She couldn't know for sure, though, because her parents had gone on a backpacking expedition in Europe. They'd left in early September and wouldn't be back for several more weeks. Communication had been limited to brief emails and attempted Skypings with poor reception.

Liese dropped into her chair and gave her school-issued computer a malignant glare. In need of a diversion, she perused the Internet for new library resources, all the while pondering whether this would be her last day at FAHL. If so, she would at least ensure the library was well stocked with acceptable literature.

A romance novel flashed on the screen: a cut male body, chopped off at the head and below the navel, took up most of the cover. Her brain immediately pasted Ryder's head onto the body and filled in the missing pieces below the waist. Flustered, she tapped the back button until the image disappeared.

"Get a grip," she told herself.

"Liese?" Blake startled her out of her self-flagellation.

"Hey! Hi. Hello." She greeted him with a little too much enthusiasm.

He leaned on the counter and adjusted her Post-it notes so they were stacked perfectly on top of each other—a square rainbow. "You all right? You look a little flushed."

"Hmm, what? Oh . . . I'm fine." Liese touched her cheek to find the skin warm beneath her fingers.

"You sure about that? You really don't look well." Blake reached out and brushed her bangs out of the way, pressing his wrist against her forehead.

She swatted his hand away. "Blake! There are students present."

"And? I'm checking for a temperature, not trying to feel up your forehead."

"Shh!" Liese hissed and shot him an irritated scowl.

Blake raised his hands in what would have been an act of contrition had he not looked annoyingly amused. "Don't get all testy with me. I'm just a concerned friend, who apparently has a better sense of humor than you."

Liese settled back in her chair, assuming a relaxed position she didn't feel. "Sorry, I don't mean to be witchy. It's been a rough day, and before you ask, no, I don't want to talk about it."

That wasn't entirely true. She did want to talk to someone, desperately. But no matter how good a friend he'd become, Liese couldn't risk confiding in Blake. He was too close to her situation.

"That's cool." He rearranged her pencils, waiting patiently

for her to spill whatever was eating her.

"I'm just preoccupied," she offered, "and maybe feeling a little under the weather." This wasn't a total lie. The nauseous feeling, however, had nothing to do with any contagious kind of sickness.

"Your eyes *are* kind of glassy. Maybe you should take off early," Blake suggested, inspecting her closely.

"I have a meeting with Mr. Whitehall after school I can't miss." Liese waved her hand and tried to appear unruffled, though her stomach felt like it held a lead weight.

"Oh? It's only Tuesday. Aren't those usually on Friday?"
"This isn't about the literacy initiative," she replied.

Blake's upper lip twitched. "Is everything okay? He can be such an asshole."

"Blake! Language."

He looked around; there were no students close enough to hear their conversation, but he issued a half-hearted apology.

"The principal has been quite supportive of the initiatives I've proposed." She cringed at how defensive she sounded. Blake made frequent negative comments about Mr. Whitehall, but Liese ignored them most of the time.

"Supportive?" Blake's fingers curled into a fist. "I can't stand the way he is when he's around you."

"What's that supposed to mean?"

"Nothing. Never mind." He picked up a pen to flip between his fingers. He had to be the most fidgety person she'd ever met. "You can't just say something like that and not explain."

Blake checked over his shoulder, looking for eavesdroppers. Tristan, a tall, lanky boy who helped with set designs for the play approached the desk, book in hand, saving him from responding.

Like most of the students who worked with Blake, Tristan

worshipped him as though he were the leader of a drama cult.

Blake greeted Tristan with warmth and energy. For a moment Liese wished she felt some kind of attraction to Blake beyond a brotherly kinship. He struck her as a diehard romantic: the kind of man who would make a woman feel like the center of his universe, which did absolutely nothing for her. Romance needed to be tempered with a heavy dose of intensity and a side of unconventional to work for her, something she had trouble finding.

All the "A" types she usually went for had been jerks. She didn't have a problem with men who were ambitious and liked to take control, but she couldn't stand being patronized, or talked down to. Lately there seemed to be no shortage of that brand of man, and the other end of the spectrum was just as bad. "Nice" guys who weren't clingy and overly needy seemed a challenge to pin down.

Blake and Tristan discussed which parts of the set needed work with flailing hand gestures. Liese watched them and tried to find Blake sexy, but failed. Sure, he was good-looking, but he just wasn't her type. Thankfully, his disinterest in collegial dating meant she had nothing to worry about. When the discussion regarding set placement and the importance of proper lighting ended, Liese checked out Tristan's book and sent him on his way.

Blake turned to her. "That reminds me, I know you've got this meeting with Ryder after school, so I understand if you can't stay to help with rehearsals too, especially since you're not feeling all that great."

"It should be fine," she reassured him, not at all confident she spoke the truth. He asked her every time if she could make rehearsals as though he expected her to tell him she couldn't, though she'd never missed one. "I'll come to the drama studio as soon as the meeting is over, provided it doesn't run too late."

A knot of anxiety twisted her stomach. She wondered what her consequences would be, and what a late meeting might mean. She would either be employed or not when she left the building at the end of the day.

"Okay, well, I guess I'll see you later." He smiled brightly, oblivious to her internal discord, and sauntered out of the library. After he left, Liese realized he hadn't ever explained what he'd meant by that comment about the principal's behavior around her, which gave her something new to fixate on.

After the final bell, Liese took her sweet time shelving the last of the returned books and organizing the stacks at the far end of the library. It shouldn't have taken half an hour to stock two dozen books. She was stalling. A million possible scenarios ran through her mind, most resulting in her termination. Others resulted in her being naked, underneath Ryder, on his desk. The latter was definitely preferable to the former, but the situation left a lot to be desired no matter the outcome.

Finished with perfecting the art of procrastination, Liese decided to give the remaining students a few extra minutes before she closed the library. She couldn't kick them out as soon as the bell rang; they needed the space to work. It seemed a reasonable excuse if the principal confronted her about not going straight to his office after final dismissal.

But stepping out of the stacks, she noticed all the computer banks were empty, as were the tables in the center of the room. That seemed odd. She paused and looked around for stragglers in the reference section, but those stacks too were vacant. Her time to put off the inevitable had come to an end.

She crossed the room to her office and froze upon opening the door. With a sharp gasp, she took in Ryder's relaxed form, seated behind her desk with her laptop flipped open, facing him. "Holy—" She pressed her hand to her chest.

"Did I startle you?" he asked, looking smug. His fingers were tented under his chin, elbows resting on the arms of the chair. He crossed one leg over the other and swiveled lazily back and forth.

"I thought I was going to meet you in your office."

"This is more private." He looked from her to the screen and back again. "Close the door, please, Annaliese."

The use of her full name had a visceral effect on her. She stepped inside and did as she was asked.

"If you wouldn't mind locking it," he prompted with a wave of his hand. Then he refocused his attention on the screen, as if asking her to lock the door was no big deal.

With trembling fingers, she turned the lock, the click so loud it echoed through the room like a gunshot.

"Have a seat." He motioned to the chair on the opposite side of her desk.

She dropped into it, fearing her legs might give out. Head bowed, she clasped hands and waited.

"Liese."

She obeyed the implied command, forcing her eyes up to meet his. When she did, the ghost of a smile curved the corner of his mouth before he grew serious. Uncrossing his legs, Ryder shifted forward in the chair. He turned the laptop so they both could see the image on the screen. It definitely fell into Liese's Top Ten, as the sub-folder was duly named. Along the bottom bar she noticed several tabs open—likely more images from her collection.

"What exactly were you thinking when you brought your laptop to work today?" Mild disapproval, or something of the like, creased his brow. His eyes moved from hers to the screen and back again. He tapped the scroll bar impatiently, then slid his thumb over the cursor, clicking on another open tab; the image that appeared was even more graphic than its predecessor. "I couldn't find my thumb drive," Liese said, her voice rough. "I didn't want to postpone showing you my new research because I'd misplaced it, so I brought my laptop, which was obviously a very bad idea." She tried to get a read on him, but he regarded her with such scrutiny that she averted her eyes again. "I had no intention of viewing pornography in my place of employment."

Ryder choked back a cough. Phrased as such, it sounded much worse than expected.

"Sugar." She sighed and slumped in her chair. Liese felt like a teenager caught drinking in the bathroom, or hacking into blocked sites on the library computers: ready for a suspension. If only that was the worst that could happen.

A dark chuckle issued from across the desk, and Liese looked up to find Ryder browsing her Internet tabs. "What are you doing? That's personal!"

He raised a brow in challenge. "Oh? And what you showed me earlier wasn't? I only looked at what was open." She worried he would think she was some kind of sexual deviant, which she wasn't. Not really—she just preferred her sex life to fall slightly outside of the vanilla range.

"It's also come to my attention that you attempted to place an order for this particular item . . ." The newest and best vibrator on the market came up on the display. "However, it appears as though you forgot some personal information. See right here?" Ryder pointed to the screen where her state and zip code didn't match up. "Shall I submit it for you now?"

Liese stared at him, unable to tell if he was mocking her. He had one hell of a twisted sense of humor, if that happened to be the case. Dignity demolished, she was about to tell him off, but didn't get the chance.

Ryder cleared his throat and rubbed the back of his neck before he continued. "My hope—" He leaned forward, a small, devilish grin spreading across his very kissable lips. "—is that in the meantime, you might be willing to have dinner with me and explain exactly what you plan to do with that item once it's in your possession."

Despite his words, his passivity made him difficult to gauge.

"I'm sorry, sir." Liese uncrossed her legs, smoothing her skirt over her thighs. He followed the movement with his eyes. She prayed he wasn't propositioning her as a means to sink the final nail into the coffin of her career, but that the months of pretending the attraction between them didn't exist had finally come to an end. "I'm not sure I understand." God, she hoped they were done pretending.

"You're an intelligent woman, Liese. I'm sure you can figure it out."

She remained silent. Tucking her chin in, she looked up at him demurely. "So, to paraphrase," she began in a conspiratorial whisper, "you'd like to have dinner with me so I can tell you about my masturbation habits? Would that be accurate, sir?"

Ryder's eyes widened. "When you put it that way—"

"It sounds inappropriate?"

"Everything that's happened between us today has been inappropriate."

"But—"

Ryder raised his hand to cut her off. "Don't misunderstand me. While I am very aware this is a dangerous path to take, I seem to have lost my ability to give a fuck. And after finding this—" He rose from the chair, gesturing to the laptop. "—I admit I would like to procure several of the other items available on this site. But I have to assume some may already be in your possession, rendering such purchases unnecessary. Again, we could discuss the items you do have as well, if you'd like." Liese blinked at him.

"Sorry, I ramble when I get excited. Of course, you already know that." He leaned forward, his hands flat on the desk, the tick below his left eye belying his nervousness.

"I really don't know what to say," Liese replied. Her initial response was to jump at the opportunity, considering she'd been thinking about that very thing for ages. But the potential repercussions gave her pause. "Do you often proposition women this way?"

"Do you often doctor pornographic images of your superiors?" he shot back.

Liese rose from her chair, her eyes narrowing as she processed his body language. "Are you trying to blackmail me into fucking you?"

"Do you *want* to fuck me?"

The question sent a wave of heat through her body. "Do *you* want to fuck *me*?" she retorted, because she'd be damned if she was going to admit it first. The time she'd spent dissecting his every glance and touch had driven her insane. The connection between them wasn't in her head, and he should be the one to confirm it.

"Yes, very much, actually."

"Oh." Of all the things she'd expected to hear, that wasn't one of them. She'd half anticipated some kind of stand-off, because Ryder could be a stubborn son of a bitch.

They stared at each other, Liese willing him to *do* something already. She allowed her lips to part, encouraging, enticing, inviting. She needed him to make the first move. The pinnacle of control, Liese wanted him to lose it—for her. For a fraction of a second she felt horrible, but he had the power, and she desperately wanted him to keep it.

In a rush of movement, Ryder's hand shot up and slid into her hair, pulling her forward until her hips hit the desk. He groaned, the sound a deep rumble in his chest as his mouth collided with hers. It was like throwing a match into a pool of gasoline. Heat slammed through her veins, and pent up yearning rocketed through her.

"Oh, God." Liese grabbed the lapels of his suit jacket. His free hand wrapped around her waist, the desk that separated them an annoyance.

"I tried so hard," he said, his fingers digging into her side as he pulled her closer. "I really did." It almost sounded like an apology.

Liese clambered onto the desk as Ryder helped lift her over the barrier. He held her steady, one hand on her waist and the other in her hair. Liese slapped her laptop closed and cleared a space to get to him. Stacks of notes fluttered to the floor, followed by the clatter of pens, pencils, and books.

With nothing to separate them, Ryder's hand left her hair, both palms moving over her hips and down her thighs to the hem of her skirt. She grabbed his shoulders for balance, their lips still fused in a panty-incinerating kiss. Even as desperation made them clumsy, Ryder's tongue moved fluidly against hers, stroking a passionate, sensuous rhythm.

He pulled away, then returned a moment later to nip at her lip, his breath coming fast. His eyes were alive with fire and want as he manipulated her body, rearranging her legs on either side of his.

"Tell me to stop." It was akin to a demand, his words at odds with his actions. Ryder shoved her skirt up her thighs, palms smoothing over the newly exposed skin, his nose skimming her cheek. His hands drifted lightly along the silky fabric of her navy thigh-highs until he reached the lacy hem and his fingers faltered. "Tell me you don't want this."

Liese shook her head in defiance, eliciting a despondent groan from him. When his fingers grazed the bare skin of her thigh, his jaw tightened.

"How very naughty of you," he slipped his pinkie under the garter and pulled, only to let it snap back against her thigh. Mouth covering hers, he swallowed her shocked protest. Ryder's hands ran along the inside of her thighs, his fingertips grazing the edge of her panties. She felt the feather-light brush of his knuckle right where the ache was deadliest.

Liese whimpered, her body jerking with the contact, desperate for the feel of his hands on her without the inconvenient obstruction of clothing.

"Shh." His thumb slipped beneath the elastic. "We wouldn't want anyone to think you enjoy your meetings with me. What if people got the wrong idea? Then I might have to discipline you for your indiscretions."

"We wouldn't want that." Liese bit back an uneasy laugh, uncertain whether to take him seriously. Something told her he meant it when he said he would discipline her, and she might very well enjoy it.

"Speak for yourself. I think I'd rather relish handing out a punishment where you're concerned." Ryder's hand tightened in her hair as his lips traveled along her jaw, drawing out the sweetest of tortures. He pushed aside her panties, finger sweeping over the smooth skin.

Liese couldn't help it; she moaned, parting her legs further.

Ryder stopped, both his fingers and mouth stilled. "What did I just tell you?" His teeth pressed softly against the juncture of her shoulder and neck, an erotic warning.

"Sorry, sir." She draped her arms over his shoulders and fingered the hair at the nape of his neck—a weak attempt to draw his attention away from her inability to follow direction and keep quiet.

"I really shouldn't do this." His lips parted against her throat.

"Please." Liese feared Ryder's conscience would kick in, and he would remember just how much trouble being together like this could cause. She chose to bury that knowledge, along with her better judgment, when she trailed her hands down his chest to his belt.

"Tell me what you want," he said.

Supplication merged with abject longing, and Ryder's fingers twitched, a reminder of how close they were to a place she wanted them to go, but shouldn't. Regardless, she didn't want him to stop.

Hands shaking, she answered the question with actions: grasping his belt buckle, she unhooked the clasp.

His breath fanned over her cheek on a warm sigh. Ryder's fingers moved lower. "You have no idea how difficult it's been," he whispered as he kissed his way over her cheek to the corner of her mouth. At the same time he circled, teased, and then suddenly pushed inside, his fingers curled, sensation radiating from the center of her body to consume her in a wave of desire.

Liese inhaled a high-pitched gasp, again heedless of Ryder's warning to stay quiet. She couldn't get enough of him, his body close to hers, his fingers moving inside her. He pushed her closer to a precipice she hadn't been anywhere near in a very long time, at least not with another person.

She fumbled with the fly on his pants, wanting to touch him as he touched her. In her haste, the button popped off and ricocheted off the desk, bouncing onto the floor.

Ryder broke the kiss and looked to where she held the two sides together. "These are expensive pants, and I don't sew," he told her.

Liese wanted to laugh at his seriousness juxtaposed with the way he caressed her body. "Would you like me to sew it back on right now?" She slid her finger beneath the elastic, dipping into his boxers until she grazed something smooth and hard and pretty damn sizable.

His eyes closed, jaw tightening and nostrils flaring. On a deep inhale he opened lust-heavy lids to watch her. "No, I was just stating a fact. I also find it incredibly hot that you'd be willing to sew it back on immediately."

"I was being sarcastic." Liese squeezed his erection, giving it a long, slow stroke.

Ryder groaned and shifted his hips, that thick, hard length sliding against her palm. Withdrawing his fingers, he leaned into her. Liese took the cue and released him, needing her arms to brace her weight on the desk as she lay back. He reached inside his suit jacket and produced his wallet. With one hand he flipped it open and retrieved a foil square. Such a boy scout. She was relieved to find him prepared.

Heat shot through her, funneling low as he nestled his hips

into the cradle of hers. Liese arched, momentarily sidetracked by what felt like a pencil behind her left shoulder and something very uncomfortable at the center of her back. Loathe to stop him, she wrapped her hand around the nape of his neck to pull him closer. The friction of his body gyrating against hers made her wish she hadn't worn panties at all.

"I want to be inside you." Ryder's hand moved between their bodies once again. Gripping his erection, he used it to push the fabric barrier out of the way, circling her sensitive skin with the head of his cock.

She lifted her hips to meet his, more items thumping on the floor as they moved with each other, so close to what they both wanted. When she sensed his hesitation, she uttered a quiet plea.

In the tense silence that followed, the weight of their actions settled around them. He positioned himself to enter her, but the muffled sound of a door clicking shut froze them both.

Their eyes locked in panic as someone called Liese's name from inside the library.

They were not alone.

5

Oh, Shit. Times a Million

RYDER'S EYES WENT wide with the same shock that had Liese closing her legs in a vise grip against his hips. "Who the hell is that?" he asked.

Before she could answer, she heard her name called a second time, closer than before—the voice unmistakable. She uttered a low curse as Ryder's alarm changed to incredulity.

"Is that Blake Stone?" His eyes zeroed in on the locked door. Liese nodded and pushed on Ryder's chest, but got nowhere. "We can't get caught," she said frantically, spurring him into action.

In a rush, she adjusted her underwear and shoved her skirt over her hips, smoothing it down her thighs. Ryder tucked his shirt into his pants and fumbled with his belt. Liese tried to re-organize her desk and pick up the items strewn across the floor. It looked like a bomb had gone off—office supplies littered the carpet like shrapnel.

Ryder knelt to help her, gathering random items to deposit

on her desk. "Why is he here?" Accusation made his tone sharp.

"I was supposed to help with rehearsal at the end of the day. He's probably checking up on me. I told him I had a meeting with you," she defended in a harsh whisper. Panic-stricken, she almost dropped the armful of papers she'd gathered.

"Let me take care of this." It wasn't a request.

He fixed her hair, tucking errant strands behind her ear before smoothing his hand down the side of her neck. "Sit down; you're shaking." He kissed her cheek before he stepped back, motioning to her chair. Liese didn't bother to argue. Barely able to breathe through her anxiety, she dropped into the chair and set to rearranging the mess of papers on her desk. Ryder stuffed the condom wrapper into his pants pocket—she wasn't even sure if he'd bothered to remove the condom. Then, calm and composed in spite of their situation, he stepped over and opened the door.

Blake stood at the threshold with his fist raised, ready to knock. The furrow in his brow deepened, and his look of disquiet morphed into confusion.

"Hello, Mr. Stone." Ryder greeted him with a smile, his tone light, posture open. But Liese could see his hand on the door knob flex until it was white knuckled. "We're just finishing up a meeting. How can I help you?"

"I—uh . . ." Blake looked from Liese to Ryder, apparently uncertain as to what the principal could do for him. "I wanted to make sure Liese was okay. She wasn't feeling well earlier, and we had rehearsal for the holiday play this afternoon."

"Oh?" Ryder feigned surprise. "Sorry if I've kept Liese from something important. Had I known, I wouldn't have let our meeting run so long." Liese could see only a partial profile of Ryder's face. He remained placidly indifferent, but she didn't miss the undercurrent of derision. Right now he bordered on furious.

"Oh, I thought she . . ." Blake paused. "Well, then—" He stumbled over his words, eyes ricocheting from Ryder to Liese and her desk. He frowned at the chaos there. Blake had been inside her office enough to know she kept her desk organized.

Ryder stepped into the doorway to block his view of the room. Liese could see him craning his neck, looking rather put out. "I'm sure if Liese and I can work through the remainder of her proposal without further interruption she'll be able to get to rehearsal soon enough," Ryder said. "Unless you're here because her presence is no longer required?"

Blake went stony. "We just finished, which is why I came to check on Liese." Despite the perilous circumstances, Ryder remained completely unfazed while Blake's obvious irritation bordered on disrespectful. Liese would have felt embarrassed for him if she hadn't been about to pee her pants.

While the two men glowered at each other, she took the opportunity to slip a handful of papers into her drawer. Blake took a step to the side, and Ryder leaned in the same direction, his hand resting high on the doorjamb. Despite his territorial stance, he looked remarkably relaxed.

Blake shifted to the left and made eye contact with Liese over Ryder's shoulder. "Are you feeling okay? You seem—" He paused, his eyes traveling over her face.

She could think of two words to describe herself currently: *terrified* and *unfulfilled.*

Ryder let his arm fall as he turned, amusement evident in the tilt of his head. "Are you not well, Annaliese?"

Liese touched the back of her shaking hand to her cheek. "I'm a little warm, but I'm sure I'm fine." She forced a reassuring smile.

"You should have told me you were ill. We could have rescheduled our meeting for another time." Ryder faked concern.

"It's fine, really. Once we're finished I'll go right home and crawl into bed." It wasn't until after the words were out that she realized the loaded context.

Ryder's eyes widened, and Blake blinked. Liese rearranged a stack of Post-its.

Blake hesitated, but when the silence grew uncomfortable, he had no choice but to leave. "Oh, okay. Well, I guess I'll see you tomorrow then."

"Sorry I missed rehearsal, Blake. I'll be at the next one," Liese assured him.

"Have a nice evening." Ryder continued to smile, but his tone revealed his impatience.

"Sure," Blake replied as he eyed them one last time. "See you tomorrow."

Neither Liese nor Ryder uttered a sound until the main door to the library clicked shut. Only when Ryder had verified that Blake was indeed gone did he truly relax. "I thought I locked that damn door." He fingered the keys in his pocket, making them jingle.

It had been too close a call. That could never happen again. None of this should ever have happened in the first place. It would be damaging enough if they tried to pursue a relationship, but to get caught going at it on her desk was unconscionable.

"I'm sorry. I didn't think he'd actually come looking for me," she offered.

Ryder moved swiftly and his hands came down on the arms of her chair, trapping her. A flash of something primal glinted in his eye as he leaned in close. "Is there something going on between the two of you I should know about?" His tone was low, controlled, and almost seductive despite the rage beneath the surface.

"Of course not." Liese didn't try to hide her offense; she flattened her palms against his chest, intending to push him away. Ryder caught her wrists in one hand and pulled her out of the chair. His other arm wrapped around her waist to hold her against him again. The charge between them sparked like tripped wire. And just like that, she forgot they'd almost been caught.

Satin-soft lips brushed over her throat, and his tongue swept out to taste her skin—an apology without words. "I don't like how interested he is in you." Releasing her hands, his fingertips moved over her cheek, and he pressed a soft kiss against the hollow beneath her ear.

"He's just a friend."

"Does he know that?"

"He's not interested, and neither am I." Liese felt a strange compulsion to reassure Ryder.

"You're sure about that?"

"Yes, I'm sure. Why?"

"I can't stand the way he is with you. It makes me want to do unreasonable, violent things to him." His hand traveled gently down her side and back up, the touch a contrast to his hostile declaration. It was kind of a turn-on. Although almost everything about Ryder seemed to get her hot.

"There's nothing going on," Liese whispered.

"Maybe he's having trouble accepting that." His knuckles traced along the column of her neck and over her collarbone. Ryder followed the action with his mouth, lips parted, tongue warm and silky on her skin. She stifled a moan as he nipped at the same spot with his teeth. The shock of pain gave way to a burst of pleasure.

"Men and women can just be friends, you know," she managed.

Ryder made a sound of disbelief against her skin, sucking lightly. She wanted to get closer, back to where they'd been before Blake interrupted.

He moved his mouth to her ear. "That issue is up for debate, but I don't want to talk about it right now. Reminds me we shouldn't be doing this."

Liese tensed, and her fingers, threaded through his hair, stilled. She'd wondered how long it would take him to come to his senses. Now what would happen? Ryder's next suggestion shocked the hell out of her.

"As much as I would love to have you right here on your desk, considering the circumstances, I think it might be more prudent for this *conversation* to continue in a more private location."

"Private?"

"That way I can discipline you properly for breaking my resolve with inappropriate pictures before I get inside you," Ryder explained as he stepped back. His eyes moved over her in a hungry sweep.

"Discipline me?" The thought of retribution did something to her, particularly when she envisioned herself bent over his desk. All the things he could do.

"You didn't honestly think you'd go unpunished for this type of indiscretion, did you?" he asked, challenging her to disagree.

She almost did, just to see what would happen. "I, uh . . . well . . . what kind of punishment?"

"You'll have to wait and see." With a sardonic smile, he grabbed a pen and a Post-it from her desk. "Do you know where I live?"

"No."

"You do now." He placed the paper in her hand and folded her fingers around it, pulling her close once again. "I'll meet you there in half an hour."

The press of his lips against her own made it impossible to deny the order. He reached around her, lifted her laptop from the desk, and tucked it under his arm.

"What are you doing?"

"Taking this with me."

"Why?"

"Don't worry. You'll get it back. Eventually. Considering the sensitive nature of the content, it would be best if I ensure your personal laptop is removed from school property safely. We wouldn't want this getting into the wrong hands, would we, Ms. Harper?"

"Of course not."

"I thought not." He gave her a sly smile. "I expect to see you in less than thirty minutes."

The *or else* was implied.

6

Desire and Deceit

WITH SHAKING ARMS, Liese propped herself against her desk and looked at the doorway through which Ryder had departed. Her constant, graphic dreams about him now seemed laughable compared to the real thing. The simple act of kissing him, not to mention the way he'd manipulated her with his hands, obliterated any fantasy she'd contrived.

Logic implied that this thing with Ryder wasn't going to benefit either of them professionally. But Liese's center of logic was fried. She wanted more. More touch, more sensation, more of whatever he was offering. Fueled by hormones, she hurried to hide the evidence of their near-encounter. Scanning the floor, she spotted the button from Ryder's pants beside the leg of her desk. She retrieved it and tucked it carefully into the top drawer of her desk.

Once her office loosely resembled its previous state, Liese shoved the piece of paper he'd given her into her purse. Leaving the scene of the crime, she opened the door and peeked out to check the halls. They were empty, but without the raucous sounds of students in the corridors, the echo of her heels made her feel conspicuous.

A soft whirring soon joined the noise of her shoes as the custodian buffed the floors down an adjacent hall. Liese slid a sidelong glance in his direction. She tried to be stealthy and would have managed if not for her footwear. He paused as she moved into his field of vision, and he raised a hand in greeting. Liese returned the gesture but didn't stop to chat as she normally would have, because today was no normal day.

Rounding the corner, she ran headlong into the one person she was actively trying to avoid. She flailed, clutching Blake's shirtsleeve to stop from falling right into his chest.

"Shit! Sorry." He grabbed her upper arms to steady her. "You're just leaving now?" He didn't let go immediately. She could feel his eyes on her, searching her face.

Her insides churned as she struggled to look him in the eye. "I had a few things I wanted to take care of, in case I can't come in tomorrow." It felt as though she had a sign on her forehead that read: *Illicit Encounter in Progress.*

"Good idea." Blake pressed the back of his hand to her cheek. "You're really warm, and kind of sweaty." His nose wrinkled. Liese would have laughed if she didn't think she might vomit.

"I feel pretty awful. Maybe it's the flu." Her voice cracked, and she rummaged for her keys so she could look away. She really hated lying.

Apparently he bought it, though, because he threaded his arm through hers, drawing her to his side. "Let me walk you to your car."

"It's really not necessary," she said weakly. On any other occasion she would have appreciated his chivalry. Today, however, his attentiveness made her paranoid.

"I'll feel more comfortable if I know you aren't passed out beside your car." He guided her toward the main entrance. *No* didn't seem to be an acceptable answer.

The temperature had dropped since morning, as it often did in late November. An unseasonably chilly wind whipped through her hair and bit at the exposed skin of her face. She curled into Blake's side, hiding from the frosty fingers of autumn as they hinted at winter yet to come. The damp heat of her skin cooled rapidly, and she huddled deeper into her jacket.

They shuffled quickly down the sprawling staircase to the parking lot. When they reached her car, Blake released her arm, and she gripped her key with a shaky hand, pushing it into the lock.

"How did your meeting with Whitehall go, anyway?" he asked as she opened the door and tossed her purse and empty laptop case on the passenger seat.

"It was fine." Liese leaned inside the car and slipped the key into the ignition. The engine turned over, and she cranked the heat.

"Liese."

She held onto the edge of the door, wanting very much to get inside and drive away. She looked up at him expectantly, wrapping her arms around herself to keep the chill at bay.

"You'd tell me if Whitehall did something inappropriate, right?"

"What?" Panic constricted her throat and made her voice too high.

Blake's eyes narrowed. He took a step closer and peered down at her. "Did something happen?"

"God, no," Liese replied, her eyes darting away. "He's never been anything but professional with me. Why? Is there something you're not telling me?"

"Is there something you're not telling *me*?" Skepticism hung thick in the air between them.

"No." A spike of anxiety shot through her. "Now answer the damn question, Blake. Has Ryder done something untoward with another female staff member? Is that why you're asking?"

"What? No." He huffed in irritation. "Until you showed up, most of us wondered whether he'd become asexual."

"What do you mean, until I showed up?" Liese shuddered against the wind and gave the parking lot a furtive once-over; Ryder's vehicle was gone, and she had no idea how much time had passed since he'd left her office.

Blake puffed out a breath and ran his hand through his hair. "I don't know, Liese. It's just the way he is with you. I don't like it. It's like he's *too* engrossed in what you have to say. How long was your meeting today?"

"What does the length of our meeting have to do with anything?"

"Nothing. Never mind. Forget I mentioned it," he said, his tone softening. "Look, you're beautiful and young and intelligent and driven. As your friend, I worry."

"Why?" Curiosity made her ask, even though she wasn't sure she wanted to hear the answer.

"Because I see the way he looks at you, even if you don't."

"I appreciate your concern. I really do, but you have nothing to worry about." Liese hoped she sounded more convincing than she felt.

"Maybe I'm being overprotective and a little too brotherly." Blake flashed an apologetic smile. "And if I am, please feel free to tell me where to shove it. Just be careful. I don't want to see you taken advantage of."

Liese sighed; she hated the guilt weighing down her limbs. "I can hold my own. If Ryder ever tries anything, I'll use the hidden power of my knobby knees to hit him where it counts." Her teeth chattered as she tried to smile. It felt more like a grimace, a product of the cold and the fabrication.

Despite his dubious expression, Blake eventually relented, giving her room to breathe. "You should go. Standing out here listening to me lecture you isn't going to make you feel any better."

Liese lowered herself into her seat and tucked her legs inside the car, welcoming the blast of heat as it warmed her face.

Blake leaned down to eye level. "Just promise you'll tell me if he does try anything he shouldn't."

"So you can file a sexual harassment charge for me?" Liese asked.

"No, so I can shove my foot up his ass."

"Blake."

"Liese," he mocked, then tapped the roof of her car. "Drive safe."

He rose to his full height and closed the door, shoving his hands into his pockets as she backed out of her parking spot. She glanced at him through the rearview mirror and waved goodbye. Judging by his expression, she wasn't sure she'd been all that persuasive in her lie.

It wasn't going to stop her from meeting Ryder, though. She'd just have to be more careful in her interactions with him, particularly after tonight. Liese tried not to think any more about her conversation with Blake as she followed the directions to Ryder's house. He'd been working under Ryder for two years, and while it had been clear from the beginning that Blake disparaged him, Liese figured it had more to do with personality conflict than anything else. Blake's laid-back attitude about most things, including curriculum, directly opposed the way Ryder operated. She could see where they would butt heads.

Pushing her reservations aside, she turned onto Sterner. The house was impossible to miss, as it was the only one on the street. She pulled into the driveway, mildly paranoid someone would recognize her car considering how isolated his property was. She cut the headlights and turned off the engine. Silence closed in on her, allowing her fear to surface. She adored her job, and the opportunities she had at FAHL were unbelievable. Beyond that, she'd made friends, and if her colleagues found out somehow, well . . . that would be complicated beyond measure.

The ding of her phone startled her out of her musings. She snatched it from the passenger seat and checked the screen to find several new messages. Marissa had left two texts asking her to call, and there were three calls from an unknown number. She didn't bother to check the voicemail—and Marissa would have to wait. Besides, Liese had a feeling she might need to chat with her after this.

Turning her phone to vibrate, Liese left it in the center console. After a deep, steadying breath, she got out of the car and rushed up the front steps. She trembled as she pressed the doorbell and tried to convince herself it had everything to do with the drop in temperature and nothing to do with anticipation.

7

THE MOTION SENSOR picked up Liese's presence and blinded her with an obnoxiously bright floodlight. Unease crept in as she stood, illuminated, on Ryder's front porch. Her imagination revved into high gear, and she pictured a news crew swarming her, snapping photos while they shoved a mic in her face, asking how it felt to get caught sleeping with her superior.

The black double doors swung inward, and Ryder stood between them, caught in the megawatt glare, looking as intense as usual. Liese drank in the sight of him, and her apprehension dissipated, replaced by the same craving that had brought her to him in the first place. His eyes were luminous in the dark, and the shadows that fell across his face made him sinister and sexy.

He hadn't changed clothes, although he no longer wore his suit jacket, and he'd rolled his sleeves up to his elbows. His top two buttons were open at the collar, and his tie hung loosely offkilter. In the time she'd known him, Liese had never seen him look so casual. While he typically exuded an aura of confidence, in his own home, that self-assurance multiplied tenfold. Seeing Ryder so clearly in his element made him more appealing than ever.

"You're late." Disapproval laced with a thread of relief—it made him sound almost vulnerable.

Liese warmed at the intensity of his gaze. "Sorry about that." He opened the door wide and motioned for her to come in. The entryway felt cavernous, the decor within sparse. Everything was pale cream and dark, rich wood, and a single large mirror adorned the wall. Its thick frame echoed the dark wood of the floor, and a side table complimented the piece, bare but for an avant-garde black bowl that held a set of keys.

Closing the door behind her, he whispered in her ear, "I worried you were going to stand me up."

"Why would I do that?" She'd considered it when she pulled into his driveway. Fear had tugged at her conscience, but desire had pushed the unwelcome emotion down and locked it away—at least for the time being.

He shrugged. "To torment me?" Circling behind her, his lips found a sliver of bare skin at the collar of her blouse. "Should I let it slide this time, or should I make an example of you?" He was playing with her, teasing, testing. "I could add some time to your detention for being late, or maybe I should make your punishment more severe."

There was a promise beneath the statement, sensuality combined with dark allure.

Excitement warred with apprehension. A detention from Ryder would be nothing like the kind doled out to tardy students. "That's probably a good idea. Wouldn't want to give me preferential treatment. That would be wrong."

"I'm glad you feel that way." She felt the curve of his lips against her neck. Then, giving her unwanted space, he asked, "May I take your coat?"

Fumbling with the buttons, Liese allowed Ryder to help her out of her jacket. Once he'd hung it neatly in the closet, he led her down an expansive hallway. His palm rested low on her back, his thumb stroking over the dip in her spine.

"What kept you?"

She debated whether or not to tell the truth. Honesty won, because he would likely see through a lie. "I ran into Blake."

Ryder tensed and angled her body to face him. "Should I be concerned?"

"He asked if you'd done anything inappropriate."

"And what did you tell him?"

"That our relationship was strictly professional."

"Good girl." He touched her cheek with the back of his fingers. The gentle caress paired with the compliment might have been offensive under different circumstances. But coming from Ryder, it sounded sinfully sexy. "Did he believe you?"

"I think so."

He nodded pensively, running his fingers through her hair and watching as it slipped between them.

Unable to bear his silence, Liese said the first thing that came to her. "He's not very fond of you."

"The feeling is mutual. I hate the way he looks at you."

"He said the exact same thing."

"Is that so?"

"It is." Liese stopped breathing as he inclined his head, ducking down until their lips met in a soft, barely there brush of satin against satin. To her dismay, and the affront of her hormones, he didn't deepen it.

With infuriating restraint, he pulled back. "And you? How do you feel about the way I look at you?"

"I feel like . . ." Liese hesitated and thought about the way his eyes had roamed her body when they were alone earlier. The intense scrutiny hadn't been new; he'd looked at her like that before, only this time she understood it better. ". . . I don't want you to stop."

He grinned. "That's reassuring." Ryder laced his fingers through hers and tugged on her hand, leading her to the kitchen.

More dark wood and cream and slate greeted her. Ryder released her and motioned to a high-backed stool in front of a large island. As Liese made herself comfortable, he rounded the island and uncorked a bottle of red wine. "Would you like a drink?"

"Please." Liese looked down at the black granite countertop, tracing the streaks of gold with her fingertips. Lust merged with uncertainty to consume her.

The soft clink of a wine glass startled her, and she lifted her head. Ryder pushed the glass toward her as he leaned on the counter. "Do you like chicken?"

"Pardon?"

"Chicken. Are you opposed to it?"

"No?"

"You sound rather uncertain."

The teasing tone made her smile. Ryder opened the fridge and held up a package of chicken before tossing it on the counter. "I assure you, it's not a trick question. I just want to make dinner."

"Dinner?" Food certainly hadn't been on her mind when she'd walked through his front door.

"Yes, dinner. What did you think?" He pried the wine glass from her fingers, setting it down on the counter. Ryder's hands slid up the outside of her thighs and back down again. Pausing at her knees, he nudged them apart, palms resting on the inside of her legs, just below the hem of her skirt. Heat spread through her limbs, her breath coming shallow and fast. She couldn't fathom what having him inside her would be like if a simple touch made her feel as though she might ignite.

"Tell me, Liese, did you expect I would take you to my bedroom immediately, with no precursor?" His voice was decadently smooth, the words inspiring her imagination.

"Something like that."

"Despite the fact that I find it torturous not to succumb to that particular option, I was raised to be a gentleman, at least to some degree." He withdrew his hands and relocated them to her waist.

She groaned in frustration. "I don't need you to be a gentleman." She fingered a button on his shirt.

His mouth hovered over hers, his hands encasing hers to prevent any attempt to undress him. "I'll keep that in mind for later. However, I should remind you, you still have a detention to serve for that folder of unseemly pictures I found this afternoon, not to mention being late this evening. I can't very well have you serving it before dinner. That would be rude."

Ignoring his words, she leaned in, her focus on the proximity of his mouth. She parted her lips in expectation and felt the warmth of his breath against her skin.

"Do you want me to kiss you?"

"Yes."

"Good." Ryder released her hands and turned away. Putting the island between them, he left her gaping after him.

Never had she been so turned on and sexually frustrated at the same time. "That wasn't very nice." She gave him a dirty look from over her wine glass.

"I promise I'll make it up to you later." He raised an eyebrow.

"After we've discussed the contents of your laptop."

A blush crept into her cheeks. Though she wanted to be angry with Marissa, Liese now knew she might wind up thanking her instead.

Ryder moved around his kitchen with efficient grace, preparing dinner. He refused her offer to help, topping off her wine periodically as he sautéed and stirred. He filled the silence with questions, gleaning personal details she would have thought trivial had he not seemed so enthralled by her answers.

"Do you have family close by?"

"My parents moved to California a few years ago. My mother likes the heat."

"And you don't?" Ryder paused to devote his full attention to her.

"I don't mind it, but I liked New York. They moved during my undergrad, and I didn't want to switch schools. My father's a military man—retired now—so we didn't stay put for long while I was growing up."

"That must have been difficult."

"I didn't know any different."

"So your father was in the military. And your mother, what does she do?"

"She's a sex therapist. They're currently making their way through Europe, so I haven't heard much from them lately. It's supposed to be a vacation, but I think my mother's using it as an excuse to visit Amsterdam and check out the red light district. She's all about freedom of expression."

"Interesting."

"Not when you're a teenager," Liese replied. "What about your parents? What do they do, and where do they live?"

"Giselle and Donovan live just outside of Allentown, less than an hour away. They're professional assholes."

Liese choked on her wine. "Pardon?"

"Sorry, that was a joke. They're lawyers." Ryder wiped his hand on a dish towel and handed her a napkin.

"Right." Liese coughed into the white square, dabbing at her mouth.

"Dinner's ready. Shall we eat in the dining room?"

The dining room table seemed unnecessarily large for one person, unless Ryder had seven roommates he hadn't mentioned. If they sat at opposite ends, they'd have to slide things across the table to each other as if they were curling.

"I usually eat in the kitchen. However, I thought a more formal environment would be welcome this evening." Ryder answered Liese's unasked question as he pulled out a chair for her. He sat perpendicular to her, close enough that her foot bumped his shin when she crossed her legs. Ryder reached under the table and grazed her knee. His eyes locked on hers as his palm slid down the back of her calf, giving it a slight squeeze.

He removed his hand far too soon and picked up the knife and fork beside his plate. He sliced into his chicken, inspecting the piece speared on his fork before he brought it to his mouth and chewed thoughtfully. Liese stabbed at a braised carrot, wondering when the hell eating had become a mode of seduction. They dined in silence for a few minutes, but it was strangely comfortable, despite the obvious tension.

He derailed her train of thought when he asked, "What made you accept the librarian position at FAHL?"

Caught off guard, Liese faltered. "I—well, I liked the environment and the foundation of the school. I, uh, thought you were a compelling administrator with an incredible background in education. I felt working under you would be enlightening."

Liese left out the fact that it had been one of the first jobs she'd interviewed for and had offered the added benefit of getting her away from the city and the presence of an increasingly annoying ex-boyfriend.

Ryder smiled with rapt amusement. "And has it been?"

"Has it been what?"

"Working under me—how have you found the experience so far?" He touched the corner of his mouth with a linen napkin, hiding a grin.

She wished he would put her out of her misery. Location didn't matter; he could take her on the dining room table for all she cared. There was plenty of room. "Ryder, please."

"I'm certainly looking forward to enlightening you later."

"You can act on that any time now."

He smiled and continued to eat, as if he hadn't been purposely antagonizing her. When he'd finished his meal, he arranged his silverware on the edge of his plate. He settled back in his chair while Liese picked at her half-eaten dinner.

"Do you like ice cream?"

"What?"

"Ice cream. Do you like it?" Ryder clearly enjoyed throwing her for a loop.

"Are we having ice cream for dessert?"

He deposited his napkin on the table. "Maybe. Are you partial to it?"

"Who isn't?"

"People with lactose issues?"

"There are pills for that." She wanted to know where he was going with this.

"True. Do you have a favorite flavor?"

"Mint chocolate chip. And you?"

"Moose Tracks," Ryder replied. "What do you typically wear

to bed?" He propped his chin on his fist.

"What does my nightwear have to do with what kind of ice cream I like?"

"Nothing. I'm just curious."

Liese took the bait. "I sleep naked. What the hell is Moose Tracks?"

"Vanilla ice cream with chocolate syrup ribbons and mini Reese's Peanut Butter Cups. Every night?"

"Every night, what?"

"Do you sleep naked every night?"

"Yes."

"Even in the winter?"

"Yes."

"Fuck."

"I thought I needed to serve my detention first, but if you want to skip that part, it's fine with me." Liese smiled angelically.

"Come now, do you really think I'd go that easy on you?" he asked, lowering his voice. "This is the part of the evening I've been looking forward to most."

Liese's fork clattered to the table. Ryder rose from his chair. "I'll assume that means you're finished." Not bothering to wait for her response, he gathered their plates.

She gulped down the last of her wine. Pushing her chair out, she followed him into the kitchen.

"Would you like an aperitif?" Ryder held up a bottle of Cognac and two glasses.

At her nod, he poured a glass of the amber liquid and held it out to her. With an unsteady hand, she accepted the drink. She would have chugged it if that wasn't so impolite. Liese put the glass to her lips and took a small sip to mask the tremor.

Ryder closed the distance between them. Setting her glass

on the counter, Liese bowed her head. Her body churned with exhilaration and uncertainty.

Ryder cupped her cheek in his palm, urging her to meet his gaze. His tenderness rendered him less severe. "If you don't want to be here, you don't have to be." "I want to," Liese whispered.

"You're certain?"

"Yes."

"That's good. I want you here, too." He smiled. "Would I be correct in assuming you're not interested in dessert?"

"I thought I was dessert."

"You will be soon enough." Taking her hand, he led her down the hall to a flight of stairs. "I'd like to show you my personal office, where we'll begin with your detention."

8

The Pleasure of Punishment

LIESE TRAILED HER fingers along the ornate banister as she ascended the stairs. Despite there being more than enough room for Ryder to walk beside her, he stayed one step behind, his hand low on her hip. At the top of the stairs he pulled her to him. His palm slid roughly over the swell of her ass, fingertips digging in as he squeezed. His head dipped, and his lips met the shell of her ear.

"I can't even begin to describe the ways I want to fuck you." Her eyes fluttered closed, certain he would spin her out of orbit.

With a hint of impatience and his hand still planted firmly on her backside, Ryder led her down the hall. He stopped at a set of double doors and opened them, sweeping out a hand to invite her inside. The room was a radical contrast to the minimalist main floor. The walls on either side were lined with cherry shelves, filled to capacity with everything from educational texts to classics. It was a librarian's fantasy room.

Along the far wall, red velvet drapes were tied back to expose windows that spanned the length of the room. An antique desk and a leather executive chair dominated the center of the space. If the sun hadn't already set, Liese imagined she'd have a perfect view of his backyard.

"Why don't you have a seat, Ms. Harper." Ryder motioned to two black leather chairs facing the desk.

Liese faltered, the use of formal address surprising her. Until she caught on. If she was serving her detention and being punished, he would be doling it out as Mr. Whitehall, not Ryder. The Ryder she met with to review her project was encouraging and engaging. Mr. Whitehall the disciplinarian was a different story.

"Yes, sir." She aimed for nonchalance and sauntered over to the chair. Purposely sliding her skirt up her thighs until it rode obscenely high, she sank into the soft leather. Crossing her legs, she hooked her hands around her knees and looked at the floor, waiting.

"Lovely."

She raised her head at the sound of Ryder's voice. His approval brought a slight smile before she could school her expression.

He leaned back in his chair and took a deep breath. "Shall we review the reason you're here this evening?" He tapped his fingers on the arm of his chair.

"Yes, Mr. Whitehall."

He smiled as his tie slid through his fingers. "I'd like you to explain it, then, so I can be sure you understand the gravity of this situation and the position you've put me in."

He looked and sounded so serious that Liese averted her gaze. "I—I was—"

"Eyes up here, please," he ordered, his knuckles rapping on the desk.

"I was viewing inappropriate material on my personal computer in my place of employment," she said, maintaining eye contact.

"Mmm, that you were. Would you care to tell me exactly what you were viewing and why?" He swiveled in his chair, waiting for her to speak.

"Um, well, as you are aware, I intended to show you the research you've so graciously helped me with as my advisor—"

"No need to suck up. You'll be doing that later." His lip twitched. "Preferably without speaking."

Liese just about fell out of her chair. Recovering quickly, she baited him. "What if I'm not the kind of woman who gets on her knees?"

"You won't need to for what I have planned," he said. "Now, explain to me why you were viewing pornographic material in a high school library, of all places."

Liese uncrossed her legs, running her hands over her thighs, her trepidation real as she thought about what could have happened. "I accidentally opened a folder I'd been perusing the night before."

"Interesting. I'd be curious to know just how long you've had that folder."

"Long enough. Would you like a copy of it?"

"What makes you think I haven't already made one?" Not waiting for a response he continued. "How long is long enough?"

Liese couldn't hide the blush that painted her cheeks. "Since early August."

"Oh?" His surprise sounded genuine.

"The image you seemed to like in my office—the one with the corset and garters?" Liese waited to make sure he remembered. "That was sent to me just last night."

"I did like that one." Ryder nodded, eyeing her legs. "What

I'm wondering, though, is why you didn't think to send me your research files before you allowed yourself to become preoccupied by images of me fucking you? Had you done that, we could have avoided this entire situation."

"That would have been a pity."

"Are you telling me you did this on purpose?"

"Of course not." She hastened to defend herself. "I'd been checking my email, and Marissa had sent me a new picture. I saved it in my folder and got distracted."

"Distracted?"

"Yes."

"And what does being distracted entail?" Ryder gripped the arms of his chair, his fingers curling around the ends.

Liese knew she was getting under his skin, her answers ramping up the tension between them. "I'm not sure it would be advisable for me to say aloud, sir. I wouldn't want to get into any more trouble than I already have." She waited for his reaction.

He switched tactics. "I'd like you to tell me a bit about your fascination with bondage, if you wouldn't mind," he said in a smooth voice.

"I'm sorry, my *what*?" She felt suddenly very aware of the bondage porn on her computer. But fascination did not equal experience.

"Don't play coy with me. Have you forgotten I've had your computer all afternoon? I've seen the entire folder, and let me tell you, I think you've been hiding some very interesting secrets from me, haven't you?"

If Ryder had found the folder-within-the-folder, denying the range of her sexual interests was a moot point. Her video collection contained a diverse array of pornographic delights. Fortunately, those hadn't been altered by Marissa. "Yes, sir," she croaked.

"I can understand why such materials might have been a distraction for you. I was quite distracted myself." He sighed, his eyes dark with lust. "If you would be so kind as to stand, I think it's time to discipline you properly."

Liese rose from the chair, more turned on and excited than she could ever remember. Ryder shuffled papers and rearranged several items, creating a space in front of where Liese stood.

He rounded the desk, stopping before her. "These clothes are in the way." He opened the top button of her blouse, followed quickly by the second and dragged his finger along the edge of her bra.

"Would you like me to resolve that issue?" she asked in a hoarse whisper.

"That would be helpful," he said, his attention fixed on the deep purple satin that peeked out from the parted fabric of her blouse.

Liese slipped free the remaining buttons. She desperately wanted to get him out of his clothes, too, but she refrained from acting on the impulse to help him. If all went well, he would be naked soon enough.

Ryder pushed the shirt over her shoulders and let it fall to the floor. Transfixed by the predatory hunger in his eyes, she remained passive, awaiting his next move. As he took in her half-naked form, Liese felt sexually alive and exposed at the same time.

His touch feather-light, Ryder's palms came to rest on either side of her neck, his thumbs brushing along the underside of her jaw. He leaned forward, his lips grazing hers. "It's a wonder I was able to keep my hands off you for this long," he murmured.

"I like your hands on me." Liese took a step closer, curling her pinkies into his belt loops, bringing their bodies flush against each other. She tilted her head up, lips parted. Ryder took the invitation, his tongue meeting hers, a slow give and take that escalated into his complete domination.

Fingers threaded into her hair, his other hand moved down her back to her skirt, traveling along the edge, back and forth, over and over. "Where is the zipper?" he groaned, infuriated. Liese laughed and pushed him away. She pulled down the hidden zipper and let the garment fall to the floor.

Ryder's jaw went slack for a moment before he composed himself. Maintaining a foot of space between them, he ran his hands down her sides and stopped just above the lace band of her thong.

"You are stunning." He took one of her hands, helping her step out of the discarded skirt.

Wrapping her in his embrace, Ryder palmed her backside and pulled her tight to him. Liese could feel the soft fabric of his shirt, the satin warmth of his tie between her breasts, the cold metal clasp of his belt on her stomach. She moaned at the firm press of his erection against her. She could care less if they made it to the bedroom. Being bent over Ryder's desk in his library would fulfill at least one fantasy.

She attempted to snake a hand between them and struggled to locate his belt buckle. A fleshy smack followed by a painful sting made her gasp. Ryder had just slapped her ass.

"Ah, ah, ah." He shook his head in disapproval as he kneaded the tender spot. "You didn't think it would be that easy to dissuade me from issuing your punishment, did you?"

Liquid heat blossomed inside her, and with it came an ache for more of his carnal discipline. "Is that all you've got?" she taunted.

"Hardly," he scoffed. "That was just a love tap." Not giving her a chance to retaliate, Ryder spun her to face the desk. "Hands here, please," he ordered, touching the polished wood.

Liese complied. His palm came to rest just below her shoulder blades, and he pressed gently, encouraging her to bend over the desk.

"Perfect," he murmured.

She felt feverish with need. Every word of approval, every soft touch contrasted with the promise of erotic punishment.

"I really do love these." He snapped the elastic of her garter against the back of her thigh.

She jumped, surprised by the lick of pain that preceded the heat of pleasure. She arched her back and widened her stance minutely. "I aim to please, Mr. Whitehall."

"I'm sure you will."

Smoothing his hands over her skin, he grazed the swell of her breasts but avoided the most sensitive areas. Liese turned her head to place her cheek on the desk, allowing the rest of her torso to follow. The cool sensation of the wood did little to calm the need building inside her. She could see Ryder in her periphery, hazy and unclear from the odd angle, but the feel of his hands more than made up for the lack of visual stimulus.

Every other sense felt heightened. The scent of lemon polish from his desk overwhelmed her. She could hear the rustle of fabric as he moved, taste the bitter residue of his aftershave lingering on her tongue, see the dust moats floating in the beam of light as it hit the edge of the desk. Most of all, her skin hummed with electric need wherever Ryder made contact. Every torturous evasion of gratification was magnified by her acute desire for release.

Focused on the movement of his hands and the way they continued to neglect the most important parts of her body, Liese yelped in shock when his palm landed again with a heavy smack on her backside.

Ryder's hand returned to the spot he'd spanked, his palm pressed firmly but tenderly against the smarting skin. "Too hard?"

"Not too hard, just unexpected." Liese craned her neck to gauge his reaction. The crease in his brow spoke to his uncertainty.

His relieved sigh extinguished any remaining nervousness. She hadn't realized she'd tensed until she melted back into the desk.

The next slap came swift and sharp, followed by the graze of his fingertips between her thighs. Liese moaned, chasing a release that had been on hold for hours. But she should have known better. Just as the welcome tingle began, Ryder withdrew his touch, alternating punishment with pleasure. His finger slipped beneath the damp fabric of her lace thong to caress her skin. The butterfly passes shouldn't have been enough, but she'd been teetering at the edge for so long, she quickly went over. Her orgasm sent her into a free fall, leaving only intense pleasure in its wake.

She tried to push up on her hands but couldn't make her arms work. Her knees buckled on her attempt to stand. Ryder slipped an arm around her waist to catch her.

"Easy. Are you okay?" He held her against him, her back to his chest, his erection pressed against her tender ass, demanding her attention.

"Uh-huh." Liese nodded dopily and let him take her weight. "I don't think I can stand, though."

Ryder chuckled, the sound strained. He turned her to face

him and lifted her carefully onto the desk. She draped her arms over his shoulders and clasped her hands behind his neck. Ryder stepped between her parted thighs.

"Lesson learned?"

"Mmmm . . ." She nipped his bottom lip. "I think so, at least for now."

"Am I to look forward to further bad behavior?"

Liese fingered the open collar of his shirt. "I have a feeling you'll be watching for misdeeds so you have an excuse to bend me over your desk again."

"Does that mean I have the authority to spank you anytime you've done something to warrant another punishment?" Ryder kissed her bare shoulder and bit down on her collarbone.

"If you promise to make me come that hard again, I'll give you the authority to do whatever you damn well please." Liese wrapped her legs around his waist, hooking her feet to secure her position.

"I was hoping you'd say that." Ryder smiled.

"Mr. Whitehall?" Liese widened her eyes, seeking to embody the picture of innocence as she ran her fingers through his hair.

"Yes?"

"I'd like to see your bedroom now."

"I was hoping you'd say that, too."

9

Upping the Antics

TOYING WITH RYDER'S tie, Liese loosened the knot until she could slip it free. Despite her eagerness to see his bed—and ultimately end up with him on top of her—she wanted to draw out the anticipation as long as possible now that she'd had some release. Hanging the tie around her neck, she let it fall between her breasts.

"What exactly do you think you're doing?" Ryder asked.

"Leveling the field." She popped the remaining buttons on his shirt. "Look how naked I am and how not-naked you are." Liese looked down at her cleavage spilling out of the satin-and-lace cups of her bra and then at Ryder's still-covered chest.

"I like you this naked." His hands drifted along the outside of her thighs to her knees. "Maybe next time I'll have you walk around in this getup until I decide what I'm going to do to you."

The promise of future possibilities combined with the feel of his hands on her body made Liese shiver. Misunderstanding her reaction, he shrugged out of his shirt and draped it over her shoulders.

"You must be cold."

She wasn't, but any step closer to undressing him was a positive one in her eyes, so she shoved the too-long sleeves up her arms. Liese flattened her palms against his chest, his muscles flexing beneath her fingers as she let them drift down toward the waistband of his pants.

"As much as I enjoy you undressing me here . . ." He fastened the button below her breasts. ". . . and while the idea of taking you on my desk is alluring, I would rather this time be in my bed." He unhooked her legs from his waist and gave her enough room to stand.

Liese slid gingerly off the desk. A bed and soft sheets would definitely be kinder to her ass than a wood slab.

"Are you all right?"

"I'm fine," she assured him.

Keeping his arm around her waist, Ryder led her from the office. They passed the same stairs they'd ascended on their way down the hall, stopping at another set of double doors. Ryder paused to open them, guiding Liese inside. She processed the space in silence. All the personality in the house resided in his office and bedroom.

The bed occupied the center of the room, set beneath the dramatic backdrop of a black wall with white designs that flickered with shadow in the dim light. The gunmetal gray duvet complimented the charcoal black headboard, and the floor mirrored the same dark cherry that ran throughout the rest of the house. The only splash of color came from a wine-red throw at the foot of the bed. Candles burned on almost every available surface, transforming the haunting quality of the room into something seductive.

She was hardly surprised by the corporeal aura of the space—Ryder exuded sensuality all the time, and his bedroom mirrored that part of him. A spike of jealousy lanced through Liese as she imagined other women here, on his bed. The thought was irrational; she'd had other lovers, and judging from the way he touched her, so had he. She squelched the possessive feelings; this couldn't be a real relationship.

A gigantic flat screen TV hung on the wall opposite his bed. Despite its blank display, the backlit black glow indicated it was on. A wire ran from the TV to her laptop, propped open on the dresser below. Liese again had the terrifying notion that Ryder had located the folder containing her saved videos.

"What's that all about?" She pointed to the set up.

"You'll see. Come with me," he whispered, his voice rough with excitement. He guided her to the bed, and she climbed up onto the mattress. Liese folded her legs under her, kneeling at the edge.

His finger traveled from the collar of her shirt to between her breasts, and he paused to flick open the button. Parting the fabric, he pushed it over her shoulders and down her arms, then tossed it on the bed. His hands went to her hips, and his thumbs hooked into the lace waistband of her thong.

Liese used the same slow movements as she followed the contours of muscle along his arms and over his shoulders. Sitting back on her heels, her fingers found his belt buckle. She gripped the metal fitting and tugged until his thighs hit the bed.

"May I?" She fingered the clasp, waiting for affirmation.

"By all means." Ryder watched her hands while she unbuckled his belt and unzipped the fly.

"I have the button, by the way," Liese offered, watching with greedy expectation as his pants slid down his thighs.

"That's a relief," he replied, kicking free of the fabric at his feet.

Her eyes fell to his black boxers and the generous erection straining against the thin fabric.

"Would you like to perform a formal inspection?" He fingered the waistband.

"More than you could know."

He moved her into the middle of the bed as he climbed up after her. Her lips parted as their mouths collided. The contact of skin on skin and the wet warmth of his tongue erased all thought in a red void of want. Liese parted her thighs, and he sank between them, that hard part of him finding the aching part of her. She groaned, arching into him, ready to feel him inside her.

"I want to show you something," he said into her neck, pushing up on his forearms to hover over her.

"Okay." Liese ran her hand down his chest and slid it into his boxers, gripping his erection.

Ryder's head dropped, his shoulders bunching as the muscles in his arms flexed. A guttural curse left him. Sitting up on his knees, he looked down his body to where she held him.

He covered her hand with his, eyes rolling back as she brushed the head with her thumb. He pried her fingers away and told her, "Not quite yet."

She protested as he tucked himself away. Ryder ignored her lament and moved behind her, one leg on either side of hers. He propped himself against the headboard and she settled into him, her head on his chest.

Ryder grabbed the remote control, and the black screen of the TV flashed blue. "I think you may recognize this." His hand spanned her stomach, fingers drawing circles on her skin while he waited for the video to cue up.

Liese suspected what she was about to see would reveal more about her predilections than she had ever shared with any of her past lovers. She didn't know how she felt about that. He moved her hair over one shoulder and followed the line of her neck with his mouth. Images popped up on the screen, the volume just loud enough to hear the woman's soft moans.

"Oh, shit," Liese breathed, recognizing the scene. She'd viewed this particular video about a week ago and given herself several orgasms in the process—all while thinking about Ryder.

"Is this familiar to you?" he asked, his palm skirting the outside of her leg. When she nodded, his hand traveled inward, his thumb traveling along the inside of her thigh.

He clicked the remote and a different video cued up. Liese's breath quickened, and her heart began to race. Ryder dropped the remote, whispering the depraved things he wanted to do to her, the places he wanted to touch, to lick, to kiss. He coaxed her thong over her hips and Liese took over when he reached her knees. Shoving it down, she tossed her panties over the edge of the bed. Her bra went next, leaving her completely exposed as he continued to show her the scenes he found most enticing.

"Should you really have been looking at these during work hours?" Liese asked, relishing his touch.

"No, but I shouldn't have been on the verge of fucking you on your desk either." He ran a knuckle over her slick skin, circling her entrance, reminding her just how close they'd been. Liese grabbed the back of his neck, searching for his mouth. "And I'm the one who got the spanking. That's hardly fair."

He kissed her hard, his fingers moving to the same rhythm as his tongue. Liese heard the click of the TV, and the room darkened, the glimmer of candlelight casting the bed in shadow. In the absence of distractions, she gave herself over to the feel of his touch and the taste of his mouth. His free hand moved to her breast, his thumb circling the pebbled skin, a gentle contrast to his work below her waist. With startling intensity, she came apart, her breath coming in ragged gasps.

While she recovered, Ryder repositioned himself. No longer sitting behind her, he pulled the covers down. Liese scooted back, reclining into the pillows. He followed the contour of her bottom lip with his thumb, then gripped the headboard above her.

With surprisingly steady hands, she removed his boxers. The muscles in his stomach tightened when she traced the length of him with a fingertip. Ryder bowed his head and closed his eyes, groaning softly.

The headboard creaked as his weight settled against the wood. With his cock inches from her face she closed the gap and touched her lips to the tip, the hot skin satin smooth. Ryder grunted a particularly obscene expletive.

"Would you like me to start sucking up, sir?"

Ryder stilled above her. The fire in his gaze wiped the grin off her face. She took him in her hand, stroking his length. With parted lips she lifted her eyes to his and licked up the shaft.

His grunt of approval encouraged her, as did the view. Ryder's muscles were corded and stark as he gripped the headboard. He shifted his hips forward with every stroke of her mouth and hand.

"God," he panted, "I can't . . ." He slid one hand into her hair and held her still, withdrawing from her mouth.

She fisted his erection tightly, and his throat bobbed as he swallowed. When she asked if he was okay, he held up a finger. It seemed like forever before he moved or spoke, and when he did, his response was so low she didn't catch it.

Ryder drew her up and kissed her. "Have I told you how much I enjoy when you suck up?" He tugged her bottom lip with his teeth. "Or how incredible your mouth is?"

Liese's laugh morphed into a moan as she felt his slick erection press against her.

His hand went to her ass, and he squeezed. "Will you turn around for me?"

"Is there another option?"

"Did you need there to be one?"

"No. You can have me any way you want me."

Ryder paused, suddenly serious. He kissed her again, but the passion was tempered with something she couldn't quite place, and it unnerved her.

Breaking the kiss, Ryder turned her to face the headboard and guided her hands to rest on the smooth wood surface. He ran his hands up her arms, over her shoulders, and down her sides. "So beautiful," he murmured. He traced the curve of her hips to her thighs and spread her legs, bending her forward slightly.

"Is this comfortable?" he asked, waiting for her affirmation before he continued. His left hand covered hers as his other arm came about her waist. His fingers splayed out over her hip and moved down, making light passes over her clit.

"Mmmm, good. I want you like this." He nuzzled the back of her neck, reaching across to the nightstand for a foil packet.

After a few moments he toyed with her, replacing his fingers with his cock, stroking back and forth before slowly pushing inside. Ryder kissed her shoulder and up the side of her neck, pausing at the hollow beneath her ear. "I knew you'd feel like heaven."

Liese released a shuddering breath when his hips eased back. His hand ghosted along her ribs, palming a breast as he pushed back in. He moved over her, slow at first, the headboard protesting the forward momentum. Chest pressed against her back, Ryder's fingers slid between her own, his grip tight on the smooth wood surface, gaining leverage as his pace quickened.

His lips brushed her cheek, and she turned into the unexpected affection. "I want to feel you come while I'm inside you," he said in a seductive whisper.

It was all too much: Ryder moving inside her, his fingers threaded tight through hers, the feel of his lips, and then his teeth against her neck. The sensations he evoked paired with his words sent her over the edge. Freefalling, Liese gave herself over to the feeling of being completely consumed. Her orgasm hit her with such force it sent her spinning, just as she'd predicted.

Ryder waited until she'd caught her breath before he moved again. His hand moved over her stomach and between her breasts, fingertips tickling hypersensitive skin. His palm came to rest gently against the base of her throat, his thumb finding its way between her lips. Liese bit down, sucking softly as his other arm came around her waist and pulled her tight against him. He pushed in deep, stilling as he lowered his head to her shoulder, a low groan of satisfaction muffled against her skin. Then he collapsed onto the pillows, taking her down with him.

"Will you stay the night?" Ryder asked on an exhale, moving her hair aside so he could kiss her temple. "Because I'd like to do this again in the morning."

10

The Aftermath of a Bad Decision

LIESE WOKE TO the soft sounds of jazz and a hard-on against her ass. Her eyes popped open as the events of the previous night came back to her in a rush.

Ryder had spanked her. And then they'd had very hot, gratifying sex.

As she lay in his bed, his warm body cocooning hers, she should have been relaxed. But the moment her eyes opened, her brain started to work. Liese became acutely aware that the moment she left Ryder's bed, real life would come crashing down on her. She would have to go to work and spend the day pretending the night before hadn't happened. In theory it seemed doable, but the reality carried a different set of complications.

The arm draped over her waist moved as Ryder's hand smoothed down her stomach. Her internal freak-out took a backseat when his fingers drifted lower.

"Good morning," he said in a sleep-graveled voice.

Liese hummed in response, pushing her face into the pillow

as Ryder burrowed his nose into her neck. She breathed into the cotton to find out how bad her morning breath was and decided *not* to roll over and face him. "Did you sleep well?"

"Mmm-hmmm," Liese replied.

"Do you feel okay?" His hand moved lower, cupping her, indicating the part he referred to.

"I'd be better if you'd stop teasing me." "Is that so?" His hand disappeared.

He palmed the back of her knee and pushed her leg up toward her chest. There was no precursor, no foreplay as he rubbed the head of his erection over sensitive skin. Liese groaned as he found her entrance and slipped in.

He paused, breathing ragged. "Okay?"

She nodded, pushing against him, urging him deeper. Ryder held her hip, keeping her still as he withdrew almost entirely before inching back in, filling her completely.

He molded his body around hers, one leg stretched out along her straight one, one knee bent to fit inside the crook of hers. It felt different than last night. There was nothing frantic about this coupling. He moved inside her slowly, his forehead pressed against the back of her neck.

Reaching up, she slid her fingers into his hair, gripping the silken strands firmly. Liese felt his mouth on her shoulder, his lips parting to suck on the skin as he continued to thrust.

He slid an arm under her waist to wrap around her, palming her breast. His other hand dipped between her legs to find the spot that made her moan his name. The slow grinding of his hips matched the lazy circling of his fingers, and a rush of warmth flooded her body. The sensation radiated through her in waves and she rode it out, desperate to hold onto the connection between them.

"God, you feel so good," Ryder whispered, holding her tight as he followed with his own release shortly after.

They lay there for a long while, Ryder's lips moving over her shoulder and neck, his fingers gilding languidly up and down her leg.

"That was a nice way to wake up." As she rolled onto her back, the sheets twisted around her calf to expose her torso.

She looked at him, and what she saw made her fear this would be her only chance to be with him this way. His contemplative frown unsettled her. The consequences of their actions seemed too big a burden to carry.

Ryder's index finger traced the valley between her breasts, drifting over the swell to circle a nipple. "Yes, it certainly was."

He bent to kiss her, sucking her breast into his mouth, and his tongue swirled around the taut peak. He released it and blew on the tip, watching it tighten.

He shifted and straddled her, rendering her secure beneath him. He looked past her to the night table where the clock glared its unwanted beacon. Their time had come to an end. "I need to get ready for work. I'm already running behind."

Liese was slow to process the electronic glow of the alarm clock. "Oh, God! We're going to be late!" She pushed on his chest and struggled to sit up with Ryder still poised on top of her. "I have to go home and change." She inhaled and blushed. "And shower. I smell like sex."

Ryder's eyes narrowed as he bore down on her. Gathering her wrists in his hands, he kept her from leaving the bed.

"What are you doing?" Panic and lust surged through her. She wanted to stay but needed to go.

"I like the way you smell." He breathed her in, his mouth hovering above the swell of her breast, his hair tickling her chin.

"Ryder, we're going to be late."

"No, we're not."

"Yes, we—"

Ryder raised his head, his lips at the corner of her mouth, and she pursed hers together. Like hell she was going to kiss him before she brushed her teeth.

"Open," he whispered.

Liese shook her head.

He shifted, his knee coming between her own. As he pressed his hips into hers she felt what seemed to be an erection but clearly couldn't be since they'd finished having sex just minutes ago. As she began to state that fact, Ryder took the advantage and kissed her fiercely. Her hesitation dissipated as desperation took over. When he finally broke the kiss, she was breathless and hot all over again.

"I really don't want to leave this bed." He released her hands and buried his face in the pillow beside her, his cheek pressed against hers.

In a consoling gesture, she ran her hand down his back, feeling the flex of muscles. "We could call in sick." Liese hated the hopefulness in her voice.

He shook his head, and although she knew playing hooky wouldn't be an option, she felt a pang of hurt.

He rolled off of her, shifting to sit on the edge of the bed, facing away. "I took the liberty of enrolling you in a professional development session that runs until noon today. Of course, you're not expected to attend, but you'll need to be at FAHL by twelve-thirty." He scrubbed his face with his palm. "You can go back to sleep for a while, if you'd like. I'll be in the shower." He pushed off the mattress, head dropping as he paused, then spun to face her with an expression that bordered on terror, his hand covering his semi-erect cock. "Fuck. What the hell was I thinking?"

"Pardon?"

At her confusion he continued, "No condom."

"Oh. I get the shot."

His shoulders relaxed a little. "Regardless, that was incredibly irresponsible of me."

"I trust you. I would have stopped you if I was concerned," she said, fingering the edge of the sheets. She'd been so preoccupied with how good it felt, she hadn't clued in to the why of it.

He leaned down and pressed his lips against hers. "Still, I apologize. I'm not so sure your trust was well earned, considering my lack of judgment."

He withdrew without deepening the kiss and turned away.

Liese took in the sinewy expanse of his back, which led to his perfect ass, as Ryder moved across the room. The bathroom door closed behind him, cutting off her spectacular view, and the patter of water from the shower filtered through the wall.

A sick feeling settled in the pit of her stomach. The doubts she'd pushed down resurfaced, gnawing at her conscience. She fought the compulsion to get dressed and leave before he returned from his shower. She didn't want to think about what would happen next. She realized again how complicated things could get from here. She should seek a different advisor. She couldn't continue to have him in that role when she wanted to be sprawled out on his desk—being spanked, no less. Now that they'd acted on the impulse, it would be impossible not to go there again given the opportunity, at least for her.

Liese stared at the ceiling and tried to figure out what the hell to do. There would be no time to talk it out this morning. Even if he hurried, Ryder would still be late. The water turned off, and she listened for sounds of movement but could only hear the fan. Several minutes later, Ryder emerged from the bathroom fully dressed, fastening the last of the buttons on his dress shirt.

The tension in the room felt suffocating. "I should go home." She sat up, clutching the sheets to her chest, and peered over the edge of the bed, looking for her clothes. Aside from her panties and bra, they were nowhere to be found. They'd been removed in Ryder's office.

"No." He headed for his dresser where he opened a small box and picked out a clip, fastening his tie to his shirt. "Stay as long as you like. Just be at work by twelve-thirty." When he lifted his eyes, he didn't look at her, but past her, above her head. "I'm sure you're aware this is a highly sensitive situation, and I expect you'll be discreet about what's happened."

Her unease transformed into humiliated despair. Ryder had shut down on her. His professional, cold demeanor—the one saved primarily for those who'd done something to displease him—loomed large. This was a look he'd never directed at her, and the sight of it now made her feel used and pathetic.

"I won't say anything to anyone," she said, willing him to meet her gaze. He didn't.

"Of course you won't. But in all seriousness, I suggest you leave your laptop at home from now on. Such a transgression would be detrimental to both of our careers." He scanned her body, his eyes never reaching hers. An emotion flickered across his face—sadness, regret maybe, but he buried it quickly. "I appreciate your discretion. There's a package on the table in the foyer with all the materials you would've received had you made it to the session." He turned toward the door.

"Ryder." Her voice cracked, betraying her emotions. This wasn't how she wanted to leave things.

He paused at the threshold, gripping the doorjamb. For a fraction of a second, Liese thought he would turn around.

Instead he straightened. "I'll see you this afternoon." And then he was gone.

She sat in stunned silence, listening as he descended the stairs. It seemed to take forever for him to leave. When the front door closed, she dropped the hand pressed against her mouth, embarrassed that she had expected anything different from this experience.

Of course it would be a one-night stand; his references to subsequent punishments last night had been founded on primal need, nothing else. A relationship with Ryder would be too complicated. She knew it, but it still hurt to have it thrown in her face. No kiss goodbye, no reassurance they would talk later or work something out. Despite herself, she wanted more. She wanted secret dates and deep conversation, passionate sex and more spankings.

She dropped back against the pillows, sinking into them as she replayed last night and this morning in her head. It dawned on her with aching clarity that both times they'd had sex it had been from behind. Not once had he looked her in the eyes or kissed her during the act.

Mortified and angry, Liese wished she could take it back. She pulled in an uneven breath. She could practically taste Ryder's aftershave and smell his skin as she huddled in his sheets. Disgusted with herself for being such an idiot, she untangled the covers and left his bed.

Striding down the hallway in her bra and panties, she retrieved her clothes from his office. It was impossible not to look at his desk as she dressed, and a fresh wave of misery washed over her when she thought about how exposed she'd allowed herself to be with him. Anger sparked, and she swiped at her tears, willing herself to hold it together. Liese yanked on her skirt and fastened the buttons of her blouse with shaking hands.

In a hurry to leave, she padded quickly down the stairs and passed his living room, a space she'd been too preoccupied to notice last night. She paused. There were no family pictures on the walls or the mantle of the fireplace. But a painting hung in isolation above a solitary wingback chair. The figure was curled in on himself, dark hair hanging over his cheek, shoulders hunched. Lean, wiry arms wrapped around his shins, and his forehead rested on his knees. The straight line of his nose reminded her of a much younger Ryder, but this version looked as helpless as she felt in this moment.

Turning away, she glanced at the kitchen. The dishes from the previous night were still on the counter, leftover food dried on the plates. Liese sighed. She needed to get out of his house. She vacillated between wanting to break his dishes or put them in the dishwasher.

Liese slipped into her shoes and pulled on her coat. She looked around for her purse, irrationally afraid Ryder would return. If that happened, she ran the risk of punching him in his gorgeous face for being such a colossal dick and making her feel stupid for having had sex with him in the first place. Her vision blurred as tears threatened to fall. A few, deep calming breaths later, she could see again.

Her purse sat on the side table, a white envelope perched beside it. Inside she found the documents Ryder had left to ensure her absence appeared legitimate this morning. Also tucked inside the large envelope was a smaller one containing a note and a key.

As she unfolded the paper, Liese wondered if she might have

misread his behavior. Ryder's neat cursive had filled the small page, but not with the reassuring message she'd hoped for.

Please lock the door on your way out. You can leave the key in my mailbox by sealing it in this envelope.

The note wasn't addressed to her, and he hadn't bothered to sign it. She shoved it into her purse along with the documents from the professional development session. If she'd had the balls, she would have left the door unlocked and taped the key to it. Instead, she slammed it harder than necessary and locked it before she stomped to her car. But she didn't leave the key in the mailbox. If he wanted it back, he'd have to ask her for it.

The second she sat in the driver's seat, her phone beeped. She glared at the device lying in the center console. She hated how much she hoped Ryder had left a message. Punching in her code, she found she had new voicemails and another text from Marissa. The request incited her to text or call within the next twenty-four hours or her friend would file a missing persons report.

Liese hastily replied to let Marissa know she hadn't ended up face down in a ditch somewhere. She desperately wanted to talk to her, but multitasking while upset seemed like a bad idea. The other new voicemail was from a number she didn't recognize with a New York area code. She left that one for later, when she wasn't in a rush to escape the scene of her poor decision making.

The shower became her primary target upon arrival at home, with her goal to remove all traces of Ryder. Now that she had some perspective, she realized she should have left the key in his mailbox. Keeping it would force a confrontation she wasn't quite ready for. Until she had her emotions under control, she would have to avoid him.

By 10:30 she was dressed and ready for work. She called Marissa's cell, but it flipped to voicemail on the third ring. Liese broke down over Marissa's recorded message telling her to "leave your deets at the tone." She spluttered out a barely coherent message, which included a request for immediate contact.

With time to spare, Liese checked her voicemail and found the two calls from the previous night to be hang-ups. She deleted them and listened to the ones from the same number that were time-stamped at four in the morning and again at five. The first was another hang-up; the next, however, was not.

"Uh—hey. Hi. It's Sean. I got a new cell, which is probably why you're not answering. I . . . uh—I was thinking about how much I missed you. I wondered if you'd gotten my texts or not. I've sent you a few. I just want to talk. I know you think we can't be together with you living in Pennsylvania and me living in New York, but I just . . . I love you and I miss you. Call me. Okay, babydoll? I really want to talk. Maybe I could come see you. Okay. I hope you call back. You can't ignore me forever." The message cut off abruptly, having run out of time to record what probably would have gone on for eons.

"Son of a bitch." Liese exhaled unsteadily. She saved the message and pressed the end button, tossing the phone down as if it might bite her. She looked out the window, half expecting to see her ex-boyfriend on her front porch. It wouldn't have been the first time she found him camped out there. Sean had slept in the hallway of her apartment the night she broke it off with him. She'd called the superintendent, and it was only when the building threatened to call the police that he finally gave up. He'd been persistent though; returning the following night, and the one after that until they did call the police.

Shaken and distraught, she left her house earlier than necessary, too strung out to stay home any longer. The local coffee shop seemed a safe bet before she headed to FAHL for her 12:30

arrival. The latte she ordered warmed her hands but little else as she sat in the parking lot, waiting until it was time to face her fate. She had to buck up. She'd made her bed and now she had to lie in it. How ironic that she'd left Ryder's a mess.

Reluctantly, she got out of the car. If all went well, she could sign in without running into anyone and hide out in the library for the afternoon. Composing herself, she headed directly to the main office. She found Blake there, chatting with Betty.

"Hey, you." He flashed her a smile. "I wondered if you were still feeling crappy since you weren't here this morning. I was worried about you last night."

"I'm okay, just a little worn out." It wasn't a total lie; she was tired, all right. "I had a PD session this morning I forgot I'd signed up for." She returned his smile and prayed it didn't look fake as she held up the package.

She could tell he didn't believe her about being okay, but he didn't press the issue. "Was it interesting at least?"

Liese shrugged noncommittally at the same time Ryder came out of his office to speak to Betty.

"That good, huh?" Blake asked. "What was it about?"

Unprepared to see Ryder, Liese blurted, "Oh, it was just some workplace harassment training session." Her vindictive side reigned as she followed with, "It was relatively unsatisfying." She tried to suppress a smile as Ryder's eyes bore a hole into the side of her face.

"Hey, Whitehall." Blake gave him a causal nod, oblivious to the nuclear-level tension.

Ryder narrowed his eyes at Blake, who was so close to Liese their arms were practically touching. "Mr. Stone, Ms. Harper."

"Sir." She donned a serene smile she didn't feel and noticed his hair, which was rather disheveled. Turning her attention back to Blake, she touched his forearm. "I should really get to the library. I'll see you later?" Liese jumped when Ryder's office door slammed.

Blake rolled his eyes. "Who pissed in his cornflakes?"

Betty leaned forward and whispered conspiratorially, "I have no idea, but he's been like that all morning. We're all used to him being a little sensitive, but this is one of the worst moods I've ever seen him in. I'd stay out his way today if I were you."

"Duly noted. Come on, Liese. Let's get out of here before you fully experience Whitehall's Mr. Hyde side."

Liese glanced at the principal's door as she heard something being dropped, or thrown, inside. "That sounds like a very good idea."

It was only Tuesday. She had all week to anticipate that experience.

11

Everything Unexpected

BLAKE FOLLOWED HER out of the office, checking the hall before he started asking questions.

"You sure you're okay?"

Liese nodded, because speaking meant lying, and she couldn't keep it together if she had to lie again to Blake.

He squeezed her shoulder. "Come on, I know you better than that."

Conflicted, she shrugged out from under his palm. She couldn't let Blake in on her secret. "Sorry. I didn't sleep well last night."

"That makes two of us," Blake said, eyes on the floor. "Look, you shouldn't be the one apologizing. I overstepped my boundaries yesterday, and if you're mad at me say so and then I can figure out how to fix it."

"Mad at you?"

He chanced a glance at her. "I grilled you pretty harshly, and I didn't have the right to do that. I know it's not my business, but we're friends, and I want you to feel like you can confide in me if someone does something to make you uncomfortable." He paused, but she didn't take the bait. "I was a jerk, and I feel bad about it."

She felt awful. "I have to go." She spun around, ready to bolt.

"Liese?" Blake grabbed her arm, and she nearly screamed in frustration.

She didn't understand how men could be so damn oblivious. On the verge of an emotional breakdown, she didn't want to be in the middle of the hall when she finally succumbed to the torrent of tears.

"I'm not mad at you, Blake—really." She raised her hand to stop his protest. "But I'm not having the best day, and I'm afraid I'm going to lose it in a second." Tears welled. "Fudge." She censored her language out of habit at school. She looked up at the ceiling, blinking rapidly, as though gravity would stop the tears from falling.

"Oh my God, you're going to cry, aren't you? Oh, God."

The panic in his voice made it more difficult to hold the tears at bay.

"I'm going to hug you now," he warned and crushed her to his chest.

"This looks really inappropriate," she mumbled into his shirt, arms hanging loosely at her sides. All she wanted to do was latch onto him and sob. He smelled like fresh laundry and incense, an oddly comforting combination.

"Who cares? It'll give the kids something to gossip about. Maybe this will dispel the rumor that I'm gay. Besides, I'm hugging you as a friend, and because you obviously need it." He gave her a squeeze.

"Thanks." She sniffed and pushed away.

You need me to get you anything? Tea? A pint of ice cream?"

"No, I'm good, but thanks for the offer."

"Okay, no problem. I grew up with four younger sisters; I'm good at the consoling thing. And if you change your mind and decide you're pissed at me, please tell me so I can give you the chance to bitch slap me for being a turd yesterday."

Liese gave him a watery smile and chuckled. "Okay."

"Oh, and there's no rehearsal until tomorrow night, so if I don't see you, have a moderately okay afternoon."

"You too." She waved him off, still feeling like she could lose it without much provocation, but thankfully back from the edge. Heading for the library, she checked to make sure no one had seen the exchange. Mercifully, the halls were empty.

Liese spent the afternoon half expecting Ryder to show up in her office. Part of her wanted it to happen so she could tell him exactly how she felt about the way he'd treated her this morning. The other part was terrified that any type of confrontation would reveal how deeply invested she was.

After the final bell of the day, her office phone rang. She looked at the extension, but disappointment dispelled her nerves when she saw it was an outside line. Irritation took hold when she remembered Sean's message from the previous night. She wondered how many of the hang-ups in the past month had been him and whether his unfailing interest was more serious than she'd originally thought. It seemed a conversation with him was imminent. She just hoped he hadn't managed to get her work number, as well.

On the third ring, she shook free of her musings and picked up the phone. "Hello?"

"Um, hi." There was a long pause before the familiar female voice spoke again. "Liese? Is that you?"

"Marissa?"

"Thank fuck."

"What's wrong? What happened?" Liese asked. The image of Marissa tied to a chair while Sean bawled at her feet and forced her to listen to him whine sprang to mind.

"What do you mean what's wrong?!"

Liese held the phone away from her ear while Marissa screeched.

"You call and leave me a message while you're sobbing and totally incomprehensible, and you have the nerve to ask me what's wrong? Are you okay?"

"Incomprehensible?"

"Like that one? I looked it up just for you before I called." Even angry, Marissa was snarky.

"I do. Thanks for that." Liese smiled in spite of her situation.

"But seriously, what the hell is going on?" Marissa demanded. "You sounded pretty awful earlier. I think we need to make some rules now that you aren't living here: no text can go unanswered for more than twelve hours. I almost had a damn heart attack today, and I'm too young to die."

"I'm sorry. I didn't mean to make you worry."

"You're forgiven. Now tell me what the hell happened."

"I can't right now. I'm at work."

Marissa sighed dramatically. "I know you're at work. I called you, remember? When is a good time?"

"Can I call you when I get home?"

"*Will* you call when you get home?" she asked. "Because if you don't, I'm driving down there and kicking your ass, proverbially speaking. I wouldn't ever really kick your ass."

"I promise I'll call the second I walk in the door."

"Fine. I'll be waiting."

Okay, thanks." There was relief in knowing she'd be able to talk to Marissa soon. "Oh, there is one thing, though. Has Sean been in contact with you lately?"

"Is that what this is about? Please tell me you're *not* thinking about getting back together with that lunatic."

"God, no. I may do stupid things, but I'm not that dumb." Liese tried not to be offended. Marissa was just being a good friend; she'd borne witness to Sean's freakish tendencies during the initial breakup. "He sent a few texts recently, and last night he left a message about getting back together." Liese fiddled with the phone cord and surveyed the room to ensure the privacy of their conversation. No one needed to know about her pisspoor track record with men.

"Maybe you should reconsider that restraining order." Marissa had wanted her to file one when Sean camped out in front of their apartment door three days in a row.

"Yeah, maybe."

"Don't think we won't be talking about this later, too. That guy's a psycho."

"I know."

"Good. I expect to hear your voice before five; any later and I'll be on my way to your house. And I won't be in a good mood, either." Marissa hung up.

In order to adhere to the phone call deadline, Liese left school shortly thereafter. A visit from Marissa was always welcome, and it had been almost three weeks since her last visit, but Liese would rather she be happy than pissed off. After four years of living together, the separation hadn't been easy.

Liese avoided the main office on her way to the parking lot. The temptation to barge into Ryder's office and give him an earful held far too much allure. The last thing she wanted to be was a stage-five clinger—she already had one of her own. The idea of becoming anything like Sean made her want to commit herself to an asylum.

As soon as she arrived home, she called Marissa. "He found the photoshopped pictures."

"Who did?"

"Ryder."

"Fuuuuuuck." Marissa exhaled loudly into the receiver. "Wait, does that mean you're fired? Are you moving back here? Why were you at work today?"

"No, I'm not fired, and no, I'm not moving back to the city."

"Boo." Marissa didn't hide her disappointment. "Wait. How the hell are you not fired?"

"I slept with him."

"With who?"

"With Ryder."

"He blackmailed you into sleeping with him?" Marissa's voice rose an octave. Or two.

"No. He didn't blackmail me."

"I'm so confused."

"That makes two of us." Liese went on to explain in the barest of details what had transpired, leaving out the part about Ryder "punishing" her because the rest of the story was bad enough. Relaying it to another person made it that much more real—and embarrassing.

"That asshole," Marissa seethed.

"I'm so stupid." Liese picked apart a napkin, creating a pile of white fluff on her kitchen table as they talked.

"No, you're not. You're human, and humans make mistakes. This is a pretty bad one, I'll give you that, but how were you to know he was going to be a huge dick about it?"

I should've known nothing good would come of this." "Probably, but you can't take it back now. I hope he was at least well equipped." Marissa tried to lighten the mood.

Liese snorted. "I'm not giving you those details."

"Oooh, so he was good? That's too bad about him being a giant penis. Or should I say *having* a giant penis." Marissa fished.

"Mar . . ."

"Okay, I'll stop. But you need to come see me and get away from the drama. Can you come this weekend? Maybe we can make a plan for you to get a job in New York again so you don't have to see that dick-smack every day."

Talk of moving back to the city tightened Liese's chest. "I can't leave my position in the middle of the semester."

"You can if you have a new one. We'll deal with that this weekend, after I get you drunk enough to spill all the sordid details."

"Good luck with that," Liese said, glad to be off the topic of leaving. She'd already run away from one problem, and that hadn't worked out very well. Sean was still harassing her, even across state lines.

They finalized plans for the weekend, and Liese promised to call if any further issues arose during the week.

Later that evening, she went to check her email, but realized she'd left her laptop in Ryder's bedroom. She also still had his house key. If things got much worse, moving back to NYC might be her only option. She contemplated driving to his house to reclaim her laptop and return the key, but she worried she might break down in front of him. She didn't want to give him the satisfaction of seeing her weakness.

Ryder was out of the office on Wednesday, preventing any chance of running into him. Heedless of the consequences, she dropped the key, inside its envelope, in his school mailbox and left a note requesting her laptop's expedient return. In defiance, she didn't sign it.

By Thursday morning, she still hadn't received a response, which infuriated her. The least he could do was acknowledge her, even if he did regret having given in to temptation.

Marissa called the same day to deliver more bad news. A new project had come her way with a short deadline, and she had to cancel their weekend plans. She apologized profusely, and they rescheduled for the following weekend, but it meant time alone for Liese to wallow. She woke up in a pissy mood on Friday, only to be sucker-punched with more disappointment when she discovered her laptop on her front porch—no note attached. She opened it, stupidly hoping to find something hidden inside, only to be disappointed further.

"Asshole," she said under her breath as she stomped to her car. The wheels sprayed stones as she floored it down her driveway. She blared industrial rock and fumed all the way to work. The itch to break something, preferably over Ryder's head, burgeoned along with her anger. His actions reeked of cowardice. Her impression of him had done a one-eighty in less than a week. To say she hadn't wanted more than a fling would be a lie, no matter how unlikely or unwise she'd known it to be from the beginning, and the way he'd discarded her like a onenight stand hurt more than she cared to admit. He had to expect a confrontation eventually. And he was sure as hell going to get one.

Unable to contain her frustration, she slammed her car into park and stalked to the front office. Ryder couldn't avoid a real conversation forever, and he needed to be taken down a notch.

His door was closed, so Liese approached Betty. She plastered a smile on her face and hoped it looked natural.

"Hi, Betty." Aggravation made her restless, and she rapped her fingernails on the desk top.

"I just called your office." Betty smiled in return, apparently pleased to see her. "I expect you're looking for Ryder."

Liese tried to mask her surprise. Anger turned to suspicion. Had he planned this? She wouldn't put it past him to orchestrate a drop off in order to avoid a conversation that might get heated. In his office, she'd have to keep her temper under control. "He's here then?" she asked through gritted teeth.

"I'm afraid not." Betty lowered her voice. "He's been out all week at the board office in Montgomery County. He didn't expect to be gone so much. He called this morning and requested a meeting with you at the end of the day. Can I tell him you'll be available?"

"You sure can." A meeting at the end of the day worked well. If timed right, the office staff would be gone, and she could give him a proper piece of her mind—provided she could stay angry that long and not slide back into her pond of self-pity. As she left the office, she wondered why he hadn't held onto her laptop until they spoke. Maybe he thought she might bash him in the face with it.

By the time afternoon rolled around, Liese was antsy. And she'd amassed quite a list of colorful names to throw at Ryder for their meeting. During her planning period, she took a break to grab a cup of tea from the staff lounge. Not surprisingly, her stomach had been in knots all day. She ran into Blake, who was filling his jumbo coffee mug.

"We're going for drinks after work. You'll be there, right?" he asked.

Liese sighed, annoyed that Ryder's impromptu meeting would infringe on her social time. "I'll be there. I might be a little late, though. I have a meeting."

Blake pulled a face, but the bell rang before he had a chance to ask questions, and he rushed off to teach his class.

Lost in thought, Liese left the staff lounge and crashed into another body, sloshing hot tea all over her arm and the floor. "Ow! Oh, God, I'm so sorry!" She inhaled a very familiar scent and looked up to find Ryder.

"We need to talk before you leave today," he said through clenched teeth. He looked beyond her.

Liese looked over her shoulder, half expecting to find someone there, but the corridor was empty. She turned back to him, their eyes locking. All the fury drained out of her as images of what she'd let him do and how he'd left things washed over her, rendering her tongue-tied and insecure.

"Yes, sir," she said timidly. She hated how weak he made her feel in that moment.

"I look forward to it, Ms. Harper." He stepped around her, his fingers brushing her hip as he passed.

Diffidence gave way to black anger in the wake of his touch. She had no idea what kind of game he was playing, but she wasn't about to let it continue.

Blake popped his head in the door after last bell. "Don't let your meeting keep you too long," he said, pointedly not asking anything further about it.

"Oh, believe me, I won't." She grabbed her purse and locked

up. She'd get this over with as quickly as possible, then drown her emotions in martinis. Blake walked her to the office, stopping to talk to Betty as Liese knocked on Ryder's closed door. Her nerves had fired up again, but at least this time they were tempered by a healthy dose of pissed.

Ryder opened the door and moved aside to allow her entrance. "Come in, Ms. Harper."

"I'll save you a seat," Blake called, louder than necessary. He winked at her before turning to Ryder, his grin widening. "Have a good weekend, Whitehall."

Ryder didn't respond, just closed the door once Liese was inside.

And then he locked it.

12

Absolutely Not

RYDER CROWDED HER, his expression grim as he occupied too much of her personal space. Liese refused to back
down, though. She wanted to win this staring contest. He looked
irritatingly sexy in his navy suit and electric blue tie. The fact
that she noticed those details incensed her further.

"Why the hell does he always have to be near you? He's like
a fucking mosquito."

"Pardon me?" Liese crossed her arms over her chest. She
didn't like his tone one bit.

"Stone. I can't stand that pompous asshole." Ryder glared at
the closed door as if he could still feel Blake's presence on the
other side.

"He's my friend, and he treats me with decency and respect,
unlike some people I know," she retorted. "You wanted to see
me?"

He inspected his tie, adjusted it, and then looked at her.
"You've been avoiding me," he said, his tone accusatory.

"How can I avoid you when you're not even in the building?" She didn't need to own up to the fact that all week she'd arrived at the bell and left as soon as the day was over. He hadn't been there to notice anyway.

"How do you know I haven't been in the building?"

"Betty told me. You've hardly been in at all this week. It's pretty difficult to avoid someone who isn't here."

"So you wanted to know where I was," he murmured. Liese couldn't be sure the comment was meant for her until he asked with honest curiosity: "Did you miss me?" "What?" She gaped at him.

"Never mind." Ryder waved a dismissive hand, his face turning red.

Liese couldn't get a handle on his motive for asking. If he'd thought they could pick things up right where they'd left off Tuesday morning, he was mistaken.

"I wanted to see you tonight," he said, looking at the floor.

"Are you *kidding me*?" Liese hissed. She wished she could yell. She wished she could slap his pretty face, but with her luck one of the secretaries would hear. As much as she wanted to embarrass him, exposing their affair would be equally detrimental to her.

"Why would I be kidding about wanting to see you?" Ryder lifted his head. "I thought maybe we could have dinner together. I could cook again."

Liese raised her hand in the air, right in front of his face. "Absolutely not. You don't want to *see* me, you want to *fuck* me, and that, *Mr. Whitehall*, isn't going to happen ever again." Even as she said it, she couldn't be certain of the truth in that statement. Angry though she was, the chemistry between them was hard to ignore. Her body remembered the feel of his hands and his mouth even as her mind tried to shut down the images. "I'm sorry? I . . ." Ryder sputtered. "I can't lie. I've certainly thought about what it would be like to be inside you again— incessantly, in fact. But that's not the only reason I want to see you." He paused, running his hand through his hair. "Maybe you'd rather me take you out somewhere for dinner instead? That way you're assured I'll be on my best behavior."

Liese put her hand on his chest, shoving him back. She tried not to think about how solid he felt. "You can't be serious. You haven't spoken to me in four days. You didn't email, you didn't text, and you certainly didn't call to see how I was dealing with this situation. Do you know how that feels after all the—"

She stopped, not wanting him to know how emotionally attached she'd become. As if he needed more leverage. "The last time we talked, you graciously told me to keep my mouth shut for the good of both our careers. Now you're trying to tell me you not only want to fuck me again, but you want to what? Date me? Is that it? Don't you think this conversation would have been more appropriate, oh, say, before you left me lying in your bed so you could ignore me for the rest of the week?" Liese whispered furiously. "I'm not some slut you can fuck when you feel like it."

Ryder bowed his head. "I know that. That's not—I never intended for any of this to happen," he said. "But that doesn't mean I didn't want it to. I know I was inexcusably rude when I left you at my house. I wasn't a gentleman, and I didn't handle things well. I didn't expect to feel—" He sighed and met her gaze. "Please believe me when I tell you I wanted nothing more than to stay in bed with you all day, and not just because of the sex. I did a horrific job of conveying that effectively. I'd like to make it up to you if you'd let me."

For a fleeting moment, he seemed sweet and awkward in his fumbling. Liese knew too well that was hardly the case.

"I'm busy tonight," she retorted, determined not to crack.

Although the way he looked at her made it a challenge.

"Doing what?" he asked, his tone just as sharp. The wounded look on his face made her want to cancel her plans, which frustrated her to no end.

"Going out for drinks with some friends—not that it's any of your business. Are we done here?" Liese put her hand on the doorknob behind her.

After a few long seconds, he sighed heavily. "You're free to leave."

Liese turned, her hands shaking as she struggled with the lock. She burst out of the room and hightailed it to the parking lot, leaving as quickly as her car would allow. When she arrived at the bar, she had to give herself a few minutes to regain her composure before she went inside.

Half of her still wanted to drive over to Ryder's house and offer to be dessert again. The other half wanted to kick him in the taint for being a gigantic asshole up until this afternoon. He'd seemed so contrite and apologetic. Regardless, she would defer to Marissa. Only when she had an impartial opinion could she make a rational decision. If she acted on her initial impulse to go to him, she was likely to do something regrettable. Again.

Resolved, Liese went inside to find her friends. Emily and Janet, the classics teacher, sat on one side of a tall table, Blake on the other. They were her Fullerton crew. None of them knew her like Marissa did, and she definitely couldn't tell them about her situation with Ryder, but at least she didn't have to be alone with her thoughts.

"Meeting with Whitehall go okay?" Blake asked as she hoisted herself into the chair next to him. He slid a fresh martini her way and clinked her glass. "I ordered it when I saw your car pull in. Cheers."

"Thanks." Liese took a hefty gulp before answering, enjoying the burn as it traveled down her throat. "He was fine. It was just about resources for the library."

"Yeah, right. That's why you're gulping down that martini. Word has it Whitehall's been in a bad mood all week," Janet said.

"We've witnessed it firsthand more than once." Blake put his arm around Liese in a show of solidarity.

"Remember when he made you cry?" Emily asked Janet and took a delicate sip of her Cosmo.

"Em!" Janet slapped her arm.

"What?" Emily asked. "Who *hasn't* he made cry? That guy is the biggest jerk in the world."

Liese ducked her head, immersing herself in the menu. She didn't want confirmation that other people saw Ryder that way.

It created more questions about him than it answered.

"He hasn't made me cry," Blake interjected.

"That's probably because you beat him up when we were in high school," Janet shot back.

Liese looked up to find Blake staring intently at his beer. "You went to high school together?" she asked. Liese tried to imagine a teenage version of Blake.

"Yeah, he was a couple of years ahead of me."

"And you beat him up? Why would you do that?"

"That's a good question. Why did you beat him up?" Emily asked.

Blake sighed, his discomfort obvious. "Are you sure you want to hear this?"

At the simultaneous *yes*, he chugged the rest of his beer and poured a new one from the pitcher, launching into his story. "So I was a sophomore, and he was a senior. I was all geared up to try out for this role in the school play because this super-hot girl was trying out for the female lead, and there was this kissing scene—" Blake paused to survey his enraptured audience. "Anyway, I got the role, which was really cool because I was just a sophomore, and usually the lead roles went to juniors and seniors."

"Stop stalling and get to the good part," Janet ordered.

"Do you already know this story?" Liese looked from Janet to Blake.

"Uh-huh. Blake and I were in a lot of the same classes in high school. Okay, continue," Janet motioned to Blake.

"I'm sure you can see where this is going."

Liese couldn't see where it was going at all. The idea of Ryder taking part in a school production seemed preposterous, but she kept her mouth shut and waited.

"Whitehall had a crush on the female lead, and I had no idea. Like I said, he was a senior. I didn't really know him. He was into track, and I did drama. We didn't run in the same circles," Blake blathered on, looking more and more uncomfortable as he continued to justify the inevitable end to his story.

"Yeah, yeah, we get it. You didn't know him, so it was totally okay for you to steal his girl," Janet cut in again.

"Will you shut up and let him tell the damn story?" Emily perched her chin on her folded hands and smiled. "Go on."

"I guess they'd been dating, but keeping it low key? Cassandra, Cassie, Carrie—"

"Caroline!" Janet interjected.

"Thanks. God, she was pretty. Not a very good actress, but

she had these full, pouty lips."

"Finish the story, Blake," Emily said.

"Well, let's just say Caroline wasn't above practicing that scene pretty much any opportunity she got. And I wasn't complaining. I was sixteen, for Christ's sake. I was a walking, talking hormone, and she was all over me."

"So what happened?" Now Liese could imagine the ending, and her heart broke for Ryder. No wonder he hated Blake.

"So we were rehearsing the kissing scene after hours. No one else was in the auditorium, and one thing led to another. I guess Whitehall decided to stop by after track practice to see her. He was still wearing those God-awful running shorts, and he had such skinny legs . . ."

"Oh, my God! He caught you guys having sex?" Emily asked.

"No, we were just making out, but there was some under-the-clothes hand action going on."

"Oh." Emily looked strangely disappointed, as if catching your significant other kissing someone else in high school wasn't enough of a punch to the heart. "Above or below?" "What?" Blake asked.

"The under-clothes hand action, was it above or below the belt?"

"Um . . ." Blake hesitated. "My hands were above, hers were below."

"Wow. It must have sucked for Ryder to walk in on that." Emily and Janet nodded to each other.

"Yeah, well, he flipped out and punched me in the face."

"Ryder hit you?" Liese couldn't picture Ryder lashing out at anyone. He was always so controlled, even when angry.

"He sure did. He broke my nose. So I started wailing on him, because I had no idea why he was hitting me in the first place.

Most of what he said to Caroline didn't make much sense at the time. It did afterward, but not in the moment. Anyway, he ended up with some stitches in his lip and bruised ribs, and I had a broken nose. Neither one of us got the girl. Which is kind of a good thing; last I heard she was working on her third marriage."

"That's quite a story." Emily swirled her drink in her glass. "I guess it must have been a tough pill for him to swallow when he came to FAHL a couple of years ago and found you on the staff. He has to relive that awful moment every time he sees you."

"So awful," Janet said. "Poor Ryder."

"All this time I thought he was just an asshole, but this explains so much." Emily sighed, her eyes watery. "Think about how terrible that would be—walking in on your girlfriend with her hands down another guys pants, and you end up being his boss later in life." Emily turned to Blake. "It's a wonder he hasn't given you a classroom in the basement."

"Seriously? Are you guys for real? *He* came at *me*. It wasn't like I hijacked his girl on purpose. I had no idea they were together."

"Does he know that?" Liese asked, taking a sip of her drink.

"Who knows?" Blake replied. "It wasn't like he let it go afterward, or tried to find out the real story. All his buddies gave me a hard time for the rest of the year. They started spreading rumors about me, and it sucked. I couldn't get a date again until senior year."

"I don't think Ryder had anything to do with that, though," Janet said. "From what I remember, he was pretty broken up about it. I think his friends retaliated on his behalf. And I'm pretty sure Caroline wasn't too kind in her references to your . . ." She pointed to her lap.

"What? There's nothing wrong with my—" Blake gestured

below the table. "I would have apologized back then, but he didn't give me much motivation, and with the way he's always breathing down my neck now, I'm not very inclined to try to set things straight. It was almost twenty years ago," he added. "He should probably just get over it."

"He's been quite civil with you, really, all things considered," Emily said.

"Change of topic, please. This one's getting old," Blake grumbled.

The conversation moved to other non-work-related topics, but Liese only half-listened. Blake's story revealed so much about Ryder. She could now understand his disdain for Blake, and see why he'd been so volatile in his office this afternoon. Liese finished her martini and ordered another, making it a double. Now that the appetizers had arrived, she could afford to cut loose a bit.

The room slanted a little while later when she slid off her seat, excusing herself to the bathroom. It took her a moment to feel steady. Liquor always hit her hard, and harder still when she hadn't eaten properly, which was the case today. When she came out of the stall, she gave her reflection the once-over. Her eyes were bright, and her cheeks flushed, but at least she wasn't on the verge of tears anymore.

Liese returned to the table and took her seat, coming back to a conversation she couldn't quite follow at first.

". . . so I guess she finally managed to get substitute work, but not in Pennsylvania. I was told by one of her former colleagues, who dates my cousin's friend, that she had to go to inner city New York to get a job, and at a public high school, of all places. They have metal detectors at the doors," Emily said, making a face.

"They're talking about the teacher-principal thing from the beginning of the year," Blake explained when she threw him a questioning look.

"Oh." Liese shifted uncomfortably in her seat, taking great interest in the fresh martini as the waitress placed it before her.

"Ah, shit," Blake muttered as Janet and Emily continued to prattle on about the alleged outcome of the affair.

"What's up?"

He inclined his head, eyes shifting right. "Three o'clock."

Liese followed to see that Ryder and Harvey Little, the assistant principal, had walked through the front door of the bar. "What are the chances?" Janet asked.

"Ugh, I hate Harvey. He always talks to my boobs," Emily said.

"Same here." Blake donned a somber expression.

Janet snickered as Blake rubbed his chest, but Liese couldn't appreciate the humor. She knew without a doubt that Ryder was headed in their direction. She could feel his molten glare.

"Oh, man, they're coming this way," Blake warned.

Liese grabbed her martini and took a gulp, glad she'd ordered it. From the look on her colleagues' faces, she was going to need it.

13

Everyone Deserves a Mulligan

LIESE PANICKED AND began to shred her napkin as Ryder approached the table. Like marionette strings being pulled, her head swiveled to seek out the man responsible for her current anxiety. She looked right at him and knew the smile plastered on his face was as fake as the one slapped across hers.

The rigid set of Ryder's shoulders gave away the tension in his body, as did the way his hands balled into fists and relaxed almost immediately. He repeated the motion, as if he was restraining himself, but barely managing. It annoyed her that she found it arousing.

"Whitehall," Blake greeted him with faux enthusiasm. He raised a hand in a half-assed wave and dropped it casually onto the back of Liese's chair.

Ryder's jaw clenched, and his eyes flashed with a level of anger she'd only witnessed once before. He eyed Blake's arm like he wanted to obliterate it. It seemed Ryder continued to read more into her relationship with Blake than there was. And she could now understand why.

"Celebrating the beginning of the weekend?" Ryder dragged a chair across the floor. It made a horrid scratching sound on the tiles as he pulled it up alongside Liese. "Mind if we join you?" He inclined his head to Harvey and took a seat.

"By all means, Mr. Whitehall," Liese said into her martini. She took a swig to occupy her mouth and hoped she hadn't sounded as derisive as she had in her head. She glanced around the table, but all eyes were on Ryder.

"Please, Liese, you needn't be so formal." The forced smile remained intact, but beneath the false façade she caught a pleading edge in his tone.

"Sorry, sir."

Liese continued to suck back her martini as conversation filled the table. Janet and Emily were quite attentive with Ryder, asking all sorts of questions and listening intently to his strained responses. Harvey was quiet, his eyes constantly straying below Emily's neckline. Liese remained silent as well, only responding when asked a direct question, and then using as few words as possible.

When their waitress came by, Liese took the opportunity to order another double martini. Coordination a little off, she took a dainty sip when it arrived and managed to dribble some on her blazer. Blake gave her a look, and Ryder frowned as she wobbled on her seat when she reached for a napkin.

"I'll take a cab home," she whispered to Blake, embarrassed that she'd managed to get so drunk—and in front of the principal and assistant principal, no less.

He nodded, a worried look in his eyes, and Liese continued to make her drink the focal point of her evening. But she sipped it more slowly, and even ordered a glass of water, which she promptly drained. Still, it amazed her how quickly a martini could disappear if you didn't engage in the conversation going on around you.

"I should probably get going." Emily stood and slung her purse over her shoulder. "I was supposed to be at a family function half an hour ago. Anyone need a ride?" Liese drained the end of her fourth martini. While the question was geared to the entire table, Emily looked at her.

Knowing it would be better to leave before she made a complete ass of herself, Liese pushed her chair back and nearly toppled over. Blake reached out to steady her, but Ryder was faster.

"Careful." He wrapped his hand around the top of her arm, his fingers grazing the side of her breast as he whispered close to her ear, "Are you feeling all right?" "I'm fine," Liese replied.

"I can take you home," Ryder offered.

"Em could take me," Liese suggested. It would have looked suspicious if she didn't try to get out of accepting a ride from Ryder, particularly considering the conversation before he and Harvey had shown up. And besides, she definitely did not want to ride with him—at least that's what she told herself.

"Sure." Emily rooted through her purse for her keys. "It's not a problem."

Liese looked pointedly at Ryder's hand, still wrapped around her arm.

He smiled, but she could see he was angry, and it served as a warning to be mindful of their present company. She wasn't sure how far she could push him before he snapped. He released her, but stayed close. He turned to Emily. "You're already running behind. Why don't you go ahead? I'm driving Harvey anyway, and I can pass by Annaliese's on my way home."

Liese had no idea where Harvey lived, but she did know her

house was nowhere near Ryder's. Emily stood rooted to the spot, keys in hand, looking conflicted. It wasn't hard to understand why; while she might want to help Liese, she wouldn't override her administrator, even outside FAHL.

Blake cut in with his own suggestion. "Or we could walk to my house, Liese. It's only a few blocks. You could take a cab from there whenever you want."

"That's not necessary," Ryder countered, and Liese caught a flicker of panic before he composed himself. "Unless, of course, that's what you'd prefer?" He deferred to her, the tension between them flaring. She prayed they weren't as transparent as she felt.

She'd reached her drama quota for the week, and if she went with Blake, she now knew she'd be sending a very poignant message to Ryder. She wasn't sure she wanted to.

"I should probably just head home." Liese gathered her purse.

"You sure?" Blake gave Ryder a suspicious glare.

"Yeah, I'm tired. It's been a long week." She offered an apologetic smile and dug around in her purse for her wallet. She realized with horror she was having difficulty focusing.

"I've got it." Ryder almost touched her arm before he caught himself. He threw some money on the table, more than covering everyone's drinks. Whether he did it out of generosity or for show, she didn't know. But it appeared she didn't know a lot of things about him.

They all filed out to the parking lot, where Ryder directed Liese to his car. Even with his hand on her elbow to steady her, she almost stumbled more than once. Harvey offered her the front seat, but she declined and got into the back.

It took three attempts to buckle her seatbelt. She tried to keep track of where they were going, but the street signs kept blurring, making them unreadable. Ryder parked in Harvey's drive-way and got out, sticking his head back inside to tell her he'd only be a minute. She ignored him.

The two men stood in the beam of the headlights while Harvey spoke animatedly. She cracked the window in hopes of clearing her head. Liese sighed, irritated that she was marinating in the smell of Ryder while he and Harvey continued to chat like she wasn't even there. If she'd taken the ride from Emily, she would've been home by now, curled up in front of the television and on the verge of passing out. After a few more minutes of waiting, she grew restless.

Harvey and Ryder's conversation had escalated to a low argument. "The issue isn't up for debate, Harvey." She caught the tail end of Ryder's frustrated response. He glanced at her through the windshield, and she resisted the urge to flip him the bird. "I should get Liese home," he said.

Harvey said something unintelligible, but his mocking smile told her it couldn't have been very nice. Ryder rolled his shoulders. Whatever Harvey had said, he didn't like it. "I'm sure she'll be fine . . ." His curt reply filtered through the window, but a motorcycle bombed down the street, cutting off the rest.

Harvey lumbered up the walkway to his front door, weaving as he went. At least Liese wasn't the only one who'd had too much to drink. Ryder closed his eyes, took a deep breath, and returned to the car. She clutched her purse in her lap and looked out the passenger side window as he got back into the driver's seat.

"I'm sorry to have kept you waiting." He buckled his seatbelt, peering at her through the rearview mirror.

"It's fine."

"You know, you're more than welcome to sit in the front."

"I'm good back here. Thank you," she replied.

"Please join me, Liese," he said, leaning across the vehicle to open the passenger door for her.

She unbuckled her seatbelt. Rather than get out of the car, she batted his hand away and climbed awkwardly over the center console. Flopping down in the front seat, she reached over and slammed the door closed.

"Better?" She yanked on her seatbelt and struggled to engage the latch.

"Much," Ryder replied, his smile infuriating.

He backed out of the driveway, and there was silence for all of ten seconds before Liese went off. "Did you do that on purpose?"

"I'm not exactly sure what you're referring to, so the answer is likely no," he replied calmly, glancing at her.

She hated how easily she fell apart and how composed he remained. The entire time they'd been at the bar, she'd felt like there was a huge scarlet "S" stamped on her forehead, branding her a slut. "You're such an asshole!" She shifted angrily in her seat.

"For driving you home?" Ryder asked, seeming confused.

"Emily would have driven me home if you'd let her!" Liese exclaimed. "Or I could have gone to Blake's."

"You're right." Ryder turned onto a side street and hit the brakes.

"What the hell?" Liese barked.

He shifted to face her, his eyes blazing. "You could have done either one of those things. But let me be frank when I tell you I am relieved beyond all belief that you came with me instead."

Of course he wouldn't want her to go with Blake. "It's not like that with him." Despite her intoxication, Liese thought better of sharing the new information she'd gained regarding Ryder's history with him.

Ryder ran his hand through his hair. "Oh no? Are you sure about that? While it's your right to do what you want, I have no desire to leave you alone with him if I can avoid it. More than that, I wanted to explain myself further before you decide that Blake is a viable option."

"You are so obtuse!" Liese said. "I can't believe you honestly think Blake would try something—ever, but particularly while I'm drunk. I'm not interested in him that way, and even if I was, I have no desire to get myself into another situation like this one. It was bad enough being fucked by you and then ignored for days on end."

Ryder looked taken aback. "We've already been over this. I didn't intend to ignore you. I was out of the building, and email definitely isn't a safe way to correspond considering—"

"Email isn't the only way to contact a person. You could have stopped by my house, since apparently you know where I live."

"Of course I know where you live. It's on file at the school." Ryder adjusted his tie. "I didn't think—"

"No, of course you didn't think," Liese cut him off. "Your dick was too busy doing that for you."

"For Christ's sake," Ryder exploded. "I did stop by your house!"

"Yeah, to drop off my laptop and run away."

"That was the second time, but I couldn't . . . You left my keys in my mailbox at work. What was I supposed to think?" Dropping his head back against the seat, he exhaled on a sigh. "I didn't want to draw any unwanted attention to us—to you. I knew I'd made a mess of things when I saw you in the office with Stone that afternoon and you made that sexual harassment comment. I thought it was a message. I figured I'd give you some time, that I would get a chance to talk to you later."

"Because I needed a week to cool down after you gave me the brush off? Whatever helps you sleep at night, Mr. Whitehall. I can walk from here." Liese grabbed the door handle.

The automatic locks clicked into place. Ryder massaged his temples. "Just let me get you home, please," he replied as he put the car in gear. "I don't think I could live with myself if something happened to you because I let you walk home in the dark."

"It's seven-thirty."

"It's still dark."

"I'm not a child."

"I'm certainly aware of that."

"Dickhead."

The rest of the drive passed in silence. Ryder turned onto her street, and the sky opened up, rain battering the windshield, making her driveway hard to see. Ryder parked as close as humanly possible to the front porch, and Liese fumbled with her seatbelt. Once she'd freed herself, she wrenched on the door handle, which didn't budge.

"Will you please just let me out?" she asked, her voice catching as she spoke. The combination of alcohol and Ryder's disapproving silence had done nothing for her composure. Only her anger kept her from a complete meltdown.

Ryder removed his keys from the ignition and stepped out into the downpour. By the time he'd rounded the vehicle and opened the passenger side door, he was soaked through, but he didn't seem to care. Liese lurched out of her seat straight into his arms. Embarrassed, she tried to find her footing, but ended up with her face mashed into his chest. Within seconds, the rain soaked through her jacket to her skin.

She pushed away from him, the physical contact too much to handle. She stumbled up the steps of the front porch and had to hold onto the doorjamb to keep from falling while she searched for her keys. Her vision blurred through a haze of unshed tears, and she realized her intoxication had increased significantly during the ride home. The world spun, and Liese worried she was dangerously close to blacking out, something that had only happened once before in her entire life—and that had been in college.

She finally managed to locate her keys but dropped them on the mat. Ryder retrieved them and unlocked the door, ushering her inside. The hall light came on, and Liese cringed in the brightness. Ryder stood beneath the harsh glow, his face a mask of disappointment.

"You can go now," she said, tossing her purse on the side table. She missed, and it dropped to the floor, the contents spilling everywhere. "You've done your job." Her hair, wet and wind-blown, hung in her face. She flicked it out of the way, another biting remark ready to fly until she made the fatal mistake of looking him directly in the eye. That was all it took for her emotions to get the better of her. She felt the tears before she could regain control.

"Are you crying?" he asked, his eyes wide with panic. She wished men didn't have that kind of reaction to tears; it only made things worse.

"Just leave!" Liese swiped at the wetness.

"You're soaked and freezing, let me at least help you get dried off and warmed up."

He started to unzip her jacket, and she swatted his hand away, the sudden movement sending her off balance. "Are you fucking sssssserious?" she slurred. "You have to be out of your damn mind if you think for a second I want to fuck you right now!"

"That's not—I'm not trying to sleep with you." Ryder raised his hands in supplication. "I didn't mean . . . shit."

She wrestled her way out of her jacket, and it landed on the floor with a wet thud. "I don't know what you want from me. I'm not going to say anything to anyone about what happened between us, okay? It's humiliating enough that you know I've been fantasizing about you. I'm not about to share that information with my colleagues, so you don't have to monitor me." She refused to look at him again for fear it would incite a fresh round of tears.

"Is that why you think I came to the bar? To monitor you?"

"Isn't it?"

"Would you please look at me?" he asked.

"Christ, even when it's a question it sounds like an order with you," Liese groused.

"I said please."

She shifted her gaze from her feet to his face. He looked so remorseful—at least she thought he did. Her inebriated state left a lot open for interpretation. But the longer she stood there, the less opposed she became to the idea of having sex with him again.

Ryder moved toward her, and she backed away. He started talking again, probably providing the explanation she'd been looking for, but Liese missed most of it, too focused on the way the room spun. She caught the last of his elucidation.

". . . You have every right to be upset with me."

Liese squinted, hoping to dispel the fuzzy edge around his form. It didn't help.

"I wanted a chance to redeem myself." He continued as though she'd heard every word.

"So you thought you'd hang with your subordinates?" Subordinates came out sounding surprisingly clear.

"It wasn't a well-thought-out plan," Ryder admitted. "I want to fix this with you. I don't know if I can, but I want to. I can't stop thinking about you."

"You can't stop thinking about me?" Liese parroted, testing the way it sounded. The impending hangover made their conversation difficult to process. She wobbled and used the wall to steady herself. It dawned on her that he wasn't trying to take her clothes off. "Wait, does this mean you didn't drive me home just so you could have sex with me again?"

She suddenly found herself in his arms, not quite sure how she'd gotten there since she'd been leaning against the wall a second ago. She grabbed the lapels of his suit and noticed how wet it was. Water dripped down her hands when she squeezed the fabric.

Ryder swept back the hair that had fallen in her face and slid his fingers through the wet strands, then cupped her head in his palm.

Liese's stomach clenched.

His lips bypassed hers and caressed her cheek, stopping at her ear. "However appealing the idea of having you naked with me inside you might be, I'd rather you be sober for the experience."

Traitorous warmth spread through her limbs, but she had enough sense to come up with a snarky, albeit slurry, comeback. "Oh," Liese breathed as she sagged against him. "Well, I guess it's a good thing I don't want to fuck you right now, 'cause I don't think I'm very sober."

"Yes, I suppose that's fortunate." And then she passed out.

14

Uncertainty is the Name of the Game

ON SATURDAY MORNING, Liese woke at a heinous hour with a hazy memory of the previous evening. She had no recollection of how she got home.

The full force of her hangover hit when she sat up. She stumbled out of bed and into her bathroom. After a round with the porcelain throne, she brushed her teeth, washed her face, and rinsed with mouthwash for good measure. She pushed off the vanity, and the room spun wildly before it let her off the carousel ride. Getting her bearings, she braced herself on the wall, looking out the window. No car in the driveway. Flashes of Ryder standing on her front porch surfaced through the fog in her brain. Had he driven her home? That seemed unlikely. But if so, had she invited him in? And what exactly had she invited him to do?

Vague images flitted through her mind, but she had no context as to whether they were real or dreamed. Unable to process anything further until she'd taken some Tylenol, Liese dragged herself to the kitchen, cracked open a bottle, and downed two pills with a huge glass of water. The clock on the stove read 5:25—way too early to be up on a Saturday morning.

Not inspired enough to make it back to her bedroom, she passed out on the couch. Several hours later, the obnoxious ring of her cell phone roused her. The sound came from somewhere down the hall, but Liese couldn't muster enough energy to get up and answer it. Whoever it was could leave a message. Thirty seconds later, her cell went off again. She groaned and rolled off the couch, landing in a heap on the floor. Using the coffee table to pull herself up, she moved toward the persistent ringing and found her phone on the entry table by the front door.

Answering the call, she sagged against the wall. "Yeah?" It sounded like her vocal cords had gone a round with a cheese grater. She cleared her throat, but it didn't help much.

"Hello?"

She should have hit the end button the moment she heard his voice, but her sluggish brain killed her ability to make speedy decisions.

"Liese? Babydoll, is that you?"

She exhaled on an obscenity. "Sean, why are you calling me?"

"Didn't you get my messages? You haven't called me back." His whine had the same effect on her as nails on a chalkboard.

"I got them. I've been busy." She considered adding "fucking my boss" to the end of that statement but decided against it.

"You couldn't even shoot me a text?" Whiny turned to angry in the flip of a switch, highlighting one of the many reasons Liese had dumped his sorry ass.

"We've been broken up for almost four months, Sean. I didn't think calling you back or texting you would be a good idea considering the number of times I've asked you to leave me alone."

"I've given you space. It's been almost a month since I talked to you last."

"Only because I haven't been responding to your messages," she fired back, her irritation mounting until her hands shook with the effort not to throw her phone against the wall. "Why am I even bothering to justify this to you? I have to go." Liese ended the call and almost screamed when it buzzed five seconds later—but her voice already sounded like she'd smoked a pack of cigarettes while yelling at the top of her lungs. She let it go to voicemail and deleted it straightaway. Sadly, she knew he would call or message her again.

Picking herself up off the floor, she went back to the kitchen, in desperate need of some caffeine. Starting her day with a hangover and a call from Sean put her in a crusty mood. She tossed her phone on the table and went about setting up her coffeemaker, opting to make toast as well to help ease her raw stomach.

Her cell rang four times between making coffee and waiting for the bread to toast. The pop of the toaster coincided with another call, and her cell vibrated again, moving across the table toward her like a stalker. She gave it the evil eye and snatched it up, answering without checking the number.

"Why the hell won't you just back off?"

"Fine then, if you're going to be a bitch—" Marissa's voice came through the line.

"Mar? Oh, God, sorry. Sean just called, and I hung up on him. I thought he was calling back."

"I have two words for you: restraining order. You need to get one stat."

"He's calling my cell, not living outside my house in a tent serenading me every night," Liese countered. It was hard not to agree, though.

"He will be soon if he keeps this crap up. Honestly, you need to get rid of this loser. I can't believe he's still calling you, even after you freaked out on him over those Voodoo bears."

"Please don't remind me." The stuffed bears had been creepy, especially the one that looked like a bear version of Sean. The effort he'd gone to was astounding, as well as disturbing, as he'd recreated his own likeness and hers in stuffed-bear format. Liese had kept them in her closet for a week before discarding them in a dumpster. "Can we not do this right now? I have bigger problems," she pleaded.

"Bigger problems? I don't like the sound of that."

"Things have gotten more complicated." Liese poured a cup of coffee. "By the way, how are you finding time to call me? Don't you have a huge project to finish this weekend?"

"It's done. Turns out three pots of dark roast and no sleep makes me ultra creative. I figured you might want to reconsider coming to visit me." Marissa sounded hopeful. "Am I to assume the bigger problems include Ryder?"

"Yup."

"What happened?"

"I'm not one hundred-percent sure, but I got drunk last night, and he drove me home." Liese rubbed her forehead, willing her memory to return.

"Oh, God, like, puking drunk? Did you puke on him?"

"No!" Liese exclaimed, then paused, not entirely sure. "At least I don't think I did."

"Too bad. That would have been awesome." Marissa lapsed into silence briefly before yelling, "Oh, shit! Did you fuck him again? You totally did."

"I did not. I'm not stupid." Liese shifted on her chair. Nope. No tenderness, which meant there had been no sex. She definitely would have felt the aftermath, even if she didn't remember the act.

"I know that. However, people do stupid things when they're drunk. I also know how long you've been flicking the bean over this guy. Anything can happen in a moment of weakness."

"Did you really just say *flicking the bean*?"

"Don't try to distract me with distractions."

"That doesn't even make sense." Liese tried not to laugh and failed.

"So are you sober enough to get your ass to the city so I can see your face and make sure you're not lying to me about riding Ryder again?"

"Ha ha, you're so witty," Liese deadpanned. "I'll pack a bag and be there in a few hours."

"Awesome. Can't wait to see you!" Marissa's excitement made Liese smile, despite feeling like absolute crap.

"Me too."

Liese hung up and nursed her coffee on her way upstairs to get ready. After packing the essentials, she crawled into the shower to freshen up. Wrapped in a towel a few minutes later, she felt much less like yesterday's garbage and more like a human being. She went to step over her clothes from the previous day, but they weren't in their usual spot on the floor in front of her closet.

More flashes of memory came back to her: her face buried in Ryder's neck, the taste of his skin on her tongue, being laid out gently on her bed. It had to be a dream. But another image popped into her mind, this one clearer than the last. She'd started to undress. While Ryder was still there. Her clothes were folded neatly on her dresser, and there were no signs of hanky-panky, which meant only one thing: she'd propositioned him, and he'd rejected her.

Liese checked herself over again, desperate to find some indication they'd been intimate, but nothing. Devastated for reasons she didn't want to own, she grabbed her bag and headed out the door . . . only to find her car wasn't in the driveway because it was still at the bar.

Twenty minutes and a ten-dollar cab ride later, she tossed her bag in the trunk and headed for Marissa's.

By midafternoon she'd arrived at her old apartment to find Marissa waiting at the door with cocktail in hand. "So, tell me what happened with Ride-Me," she said as she ushered Liese inside, evidently not interested in preliminaries such as "Hi" and "How are you?"

"His name is Ryder." Liese shot her an unimpressed look, and Marissa handed her a cocktail of her own. "Thanks for the drink."

"What are friends for if not to help your hangover by giving you another one? Now fill me in on the Ry*der* situation, and start from the beginning."

Liese followed Marissa to the modest living room, and they both dropped onto the couch. Liese adjusted the pillows and sank in, immediately comfortable. "I don't know why I'm so worked up about this man." That was a bald-faced lie; she knew exactly why. "First he propositioned me after he found the photoshopped pictures, then later that day we almost had sex in my office, except we were interrupted. That in itself should have been a sign. But he invited me to his house, and I was hormonal enough to go. Then he buttered me up by making dinner before getting down and dirty." She flushed at the memory of how down and dirty things had gotten. "And as if that wasn't enough, he coerced me into staying the night, and we had sex again the following morning. All of that would have been fine, except he didn't talk to me for the rest of the week." She paused, raising her finger to drive home the next point. "Then . . ." Liese waited for dramatic effect. "Oh my God, just when I think maybe I'm going to be able to get over it, do you know what he did?"

Marissa shook her head, remaining silent while Liese continued her diatribe.

"He called me into his office at the end of the day yesterday and told me he wanted to see me—after not speaking to me for four days. What the hell am I supposed to think?" Liese took a sip of her drink and coughed. Vodka. Nothing beat the hair of the dog.

"That he's a huge wang," Marissa supplied sympathetically.

"So I told him I had plans, because I did." Liese shot up off the couch. Running her fingers through her hair, she began to pace. "I wasn't going to cancel for him, even if the sex is out of this world. There's just something about the way he words things, as if it's a suggestion, but it's not . . ." Liese trailed off, her fingers at her throat as memories of their night together came flooding back.

"But that wasn't the end of it. Do you want know what happened next?" Liese barreled on, the question rhetorical. "He showed up at the bar with the school's other administrator, crashed our table, and I got so blitzed I couldn't drive my own ass home." Liese flailed her arms and circled the living room like a caged bird, unable to escape the rising fear that came with not remembering how she'd acted.

"Which is when he swooped in and saved you by driving you home and trying to get into your pants again?"

"No. Yes." Liese shook her head vehemently. "I mean, yes, he drove me home, but no, he didn't try to have sex with me. At least I don't think he did. I have a feeling I may have propositioned him, but apparently I'm not all that fuckable when I'm wasted," Liese replied.

"Well, that's one redeeming quality about him, isn't it?"

"How is that redeeming?"

"Um, well, Liese, don't you think it's more respectable that he *didn't* try to have sex with you when you were passed-out drunk?" Marissa asked. "Or would it have been better if you'd woken up sore with no recollection of how you got that way?"

"Good point." Liese sipped her drink. In her post-hangover haze, his rejection had seemed to mean he didn't want her, period. But when she considered the conversation they'd had before the bar fiasco, it made sense. "What the hell am I supposed to do? He's telling me he wants to take me out again after being an asshole all week. Driving me home and not taking advantage of me doesn't negate that." Liese flopped back down on the couch.

Marissa patted her shoulder. "If he wasn't your boss, I'd tell you to play mind games with him, but for some reason I don't think that would be the best idea."

While they drank, Liese filled Marissa in on some of the parts of the story she'd previously left out, particularly how the doctored photos were involved and how Ryder had managed to come across them.

"The bondage ones were a joke—you know that, right? I didn't honestly think you were into that kinky shit," Marissa mused.

"I think that's the least of my problems right now." Liese downed the rest of her cocktail.

"I'll let that go for now, but we'll be returning to the subject, just so you know." Marissa grabbed Liese's empty glass and went to the kitchen. The small loft apartment made it easy to continue the conversation while she made more drinks. "I guess the question is, what do you want to do? Bear in mind, you have a horrible track record with men in general, particularly with clingers, and this guy is your boss until the end of the school year."

"I don't know. Honestly, I have absolutely no idea what I *should* do. I know I *shouldn't* want anything to do with him for a multitude of reasons, some of which you've just stated. It could damage both our careers if the wrong people found out. We can't have a real relationship, at least not while we're working at the same school. Besides, I'm pretty sure that's not what he's looking for anyway."

"I don't get it," Marissa countered. "Why would he want to risk being exposed by taking you out for dinner if he didn't want a real relationship? That doesn't make any sense."

"I don't know. I'm so confused," Liese groaned.

"Think about it, though. If he didn't want anything from you, do you really think he'd have followed you to the bar?" Marissa set the shaker down and leaned on the counter. "If he hadn't asked you out for dinner, I might agree with you about him not wanting more or just wanting to check up on you. But I think this guy has it bad for you, and really, who wouldn't? You're a stellar lay, based on previous reports."

Liese sniffed. "Hardly."

"Don't even." Marissa picked up the shaker. "I can't begin to tell you how much information Sean imparted after you broke up with him. And remember that guy Irving, or Ivan, or whatever his name was? He talked about how amazing you were in bed every damn time I ran into him. It was really annoying, and kind of gross. I bet Ryder is already addicted to riding you, and now he can't get enough."

"You really love the play on words, don't you?" Liese sent her a dirty look. "And how is rehashing my previous sexcapades helpful?"

"I can't resist the pun, but that's beside the point. Look, you were obsessing over this guy before you even went to the interview, and when you came back, he was all you talked about. I'm not an idiot, and neither are you. Clearly you want this to go somewhere, even if you refuse to admit it."

"It doesn't matter what I want. It can't happen."

"Why not? If he wants to try to date you, and you want the same thing, it's pretty much a go, isn't it? I'm not getting what the issue is." Marissa cracked the shaker and split the cocktail between two glasses. She topped Liese's with ice and juice.

"He's my superior. Teachers have been cut out of the pool for things like this," Liese explained, taking the highball.

"The pool? What the hell does swimming have to do with anything?"

"The teaching pool, not a real pool; it's the substitute list." Liese grew serious. "Another teacher lost out because she had an affair with her principal."

"Well, you're a librarian, not a teacher, so that takes care of that, doesn't it? Besides, doesn't an affair imply one of them is married?"

"You're splitting hairs. It's that they were involved with each other that's the problem."

"I don't think so. The point is, you're both adults who are capable of making adult decisions. Talk it out if you want to, ignore him if you don't. Either way, you'll figure it out." She grinned. "Now I want to hear about your bondage fetish."

Liese felt her cheeks heat. "I don't have a bondage fetish."

"Right. So did he tie you up or what?"

Several cocktails, a deep dish pizza, and a few overly informative conversations later, they called a cab, ready for a night out on the town. Liese hadn't been to a nightclub since her move to Fullerton, and it wasn't usually a scene she missed. Tonight, however, she wanted to cut loose and forget about her problems.

Unfortunately, after one Cosmotini, a Sean-spotting forced Liese to drag Marissa away from a flirty, well-dressed business man.

"Sean's here," she shouted in her friend's ear. Surveying the club, she tried to locate him in the crowd again before he could find her.

"What?" Marissa scanned the room. "Does that guy have a tracking device on your phone or something?" Business Guy tried to reclaim her attention, but she ignored him and continued to search the throng of clubbers for Sean.

"Liese! Hey, Liese!" Sean's shrill voice rang out over the pounding music.

"Oh, no." She could see her panic reflected in Marissa's eyes. Judging by the volume, he was close.

"Just pretend you can't hear him." Marissa squeezed her shoulder.

"He sounds like he has a megaphone."

"He does."

"Really?" Liese turned around to find him right behind her, sans megaphone.

"Liese!" he yelled in her face, grabbing her arms. He yanked, and she stumbled into him.

"Sean!"

He wrapped her in his arms, giving her a tight hug while he pressed his face into her hair and said something indecipherable. When he pulled back he ran his hands up and down her arms, looking her over.

"God, you look amazing. How have you been? I've missed you."

"I'm good," she replied slowly, desperate to extricate herself so she could run screaming from the club.

"I just . . . God, it's so good to see you again. I saw your car parked in front of your old apartment building. I thought I might find you here. It's like we're connected, you know?" He pounded on his chest, much like a gorilla. "I could feel you close by, and I needed to see you." His eyes were wide and frantic as they bounced over her face. He gripped her far more firmly than was comfortable.

Liese gently pried his talon-like fingers from her waist. "I, uh . . . I didn't expect to see you at all."

"Hey, Sean, you creepy stalking asshole, why am I not surprised to see you here?" Marissa said loudly enough that several people turned to look at them.

"I'm not stalking Liese."

Marissa slipped between them, acting as a shield. "Right, because all the phone calls and texts and dropping by our apartment just so you can sniff her old pillows or whatever it is you want to do isn't considered stalking." Marissa grabbed Liese's hand and backed away from Sean. "Anyway, it's been a slice, but we have a restraining order to file, and it would be in your best interest not to bother escorting us out."

Marissa spun and shoved the guy next to her. He turned, looking angry, and she pointed behind her to Sean as she seized Liese's wrist and dragged her through the crowd. A quick glance over her shoulder confirmed Marissa's ploy had worked. The guy she'd shoved was in Sean's face. Liese didn't see what happened next as the crowd swallowed them up, and she and Marissa burst out of the club into the cold, blustery wind of the city street.

"Honestly, that guy is psychotic." Marissa hailed a cab and dove inside, hauling Liese after her. "He practically camped outside the building for the first two weeks after you moved."

"You should have told me." Liese chewed her fingernail as she studied her friend.

"Why? So you could worry more?"

Liese dropped her hands to her lap, clasping them tightly so she wouldn't ruin all her nails.

Marissa sighed. "Well, I really hope Ryder isn't a psychotic stalker. It's going to be awfully challenging for me to be your bodyguard when I'm more than two hours away. Also, I have no immediate plans to move to Fullerton."

"He's not a stalker, or psychotic."

"He better not mess with your head, or I'll send Sean after him," Marissa joked, although she looked serious.

Morning brought a hankering for greasy breakfast food. They drove in separate cars to a diner half an hour outside the city to avoid any further run-ins with Sean.

Afterward, Marissa walked Liese back to her car. "I'll be down to visit soon, okay?" she promised.

"We'll make a plan," Liese agreed, getting into her car.

"I expect to hear an update as soon as you've made up with Ryder."

"If I make out with him."

"That's what I thought." Marissa laughed.

"I didn't mean—"

"Don't even try, Freudian slip. Call me when you get home, okay?"

"Promise." Liese gave her a Girl Scout salute and pulled out of the parking lot toward the freeway.

She wished she knew what to do about Ryder. Regardless of how good it would feel to be with him again, it was too dangerous to want because it wouldn't stop there. Marissa was right. Liese wanted more than a bed partner, and if he wanted the same, then what? What if it didn't work out? What if someone important found out and their relationship became public? Even as consenting adults, most of her colleagues wouldn't look favorably on her. People would think she was trying sleep her way to the top, and Ryder would look like he was taking advantage of her.

More than that, his actions over the past week had made her cautious. She would be better off without more drama in her life. Whatever his intentions had been, she'd had enough bad relationships; she didn't need another.

So tomorrow she would talk to Ryder. Despite the heavy feeling it left in her stomach, perhaps it would be best if they didn't see each other in anything but a professional capacity.

15

Conversations without Words

ONCE HOME, LIESE let Marissa know she'd arrived safely and then turned off her phone. She didn't want to field another call from Sean or continue to stew over the fact that Ryder hadn't checked on her over the weekend. Exhausted, she went to bed early but still felt emotionally spent when she woke Monday morning.

Unable to stomach anything solid, Liese blended a fruit shake and left for FAHL a half-hour earlier than usual. She wanted to speak with Ryder about keeping things strictly professional so she wouldn't feel like puking for the entire day.

The parking lot was practically empty when she pulled in, with Ryder's Lexus nowhere to be seen. She bypassed the main office. If Ryder hadn't arrived yet, she had no reason to stop in apart from picking up her mail, which she could do later. She hadn't been in the library two minutes when someone knocked on her door. Logic told her it couldn't be Ryder; he'd go to his office before he came to her.

"Come in," she called, her voice wavering.

Blake stuck his head in. "Hey, you're here early."

"I wanted to get a jump on things." She motioned to the stack of boxes beside her desk. "How was your weekend?" Liese smiled, assuming an air of calm, though she was too edgy about talking to Ryder to be very social. She had a vague, nagging memory that part of her conversation with him on Friday night had revolved around the man currently occupying her office doorway.

"It was okay. Friday night was the most exciting part, I'm afraid. Speaking of which, how was the ride home with Whitehall? We all felt horrible for you, but he was kind of pushy about it. That guy never takes a break from being a dictator." Liese threw him a withering glare.

"Sorry, my mistake. I mean administrator." His smile smacked of insincerity.

"I made it out alive." She wished she knew how she'd ended up in Ryder's car, but everything after her third martini blurred together. A two-drink limit would be instated from now on when out with colleagues. And no doubles.

"That bad, huh?" Blake put his arm around her shoulder in a sympathetic hug. "I would've let you crash at my place if he hadn't been such a dick about it."

"It was fine. He didn't even make me cry." It should've been a joke, but for some reason Liese felt like it might be a lie.

"I'd solicit a student to egg his car if he did," Blake replied.

"You wouldn't."

"Probably not, no. But it's fun to pretend, don't you think?" He hung around and chatted until his bucket of coffee was empty. "Well, I need a refill before class, and I should probably get ready for first period. I just wanted to see for myself that you'd escaped the clutches of our dreaded headmaster." "Overdramatic much?"

"Never. I figured you could hold your own. Lunch in the staff room? You know the girls will be dying to hear the details about your excursion now that they're all sympathetic to Whitehall's plight."

"Um, possibly? It depends on whether I can get my final proposal for the reading group together by the end of the morning and stock the shipment of books that just came in." Liese glanced again at the boxes beside her desk, which had arrived Friday afternoon.

"Oh, okay. If I don't see you at lunch I'll save you a seat at the staff meeting." Blake rushed off as the first bell rang, signaling five minutes until class.

Liese slumped back in her chair; she'd completely forgotten about the staff meeting. The thought of having to sit through a meeting led by Ryder while surrounded by her colleagues made her want to vomit. On the up side, at least she knew he'd be at work sometime today.

But he wasn't in all morning, and when he finally did arrive, he stayed behind closed doors with the school security officers for the remainder of the day. According to Betty, he was dealing with a student issue from the previous week.

Liese thought she might need a Valium by the time she heard the final bell. Her office phone rang as she was about to go to the lounge for the staff meeting. Ryder's name showed up on the digital screen. She let it ring so many times it went to voicemail. Five seconds later, it rang again, and Liese dove for the receiver.

"Liese Harper, Library Resource Center, how may I help you?" she exhaled breathily into the phone.

"Christ," Ryder muttered. "Do you answer the phone like that for everyone?"

"Um, yes," Liese replied, in the same breathy voice.

"I'd like you to stop doing that, please." He sounded irritated, which annoyed her.

"Pardon? What's wrong with the way I answer the phone?"

"Nothing. Never mind. I just . . . you sound . . . I wanted to talk to you about your decision."

"My decision on what, exactly?" She really had no idea at this point.

"Your decision regarding our conversation Friday evening." He paused and sighed into the receiver. "Which you probably don't recall."

"Not really," Liese hedged.

The PA system crackled, and Betty's voice filtered through the building, "The staff meeting will begin in the lounge in five minutes."

"Damn it," Ryder said. "We'll have to talk later."

The line went dead. She willed her brain to give up something—any recollection from Friday to help her figure out what kind of decision she was supposed to have made—but her mind remained blank. Ryder's call made her question the decision she *had* made about keeping things professional between them. She grabbed her coffee mug, a pen, a notebook, and a piece of gum and trudged to the staff meeting.

When she arrived, Blake sat with Emily and Janet close to the back of the room; the two women were deep in conversation, whispering back and forth with a magazine spread open between them. Liese peeked over, curious. It was an article on the do's and don'ts of inter-office dating, the number one no-no being getting involved with one's boss. She looked away quickly. He patted the spot beside him. "Hey, saved you a seat."

"Thanks." Liese slid into the uncomfortable plastic chair.

"We missed you at lunch." Blake appraised her, unsettling her further.

At the front of the room, Ryder cleared his throat and saved her from making an excuse for her absence. The staff lapsed into silence. Compelled to look at him, she lifted her gaze forward. Ryder stared directly at her, his expression stormy. Liese commenced leafing through her notebook.

She shifted forward, pulling her seat closer to the table, and Blake's arm dropped from the back of her chair. Now she understood why Ryder looked so worked up. Even if Blake's actions were more accidental than intentional, she wanted to smack him for making the situation worse. A few seconds later, Blake kicked her ankle, but she shook her head without looking at him, the universal signal for "not now." Thankfully, he let it go. Liese grabbed her pen and jotted senseless notes to keep her hands busy. It didn't work. Her mind kept wandering.

"Ms. Harper." Ryder cleared his throat.

"Sir?"

His eyes flashed briefly. "I thought you had a question, my mistake."

Liese realized she'd been twirling a piece of hair around her finger. She'd also been staring at Ryder's crotch. She felt as transparent as a jellyfish—except her emotions were on display for everyone to see rather than her insides.

Ryder sped through the agenda, his tension palpable, at least to Liese. He seemed to stiffen each time he looked over at her and her comrades. His physical response sparked her guilt—a sort of panic merged with an unsettling need to fix things between them, even though he'd been the one to screw things up. In spite of knowing what would probably be wisest, considering the situation, Liese found herself more uncertain about how to handle Ryder than ever.

When Ryder called for any additional business, Blake raised his hand. Reclined in his chair as usual, he balanced precariously on two legs with his arms crossed behind his head, one suspended in air, the picture of ease.

Ryder gave him a tight-lipped smile. "The floor is yours, Stone." He leaned against the table behind him, posture relaxed, a contradiction to the way his hands gripped the edge.

Blake let his chair settle on all four legs and slowly got to his feet. Too lazy to hold up his own weight, he grabbed the back of Liese's chair and leaned on it. Liese didn't hear much of what he said, the buzz of anxiety far too prominent in her ears. At some point he fell into a huge diatribe about her gracious involvement in the school's upcoming production. By the end of his gushy monologue, Liese wanted to crawl under the table.

Ryder dismissed everyone shortly thereafter, and Liese packed her things, desperate to escape her colleagues. They all wanted the dirt on her ride home with their illustrious principal. But she pushed back her chair to find Ryder barricading her only exit.

"I'd like to see you in my office, Ms. Harper."

"Of course, Mr. Whitehall."

"Immediately." He spun on his heel, turning toward the door.

"Jesus, what the hell is his problem?" Blake griped.

"Looks like I'll be seeing you all tomorrow." Liese sighed. And she thought *she* had trouble keeping a lid on her emotions. Ryder looked like he was about to blow. If he continued to act this way, he would inevitably expose them—all the more reason to make sure there was nothing left to expose. No matter how much he'd disliked Blake before, his current attitude toward him bordered on hostile.

The main office was deserted. She dropped her things in her mailbox and knocked on Ryder's half-open door, much harder than she'd intended. On the third loud rap, the door swung open, and he motioned for her to step inside.

He slammed the door behind her and locked it. "Do you mind telling me why the *fuck* you're lying to me?"

16

Interruptions

"WHAT THE HELL are you talking about?" she shot back. "How can I lie when I haven't even spoken to you?" Liese folded her arms across her chest, mostly to prevent launching a physical attack that had nothing to do with the ever-present sexual energy in the room.

"Don't play dumb with me, Liese," Ryder whispered angrily. "You think I don't see what you're doing?"

"What I'm *doing*? What does that even mean?" A hot rush of ire surged through her.

"Fucking Blake and his fucking hands all over you— touching you. That's what I mean," he seethed, his eyes alight with fury. "I would have thought after Friday—" He stopped, closed his eyes, and inhaled. When he opened them the rage had diminished, tempered with hurt and confusion.

"Honestly? I barely remember Friday evening, apart from when you told me you wanted to . . . what was it you said? I'm sure it had something to do with you being inside me." Liese exhaled heavily as the memory came back to her in vivid flashes: his mouth close to her ear, the words burning through her mind and her body. They'd been in her front hallway.

Ryder's face turned a shade of red usually reserved for the primary color wheel. "Well, I . . . I—" His hands waved around in the air before he shoved them into his pockets. "Is that the only part you remember?"

Liese blinked at him. "No," she replied defiantly.

"For the love of . . ." Ryder sighed. "What else do you remember?"

"You undressed me."

"Oh, no. You undressed yourself despite my request that you remain clothed." His eyes swept over her, as if recalling the event. "I was kind enough to find you something to sleep in."

"I sleep naked."

"Oh, I remember." He took a step closer. "However I didn't feel it would be in my best interest to have you so exposed in your condition. Particularly while I was trying to put you to bed. You are incredibly difficult to resist when you're clothed, let alone when you're naked and willing." He lowered his voice to a whisper. "And you were very, very willing."

She scoffed to hide her indignity. "I highly doubt that."

"You were quite insistent that I stay and get naked along with you." He paused as his eyes searched hers. "I didn't think it prudent, though, considering your state of intoxication, no matter how badly I wanted to accommodate your request."

Liese opened her mouth, but only a squeaky, embarrassed sound came out. Being turned on wasn't going to help her resolve to keep their relationship professional.

"I also didn't think you'd appreciate waking up on your bathroom floor, which is where you originally intended to go to bed."

"Oh my God." Another memory broke free, screaming its way into her consciousness. Ryder had lifted her onto the bathroom vanity and reached behind her for something, her toothbrush possibly? She couldn't recall exactly, having been too fixated on his proximity at the time. She'd grabbed his tie and yanked him forward, fumbling with the buttons on his shirt and the buckle of his belt. He had been gentle but persistent when he'd clasped her hands in his, lips moving over her temple to press against her forehead. More images surfaced, and her mind settled on one where she'd been on her knees in front of the vanity, her hands on Ryder's belt. She'd tried to blow him in her bathroom?

"Did I—" Horrified, she choked on the words. "Did we—"

"I didn't let anything happen. But you were quite entertaining when you weren't scaring the hell out of me. I can't imagine how much you drank to achieve that state." He remained serious, but hurt lingered behind his eyes.

"More than I should have, obviously," Liese admitted, eyeing him as he rubbed the back of his neck, looking lost. "A lot of the evening is foggy."

"How much of it?" he prodded.

"I don't know . . . most of it? I have snippets, bits of memories, but nothing solid." That she'd blacked out scared the crap out of her. She didn't like that she'd lost control.

"I'm sorry. I know this is my fault." Ryder's voice was soft, meek almost. He bowed his head.

Liese didn't want to feel sorry for him, but damn it, she did. She clung to the fading wisps of anger that remained, determined to make him understand why they'd reached such a critical mass. "You ignored me all week and then pulled that garbage about wanting to see me. Showing up at the bar? Not the best move, I'm afraid. How did you think I would react?"

His shoulders slumped. "I knew I'd made a mistake. I thought I could fix it." He lifted his head. "You told me there wasn't anything going on between you and Blake."

"There isn't."

"I'm not blind. I saw his arm around you at the bar and the staff meeting. That's not nothing."

"He's a drama teacher; he's touchy with everyone." Liese's defenses came up. She would be having a conversation with Blake about boundaries, though. Ultimately, she could see why Ryder had the wrong impression of their relationship.

"Maybe he wouldn't be so touchy if someone broke his fucking fingers."

"Ryder!"

"What? Think about it: how would you feel if I went around touching every woman in the building the way he touches you? Does that seem professional to you?"

"You mean the way you're always touching me? Or didn't you realize you do that?" She knew she was being unfair. Ryder rarely touched her in public, and when he did, it was fleeting at best, nothing like slinging his arm over her shoulder.

Even before the tension between them had come to a head, he'd kept his physical contact limited to infuriatingly innocent brushes. But backing down meant owning that maybe, just maybe she'd let Blake get away with his friendliness because she'd wanted to make Ryder jealous. It had worked, but at what cost? Their conversation was going nowhere fast.

"I—what? Damn it, this isn't want I wanted," Ryder said. "I don't want to argue."

"Well, that's difficult when you accuse me of *fucking* lying to you, isn't it?" she said, mocking his earlier question.

Ryder sighed in frustration. "This is why I don't do this."

"Do what?" Even angry, Liese felt her stomach sink, and she grew irritated with herself all over again. She wasn't supposed to want to do it anymore either.

The abrasive strains of dance music filled the room, startling them both. Ryder felt around in his pockets, mumbling profanity. Liese had never heard him swear so much, not even when they'd had sex.

He pulled his phone out of his breast pocket and touched the screen before putting it to his ear. "How many times have I told you not to change my damn ringtone? It's embarrassing." His face reddened, and he turned away.

That he'd answered the phone in the middle of what she'd thought was an important conversation stunned her, but not as much as the harsh way he spoke to the person on the other end.

"Tiffany? Tiff? Sweetheart, don't cry. I didn't mean to yell. It's been a difficult day. Of course not, sweetie . . . It's okay. I'm not angry with you, just tell me what happened, and I'll see if I can deal with it," he murmured. He scrubbed a hand over his face as he paced toward his desk.

Liese's shock deepened. Who was this soft man who practically cooed into the phone over some woman named Tiffany? A cold, sick feeling settled in her stomach. Not once had she entertained the idea that Ryder might be involved with anyone else, but the way he spoke to "Tiffany" left little room for doubt.

Liese struggled with the door to unlock it. She bolted from his office, not stopping when she heard him call her name. Dashing down the hall, she burst into the library, went to her office and threw her jacket on, hastening to grab her purse and vacate the building as quickly as possible. She made a mad dash for the side exit in hopes of avoiding any further confrontations with Ryder. Forget telling him they'd be keeping things professional.

He could just figure it out.

Once home, she tried Marissa, but got voicemail. She put away her things from school, but no matter what else she did to occupy herself, she kept returning to the events of the past week and how badly they'd gone wrong. Sometime close to eight o'clock, Liese poured a glass of wine. She needed to unwind, and a bath was the perfect way. She waited while the tub filled and sipped her drink. Absently swirling a finger in the rising water, she tried to come up with a valid explanation for the phone call from this Tiffany person. It made sense that Ryder thought he saw signs of a relationship with Blake if he had another one of his own on the back burner.

Liese slipped into the hot water. Submerged completely, with only her nose and mouth remaining above the surface, she didn't catch the muffled ring of her phone, or the sound of a car pulling into her driveway.

17

Apologies

LIESE SLIPPED FARTHER into the water and held her breath. She stared up at the ceiling, the light fixture distorting as bubbles escaped her mouth and caused ripples in the water. Her hair floated around her face like silken seaweed. When the pressure in her chest became too much, she broke the surface with a gasp.

The tranquility of her bath ended abruptly as the sound of someone banging on the front door carried up the stairs. Liese bolted out of the tub and nearly cracked her head on the vanity when she slipped on the wet floor. Nothing quite like a potential head injury to negate any relaxation her bath had achieved. She threw on her robe, cursing as she grabbed a towel to squeeze the ends of her soaked hair. She peeked out the window to see Ryder's Lexus kissing the bumper of her car, he'd parked so close.

She felt a rush of relief, followed by one of annoyance for even wanting to see him.

The knocking grew more insistent. She dumped the towel on

the floor and headed for the stairs. "I'm coming!" she yelled. "Hold your horses." She flew down the steps, skidding at the bottom as she rounded the corner and stopped at the door. Taking a deep breath, Liese gathered her courage before she flipped the lock.

She rolled her shoulders and straightened her spine, then threw open the door in a dramatic flourish and cringed when it banged against the wall. Recovering quickly, she assumed a defensive stance. "What are you doing here?"

Ryder's fist was poised to knock again, and it stilled in midair. A look of confusion shifted to astonishment. His mouth opened and he sputtered, no words coming out as his gaze found its way to the front of her robe.

Liese followed his eyes to the gaping V and scowled, drawing the lapels together. The thin silk fabric clung to her damp skin. A cold night breeze blew, and her nipples tightened. They pointed in admonishment at Ryder, who stared right back at them.

"Were you in the bath?"

Liese crossed her arms over her chest. "No, I was playing in the sprinkler in the backyard."

He stood for a long moment, saying nothing, his eyes still on her chest. Eventually he nodded, like a jaunt through the sprinkler at night when it was almost December made perfect sense. Then he finally seemed to remember himself and blurted out, "I got these for you."

He thrust a bouquet of flowers at her, which looked suspiciously like the kind she'd seen at the drugstore down the street. Liese glowered and kept her arms firmly secured over her still-hard nipples. She was rather insulted by the lack of effort.

Still holding the flowers out awkwardly, Ryder cleared his throat. "I'm sorry about this afternoon. I wanted to talk to you about us, about our . . . relationship."

"Relationship?" Liese said with scorn. "I think your conversation with *Tiffany* this afternoon pretty much showed me where I stand. Thanks for the condolence flowers, but I don't need them." She moved to close the door, but Ryder raised a hand. She hesitated long enough for him to begin pleading his case.

"I think you might have misunderstood. Tiffany is my sister."

"Pardon?" She could have sworn he said sister, not mistress or submissive.

"She's my sister; you'll likely meet her on Friday. She's coming to FAHL in the afternoon because she's staying with me for the weekend." Ryder dropped his still-outstretched arm. One of the flowers broke against his leg and the head snapped off, falling onto the front porch to land beside his shoe.

Liese pictured a female version of Ryder. Based on the conversation she'd heard, the woman might be a little neurotic. "I can't believe you have a sister." She knew she must sound like an idiot, but she'd never seen so much as a picture of his family.

"Well, I do. She's almost twenty years younger than me."

"Are you serious?" That would explain his voice when he spoke to her, more like a parent than a brother.

"Completely."

"And she called you this afternoon?" Liese clarified.

"Yes, she was upset and is convinced she hates our parents. Although, in her defense, they are assholes," Ryder explained.

"You've mentioned that before. I thought it was a lawyer joke."

"It wasn't."

Liese agreed as if she could relate, although she couldn't; her parents were unconventional but awesome. Some of her anger melted away, turning to guilt over assuming the worst. "I thought she was your girlfriend."

Ryder scoffed. "I think I've proven thus far that I'm not the most relationship-savvy person. I can't even manage one woman without messing things up."

Liese could hear the apology in his voice, and as much as she didn't want to be swayed, she could see his point. She'd jumped to conclusions.

"Would it be all right if I came in?" Ryder asked. "We could talk? I could grovel?"

After a moment she stepped back to let him in, even though allowing him into her personal space definitely wasn't in line with keeping things professional. "I guess that would be okay."

She took the flowers from him and waited while he hung his suit jacket on her coat rack. Then he stood there, hands shoved in his pockets, looking entirely edible. Liese sighed and motioned for him to follow her. Having him in her home felt strange, but nice. Though her housekeeping skills had suffered this past week, and the disarray made her self-conscious, particularly when contrasted with Ryder's pristine house.

She led him toward the kitchen. He kept a respectable distance, presumably to give her some space. Now that she knew Tiffany wasn't her competition she didn't know what to say— not that competition should have been an issue since she was supposed to be telling him they'd no longer be having a notquite relationship. Depositing the flowers on the counter, she opened the cupboard and searched for a vase. Of course, it was on the very top shelf.

"I can get that for you." Ryder was right behind her now, close but not touching. Liese sidestepped out of the way as he reached up to retrieve it. "I would have picked up a nicer bouquet, but the drugstore was the only option on the way here.

I didn't plan this very well, I'm afraid."

"It's fine. They're lovely," Liese lied.

"No, they're not. They're terrible, but I didn't want to come empty handed, and the boxes of chocolate were past their expiration date." Ryder hovered near her and pulled on his tie. "The dying flowers seemed like a better option, but now that I think on it, maybe I should've bought the chocolates since you likely wouldn't have checked the expiration date until after I left."

Liese turned her back so he couldn't see her smile. "I think you made the right choice considering the selection." She arranged the flowers, discarding the wilted ones, and set the vase on the kitchen table.

When she could no longer justify stalling, she turned, keeping the table between them. "What are we doing here?" She motioned at the air between them.

"That depends."

"On?" she prompted, her heart stuttering.

"On what you want."

"I'm not sure what that should be." All day she'd been prepared to tell him they couldn't do this anymore, but once again, being in his presence had changed things.

It was as close to the truth as she would allow. She stuck her head in the fridge and dug out a half-empty bottle of white wine. If they were going to have this conversation, she needed alcohol. She filled two glasses and handed one to Ryder.

"Come on." She moved past him, her shoulder brushing his arm. Even minimal contact made her flush. She motioned to the sofa when they reached the living room. "Make yourself comfortable. I'll be right back." She left Ryder on the couch as she ran upstairs to put on some clothes.

Liese waffled over an outfit, settling on a pair of yoga pants and a hoodie. She didn't want to appear sloppy, but a vibe that said "I'm not trying to impress you" seemed important.

She resisted chugging her wine as she descended the stairs; intoxication, though alluring, would not be helpful. When she reached the living room, Ryder was lounging on her couch—looking more at home than he had any right to—and flipping through a coffee table book of erotic art: Marissa's version of a housewarming present.

Liese blushed, her embarrassment ironic considering that the artistic content didn't hold a candle to the pornographic images he'd seen on her laptop. Ryder pulled at the collar of his shirt; his eyes widened. He cocked his head to the side and changed the angle of the picture. When she cleared her throat he slammed the book shut and dropped it on the floor with a loud thud. She choked back a laugh as his cheeks flamed the same shade of red as she knew hers must be.

"Interesting reading." He retrieved it from the floor and set it on the table, exchanging it for his wine.

"There's not much in the way of text in there."

"You know what they say about a picture speaking a thousand words." He ran his hand down his thigh and patted the cushion next to him. "Sit with me?"

Liese eyed the chair on the opposite side of the room. It would be much safer not to sit too close—and smarter. But as much as she didn't want to give in, her desire to be close to him drove her toward the couch. She sat down, leaving as much space as possible and hoping he would get the message that she hadn't forgiven him. Not yet, anyway. If they were going to take a chance on a relationship, he'd damn well better make it worth her while. She pulled her legs up, wrapped her arms around them, and leaned into the backrest.

"I've done a pretty good job of botching this up." Ryder twirled his glass between his fingers, watching the liquid swirl.

"That's a rhetorical statement, right?"

He closed his eyes and let his head drop back, exhaling heavily. "I never should have hired you in the first place."

"Are you serious?" Liese sat forward, her foot hitting his leg, startling him.

His wine spilled into his lap, and he swore quietly, looking around the room for something to mop up the mess. Resisting the urge to help, she pointed to the Kleenex on the side table, trying not to look at his crotch. He dabbed at the spot with a tissue, which didn't help his cause much. After a moment he looked at his soaked lap, the outline of his equipment glaringly obvious as his pants stuck to his skin. Thankfully he untucked his shirt to hide the problem from view, allowing her to concentrate on the real issue.

"If this is your idea of an apology, you can shove it."

"I didn't mean that the way it came out. I'm not explaining myself very well." Ryder set his wine glass on the table and propped his elbows on his knees, leaning toward her.

"Understatement of the decade." Liese retreated further into the safety of the cushions. She had the juvenile inclination to use the throw pillows as a barricade. "You have one minute to stop wasting my time and explain what you mean."

"You're amazing at your job, and you've done wonderful things for our student resources department from the day you started at FAHL," he said.

Liese nodded. This she knew.

"What I should've said is that I've been dangerously attracted to you from the beginning. I enlisted Harvey to make the final decision on hiring you because I didn't think I could be impartial enough. On paper you were extraordinary, and in person you were . . . more than I could have hoped for. I spent the majority of our interview trying to get my erection and my imagination under control."

Liese had been in the middle of a sip of wine, which she now sprayed all over him. "I don't even know what to say."

Ryder casually wiped his face, pretending she hadn't just showered him with alcohol. At least the wine was white. "I know it's disturbing. I probably shouldn't have told you that."

"Not disturbing . . . well, maybe. Unexpected might be a good way to put it."

"You remember when you came in to sign the paperwork?"

"What about it?"

"Why do you think I never came out from behind my desk?" Ryder's face flushed as though he was reliving the event. Liese remembered too. He'd been dressed casually in a school-issued golf shirt and dark pants, the latter of which she had only seen when he ushered her into his office. Even then she'd scoped out his behind—and his arms. He had nice arms, all long, lean muscle.

"Oh." Her eyes widened as she connected the dots.

"I've never had an issue like that before. Well, maybe when I was a teenager, but going over a speed bump would've given me a hard-on back then." He rubbed the back of his neck. "What I'm trying to tell you, and making a fool of myself in the process, is that the attraction for me was instant. Intellectually, you were my ideal, but when I met you, you exceeded my expectations in every way possible. Hiring you was a bad move on my part because I already found you so enticing."

"So why hire me, then? Why put us both at risk if you knew I was going to be a problem for you?" Liese couldn't decide if she should be flattered or unsettled. That he'd suffered as long as she had made her feel a little better.

"I tried to convince myself I could remain professional, and at first I did. That is until you asked me to be your advisor, and then I screwed myself."

"And me."

"Believe me, I tried not to give in. If I'd said no to being your advisor, maybe things could have stayed collegial between us. But spending all that time with you—" Ryder's guilt was evident in his tone. "I devised ways to make our meetings last longer than necessary. It was wrong of me to indulge my infatuation. I thought it would remain one-sided, that you wouldn't feel the same way for me. I was sure the age difference would be enough of a barrier."

"Age difference? You're hardly old."

"I've got a decade on you, and as you've probably noticed, I can be somewhat of a domineering asshole at times. I thought that would be a deterrent as well."

"Apparently I like domineering, asshole-ish older men."

"Lucky for me."

Liese narrowed her eyes, and he had the decency to look somewhat remorseful.

"Then I saw those pictures and, Christ, I'd been so close to the breaking point so many times already. It was . . . challenging to be near you and not give in to the compulsion to do something about the way I felt. I couldn't have stopped myself at that point if I tried."

"If you felt that strongly, why were you so cold the morning after?" Liese asked. Tears pricked at the corners of her eyes. "I was humiliated."

"It wasn't my intention to ignore you after you spent the night at my place."

"You mean the night you spanked and fucked me?" Liese took another gulp of wine, the crassness of her comment appalling even her.

His eyebrows climbed his forehead. "Are you telling me you didn't want that? Because I certainly didn't hear you complaining."

"There was nothing to complain about until you acted like a giant douchebag the next morning."

His shoulders curved forward, reminding her of the painting in his house, the one where the subject looked so forlorn and innocent. "I haven't handled this situation well. I didn't want to pretend nothing happened, but I wasn't sure what your expectations would be. I had no idea how to manage the way I felt, and talking about it . . ." He paused, pensive. "I'm sorry we didn't discuss it that morning. I'd planned to before I left, but I got sidetracked, and we ran out of time."

Liese remembered just what "sidetracked" had looked and felt like. "That sounds awfully close to a cop-out to me."

"I don't mean for it to be. I had no intention of making you feel like you were just some fling," he said.

"The note you left didn't help."

Ryder leaned in, but she recoiled and tucked her feet between the couch cushions. He withdrew. "I never wanted to hurt you, or make you think I have anything but the highest regard for you. It took until the evening at the bar for me to realize what an insensitive, self-absorbed jerk I've been."

Liese felt her cheeks color with embarrassment. With deliberate slowness, he reached out and skimmed the top of her hand with his fingertips.

"I want to try to make it better. Unless, of course, you're no longer interested . . ."

She picked at a loose thread on her cuff. She yearned to take him up on his offer to fix things, now that it definitely seemed like he wanted to, but fear of being hurt by him made her cautious. "I don't know, Ryder."

"Is it because of Stone?"

She hesitated longer than necessary just to see him squirm. "We've been over this. What is it going to take for you to believe me when I tell you it's not like that with him?"

"My history with him makes it difficult." Ryder shifted closer. "I'm not sure if you're aware—"

"That you went to high school together? I found that out on Friday."

"Ah. I see." He picked at his untucked shirt. "So Stone's informed you about our previous interactions?"

"You mean when you punched him out?"

"He wasn't the only one to incur damage." Ryder's tongue touched the scar on his lip. "Did he also make you aware of the reason behind the violence?"

"He might have mentioned you had a crush on the same girl."

Ryder's expression hardened. "It wasn't a crush. She and I had been dating for several months. I'd been under the impression we were exclusive."

"I didn't realize—"

Ryder waved her off, as if the whole thing were inconsequential. "It's irrelevant now. But I can't tell you how paranoid I've been, thinking I pushed you right into the mouth of the lion. The way he's always touching you, always around you . . . I wondered if I'd taken things too far, especially with the spanking—" He chuckled darkly, but there was no humor when he spoke. "Of course, I know I've already gone too far. This is probably the last place I should be, but I can't pretend this thing between us doesn't exist."

"Well, that would be difficult since we work in the same building." Precisely the reason she'd thought it best not to pursue this with him.

"You'd be surprised at how little I see some of the staff. I could avoid you entirely if I wanted to."

"But you don't want to do that?"

"Definitely not. As aware as I am of the peril of this relationship, I want you, unquestionably." Ryder edged closer until his knee touched her leg.

His affirmation of the danger reinforced her worries, as did the way her colleagues continued to gossip about the demise of the teacher who'd been with a principal. She didn't want to tarnish her reputation or run the risk of not being able to secure another position if things went horribly wrong. And based on her relationship history, the possibility wasn't all that outlandish.

"What if it doesn't work?"

"What if it does?"

Liese met his pleading gaze. He looked as vulnerable as she felt. It might be the worst decision she'd ever made in her life, but she couldn't ignore how well they seemed to fit together, both in and out of bed.

"We'll have to be very careful, won't we?"

"Extraordinarily."

"I'll need a new advisor, won't I?"

"That would probably be for the best." Ryder's fingers trailed gently along the contour of her cheek down to her chin. He leaned in, lips hovering close, but paused just short of contact. "Is that a yes?"

"Yes. It's a yes."

"I can't begin to tell you how glad I am to hear you say that." Ryder smiled against her lips.

"You can be very compelling when you want to be." Liese put her palm on his chest.

He put his hand over hers, twining their fingers together. "I'm rather lucky I can talk my way out of my own idiocy, and even more fortunate you're so understanding."

"I am very understanding, aren't I?" Liese agreed.

"Very." Ryder raised her hand and placed a soft kiss there, his lips warm even against her heated skin.

"It wouldn't do you any harm to express your gratitude for my unparalleled understanding," she added.

Ryder prowled over her, covering her body with his. Nudging her thighs apart, he settled between them and cradled the back of her head in his hand.

"How does this feel to you?" He nipped at her bottom lip, the sensual swivel of his hips bringing his erection flush against her.

Liese sighed, tilting her hips up to add to the friction she needed. She wanted to punish him for having been so imperceptive, but her own need took charge. He moved against her, a slow, stroking rhythm that took her higher, but not high enough.

"Ryder," she groaned, arching into him. She should make him wait a little longer before she invited him to her bed—like five minutes, give or take a minute or two.

He shifted, robbing her of his delicious weight. Gentle fingertips traced her thigh to the waistband of her pants. He slipped his hand beneath the fabric, passing over bare skin to dip lower. Liese followed with her own hand, covering his as though he might stop. The notion was ridiculous, because his actions told her he had no intention of doing any such thing.

Warm, strong fingers slid inside her, bringing her to the edge over and over again until she was writhing, begging for the release she craved. The press of his thumb and the curl of his fingers, combined with dirty promises of future orgasms, sent her headlong into the abyss of pleasure.

When she surfaced, Ryder smiled down at her. "Have I sufficiently expressed my gratitude?"

"It's a start." Liese ran her hand down his chest, but he caught it before she could get past his belt buckle.

"That's not necessary." He sat up, pulling her with him.

Her eyes went to his pants, where his erection strained against the wine-dampened fabric. "It looks pretty necessary to me." She tried to extricate her hand from his grasp, but he held on tighter. Instead of fighting his hold, Liese maneuvered her body to straddle him. He groaned at the contact, and his head fell back against the cushions.

He released her wrist, his hands moving to her hips to keep her still. "Really," he rasped, "I'd rather you didn't do that."

"I think your cock begs to differ."

He let loose an expletive as he lifted his head, his lids heavy. His fingers dug into her hips—not painfully, but with enough pressure that Liese knew his control was tenuous. Why he held back she had no idea, but curiosity made her compliant.

"I'm sure it does." He cleared his throat. "However, before I can in good conscience permit my cock the exquisite pleasure of your touch." He paused to breathe. "I would like to take you on a date."

"A date?"

"Mm-hmm, a date," Ryder repeated.

"Uh, not that I don't want to go on a date with you, because it sounds really nice, but don't you think that's going to be difficult to pull off considering how small Fullerton is? Doesn't that defeat the purpose of a covert dating operation?"

"Fortunately, I have a car."

"Right. Good point."

"Will you let me take you out?" Ryder looked so hopeful Liese didn't have the heart to say no, even though she worried.

"When?"

"How about tomorrow?"

"I can't. We have rehearsal for the play after school. It usually runs late." Liese grimaced. Blake again.

Surprisingly, Ryder didn't say anything derogatory. "Wednesday I have a meeting. What about Thursday?"

"I'm free then."

"Perfect. I can pick you up just after six?"

"Okay."

"Okay." Ryder grinned and patted her bottom. "I should go."

"What? Why?" Liese wrapped her arms around his neck as he stood. She tried to do the same with her legs, but they were still rubbery post-orgasm and wouldn't comply. Instead they slid down the outside of his thighs until her feet touched the floor. "It's not even that late. You could stay a little longer."

"I don't think that's a good idea." Ryder clenched his teeth as she rubbed shamelessly against his erection. "You see, if I do, I run the risk of taking you against the closest surface, and that just happens to be the coffee table."

"That sounds fun."

Ryder wrapped his arms around her waist, pulling her tightly to him. "My fear is that in my current state I won't be able to control myself." Ryder kissed her neck, his fingers trailing a slow line down her spine. "And the possibility that I might inadvertently break your lovely table as I fuck you until you see stars doesn't sit well with me."

Despite her telling him how much she loved stars and wouldn't miss her coffee table, if it happened to break, he remained resolute. Liese remained a bit baffled. It seemed pointless to wait when clearly they both wanted the same thing.

To make matters worse, Ryder's stupid conscience kicked in, and he instituted a clause stipulating no post-date sleepover for Thursday. He said he intended to prove he was serious about wanting more from her than just spankings and sex. Liese smiled, and at first she thought she'd found a loophole: there were a million locations on which to fornicate that didn't involve a bed. But then he clarified that he meant no getting naked in any way. No naked, no sex. Not on this next date.

Getting out of an agreement with Ryder would be similar to trying to escape from a straitjacket. When he set his mind to something, he didn't back down. Stubborn sexy asshole. No matter; two could play at that game. She'd be sure to make adhering to his clause as difficult as possible.

18

The Covert Date

LIESE SPENT THE days leading up to Thursday attempting to act nonchalant at work, which proved difficult. She limited her visits to the main office as much as possible but still ended up running into Ryder. Every time she saw him, lurid fantasies popped into her head, her imagination running wild. Ryder's "no hanky-panky" clause was going to be a giant problem.

She hadn't factored in the impact such a bargain would have. Being the kind of person who never backed down from a challenge, she'd just agreed. In the interim between their conversation and the planned date, her "plastic friends" were getting quite the workout. Liese was almost relieved that she and Ryder would be in a public place for their evening together, because she didn't want to be the one to forfeit.

If she could entice him enough, surely Ryder would cave and at least help *her* out since he'd given in before. He'd gratified her after they made up; she banked on the fact he would do it again. She'd even keep most of her clothes on, if that's what he wanted.

On Thursday after work, Liese rushed home to get ready. She donned a slinky dress with a plunging neckline and her best push-up bra. The power of cleavage should never be underestimated. To deter potential nudity at the end of their date, she wore the one pair of granny panties she owned. Even though inviting him back to her house might be a no-no, the backseat of his Lexus was roomy. Wearing ugly underpants would deter her from making use of that option.

Ryder arrived five minutes early, looking adorably nervous and carrying a box of decadent truffles and a much nicer bouquet of flowers.

She brought the blossoms to her nose and inhaled. "These are beautiful," she sighed as she discarded the wilted flowers from earlier in the week and replaced them with the new bouquet.

He smiled, looking pleased with himself. She sidled up to him, running her hands over his chest as she brought her body flush to his. "That was very thoughtful of you," she whispered, batting her lashes as she kissed his lips. His hands came up to rest on her waist. Liese stepped back but he followed, pressing her against the counter as he caged her with his arms.

"I know what you're trying to do," he said against her mouth, the evidence of her effect on him pressed against her stomach.

"Is that so?" She snaked an arm around him.

"Mm-hmm, and it's not going to work."

"I have no idea what you mean." She gave his ass a squeeze, then pushed him away and stepped around him, heading for the door. If they didn't leave now, they'd end up on the kitchen floor. "We should probably go. Don't want to be late."

He dropped a juicy curse. She hid a satisfied smile as she slipped on her heels and shrugged into her coat. Ryder guided her down the porch steps to his car. Part of the charm of her tiny house came from the evergreens lining the drive. Plus, they offered privacy from neighbors, something she certainly wasn't used to after living in New York.

Ryder waited as she folded her legs into the car. Liese sucked in a breath when his fingers brushed along the outside of her thigh to adjust her dress. She had no idea how she would make it through this evening, let alone wait for another opportunity to spend some time in the privacy of one of their bedrooms. Ryder wore a mischievous grin as he shut the door and rounded the front of the car, his eyes on her the entire time.

On their way to the restaurant, Liese tried not to focus on the car-sex fantasies that inundated her. She kept up a steady stream of questions, only half paying attention to his replies. Ryder glanced at her and reached over, his fingers grazing the back of her wrist. Liese flipped her hand so he could lace his fingers through hers.

"You okay? You seem a little antsy," he observed as she uncrossed her legs for the third time in less than a minute.

"Yes, I need a distraction."

"From what?"

"You."

"Me? Am I making you nervous?"

"No, you're making me horny," Liese said and slapped her hand over her mouth. So much for maintaining the upper hand.

"Really? I'm not even trying," Ryder said in a smooth voice that made her want to climb over the center console.

"I can resist temptation." Liese pulled her hand away and linked her fingers in her lap.

"What if I don't want you to?"

"Then I'd tell you that's too bad since you're the one who

enacted the stupid clause in the first place."

"Clause?"

"Yes, the no-naked clause."

"I thought it was a mutual agreement." Ryder raised an eyebrow but kept his eyes on the road. "I wouldn't want to be responsible for acts of coercion. Heaven forbid I come across as domineering." There was that smirk again, as infuriating as it was charming. "If it's too difficult for you to resist me, by all means let me know. I wouldn't want to cause you undue sexual frustration."

"You're not egotistical at all, are you?" Liese shot back, crossing her legs. The fabric of her dress rode up, and she tugged it down over her thighs.

Ryder's eyes moved from the road to her lap, fixated on her hands moving along the satin. "So I'm not only domineering, I'm egotistical now? Maybe I need to be punished for being so difficult."

"You do know the road is in front of you, not in my lap, right?" Liese ignored the comment. The conversation needed to end.

"Right." Ryder sighed and turned his attention forward.

"And you're the one who said you were domineering, not me," Liese noted.

"Am I?

"Sometimes."

"Sorry."

"That's okay; sometimes it turns me on," Liese murmured, fiddling with the hem of her dress.

"And other times?" Ryder prompted.

"Okay, it turns me on most of the time. Although there are occasions when it irritates the hell out of me. Now stop asking these kinds of questions. Are you purposely trying to torture me?

If so, I can assure you it's working."

Ryder took her hand again, bringing it to his lips. "I would never torture you intentionally—unless you wanted me to."

Liese snatched her hand away. The warmth of his lips on her skin made the persistent ache low in her belly flare. "Not helpful," she said. "Change the subject, please, or pull over."

Ryder took his foot off the accelerator, clearly considering the request. His eyes moved over her in a feral sweep. Liese bit back a smile of triumph, trying to maintain her composure. Then the car sped up, much to her dismay.

"My apologies," he said. "What would you like to talk about?"

Liese grumbled under her breath.

"What was that?" He turned the soft strains of music down until they were barely audible.

He was playing with her. "Nothing." She shot him a dirty look. "You pick the topic."

Ryder spent the rest of the drive sharing stories about his dysfunctional family. Soon the idea of meeting his parents terrified her. What if they didn't like her? She pushed the thought out of her head; the present was already so complicated.

Liese stretched as she got out of the car, the remnants of sexual tension making her stiff. She followed Ryder inside to find the restaurant small and lovely, perfect for their first date. The converted main floor of the old brick house created an intimate environment, made all the more private by the highbacked plush benches. Each was wide enough to seat two and looked like a giant throne with its ornate wooden frame and red velvet cushions. The hostess brought Liese and Ryder to the table nearest the wood-burning fireplace at the back of the restaurant.

The side of Ryder that had initially enamored Liese came out during dinner. She hadn't realized how much she'd missed his companionship over the past couple of weeks. The change in their relationship had taken away the opportunity to spend time together the way they used to—when they'd been busy pretending to be *just* colleagues. Only for her did he drop his guard and show his softer side. He was sweet and attentive, charismatic and charming.

The more they talked, the more she realized how much they'd been holding back. The chemistry between them was so powerful; she couldn't understand how they'd managed to resist each other for nearly three months in the first place.

Halfway through appetizers, Ryder leaned toward her, bringing into view a couple seated across the room. The woman looked away as Ryder adjusted the strap of Liese's dress, finishing with a kiss on her shoulder.

"Do you know her?" Liese inclined her head in the direction of the bimbo who'd been staring at them.

Ryder turned and studied the woman briefly. He twined their fingers and, raising their clasped hands, kissed each of Liese's knuckles, one by one. "No, I have no idea who she is."

"She keeps looking over here," Liese said. "It's like she's trying to undress you with her eyes."

"Maybe she has x-ray vision."

"I hope not. No one should see you naked but me."

"Is this something you were hoping for?" She felt his teeth scrape across her finger.

"Ryder," she exhaled softly.

"Hmm?"

"Behave."

"I believe you started it." He flipped her hand over and pressed her palm to his lips.

"I did not," she protested.

"Shall we debate the indisputable fact that you want to undress me?" he asked, running his nose along the inside of her wrist. He leaned closer. "You smell incredible."

The sound of a throat clearing surprised Liese, and she pulled free of his grasp. The waitress smiled apologetically, meals in hand. Liese wanted to be angry, but she knew she should probably say thank you. The waitress had saved them from themselves.

Conversation for the remainder of the evening included periods of heavy innuendo between bouts of normal discussion. The tension between them had ratcheted up to an almost unbearable level during dinner, and the hour spent in the car on the way home felt claustrophobic as they continued to taunt each other. Ryder must have adjusted himself half a dozen times. By the time he pulled into her driveway, Liese was biting her tongue to keep from inviting him inside—granny panties be damned.

"I had a wonderful time," she told him.

"As did I."

"I should probably go inside," she whispered.

Ryder took an unsteady breath. "That would likely be best."

The stare down had barely begun before they lunged at one another, their lips colliding and teeth clashing. Liese fisted his hair as their tongues met and retreated over and over. Within seconds she was halfway into the driver's seat. His hands were on her hips and moving along her sides until he was at the swell of her breasts.

Liese broke the kiss only to go back for more. Then she got a handle on herself and remembered she wasn't going to be the one to forfeit on the *clause*. "Thanks for dinner," she panted, kissing his cheek before she returned to her seat.

"It was my pleasure," Ryder replied, his breathing as labored as hers.

"I'll see you in the morning." She backed away, searching blindly for the door handle. She wrenched open the door, escaping before she did the unthinkable, despite her hideous underwear.

19

New Developments in Secret Places

LIESE PRESSED HER forehead against the doorjamb, taking deep breaths. The crunch of gravel filtered through her front door as Ryder backed out of her driveway. She was too late to call him back to take care of the volcanic-level problem below her waist without looking pathetic. His headlights disappeared as he pulled onto the street.

If she'd been smarter, she would have invited him in for a drink and ditched her ugly panties—screw the no-hanky-panky garbage. Instead, like an idiot, she'd allowed him to leave. Now she had to take care of the issue on her own—not nearly as satisfying as having Ryder do the honors. She technically wouldn't have had to get undressed either. Losing the granny gitch and lifting her skirt would have done the trick.

Frustrated, she kicked off her shoes and stomped up the stairs to her bedroom; exasperation paired with unrequited lust doubled her need for relief. She went straight for the laptop on her nightstand and opened her folder of pictures. While the photoshopped images weren't the same as the real Ryder, she made due.

Several orgasms later, she grabbed her phone. Ryder deserved a little payback in the form of naughty texts. The phone buzzed when she turned it on, indicating new messages. Maybe Ryder had had second thoughts. She could always invite him back over for a personal tour of her bedroom. But Liese's grin faded when a familiar but unwelcome number flashed on the screen. Sean had sent her a total of sixteen messages in the last six hours. Talk about unnerving. And if that wasn't cause enough for concern, he'd also left three voicemails.

Since he'd gotten hold of her new number—she still didn't know how that had happened—he seemed incapable of going more than twenty-four hours without contact. Ignoring him had seemed the best option, but now that approach had increased his efforts.

The voicemails she deleted—she could predict the content without listening. But with her finger poised to delete the texts, Liese paused. One message caught her attention, and the words on the screen made her throat close. Dread hit her like a sledgehammer:

> R u dating someone?
> Is that why ur IGNORING me?

The all-caps freaked her out; it reminded her of just how angry Sean could become, and it didn't take a whole lot to ramp him up. The fine hairs on her neck rose, and she flipped on the lights in her room to make her feel safer. She scrolled down to the next message, the content more troubling than the first:

> I thought we had something
> special. I WILL NOT SHARE U

There he went with the shouty-caps again. The threat in the message made her skin crawl. As she reread the texts, she decided he couldn't possibly know anything about her date with Ryder. Sean lived in the city, hours away, and she didn't have a landline, so he couldn't look her up to know where she lived. Only her closest friends and family had her new address. And Liese had asked her previous landlord not to give out her forwarding information.

As she reread the message, which he'd sent about thirty minutes ago—coincidentally about the time when Ryder had dropped her off—another one arrived.

> miss u, babydoll.
> We need to talk.

The man was delusional. One moment he was the jealous ex-boyfriend, and the next he was sweet and pleading. He hadn't changed at all since she'd broken up with his crazy ass. Marissa might be right about a restraining order. The thought of running into him, even in a public place, scared Liese crapless.

Paranoid, she gathered her robe around her and tiptoed down the darkened hallway to the bathroom. She peered outside, but could only make out the reflection of the moon on the windshield of her car.

She debated whether to go downstairs and flick on the porch light, call Ryder and have him come back to her house, or make a run for her car and go to Ryder's instead. She imagined herself sprinting the short distance from her front porch to her car, only to have Sean burst out of the shadows and tackle her to the ground. It seemed unlikely and ridiculous, but her imagination instilled enough fear that she stayed put.

In the end, she decided not to respond to Sean's messages and not to text Ryder. She would need to tell him about her ex and his unpredictable behavior, but she wasn't quite ready. It was embarrassing to have dated such a loser.

Once calm enough to be rational, she read the remainder of Sean's texts—most of them ranting about how he missed her and wanted to talk to her. Only the last few focused on the possibility that she might be seeing someone else, and how could she if she was, *blah, blah, blah.* His tirades knew no bounds. Tired of the incessant ding of new messages, Liese turned off her phone and climbed into bed. But sleep evaded her.

It was almost two in the morning before she finally passed out, and when she woke three hours later, thanks to a family of raccoons pilfering through her garbage, she couldn't fall back asleep. Groggy and grumpy, Liese forfeited rest for a shower. She put on coffee and milled around her kitchen. Even at her leisurely pace, she was still more than an hour ahead of schedule. But not wanting to be alone any longer, she left the house at six-thirty, just as dawn broke through the thin cover of clouds, coloring the world a soft pink over the inky grey of morning.

Liese stopped for coffee on the way to work, the extra caffeine a necessity to get her through the day. By the time she arrived at FAHL, the coffee had taken effect, and her tension had grown exponentially. Other than those of the janitorial staff, the parking lot was devoid of cars. She passed through the office to check her mailbox and debated whether to leave a note for Ryder. But waiting until the end of the day seemed better to tell him about her stalkerish ex. An angry Ryder wasn't easy for anyone to work with. The less interaction they had at work today the better, as her body hummed with pent up energy, fretfulness superseding the residual sexual tension from the night before. Sean was magical in that respect: capable of killing a sex drive in one text.

Half an hour before first bell, her office phone rang, scaring the crap out of her. She rushed to answer it, recognizing the number as Ryder's.

"Hi," she whispered as she turned her back to the students working on assignments.

"Hello, Ms. Harper. How are you this morning?" Ryder's formal tone was laced with a hint of teasing.

She hesitated and then answered with a lie. "I'm fine. You?"

"I'd be better if I didn't have a meeting. I won't be in until lunch, but I wanted to talk to you. Do you have any free time this afternoon? I thought we might need to debrief after our meeting yesterday."

"Debrief? Is that code for something?" Liese twisted the phone cord around her finger.

"I suppose. I wanted to make sure you felt okay about last night."

"I would have felt much better if there had been an option for extracurricular activities."

She heard a rustling sound and then the distinct click of a door through the phone line. "Are you saying my company and conversational skills are lacking?"

"Not at all. Your conversation skills are phenomenal— orgasmic even." She glanced at the students on the far side of the library. No one was close enough to overhear. "However, your mouth is equally skilled in other areas, and I worry those were not adequately explored. I entreat you to reconsider your ridiculous clause before our next meeting, so I'm not forced to take matters into my own hands—again."

"Again?"

"Mmm. Had you been able to assist me in the endeavor, I

wouldn't be so tired this morning."

"Maybe this is something we might rectify later." Ryder's voice cracked ever so slightly.

"Does that mean the parameters of your clause have expired?"

"Possibly." Liese could hear the faint rustle of fabric followed by throat clearing.

"What are you doing?"

"Adjusting myself. What are you doing?"

"Making sure none of the students is listening to our conversation. I'll see you later today? We can discuss it then? Privately?"

"Most certainly, Ms. Harper."

She managed to keep busy for the remainder of the morning, but her thoughts drifted no matter what she did. Sometimes she thought about Ryder, but mostly she worried about Sean.

At the start of lunch, Liese headed to the main office to drop off paperwork for a new series of novels she wanted to purchase. It could have waited until the end of the day, but she was hoping Ryder had arrived and they could have the discussion he'd promised her. She also hoped somehow she'd be able to work in a segue to the Sean issue.

She came in through the side entrance, which led directly to the mailboxes rather than the front desk. From her vantage point, she could see the door to Ryder's office, yet remain undetected by the secretarial staff. The sound of male voices drifted over to her as she peered around the corner. She froze when she heard the familiar whine that had inundated her voicemail recently. Sean was in the main office.

She couldn't quite make out who the other person was until Blake's voice rose ever so slightly. "I'm sorry, who did you say you were?"

"Her boyfriend." Sean sounded like his typical insecure self. "Really? Liese never said anything about having a boyfriend. Betty, did you know Liese had a boyfriend?" There went Blake, poking the proverbial bear.

Betty made a noncommittal comment, but Sean cut her off. Their voices were too low for Liese to hear anything beyond an occasional word or phrase.

"Why don't we call her extension again? If she's in the library, she'll pick up," Blake suggested.

"I don't understand why I can't just go there and see for myself," Sean protested. "I'm her boyfriend."

Liese wracked her brain for a way Sean could have discovered where she worked. Marissa would never divulge that information, but maybe a former neighbor in her building? After another minute or two, when it became clear she was not in the library, she heard Blake offer to personally deliver the message that Sean had stopped by.

"It might be a good idea to plan a visit in the future so Liese can let the administration or one of our secretaries know you're coming," he offered.

More irritated mumbling from Sean followed. Feet shuffled, and the main door of the office opened and shut with a loud bang. Liese exhaled in relief as Blake and Betty resumed a hushed and anxious conversation. She backed toward the exit through which she'd come, intent on returning to the library to hide out.

Before she could make her escape, Ryder came through the door Liese was propped against, nearly knocking her down. He grabbed her arm to steady her.

"Liese—"

She cut him off with a wave of her hand, shushing him. When he began to question her, Liese held up a finger, signaling him to wait until she heard Blake leave the office.

"I need to talk to you," she hissed.

"Is everything okay? You look pale."

"Yes. No. Can we go to your office?"

Ryder ushered her forward with a sweep of his hand. Liese peeked around the corner to make sure the office was empty but for the secretaries. Finding it all clear, she bee-lined it for Ryder's office.

"Liese, I'm glad you're here." Betty smiled tightly. She hesitated, speaking slowly as though she wasn't quite sure she believed what she was saying. "Your boyfriend just left. He was headed toward the parking lot." The word *boyfriend* came out a question.

Liese could practically feel Ryder bristle behind her. Clearly she should have called him last night instead of waiting until today to deal with the Sean bullshit. "He's not my—"

Ryder cut her off. "Annaliese has a meeting with me right now. Her *boyfriend* will have to wait," he said. "Isn't that right?"

"Of course, Mr. Whitehall." She waited as he brushed past her and unlocked his door. He fumbled the key once before sliding it home, strain apparent in the set of his shoulders. She hoped Betty hadn't noticed.

Ryder shut the door and locked it. "Based on what's going on between us, I'd like to think Betty has been misinformed."

"He's my *ex*-boyfriend," Liese said as he crossed the room. She raised her hands in supplication, and he stopped just before he collided with her upturned palms.

"Why would he show up here and tell my secretary he's still dating you?"

"I don't think he's gotten the message yet." Liese chewed the inside of her lip. "I was going to tell you about him today; he's been texting me. Harassing me."

"Harassing you? In what way?" Concern replaced suspicion.

"He sent me sixteen texts between the time you picked me up and dropped me off last night."

"Sixteen?" His voice rose in shock.

It sounded way worse when repeated back to her.

"And three voicemails," she added meekly. "I haven't checked my phone since midnight though, so there might be more. I'm sure my lack of response is the reason he showed up here." Liese gave in to the impulse to touch Ryder, her fingers clutching the lapels of his jacket. He looked down at her hands, and she snatched them away, unsure if the contact was welcome.

"Sit down." It sounded like a command. Liese began to protest until he guided her to a chair. She hadn't realized she'd been shaking until he folded her hands in his and encouraged her to take a breath.

Rolling his chair over so he could sit knee to knee with her, he gave her a few minutes to collect herself. Then he fell into administrator mode and asked questions. How long had this been going on? How long had they dated? Was he dangerous?

Until last night, Liese hadn't thought Sean was dangerous. A whack job? Sure. In need of therapy? Suffering from an attachment disorder? Probably. Dangerous? What had once been an adamant *no* now changed to an uncertain *maybe*. Sean's tracking her down and impromptu visit made her question her safety, especially since she lived alone.

"The man sounds like he's a few bricks short of a load," Ryder said, his hands stilling as she told him about the effigy bears he'd given her when they first broke up. Liese nodded in agreement. "Marissa keeps telling me to get a restraining order."

"Have you?"

"I hadn't thought it necessary," Liese admitted. "I'll file one this afternoon on my way home."

"I'll have the police come here instead," Ryder said. "That way you don't have to deal with them on your own."

"I don't know, Ryder. Won't that look bad?" Having a psycho ex-boyfriend pop into work looking for her was bad enough. Ryder's reaction to the term *boyfriend* had seemed like another red flag in the not-so-covert-behavior department.

"I can make it look like a school-related investigation," he said, not taking no for an answer. "In the meantime, we should check to see if he's still in the building."

Liese didn't argue. The more she thought about her current situation, the less comfortable she felt being alone. The ever-green trees lining her driveway offered privacy, but they also provided protection for would-be stalker exes. She wanted to ask Ryder if she could stay with him, but his sister was visiting this weekend. She couldn't crash that party. She'd call Marissa later to see if she was available.

Ryder released her hands and rolled his chair over to his desk. He flipped on his monitor to check the school video cameras, focusing on the ones outside, specifically those leading to the parking lot and the main entrance.

She could see Blake just inside the doors, talking to a student. Ryder pulled up the feed overlooking the parking lot and zoomed in to focus on her car. There was Sean with his hands on his hips, glaring at the vehicle. He tried the driver's side door, but Liese had locked it. Living in the city made it a habit. He leaned down, pressing his face to the glass.

"What the hell is he doing?" Ryder asked, zooming in closer.

"Looking at my grocery list on the front seat?"

"And you're telling me you only went out for a few months?"

"He's been trying to get back together with me for longer than we dated." After a few more minutes of peering inside her car and searching for a way in, Sean finally gave up. He surveyed the parking lot, tapping his foot. Suddenly he headed toward the school again, veering right when he reached the stairs, which took him off the camera's radar.

Ryder brought up another view of the school. Liese recognized it as the west entrance. Sean yanked on the door, but it remained closed. After second period, all doors except the main entrance were locked from the outside for the day. Liese hadn't understood the reasons behind it, but now she was grateful. Sean went from cntrance to entrance, trying them all unsuccessfully.

"I should escort him from school property," Ryder said.

"Do you think that's a good idea? I mean, he can't get in, can he?" Liese gestured to the screen. "What if he followed us last night? He could have seen you when you picked me up or dropped me off. What if he recognizes you and says something incriminating?" Watching the feed, she could see the moment Sean decided not to push his luck. He stepped away from the building.

"I'll have a trespassing order filed against him when we meet with the police."

"Okay," Liese said. "I'm sorry."

"You've no need to apologize. You can't control other people's actions."

"I should have told you before. I just didn't want you to think . . . I don't know." That was untrue; she knew exactly why she hadn't told Ryder about Sean.

Ryder pushed his chair back and pulled her into his lap, his hand moving slowly up and down her back. The warmth of his embrace made her feel safe, and she snuggled in closer, wanting to forget what had happened.

"You've told me now, so we'll deal with it. And you'll have a restraining order filed against him before you leave today."

"Yes."

"Good girl." The rough cadence of his voice struck a match inside her, igniting like napalm to burn away the fear and replace it with primal need.

She was on him before he could utter so much as a syllable; she wrapped her arms around his neck and pulled his mouth to hers. She sighed as his hands tangled in her hair and kept her mouth fused to his.

"We shouldn't be doing this right now," he murmured.

"Probably not," Liese whispered and bit his bottom lip while fumbling with his belt. No amount of reasoning could justify what they were doing, or the fact that they were doing it in his office right after they'd had a conversation about her stalker ex-boyfriend.

"Fuck," he muttered as his hand moved lower to search for the hem of her skirt.

"Funny. That's exactly what I was thinking." Liese grabbed his shirt and yanked it from his pants.

Frantic hands pulled at clothing, untucking and unbuttoning until Liese's skirt was shoved up around her waist and Ryder's erection left his boxers. She pushed him down into his chair and tried to straddle him, but it was too awkward. The driving need to touch each other made them both impatient. Ryder spun her around, and Liese groaned quietly as his fingers dipped low to find her ready. He kissed her lower back and pulled her down onto him.

They exhaled a soft moan in tandem as he slid in deep and stilled. Ryder pressed his face against the back of her neck, kissing her skin as he inhaled.

"We really need to be quiet," he said, his voice muffled by her hair.

Liese pressed the heel of her palm to her mouth. Lips parted, she bit down to stop herself from making audible noise. They stayed motionless for a few moments, breathing heavily together.

Eventually he began to move. Liese closed her eyes, absorbed in the sensation. She dropped her hand from her mouth to grip the armrests as he lifted her—retreating and filling, again and again. He took control, moving her over him at an unyielding pace. The chair squeaked softly with each thrust, but their need for each other trumped the fear of getting caught.

"I want you to come," Ryder entreated in a desperate request.

His fingers traveled lightly between her breasts and over her stomach to graze the place where they were joined. Liese parted her legs farther, then dropped onto his erection, grinding in a slow rhythm.

He wrapped an arm around her waist and pulled her against his chest. The hand between her thighs found the place in need of his attention, and Liese bit her tongue to stop her moan.

Her fingernails dug into the nape of his neck as she turned and brought his mouth to hers. A strangled sound left him when she sucked his tongue between her lips. Sensation washed over her, warmth flooding her body to drag her into the sweet undertow.

Ryder shuddered beneath her, peppering her lips and jaw with soft kisses.

"I'm so glad the no-naked clause is over," she said.

Ryder hummed and kissed her neck. "You don't look naked to me."

"You sneaky—"

The phone rang, startling them out of their post-coital bliss. As the haze lifted, Liese became very aware that they'd just had sex in his office in the middle of a school day. She scrambled off his lap, and Ryder rolled forward, taking several deep breaths before slamming his thumb down on the speaker button.

"Yes?" he barked.

Liese cringed at his tone as she hurried to fix her skirt and retrieve her panties from the floor beside his desk.

Betty's voice filtered into the room. "Sorry to interrupt you, Mr. Whitehall. But you have a visitor."

20

Visitors

LIESE DIDN'T WANT to imagine who could be waiting for Ryder in the front office. It had to be someone important to make him look so frantic.

He covered the mouthpiece and turned his head to the side to clear his throat. At the same time he furtively tucked himself back into his pants. "Pardon me?" He shot Liese a panicked glance as she shimmied her panties up her legs and smoothed her skirt. She surveyed his reaction, tempering her own unease based on his body language.

His rigid posture relaxed, albeit minutely, but his eyes reflected a new kind of disquiet. "I thought she wasn't going to be here until the end of the day," he bit out irritably. "Tell her I'll be with her in a minute."

He hung up and met Liese's petrified gaze. She hastily buttoned her navy blazer, thankful she'd worn it, seeing the rumpled mess her blouse had become.

"My sister is early," Ryder said. He tightened his tie and fastened his own suit jacket to cover the majority of his dishevelment.

"Oh, God! That's not good." She ran her fingers through her hair, trying to tame it.

"It could be a hell of a lot worse." Ryder stepped forward and brushed her hands away from her hair, smoothing it out for her. His fingers caught in a tangled section, and he had to work to free them.

"It smells like sex in here." She straightened his tie and stepped back, looking around the room for a secret exit; there wasn't one.

Ryder opened the top drawer of his desk. Wielding a can of room deodorizer, he released a spray of overpowering scent into the room. "Better?"

Liese grabbed the can, covering her mouth and nose so she didn't breathe in the fumes. "Now it smells like sex in a flowerbed. This stuff is horrible. Where did you get it?"

"It was in there when I took the job." He motioned to the drawer. "It's better than my office smelling like sex. Isn't it?"

"Not really."

"Well, does it even mask it at all?"

"I think so. It's hard to tell though." Liese sniffed the lapel of her blouse. "I'm saturated in the smell of you."

Ryder's eyes lit with dark fire. "This was a terribly bad idea." He took her face between his hands and kissed her fiercely.

"The room spray or the kiss?"

"Neither—the sex in my office."

"Oh, right." Liese adjusted his tie again. "So much for all our declarations. It felt good, though."

"I can't disagree with that." He smiled wryly. "You should go back to the library. I'll send someone to get you when the police arrive."

"Okay." She'd forgotten all about the police.

Liese checked herself over one last time. Priority number one was finding something to mask the smell of Ryder. He opened the door and stepped aside to allow her to exit, careful to avoid physical contact. Her cheeks felt hot as she left the safety of his office, but she couldn't miss the tall, lanky girl with hair the same color as Ryder's that leaned against Betty's desk. At the sound of the door opening, she turned to Ryder with an excited smile.

"You're early." Ryder's tone was chastising but his grin told another story. "I thought Donovan was dropping you off at the end of the day. Aren't you missing classes?"

She shrugged. "I took the bus. Sitting in a car with Dad for an hour is torture. You'll call in for me, right?"

She gave him one of those typical teenage looks, halfway between expectation and apology. Tiffany inspected Ryder as he tugged on his tie. Out of the corner of her eye, she could see Ryder's sister appraising her next. Liese prayed she didn't look as guilty as she felt.

"I'll speak to you later this afternoon," Ryder told Liese, his tone all business. He in no way looked like someone who'd just had sex in his office with the school librarian. Aside from the tie-tugging, he was maddeningly unflustered.

"Great. Good. Thank you, sir." Liese forced herself to look at him despite her desperation to escape the office and all the eyes therein. She caught a twitch at the corner of his mouth but couldn't be sure if her jumpiness was the cause.

She realized she'd been staring at him, probably for longer than was comfortable. He broke eye contact first. "Annaliese, I'd like you to meet my baby sister, Tiffany. Tiffany, this is Ms.

Harper, our resident librarian." He gestured between them.

As Ryder's subordinate, meeting his sister shouldn't have been a big deal, but Liese wasn't currently feeling confident about her ability to speak coherently.

She smiled at Tiffany and waved. "Hi."

"I'm not a baby, RJ!" Tiffany half-shrieked and flapped her hands in a dramatic display of displeasure. "He's always trying to embarrass me like that." She directed the comment to Liese before cutting a scathing look at Ryder. "I don't go introducing you as my geriatric brother, do I?"

"I'm hardly geriatric." He crossed his arms over his chest.

Liese stifled a laugh. She could definitely see the family resemblance.

"Whatever." Tiffany faked indifference.

The warning bell rang, signaling the end of lunch. Liese hadn't realized how long they'd been alone in his office. "Oh! I should get going. There's probably a line of students waiting for me. Nice to meet you, Tiffany."

"You, too." Tiffany called as Ryder ushered her into his office and shut the door.

Liese forced down a wave of nausea as she headed for the library. Talk about awkward introductions. Yet another reason why people who worked together shouldn't hook up. Especially if, like her, they didn't have the best poker faces in the world.

She entered the library, taking comfort in its quiet familiarity, but the full impact of how close they'd come to being caught hit Liese when she stepped inside her office. They were lucky no one had interrupted them mid-fornication. It could have been anyone at the door—another staff member, the superintendent, some other board employee who could destroy their careers. She sanitized the crap out of her hands and slathered her arms in lotion that made her smell like a piece of cake. She hoped it covered the pervasive scent of Ryder's cologne.

Students began to file into the library, allowing her to divert her attention to something less stressful. Then, as if she needed more drama, Blake showed up.

"You had a visitor at lunch today." He tried for casual, but she could tell the curiosity was killing him.

"I know. I was hiding behind the mailboxes and heard most of it." There was no point in lying.

"What?" His voice rose.

Liese glared at him, looking pointedly over his shoulder at the students. "I said I know," she whispered. "He's my exboyfriend. It's complicated. Thanks for getting rid of him though—it could have been disastrous."

"Ex-boyfriend? I wondered what his deal was. He was pretty damn persistent about seeing you."

"He's delusional," she clarified, feeling compelled to provide some sort of explanation. "We broke up months ago, but he can't seem to take a hint. It's really frustrating."

"That's kind of messed up. I'm sorry." Liese could see him putting things together. "I'm glad it was me who ran into him instead of you."

"You have no idea how thankful I am about that," she said.

Blake gave the room a quick scan, then lowered his voice. "I caught him trying to sneak in one of the side doors even after I told him you weren't available."

"Yeah, I saw. I was in Ryder's office watching the surveillance cameras. I'm glad he didn't get back inside the school."

"Me too, from the sound of things." Blake fiddled with her Post-it notes. "Wait, so Whitehall knows? He'd better not have been a jerk about it."

"He's being quite nice, actually," Liese said. She focused on softening her tone. "He's helping me file a restraining order this afternoon."

"Oh? That's a good idea." He looked surprised that Ryder could be something other than an asshole. "If you need someone to walk you to your car or anything, let me know. I'm a great bodyguard." Blake flexed a bicep, and Liese tried not to laugh. Blake, while attractive, was tall and lean, not a typical bodyguard physique.

"What?" He pretended to be hurt. "I'm wiry but strong. Anyway, I'm around all weekend if you need company."

"Thanks. I'll keep that in mind."

Halfway through study hall, Ryder called Liese for a favor. He had things to take care of, and Tiffany was bored. She could hear the apology in his voice. And the plea for understanding.

"Send her down. I'm happy to have her here," she said. Maybe she'd have an opportunity to make a better impression on his sister this time around, now that she was less frazzled. Ryder arrived a few minutes later, Tiffany trailing behind him.

She perked up when she took in her new surroundings. "This library is awesome!"

Ryder shushed her when half the students in the room swiveled their heads to stare.

"Sorry," she whispered. She turned to Liese. "Can I look around?"

"Have a ball." Liese motioned her forward. She didn't need to be told twice. Tiffany dropped her backpack on the closest table, disappearing into the stacks.

Once his sister was out of earshot, Ryder inclined his head toward Liese's office. From her place behind the door, she could still see most of the students at the tables, but she and Ryder were hidden enough to escape notice. He maintained a safe distance.

"Are you okay?"

"I'm fine," Liese said, but she wasn't sure she meant it. She was a lot of things: incredulous over her recent tryst in Ryder's office, terrified Sean might be more dangerous than she'd first assumed, and distraught that she and Ryder wouldn't be able to adequately hide their relationship, compromising their jobs. Now she was responsible for his baby sister, and Liese wanted her to like her. Of course she was fine.

"I never should have put you in that position."

"I don't mind your sister being here. She'd be bored out of her tree if she had to sit in your office all afternoon."

"That's not what I was referring to."

"Oh."

"I won't let it happen again."

"I'm sorry?" Confusion made her slow to understand.

"I promise not to take advantage of you like that. You were distraught. I was angry and feeling . . ."

"Um, I was a willing participant, and I think I started—"

"—who was anxious about an ex-boyfriend who showed up and wouldn't leave."

"Well, there is that," Liese conceded. "I think we should probably agree to be hands off when we're in this building—or in any public place, for that matter." Ironically, they'd leaned toward each other as they spoke, inching closer with every exchange. She took a step back.

"Agreed." Ryder mimicked her movement and leaned against

the doorjamb, looking over his shoulder at the students, who were busy studying. "Do you have somewhere to stay this weekend?" he asked. The abrupt subject change caught her off guard. "I don't like the idea of you being alone. I'd invite you to stay at my place, but with Tiffany there . . ."

"Blake offered to hang out with me." Liese gave him a lopsided smile. She didn't have to wait long for a reaction.

"Not funny." Ryder gave her a hard look. "That man is like a fucking vulture."

"He's just worried." Liese held up a hand to fend off his verbal bashing. "And that was a joke."

"Worried, my ass," Ryder grumbled.

"I can call Marissa and see if she's available." When Ryder didn't move she added, "Right now?"

Liese hadn't expected to get Marissa on the phone, but she answered on the first ring. After a brief explanation of the situation, Marissa cursed a blue streak and promised to be in Fullerton in less than three hours. Liese told her not to speed.

Marissa "pffted" and hung up.

"Happy now?"

"I'd be happier if you were spending the weekend in my bed," Ryder said. "But this will do."

"Raincheck?"

"The sooner the better, Ms. Harper." His hand jerked at his side, as if the compulsion to touch her was too strong to deny. She could relate. "I should get back to my office."

"Probably a good plan."

"Oh, and the police will be here by the end of the day. I'll call you when they arrive."

"Okay."

As Ryder turned and left the library, Liese looked out over the students. She had to wonder whether she and Ryder were more obvious than either of them realized.

Liese spent the afternoon being enchanted by Tiffany. She in no way shared her brother's reserved demeanor, but offered the same level of charisma. Tiffany was a fiery, funny girl who clearly loved her brother. Ryder would've spit nails if he knew how much information she offered up about him. But Liese pinkie-swore not to say a word.

The "J" in RJ stood for Jackson, and only Tiffany was allowed to use the nickname. She revealed that Ryder had been kind of nerdy in high school—not new information based on the conversation at the bar. But she gained Liese's rapt attention when she talked about his first girlfriend. Or at least the first girl he'd introduced to his family. It was a long time ago, and, according to Tiffany, she was the only woman he'd ever brought home. His parents hadn't approved, which could explain the lack of subsequent family introductions.

Tiffany told Liese she'd already had three boyfriends, but all of them were idiots. She swore up and down she wasn't going to date again until she turned twenty.

But less than five minutes later, Tristan, one of Blake's drama students, came in search of some resources. Tiffany jumped at the chance to take him to the reference books. By the time she returned, they were exchanging phone numbers.

"You won't tell RJ, right?"

"Tell him what?"

"Thanks." Tiffany's smile was radiant. "I think I'm in love."

Liese stifled a laugh. If only life could be so simple.

Blake came by near the end of the day to relieve her of her duties so she could join Ryder and the police in his office. Tiffany stayed behind, per Ryder's request, so Liese left Blake sitting at her desk with Tiffany close by, scoping out the library for cute, studious boys.

The interview with the police was thorough and unnerving. Officers Tanner and Cooke got straight down to business, diving right in with personal questions about her relationship with Sean. Ryder offered to leave, much to her relief. Rehashing the details of her previous, failed relationship in front of him would have been beyond embarrassing. Liese swore the officers must have noticed the tension between them.

She couldn't explain how Sean had managed to acquire her new cell number or find out where she worked. But if he could do that, they determined it wouldn't be unlikely for him to discover where she lived, and that prospect scared her half to death. Liese knew Sean could be charming, so it wouldn't be that difficult for him to persuade someone to provide her forwarding address. He'd certainly pulled the wool over Liese's eyes for the first couple of months, after which things had gone downhill fast.

"Do you believe him capable of violence?" Officer Tanner asked while his partner took copious notes.

Liese hesitated. "Maybe? I'm not sure."

"Has he ever physically assaulted you, or threatened physical harm?"

"No. Never." Liese was adamant about that.

Officer Tanner kept the questions coming, making inferences about emotional abuse, potential threats, and Sean's recent increase in obsessive behavior. Officer Cooke asked if Liese was aware of whether or not he owned a firearm, which unfortunately, she was not.

Ryder returned when the officers requested to see the video surveillance from the school. In conjunction with the texts and countless emails she'd saved from Sean, along with her statement to the police, there was sufficient evidence to warrant a restraining order. The document also stipulated that he couldn't come within a hundred feet of FAHL.

"Oh, one last thing, Ms. Harper." Officer Cooke stood, flipping his note pad shut. "Are you currently involved with anyone?"

21

Speculation and Undercover Operations

LIESE SPUTTERED. "I'VE gone on a date recently."

"How recently are we talking?" Cooke put his pen back to his pad and scribbled some more.

"Um, last night."

"This would be important information, Ms. Harper." Officer Tanner gave her a hard look.

"She's been under a lot of stress today," Ryder cut in. His hand came to rest over hers, and he gave it a squeeze.

"That could explain the increase in erratic behavior. I suggest you let the individual you're seeing know about your ex."

Officer Cooke looked at Ryder. "Unless he's already aware."

"I'll do that," Liese managed.

Ryder rose from his chair to escort the officers out. At least he could keep his cool when she was falling apart.

Officer Tanner diffused the sudden awkwardness when he promised to call once he'd issued the restraining order. All she could do now was wait.

As he opened the door, Liese caught a glimpse of Marissa standing at the front desk, talking to Betty. Her friend stopped mid-sentence and tackled her with a hug, practically bowling over the officers and Ryder to get to her.

"I'm so glad you're okay." She kissed her on the cheek and held Liese at arm's length to inspect her. Apparently she passed the test. Marissa heaved a huge sigh of relief and hugged her again declaring, "I'm going to fuck Sean up the next time I see him. That guy is such a loser."

"Um, Mar . . ." Liese felt the heat in her cheeks as she sought to extricate herself. It seemed to take her friend a second to realize what she'd said and where she'd said it. Unfazed, Marissa released her and tossed her hair over her shoulder, smiling brightly at the officers. She gave them both a cursory inspection—Marissa never discounted any man as not being her type. "I meant that figuratively, not literally." Officer Tanner arched a brow.

"I'm Marissa, Liese's girlfriend."

Officer Tanner's expression turned to mild confusion. He looked from Liese to Marissa.

Understanding dawned on Marissa. "I mean her best friend, not her girlfriend as in *girl*friend. We don't sleep with each other. Well, sometimes, but not like *that*." She backtracked—or at least tried to and failed miserably.

Ryder sounded like he was choking to death beside her. Liese gave him an exasperated look and rolled her eyes. Men could be so damn predictable. Marissa was tall, gorgeous, and willowy. It was a wonder the image she'd just planted in their testosteroneaddled minds hadn't made their heads explode.

"Way to introduce yourself, Mar," Liese whispered. She turned to the officers. "Marissa used to be my roommate. She's staying with me this weekend so I'm not alone."

Officer Tanner cleared his throat. A slight smile gave away his amusement. "We can send a car to patrol your area, Ms. Harper, to give you a little additional piece of mind."

"That would be amazing," Liese said, thankful stalking was considered a big deal in Fullerton. In the city they just asked if you owned a registered handgun. "I really appreciate your help."

"We're doing our job, ma'am," Officer Cooke replied and tipped his hat.

"Here's my card." Officer Tanner handed it to Liese, his eyes moving to Marissa. "We're just a phone call away should you need anything."

"That's so kind of you, officer," Marissa gushed, swiping the card out of Liese's hand. She shoved it in the back pocket of her jeans. "I'll hold onto it, just in case."

"You do that," Tanner replied. He winked as he followed his partner out of the office.

"I can't believe you just did that."

"Did what?" Marissa batted her lashes and flashed a mischievous grin.

"I believe Liese is referring the blatant flirting," Ryder cut in.

"Was it that obvious?"

"If it makes you feel any better, he was just as obvious."

"It does." Marissa held out her hand, offering Ryder a knowing smile. "You must be Ryder. I've heard all *sorts* of things about you."

Liese elbowed her in the side, afraid someone might overhear. But the main office was empty. Betty and the other secretaries had slipped out sometime during Marissa's embarrassing conversation with the police.

"All good things I hope?" he asked.

"Some," Marissa replied honestly, much to Liese's chagrin.

She knew Marissa still worried about their relationship.

"That doesn't sound very promising."

"You seem to be doing an excellent job of redeeming your-self for past indiscretions." Marissa patted him on the shoul-der. "But what I'm wondering right now is, why exactly have I been awarded the pleasure of a sleepover with Liese? I'm sure it would be far more satisfying for her if it were you. Not that I'm complaining. I'm more than happy to snuggle with my bestie."

Ryder stiffened. "Did you just imply . . . should I be con-cerned?" Liese had never seen him so flustered.

Marissa burst out laughing.

"She's just giving you a hard time." Liese directed her com-ment at her friend. "Ryder's sister is staying at his house for the weekend, which is why I called you."

"So? Why should that matter? You're both adults." "Yes, but my sister is seventeen," Ryder replied.

"Oh. Right. Gotcha. Not really good for teenagers to witness bondage and all that jazz."

"Marissa!"

"Exactly how much have you told her?" Ryder asked.

"That was actually a joke." Marissa slung an arm over Liese's shoulder. "But methinks we have much to discuss, my friend."

"For the love of . . ." Ryder glanced at his watch. "I should probably get Tiffany from the library. I'm sure Stone is having a hissy fit."

Liese let the barb go. Ryder gathered his things from his of-fice, and the three of them left for the library. Marissa kept whis-pering under her breath, but Liese couldn't quite make out what she said. However, it was likely inappropriate.

They found Blake sitting where Liese had left him: in front of her computer, chin propped on one hand, clicking away on the mouse with the other. Tiffany and Tristan sat in the back corner, looking a little too cozy for having met just a few hours earlier.

When the door opened, Blake looked up. He seemed like he was about to drop a snarky comment, but froze as his eyes moved past Liese to Marissa. He rolled his chair back to stand, but crashed to the floor instead.

"Blake? Are you okay?" Liese leaned over the desk, catching a glimpse of the top of his head.

He sprang to his feet, dusting himself off. "Hey, hi. Hi, guys. Whitehall, Liese." His head bobbed up and down comically as he planted his hands on the desk. Today seemed to be a banner one for embarrassing moments.

"Stone." Ryder didn't seem the least bit concerned about whether Blake had hurt himself. He looked over at his sister, who was very nearly sitting in Tristan's lap. Liese had a feeling if they'd come in a few minutes later, they might have found the pair in a much more compromising position.

Tiffany jumped at the sound of Ryder's voice. "Okay, well, thanks for all your help," she told Tristan. "Nice to meet you."

"Is that what they're calling it these days?" Ryder muttered.

She felt sorry for the poor boy as he gathered up Tiffany's backpack and helped her put it on before slinging his own over his shoulder. Tiffany gave Ryder an imploring look that clearly said, "Please don't humiliate me."

"I believe you usually spend most of your time in the theater, Mr. Emerson. It's good to see you taking such a strong interest in your studies," Ryder said as he turned to

Tiffany. "Are you ready to go?"

Tristan glanced from Tiffany to Ryder. "Mr. Whitehall is your *dad*?" he asked.

"No, Mr. Emerson, I'm not her father. Fortunately for you,

I'm just her brother." Ryder smiled.

"Oh." He looked back and forth between them, his face scrunched in confusion. "But you're so old."

"What is it with people telling me I'm old these days?" Ryder threw his hands in the air.

Tiffany burst out laughing, startling Tristan, and Liese stifled a snicker as the poor boy continued to back toward the exit.

"Sorry, sir." Tristan pumped the push bar. "See you later." He waved at Tiffany without actually looking at her. "Have a nice weekend, Ms. Harper, Mr. Stone. Sorry I called you old, Mr. Whitehall." The words blended together at the end as he struggled with the door. He almost tripped over his own feet in his haste to leave.

"I hate you. I hope you know that." Tiffany narrowed her eyes at Ryder.

"If he really likes you, he'll call," he assured her.

"Uh, no, he won't, and it's all your fault. You'd better buy me pizza for dinner to make it up to me, and take me shopping for new shoes. Mom refused to let me get the ones I want. She said they weren't feminine enough." Tiffany grabbed the keys from him and stomped across the library, pausing before she pushed the door open. "Bye, Ms. Harper. Thanks for letting me hang out this afternoon. And you—" She pointed at Blake. "Thanks for the warning. I'll meet you in the car, RJ." With that she disappeared down the hallway, sticking her tongue out at Ryder as she passed the windows.

"Well, this should be a fun weekend." Ryder sighed. "Thank you for watching the library while Liese was indisposed," he told Blake. And while his posture was stiff, he sounded sincere.

"No problem," Blake replied, his hands clasped behind his back.

"Okay, well . . . have a lovely weekend." Ryder hesitated at the door, his eyes lingering on Liese before he followed his sister down the hall.

So much had happened in this whirlwind of a day that Liese could barely get her head around it all. Meanwhile, Marissa eyed Blake, who was busy shutting down the computer. Liese knew the look on Marissa's face; it meant she was sizing him up—otherwise known as "mentally undressing him and determining his penis size" in Marissa's world. Liese suppressed a cringe. The minute they were alone Marissa would give her unsolicited opinion on his assets and drawbacks, just as she would for Ryder.

"Blake, this is my friend Marissa. Marissa, this is Blake, our drama teacher."

"Ooooh, hey," Marissa drew out the words as the pieces of the puzzle fell into place. "It's nice to meet you. I think Liese might have mentioned you before."

"Oh?" Blake rubbed his palm on his pant leg and smiled. "I hope it was only positive."

"Definitely positive," Marissa nodded slowly.

"Well, that's . . . positive."

"Did you still want to go to the bar?" Liese directed the question at Blake, feeling absurdly awkward.

"Yes!" Blake and Marissa responded in unison. They looked at each other and then away.

"Great." Liese clapped her hands together, startling them into action.

She grabbed her purse and closed up the library. They accompanied Blake to the drama studio to retrieve his jacket, and he used the opportunity to show Marissa the set of the play that would open the following week, pointing out all the pieces Liese had worked on. Marissa ooh'ed and ahh'ed over it, asking lots of questions, as was her personality. It took another twenty minutes before they finally left the building. Concerned Sean might be lurking outside the school, Blake and Marissa flanked Liese as they crossed the parking lot. If he was around, he went undetected.

Blake suggested they drop off Liese and Marissa's cars and allow him to drive. Marissa was enthusiastic about the idea, which meant she wanted to tie one on. So they drove separately to Liese's and then piled into Blake's car to meet up with the rest of their colleagues.

Marissa fit in seamlessly, striking up easy conversation with the group. Liese felt relief in being able to merge these two facets of her life, particularly since she still worried about how she would manage this with Ryder in the future. Even if things did work out between them, it wasn't as though she could bring him out for a drink with her work friends.

Embarrassingly, everyone seemed to know about Sean showing up at work. The story had mutated in to a ridiculous rumor that Sean was her ex-husband and had come to the school to confront Blake. Both Liese and Blake were quick to correct this. Liese didn't like how easily her colleagues had believed the initial story, or the curious glances she received when she shut the conversation down.

The buzz of her phone served as a diversion, and she checked her messages. Ryder had sent a text.

Liese nearly choked on her beer.

> Restrained?

The next text came more quickly, with the dictionary definition of restrained sent as a link.

> Yes. Restrained.

Liese smiled.

> Does this have anything to do with Marissa's comment?

The next message made her wish she could drive to his house to make it happen.

> Possibly. I rather like the idea of you tied to my bedposts.

Liese checked to make sure no one was paying attention to her before texting

> That could be arranged.

After drinks, Blake drove her and Marissa home. He walked them to the door, checking the perimeter of the house even though they'd passed a cop car parked under a streetlight just down the street. It made Liese feel safer knowing people were watching out for her. Sean would have to keep his distance.

Blake said an awkward goodbye before he left. He'd been gone less than thirty seconds when Marissa started in.

"You didn't tell me Blake was hot," she accused as she flopped down on the couch.

"He's all right. I mean, yeah, he's a good-looking guy; he's just not my type. Ryder on the other hand . . ."

"Is. I get it. But still, it would have been easier to date your sexy colleague than your boss."

Liese sighed and sunk into the cushions. "Blake is a great friend, but he doesn't do it for me."

"Because he's not into spanking and black latex?"

"Oh my God! Would you seriously stop?" Liese smacked her on the leg, mortified. Mostly because the comment rang more true than she wanted to admit.

"What? There's nothing wrong with a little kink. And don't even try to deny it. That man is so reserved and in control, there's no way he's not bringing it in the bedroom."

"I don't even want to know how you know that."

"Ha!" Marissa's eyes lit up, and Liese knew she'd been duped into divulging. "You're such a deviant!"

"You're the one who made all the photoshopped porn," Liese pointed out.

"Only because you kept thanking me for it."

"Can we please change the subject?"

"Sure," Marissa placated. "So, what kind of heat is Ride-me packing?"

"Why do you always insist on referring to men's junk as a firearm?"

Marissa gave her a hurt look. "I do not."

"Actually, you do. And I'm not telling you about *Ryder*'s package, because you don't need any more ammunition where he's involved."

"Now who's using gun references?"

"You're impossible."

"I know. But you love me anyway." Marissa nudged her shoulder.

"As much as you love me."

"But just like a sister, so don't get any ideas."

Liese snorted. "I'll try to control myself."

At three in the morning Liese's phone buzzed, pulling her out of a dream she didn't want to leave. She scrambled for her cell, punching buttons until the screen lit up. She grunted into the receiver only to be met with silence.

"Hello?" She blinked groggily and pulled the phone away from her ear to check the number. It read unknown. She listened intently, trying to pick up a sound, something to indicate someone on the other end of the line, but nothing registered.

"Hello?" she asked again, louder this time.

A long sigh came through the line, sounding plaintive and sinister at the same time. A chill ran up her spine.

"Liese? Who are you talking to?" Marissa asked.

"Just some stupid pervert breathing into the phone," she replied and hung up. She turned off the device and tossed it to the floor. She knew of only one person who would call her and do something so creepy.

Sean must have gotten another new cell phone.

22

Dating in the Dark

EARLY THE NEXT morning, Marissa retrieved Officer Tanner's card from the pocket of her jeans and called the station before handing Liese the phone. Sean's recent visit screamed of his obsession, and the middle-of-the-night phone call from the mouth-breather had made sleep elusive for her once again. Officer Tanner answered and informed Liese he'd been about to contact her. He'd issued the restraining order less than an hour prior, when he and his partner found Sean parked down the street from her house.

Liese contemplated her father's previous offers to take her to a shooting range, something she'd avoided until now. Maybe being able to handle a firearm wasn't a half-bad idea. Might be just the thing to move Sean along to his next lucky victim.

"Everything okay?" Marissa asked after she ended the call.

"Officer Tanner issued the restraining order this morning. Sean was skulking around near the house."

"I knew he was a whack job, but I didn't know he was that

much of a creepy douche. At least now he *has* to stay away from you," Marissa replied.

Beyond her concerns over his increasingly erratic behavior, Sean's continued presence in her life further complicated the situation with Ryder. "I really hope he follows the order," Liese agreed. "If he keeps this up, he could very well expose my relationship with Ryder. And that would be a mess."

"I'm sure he'll back off. He has to, otherwise he'll be charged. I'm pretty sure even Sean isn't all that keen on being someone's prison bitch."

While Liese prepared lunch, her cell rang, bringing with it a fresh wave of fear. Marissa answered on her behalf, and apparently it was just Blake wanting to make sure their night had been uneventful. Marissa chatted with him for a few minutes before handing the phone to Liese.

"You're still okay to come tomorrow?" he asked.

"Oh, no!" Liese smacked her forehead. "I totally forgot." In the chaos of Friday, the dress rehearsal Blake had scheduled for Sunday had slipped her mind.

"If you can't make it . . ." He let the sentence hang unfinished.

She knew he needed her help. He couldn't run a full dress rehearsal on his own, and Liese had been there with him from the beginning. He conferred with her on everything.

"No, no," Liese rushed to reassure him. She promised to be there on time.

"Great. Looking forward to it." Blake paused before tacking on, "Feel free to invite Marissa if she's still around."

"Will do." Liese ended the call and set her phone back on the table.

"What's doin'?"

Liese explained the situation. Although Marissa came across

as indifferent, Liese could tell she was disappointed. At her reaction, Liese began to devise a plan.

"We're not starting until later in the morning. You can come if you want."

"Yeah?" Marissa's face lit up. "I won't be in the way?"

"Not at all. Blake even invited you."

"Cool." Marissa ducked her head and toyed with a lock of hair, twisting it around her finger as she leafed through the day-old newspaper on the kitchen table.

Liese observed her friend with growing curiosity. She had an inkling Marissa's sudden interest in high school productions had less to do with theater and more to do with the director. If she set Blake up with Marissa, maybe Ryder would ease up on him for good. It was worth a shot.

Mid-afternoon, Marissa had a shopping attack. Liese attempted to dissuade her: Fullerton wasn't like the city, and the stores wouldn't meet her expectations. Marissa wouldn't hear it, though. The restraining order had taken care of Sean; they didn't need to stay holed up all weekend, so Liese stopped arguing. Shopping with Marissa was its own form of entertainment, and Liese could use the diversion.

A little while later, she trailed behind Marissa as she ducked into stores, the names of which she'd never heard before. She held up a sparkly gold tunic, and Liese made a noncommittal noise. On most people, the top would look awful; on Marissa it would look amazing.

"Could you at least pretend to be enthused by something I show you?" Marissa scowled and hung the shirt back on the rack.

"Huh?" Liese looked up from her phone, having checked her messages for the hundredth time since they'd arrived at the mall. "This." Marissa held up a red sequined top. "Or this." In her other hand she dangled a long-sleeved black shirt with a silver pattern on it.

"Depends. If you're thinking of wearing that out tonight—" Liese pointed to the sparkly top. "—you might want to reconsider. The bar we went to last night is about as exciting as it gets here. However, the black one won't make you stand out like a sore thumb."

"Hmm, good point." Marissa headed for the changing rooms, taking both options with her anyway.

Two hours later, Marissa had combed the entire mall and succeeded in purchasing enough new clothes to dress an entire family. Or at least a nightclub of go-go dancers.

As they passed the movie theater, Marissa eyed the billboards. The half-naked body of a warrior promised both violence and partial nudity. "Ooooh, want to see an action flick?"

"Sure, why not?" If nothing else, a movie would help keep her mind off Ryder and what he might be doing, or what he might be doing *to her* the next time they were alone. He'd sent messages earlier in the day alluding to a very interesting fantasy involving her and a pair of furry handcuffs. If his sister hadn't been there, Liese would have driven right over and enacted the entire scene—after she stopped at the nearest adult store to purchase said handcuffs.

Yet despite her eagerness to fall back into bed with him, she knew they needed to deal with what had happened yesterday. She couldn't keep defaulting to sex when things were too stressful to talk about. There was a therapy session waiting to happen somewhere in there.

She followed Marissa into the lobby of the theater and purchased two tickets. At the concession counter she ordered a large popcorn, an enormous chocolate bar, and enough Coke to bathe in.

"Thirsty?" Marissa asked as Liese pulled money from her wallet.

"I thought we could share."

"Like I'm your date?" Marissa waggled her eyebrows.

"You know, one of these days someone is going to take you seriously and think we're actually dating," Liese warned.

The teenage boy behind the counter dropped her change and coughed as he swept it back into his hand.

"My mom already does."

"She does not."

"No, but she did when we were in college and you went through that phase where all you wore were army pants and combat boots," Marissa said.

"That was you, not me." Liese gave her a look and pocketed her change. "And I think that phase lasted two weeks—about the same amount of time it took you to decide the main reason you wanted to take art was so you could pick up the nude models."

She handed Marissa the popcorn, and they headed for their theater, taking two seats in the second-to-last row. The lights were already low, the first of many trailers playing on the screen. Liese settled into her seat. She checked her phone again and adjusted the volume. Still no new message from Ryder. She tried not to feel disappointed.

The trailer for some ridiculous romantic comedy she would never pay to see began. Marissa elbowed her side and leaned in close. "Hey, isn't that Ryder?"

Liese sat up in her chair, peering around the darkening theater, but didn't see anyone who resembled Ryder. She sank back into her seat. "Don't do that; it's not funny."

"I'm serious." Marissa pointed to two figures standing at the base of the stairs. The glare of the screen cast them in shadow, their features impossible to discern.

Liese squinted as they ascended the stairs, but the first figure—obviously female—blocked her view of the person following.

"How about here?" Ryder's voice was unmistakable.

She glanced at Marissa who grinned. "Told you so."

Liese was about to retort but stopped when she realized Ryder had paused a few rows in front of them.

"No way. I want to sit at the back," Tiffany replied, climbing higher, pausing at the row where Liese and Marissa sat. The three seats to their left remained vacant.

Ryder sighed as Tiffany sidestepped down the aisle toward them. Marissa flashed Liese a conspiratorial smile as she stood up to allow them to pass. "What are the chances?" she whispered.

"Slim to none?" Liese murmured in return.

"Excuse me." Tiffany sidled past Marissa and Liese, leaving an empty seat between them. She did a double-take as Ryder approached to pass. "Oh my God! Ms. Harper?"

Liese waved in silent greeting. Ryder moved past Marissa, apologizing more than once for the disruption. And then he was right in front of her. His back brushed against her chest, and Liese barely mustered the restraint not to rub up against him. Tiffany reached over Liese and grabbed Ryder's arm, nearly pulling him into Liese's lap.

"Tiffany," he hissed, dropping into the seat beside her. He turned to apologize. The words died as he realized who occupied the seat next to him. "Liese?"

"Hi."

"That's what I was trying to tell you," Tiffany whispered, sitting forward so she could wave at Liese and Marissa again.

"How cool is this?"

"How . . ." Ryder paused, surreptitiously checking her out. ". . . unexpected." Liese didn't miss the rapacious gleam in his eye.

"Is it okay if we sit with you?" Tiffany asked, bouncing in her seat. She gripped the sleeve of Ryder's shirt, willing him to stay put. Liese mentally did the same. However risky it might be for them to be seen together, she didn't want him to switch seats.

Marissa spoke first. "Sure."

Ryder glanced around the theater.

"Sorry," Liese whispered.

"For what? How could you have known I'd be here?" He smiled faintly.

"RJ tried to make me see some stupid PG crap, but I thought this would be way better." Tiffany injected herself into the conversation.

"Yeah, same with this one." Marissa thumbed at Liese.

Liese rolled her eyes. "Hardly."

The screen threw a pale glow over the audience, and Ryder shifted in his seat, shedding his jacket. She thought he might be wearing jeans, but it was too dark to tell. He smelled amazing, though. His cologne wafted over, making her mouth water. She could imagine the bitter taste of it on her tongue when she kissed her way over his jaw.

Tension buzzed through her body. She gave the theater a quick perusal, praying no one would recognize them. She hadn't seen anyone familiar, but she didn't know all four hundred students who attended FAHL, or their families.

Halfway through the film, Tiffany went to the bathroom, followed by Marissa, who graced her with the most obvious thumbs up in history. Once they'd disappeared through the doors, Ryder's hand settled on top of hers, fingers sliding between her own.

"Do you have any idea what's going on?" he whispered in her ear.

"What?"

"The movie, are you following it?"

"Not really," she admitted, flipping her hand over so they were palm to palm.

"Me neither." He ducked his head and raised their hands, sweeping his lips over her knuckles. "I've been wondering—" He bit down gently on the pad of her thumb.

"Hmm?" Liese turned so she could see his profile. God, he was gorgeous. His mouth pouty and sensuous, he continued to torment her by kissing along her fingers.

"What are you doing tomorrow night?"

"I don't have plans." Liese shifted closer to him. The damn armrest was in the way.

"I'm dropping Tiffany off at my parents' house in the afternoon. Would you like to have dinner with me?"

"I'd love to have you for dinner," Liese replied breathlessly. She felt the wet warmth of his tongue as he kissed her wrist.

Ryder's eyes blazed, and he dipped his head until his lips were at her ear. "That could be arranged."

"Huh?"

"Think about what you just said." His mouth was hot against her neck as his teeth grazed her skin, and she almost whimpered.

Lost in a haze of lust, Liese couldn't figure out what he meant until she replayed her response in her head. Several times. "I meant *with you*, I'd love to have dinner with you."

"I'm sure you did."

She wanted to lick the arrogant smirk right off his face. "If you weren't so busy distracting me with your mouth, I might be able to string a sentence together properly," she whispered.

"I can't wait to have my mouth all over you again," Ryder replied, sitting back as Tiffany and Marissa ascended the stairs and shuffled up the aisle.

Liese spent the remainder of the movie thinking about all the ways she'd like to "have" Ryder. By the time the lights came up, she felt ready to explode. She gathered her things, and Ryder bent to help her, arranging the strap of her purse on her shoulder, his fingertips brushing over her collarbone. He was torturing her on purpose. He ushered Tiffany down the stairs in front of him, creating physical distance that somehow resonated emotionally as they vacated the theater.

"I need to use the ladies room before we go." Liese stopped just outside the door, shifting uneasily. She discreetly surveyed the corridor for familiar faces. Sitting in a darkened theater with Ryder seemed innocuous enough, but under the bright lights outside, she felt exposed and anxious.

They managed a rushed and slightly awkward goodbye, parting ways when they reached the bathroom. Liese hated the wave of relief that washed over her when the danger of being seen together passed.

"So, talk about a coincidence," Marissa commented as they pulled out of the parking lot.

"That was nerve-wracking."

"Yeah, I guess I can see how you might have been paranoid, what with how bright the theater was," Marissa said, throwing in an eye roll.

"Your sarcasm is not appreciated."

"Seriously, though, no one could see us. He didn't even know it was you until he practically sat on top of you."

"Running into him was still unexpected."

"I can imagine." Marissa sat in silence for a moment. "You know, I had my doubts about him, and I hate to admit it, but after the way he was with you yesterday and again tonight, I guess I can see why you're into him. And he's definitely into you."

"You think?"

"Uh, yeah. I think." Marissa looked at her like she had two heads. "He'd be an idiot not to want you."

"That's not what I meant. Sometimes he's hard to read. He's always so in control."

"That I did notice, but I didn't think he was hard to get a handle on." Marissa reclined her seat, getting more comfortable. "Think about it, Liese. He wouldn't take the risk if he wasn't serious about being with you. That part still confuses me, by the way. You're two consenting adults. If you want to bang each other, you should be able to. It's not like it impacts your actual job."

Liese choke-coughed. "It's not that cut and dry. Working in education is different; there are ethical standards."

"Whatever. I think it's stupid." Marissa waved dismissively. "Anyway, it's pretty obvious he's got a boner the size of a cannon over you."

"There you go with the explosive weapons/genitalia comparisons again."

"It's fitting, don't you agree? They're always blowing up."

"You're ridiculous."

"I know. It's part of my charm. Anyway, I'm glad things are working out between the two of you, but believe me, if he screws you around again I'm going to take him down—proverbially speaking, of course."

23

Close Curtain Calls

LIESE AND MARISSA spent the remainder of the evening playing cards and drinking copious amounts of wine—not their typical Saturday night adventure, but Liese didn't want to give Sean an opportunity to "run into" her again, should he still be hanging around. And anyway, Fullerton's night life would inevitably fall short of Marissa's expectations. But even with the modified activities, they still went to bed far later than they should have.

"We really need to stop drinking so much when we get together." Liese groaned as she reached for a bottle of Tylenol on her nightstand and shook out two pills the next morning.

Marissa grunted something incoherent and shoved her head under her pillow.

"We have to be at the school in less than an hour." Liese sighed, rolling over to sit on the edge of the bed. She eyed the alarm clock with contempt.

Marissa popped up, sheet lines etched into her cheek, hair a mess. She vaulted off the mattress. "Dibs on the shower," she called over her shoulder, slamming the bathroom door behind her in haste.

Liese went downstairs to put on coffee while she waited. A full twenty-five minutes and three warnings later, Marissa emerged from the bathroom looking infuriatingly perky. Liese had to rush her own shower as a result. She pulled her hair up in a messy ponytail, dabbed concealer under her eyes, and forewent her usual makeup routine so they would make dress rehearsal on time. Late wasn't an option. Blake might be laid back in most respects, but he took nothing more seriously than theater.

They pulled into the parking lot just before eleven and rushed to the auditorium. Blake was already there, performing a lighting and sound check with the tech crew. The cast had settled in the chairs near the stage, waiting for Blake to give orders, and some of the backstage crew already worked on setting up for the first act. Liese expected Blake to be snippy, given how close they'd cut it, but he turned to greet them with a wide smile.

"Great! You're here." He pulled Liese into a half-hug and greeted Marissa warmly. "I'm so glad you decided to join us."

He held out a hand, and Marissa slipped her fingers into his grasp, giving him a coy smile. "The pleasure's all mine. Just tell me where you want me."

While Liese doubted Marissa intended to sound like a phone sex operator, her husky voice made her offer seem lewd. Blake shook her hand long past what would be considered normal. They looked like love-struck teenagers as they beamed. Blake finally dropped Marissa's hand and motioned to the gathering of students near the stage.

"How are you with makeup?"

"Decent?"

"Decent works for me." He ushered them down the aisle.

Liese went first, glancing over her shoulder to find Blake checking out Marissa's rear assets. He exhaled a long breath, then turned to address the lighting and sound crew. Setting up those two looked like it would be a cake walk. Better yet, if things panned out, Marissa would have reason to visit more often.

By mid-afternoon, they were preparing for the second act for the second time, and Liese's setup was going according to plan. Marissa had glued herself to Blake's side, and it hadn't taken much convincing. Marissa was a take-charge kind of woman. If she wanted something, she went for it, and she clearly wanted a piece of Blake—particularly the piece of him nestled in the crotch of his pants. Liese kept catching Marissa staring at his package.

While the two of them were busy directing the cast—or rather Blake directed, and Marissa watched Blake in his element—Liese headed backstage. She intended to make sure the stage crew was ready for the next set change as the scene drew to a close. It had been a long day, and some of them were getting a little lazy.

Darkness enveloped her as she stepped into the wings, so she let the curtain guide her to the prop room. She blinked against the shadows, adjusting to the lack of light and allowing the soft velvet to lead her as it slipped under her fingertips. She could hear the protagonist break into song, and she paused to peek through a split in the curtains.

He commanded the stage with his performance, and though she admired his work, Liese had never been interested in the limelight herself. She'd preferred to remain backstage most of her life. Even the acknowledgements at the end of a performance made her stomach churn.

She jumped at a whisper in her ear.

"Ryder?"

"Sorry. I tried not to startle you." His arm came around her waist, bringing her back flush against his chest. She stifled a gasp and dropped the curtain, erasing what little light filtered through the gap.

"At least I announced myself before I pressed my hard-on against your ass."

"Very considerate." She scanned the darkened hall, but there was no one there to witness their stolen moment—at least not that she could see.

"What are you doing here?"

"Taking an interest in our school production. Tiffany insisted we stop by before I drop her off at home. I could hardly deny her the pleasure."

Liese smiled. Tristan, the boy she'd been cozied up to on Friday, was in the play. He must have called her, despite Ryder's obvious disapproval. He was a nice kid, particularly for a hormonal teenager.

"How nice of you to accommodate your sister's wishes," she said.

His grip on her waist tightened as his lips touched her cheek. "I'm trying to win the Brother of the Year Award, but I do have selfish intent. This gives me an excuse to see you." "Is that right?" She relaxed into his embrace.

"Yes." His nose skimmed along her neck. "It seems I've developed quite a fondness for your company, and I'm reluctant to be without it."

Liese made a noise in the back of her throat that came out somewhere between a groan and a sigh.

"Although I suspect my younger sister may have other reasons for wanting to be here. I noticed Mr. Emerson in the audience."

"Something like your ulterior motives?" Liese turned in his arms, glancing down the hall to be sure they were alone. Her eyes had adjusted to the dark, and she could make out the hazy outline of Ryder's features. She let her hands drift lazily up his chest to fiddle with the collar of his shirt.

"I hope to hell not. My motives are as impure as you can get." He leaned down to kiss her lips. "I can't wait to get you alone tonight. When do you think you'll be done here?"

"Another hour or so?"

"Perfect. Are you hungry?"

"Starving," Liese answered, sliding her fingers into his hair.

"Me, too." Ryder's mouth hovered over hers.

Liese closed her eyes and melted into the kiss. She felt the warmth of Ryder's tongue as it swept along her upper lip and just barely inside her mouth. She tilted her head to the side, her fingers tightening in his hair. As much as she wanted the kiss to continue, she was well aware the darkness and curtains didn't truly provide the privacy they needed.

The music came to an end and Liese pushed away, putting space between them as the shuffle of feet on stage filled the silence. She took a moment to compose herself and pulled back the curtain to reveal a drove of costumed teens coming in their direction.

Ryder ran his hands through his hair and clapped them together enthusiastically. He donned a mask of implacable calm, greeting the students with a warm smile and patting them on the back as they headed offstage, making a huge deal about how well they'd done and how proud he was. Liese plastered on a smile and gave them high fives, relieved she'd had the where-withal to control herself for once.

Ryder paused on his way to collect Tiffany. Whispering a hasty apology, he swore he would keep his hands and mouth to himself until he could get her alone, beyond the walls of FAHL. Liese didn't think that could happen soon enough. Although Friday had taken the edge off—while also probably taking years off her life—it hadn't sated her the way she wanted or needed. She hoped for a no-holds-barred session that would last for hours.

In the end, rehearsal didn't finish until after four-thirty. Once all the costumes were returned to their rightful places and the set had been cleaned up, the students filtered out, looking worn but pleased.

Liese found Marissa talking with Blake in the sound booth as the last of the students departed. They looked quite comfy sitting together. Though Liese was not inclined to interrupt their intense conversation, she wanted to get home before Ryder came over so she could freshen up—and send Marissa on her merry way.

Liese leaned against the doorjamb, taking in their intimate posture. Marissa was as close to Blake as she could get, considering they sat in separate chairs. Their knees touched, and every time Blake made a hand gesture, he brushed the outside of her thigh. He was definitely interested.

"What's going on?" Liese asked when it became obvious neither one of them would notice her unless she made her presence known.

Blake rolled his chair back, creating space where there had been none. He looked guilty, like he'd gotten caught doing something he shouldn't have. Marissa crossed her legs and shot Liese a pissy glare.

She felt bad for interrupting. "So what did you think?"

"It was great." Marissa motioned to Blake, allowing her hand to rest briefly on his forearm. "I was just telling Blake I would try to come see a performance—maybe the last one, on Wednesday evening? I could stay the night."

"Of course!" Liese said. "We'd love that, wouldn't we, Blake?"

"I'll hold a ticket for you," he offered. He couldn't stop smiling, or fiddling with the papers on his clipboard. He was smitten.

On their way home, Liese checked her phone messages, but no word from Ryder. She didn't know where his parents lived, so she couldn't gauge how long it would take him to drive his sister home.

Clouds had rolled in during the afternoon, threatening a storm and dropping the temperature. The short jaunt between her car and her house set her teeth to chattering. At least tonight she'd have someone to curl up with and snuggle by the fire—or get freaky, the latter being the preferable way to stay warm.

Once inside, Marissa packed her bag and checked the weather forecast. The looming storm was scheduled to hit Fullerton sometime in the next hour, moving east. She hustled her things into her car in a bid to outrun the weather. Liese wasn't too worried; Marissa had a lead foot. She'd likely be home in less than three hours, even with city traffic.

Liese pulled her into a tight hug, happy to have had her stay the weekend. Beyond the opportunity for some much-needed bonding time, she'd felt much safer with her friend close by.

"I'm really glad the Sean shitshow is done with," Marissa said as she settled into her car. "There's no way he can get away with stalking you in such a small town."

"I know. It's definitely a benefit of living here," Liese agreed. "Thanks so much for coming down and keeping me company this weekend."

"Anything for you. I'll call when I get home."

"I may not answer if Ryder is here."

"I'm sure you can take ten seconds to shoot me a text, unless he's got you tied up. Then you'll have to trust him with your passcode."

"You're never going to stop with this, are you?"

"It's unlikely."

"Drive safe." Liese kissed her on the cheek and closed the door. She flipped up the collar of her coat to protect her face from the bitter wind as Marissa's car disappeared down the drive and onto the street.

Not wanting to waste another minute, she went back inside to prepare for Ryder's arrival. Excitement and nerves abounded. She couldn't wait to see him, touch him, be with him—without any reservations this time.

24

Unleashed Restraint

LIESE WANDERED INTO the kitchen and put the kettle on, restless now that there was nothing to do but wait for Ryder's call. The house felt empty without Marissa. Their years of living together had made them comfortable with each other, so it had been easy to fall back into sharing space over the weekend. Liese didn't like how vacant her house now felt without the companionship.

As she poured hot water over a teabag, she thought about the events preceding her weekend. Although Sean had been on her mind since then, a feeling of safety had come with the restraining order and having a trusted friend around, but unfortunately it had dissipated in Marissa's absence.

In New York, the streets were always teeming with life, even in the middle of the night. Billboards and neon signs provided an endless supply of artificial light, and the high-rises created a protective barrier, a safety net of human availability. It had been impossible to feel alone. But here in Fullerton, Liese could barely make out the lights of the house across the street with the dense cover of evergreens surrounding her tiny yard. And now that it was winter, night came earlier, descending like a menacing shadow. She stood at her kitchen sink, gazing out the window as gathering clouds blocked out the sun on its journey below the tree line. The imminent storm promised to break the eerie calm. The solitude was oppressive.

The restraining order against Sean should have put her mind at ease, but it didn't. Instead a new fear took root: this development might fracture his fragile state and send him off the deep end. She didn't want to know what such a breakdown could entail. Liese hoped Marissa was right about Sean keeping his distance now. In spite of that, she turned on every light—inside and out—and drew the curtains to drive away the darkness and her worry.

Nevertheless, Liese startled at the slightest sigh of wind or the whistle of the furnace as it kicked on. Unable to bear the sound of tree branches scratching against the siding, she turned on some music. Her imagination had become a festering pit of craziness in the absence of something or someone to help keep her thoughts occupied.

Maybe it was time to get a dog.

She fired off a message to Ryder, hoping he'd be over soon. Shortly after she sent the text, her phone rang. She screamed and then laughed at her own nerves, answering the call when she recognized the number. Ryder's tone deflated her mood further and for good reason: Tiffany had skipped her afternoon classes on Friday, and in doing so, she'd missed an important tryout. She had no interest in being on the ski team, but her parents had insisted she join. Ryder needed to run interference, which meant staying for dinner in an attempt to reason with them and prevent his sister from being grounded.

Though she was disappointed, Liese understood. While she didn't have siblings, she would have done the same for Marissa, who was as close to a sister as she'd ever found. She found Ryder's compulsion to stick up for Tiffany rather endearing. She liked the dichotomy this side of him presented.

He promised to call as soon as he was on his way, but she had no idea how long he'd be. Family crises in her house could last for hours, although with a therapist for a mother and a retired military man for a father, that was hardly a surprise. Unable to deal with an unknown span of time, Liese needed a way to relax. The comfort of bubbles and hot water seemed a good way to accomplish such a mission.

At 7:42, Ryder called with an ETA of less than twenty minutes. She jumped off the couch and sprinted to her bathroom to check her appearance, even though she'd barely had time to warm the couch cushion post-bath. Under her jeans and shirt were the bra and panties set she'd purchased on Saturday during Marissa's effort to revamp her lingerie drawer.

She paced around her bedroom, straightening the comforter and rearranging the pillows until she heard the sound of gravel crunching on her driveway. Running to the bathroom, she looked out the window to see Ryder's Lexus. She bounded down the stairs to meet him at the door, throwing it open before he'd knocked. Despite her obvious eagerness and labored breathing, she feigned calm, leaning casually against the doorjamb. The dark sky provided an ominous backdrop as she looked out at him. Flakes of snow swirled around and settled on his shoulders and in his hair, melting into crystalline beads. The wind had picked up.

"Hi." So much for nonchalance; her voice came out a sultry

whisper.

"I'm sorry I ruined our plans." Ryder crowded her in the doorway, waiting for her to retreat into the warmth of her tiny foyer before he crossed the threshold.

"You should be. I've been waiting for hours, and I'm starving."

"I assure you, it won't happen again." He held up a bag of takeout, which Liese ignored.

She grabbed him by the lapels and tugged him farther into the small space, closing the door with her foot. Plucking the takeout from his hand, she discarded it on the side table.

"I didn't say I was hungry for food." She stepped into him, trying to get closer, his winter coat a serious impediment.

"Oh no?" He wrapped his arms around her, the palm of his hand flattening against the small of her back. The other drifted up her side.

She loosened the black scarf around his neck, running her index finger along the edge of his collared shirt. As much as she'd loved him in a suit and tie, she also appreciated how sexy he looked in jeans and a dress shirt. Or nothing at all.

His fingertips moved along her jaw, sweeping her hair over her shoulder, his eyes dark. "I'd like to kiss you, if that would be permissible."

"I suppose I could allow it." Liese smiled.

His mouth covered hers, and she clasped her hands behind his neck, keeping him close. The kiss started slow and sweet, soft brushes of his lips against hers. A teasing nip of teeth on her bottom lip turned into gentle suction, and Ryder's tongue parted her lips to slip inside her mouth, exploring, retreating, tangling with her own. The kiss gained momentum until the inferno of lust built up over the weekend detonated, and Liese found herself backed against the wall, grinding against him with desperate need.

She scrambled to undo the buttons on his coat, and Ryder released her with a despondent groan to finish the job. She shoved his coat over his shoulders, pushing it down his arms. He cupped her cheek in his hand, his free hand returned to the bottom of her shirt, sliding beneath and moving up her ribcage to palm her breast.

"Fuck." It came out a low, almost intelligible grunt.

"I'm happy to accommodate that request." She undid the clasp on his belt and jerked it through the loops, dropping it on the floor.

"Where's your bedroom?" Ryder's lips moved in a fiery trail from her cheek to her ear.

"Upstairs."

"I'd like to go there. Now, please."

Liese felt the hairs on her arm raise at his tone, more of a command than a request. She pushed on his chest, and he obliged by taking a small step back, enough for her to slip out of the narrow space between his body and the wall. She grabbed his hand and tugged him down the hall and up the stairs.

The moment they passed through the door to her room, Ryder had her in his arms again, moving her across the floor until the back of her knees hit the mattress, and they tumbled onto the comforter.

His hands were everywhere but where she needed them, his mouth much the same. And then he settled into the cradle of her hips. She gasped, shifting against him, her desire so acute it was almost painful.

"I can't stand being away from you. It drives me fucking crazy." Ryder echoed her feelings as he rose to his knees. Shoving her shirt up with both hands, he pulled it over her head. "All weekend, the only thing I could think about was you: being with you, inside you." His fingers moved to the fly of her jeans, flicking the button open. He unzipped them and dragged the denim down her legs.

Then he paused, his chest rising and falling rapidly as he took in the lingerie she'd purchased. His thumbs followed the lace edge of her bra. "This is lovely on you."

"I thought you might like it."

He cupped her breasts, pushing up to create even deeper cleavage. His head dipped down to kiss the exposed skin. "You have been known to be an incredibly thoughtful woman."

"I try," Liese replied, her hips undulating as she sought some kind of friction.

He kissed over her stomach, nose skimming along the lace band at her waist. He hooked his fingers into the material and gave a gentle tug. "As pretty as these are, I need them gone." He pulled the fabric down her thighs and discarded it on the floor. Hands clamped on her hips, he dragged her to the edge of the bed and spread her legs wide. Hooking them over his shoulders, he sank to the floor.

Liese's mouth dropped open in a silent moan as his lips traveled along her inner thigh, his journey to where she wanted his mouth excruciatingly slow. Then warm breath fanned over her most sensitive part. She arched, hips lifting off the bed. And then his mouth was on her, his hot tongue sliding over even hotter skin.

Liese fisted his hair, holding him against her as she writhed. It didn't take long for her to reach her peak, and as soon as she crested he paused, gracing her with a self-satisfied smile before drawing out another orgasm with his mouth.

Liese felt like she was on overload, the barest of touches pushing her limit of control. Ryder kissed over her body, taking his time, nipping and sucking as he went. He focused his attention on her breasts, his lips parting over their swell. He flicked his tongue out, catching a nipple and closing his mouth over it.

With lidded eyes she watched him, his broad back flexing as he held himself above her. His teeth grazed the delicate flesh. Liese moaned; the sight of him looking so primal coupled with the feel of his mouth drove her to the edge, dangling her from a precipice she couldn't wait to drop over.

She slipped her hand between their bodies to unbutton his pants. Yanking down the zipper, she shoved them down his thighs, along with his boxers. She wasn't interested in any more preliminaries. She needed him moving inside her, eradicating the anxiety that had consumed her.

"Eager, aren't we?" Ryder teased, his lips at her neck, her chin, the corner of her mouth. She turned into his kiss, and he withdrew, leaving the barest amount of space between them.

"I want you in me." She spoke with urgency. Her hand closed around his shaft, stroking up. Her fears and longing collided, making her nearly frantic with need. She didn't want to think about the uncertainty of the future, about how intense her feelings had grown for him. All she wanted was to feel.

Ryder's eyes closed, his lips parted, and he exhaled slowly. When they opened, his expression grew dark. "Do I need to restrain you so I can take my time?"

Liese's grip on him tightened at the mention of restraints. She'd considered buying those fuzzy handcuffs, but hadn't had time yet. The idea of relinquishing control elicited both fear and exhilaration. She wanted to give herself over to Ryder in such an intimate way, but allowing him to dominate her touched too closely on the depth of her feelings for him.

"You don't have anything to restrain me with." Liese taunted, arching against his hold on her.

"I have a tie and a belt." He smiled as her lips parted, pausing before he continued. "And I'm certain if I looked hard enough I could find a pair of pantyhose." His hips eased forward, his erection sliding in her grip.

"I've already come twice. Why would you need to take your time with me?" Liese countered, stroking down and then up again, brushing her thumb over his swollen tip.

"Because—" Ryder groaned and reached between them, prying her hand away. He threaded his fingers through hers and pressed the back of her hand to the sheets. "It's been far too long since I've had you in a bed. I want it to last as long as humanly possible." She felt the thick ridge of him against her pelvis.

"We could always have sex again in the morning," Liese suggested, squirming but getting nowhere now that she was trapped under his weight.

"Oh, I plan to have sex with you again in the morning, and possibly in the middle of the night—more than once, if you'll allow it."

Liese gave up the fight, melting into the bed as his lips found hers in a liquefying kiss. She didn't try to touch him, even when his hands moved from hers to skim along her body. She gave herself over without reservation. And when he finally entered her, he stayed close, their bodies flush, his lips pressed to hers.

He moved slowly, taking his time as he'd promised.

25

The Last Curtain Call

LIESE WOKE UP at five-thirty in the morning to find Ryder's arm draped over her waist, his hand nestled between her thighs, and his fingers twitching as he nuzzled into the crook of her neck. His breath tickled her shoulder every time he exhaled. All was well until the alarm on his phone interrupted the moment, blaring an annoying pop song.

"I'm going to kill my sister for messing with my phone again," Ryder grumbled in a sleep-heavy voice. He rubbed his stubbly jaw against her shoulder and followed with his lips.

She laughed, then moaned when Ryder's hard-on pressed against her lower back.

They'd had sex twice last night, which should have been enough to abate her need for him. He'd taken his sweet, dirty time with her at first. Later, after they'd gone downstairs to devour the takeout they'd abandoned at the front door, he'd deposited her on the counter and fucked her into oblivion.

"Why is your alarm set for such an ungodly hour?" Liese

pressed back against him. Ryder's hand, still snugly situated between her legs, clenched around her inner thigh.

"So I can get inside you again before I have to leave for work. What other reason would there be?"

"I don't know. Maybe you wanted to make me breakfast in bed?"

"Oh, I'll make you breakfast in bed, all right." He rolled her onto her stomach, covering her body with his. She wriggled under him, and he grunted out an expletive as his cock slid along the cleft of her ass.

He reached over her, grabbed his phone from the nightstand, and silenced it. "That's better." He sighed and rested his weight on top of her again.

Liese hummed an affirmation, punctuating with a swivel of her hips. Ryder swept her hair over her shoulder to kiss her neck. She turned her head toward him, but her position didn't leave much room for movement. She could barely catch his profile in her peripheral vision.

Ryder's lips moved over her shoulder and down her spine. The weight of his body left her, and his hands stroked down her sides to her hips, skimming the curves of her bottom. He kneaded the supple skin, his thumbs grazing the crease, and the warmth that spread through her body shocked her. Trusting Ryder to make her feel good, she allowed sensation to take over and relaxed into his touch. She could hear his breathing quicken and feel his erection jump on the back of her thigh.

Just when Liese thought she couldn't handle any more of his gentle, teasing touch or the soft sweep of his lips between her shoulder blades, he stopped. The absence of touch became just as overwhelming as the softness. Then his hand came down on her backside with a loud slap, leaving a hot sting in its wake.

Liese shrieked and bucked, her struggle useless; his weight rested on her thighs, securing her beneath him.

"Sorry, I couldn't help myself." Ryder sounded anything but apologetic as he ran a hand over the place he'd just spanked. Of course he followed the request for forgiveness with another smack, and another and another until Liese was breathless. Her position made her vulnerable, but she trusted him to anticipate her limit. The promise of pleasure allowed her to relinquish control in a way she'd never been able to with anyone else.

He circled her entrance and slipped a finger inside, adding another and yet another. He penetrated and retreated over and over until she came to the brink of an orgasm, unable to fall.

Liese closed her eyes, no longer straining to see him. Instead, she allowed herself to give in to the ecstasy he teased out of her. Her soft moans must have encouraged him, as he nudged the head of his cock to where his fingers had been exploring. He pushed forward slowly—so slowly that the expectation of fullness was an excruciating torture. When he was fully seated inside her, he covered her body with his. Then he slid one of his hands between her body and the sheets. Palm facing up, he wrapped his fingers around her shoulder, anchoring him to her.

"I'd like to spend an entire week with you in my bed," he whispered against her neck as he began to move, his thrusts achingly controlled.

"I can check my calendar; I think I have one free soon."

Ryder's husky laugh was followed by a groan. His legs remained on either side of hers, keeping her confined beneath him. The position made her feel much fuller, her sensations more intense. The exposed feeling remained, and heightened even, as he moved inside her. She'd always been of the mind that the most intimate sexual encounters had to be face to face, but Ryder had shattered that notion. With his mouth beside her ear whispering charged words of desire, she felt more connected than ever. He shifted his knee to nudge her legs apart, spreading them enough to penetrate deeper, go harder, move faster. Warmth settled low in her belly, gradually suffusing her entirely. She clung to the burgeoning sensation, ready to come undone.

He snaked his other arm around her waist and hauled her up onto her hands and knees. Now Ryder slammed into her from behind, holding her hips to keep her from falling forward as he picked up momentum. He sat back on his knees, taking her body with him, crushing her to his chest. She straddled his thighs, her knees on either side of his, but not touching the bed. The balls of her feet rested near his calves, but she abandoned the need to find footing, given how securely Ryder held her.

One palm found her breast and squeezed, while the other moved down over her pelvis. He slapped her clit lightly and then rubbed a slow circle as he ground into her. She moaned his name in a plea, aching for a release that promised to shatter her nerves.

The hand on her breast came up to brush over her throat, his fingers tangling in her hair. He turned her face toward his and captured her lips. "I'm going to come," he warned, sucking on her bottom lip.

"I'm right there with you," Liese reached around and grabbed the back of his neck, keeping their mouths fused.

He pulled out all the way to the tip, leaving her empty before he filled her one last time. Her legs locked down, hips shifting in time with his deep thrust. The release she'd been after tore through her as Ryder shuddered, his own orgasm overtaking him. He exhaled a fevered breath against her cheek, his tense body enveloping her.

Liese let her head drop against his shoulder, her body contracting and releasing as she rode out the aftershocks. "Oh, God." She sighed.

"I know it's a difficult distinction since we have such similar qualities . . ." Ryder held her limp body to his. "However, I'd like it if you at least got my name right in the throes of passion."

Liese smacked his thigh. Well, she tried to smack him, but her hand barely obeyed the command to move. "Get over yourself."

She rose to her knees, her thighs wobbling from the strain, and broke the connection between their bodies, a sensation she didn't much like. But her feelings for Ryder were spiraling out of control, and she needed to rein them in. She joked to keep the intensity of her emotions at bay.

"I'm going to have a shower; feel free to join me if your ego can fit through the door." She slid off the bed on jelly legs and attempted to saunter to the bathroom to cover her near inability to walk.

She smiled when she heard Ryder's feet hit the floor. He grabbed for her hand and spun her into his arms. Head bowed to hers, he pressed a lingering, close-mouthed kiss to her lips. He didn't try to deepen it, which for some reason made it more intimate.

"I wish we had more time to talk," he said.

"Talk? About what?" Liese's throat tightened. More than once in her life she'd been the one to initiate a "talk." Typically it didn't mean good things.

Ryder must have picked up on her panic. "Nothing bad," he assured her, pressing another soft kiss to her lips. "I wanted to talk to you about the holidays, that's all. Now isn't the time, though." He inclined his head to the clock on her nightstand, his eyes raking over her. "Didn't you request help in the shower?"

Ryder left her house just after seven, giving Liese time to center herself. She wanted to feel reasonably normal before she went to work, but she found it impossible not to experience some level of paranoia after a night with Ryder. She knew the second she walked into the building she'd begin to postulate all the ways she might reveal their secret. She remained amazed they'd managed to get away with it for this long, given all the ways they'd slipped up.

She needn't have worried about worrying, however. Blake dogged her as soon as she pulled into the parking lot. He trailed her to the library, talking a mile a minute about what they still needed to do for the play opening this afternoon. She didn't even have a chance to go to her mailbox before the first bell rang.

Her morning consisted of several frantic calls from Blake regarding last-minute details. He fretted over whether the costumes would be dramatic enough, and whether the set was too minimalist. Liese assured him they would balance each other out, having been the one to help design them in the first place. She also had to deal with students desperate to sign out research texts and novels. One grumpy teenager informed her of the importance of getting a head start on studying for midterms, which took place soon after they returned from the holidays.

Over the days that followed, Liese remained incredibly busy. She didn't have a spare moment to give in to the temptation to seek out Ryder and was almost grateful for the unending list of tasks Blake assigned her. The matinee performances took place just after lunch and meant she needed a substitute to cover the library. Her replacement left a lot to be desired in the organizational department, so between the day and evening performances, she catalogued and shelved the bins of returned books, setting aside those on reserve, and rushed back to the auditorium for performance round two.

By Wednesday, she'd sworn she would never help with another theater production again. The final matinee would begin in less than a half-hour, and Liese found herself fixing the female lead's makeup for the third time because she kept breaking down. Apparently she'd been dating someone in the cast—Liese couldn't quite understand the boy's name through the sobbing—and had caught him kissing another cast member.

She tried to calm her down, but everything she said seemed to cause more tears. Liese dabbed at the girl's eyes, thankful for waterproof mascara. Just when she thought she was going to start crying herself, Ryder walked through the door. Liese had only passed him in the office once in the past three days, although frequent text messages kept her linked to him at all hours of the day and night. Because the play kept them both at the school well into the evening, they'd not had any private time since Sunday.

"I brought reinforcements." He stepped aside to reveal Marissa.

"Oh, thank God you're here!" Liese exclaimed.

Marissa had called the night before to confirm she was coming to the final performance, and her arrival couldn't have been better timed. Liese's current state of crisis must have been written on her face because Ryder approached the teary female lead.

He sank down on one knee, bringing him level with the sniffling girl. "Are you all right?"

Her garbled response must have made sense to Ryder because he asked several more questions, his voice taking on the soft, almost lilting quality Liese had become so familiar with. He used it on her whenever she was stressed out.

Liese stood with Marissa and watched in fascination as Ryder worked his magic. It seemed very few people were immune to his charismatic ways. Within three minutes, the lead stopped crying; after five minutes her sniffles and hiccups subsided, and she even cracked a smile. Ryder patted her on the shoulder and winked at Liese before heading for the door. She longed to follow him and find a dark corner.

"Impressive," Marissa said.

"Sometimes Mr. Whitehall is so nice." The lead sighed dreamily.

"Isn't he, though?" Marissa directed the comment at Liese.

She made a noise of agreement before going back to work fixing makeup. She smiled brightly and changed the subject. "Blake's with the sound and light crew if you want to say hi."

"Yeah?" Marissa's face lit up. "Okay, I'll do that." She turned toward the door and added, "Plus he can tell me where I'll be the most useful."

Liese refrained from mentioning that Marissa could have easily asked *her* where she'd be most useful. "Great idea," she said with a smile. "See you in a few minutes."

But Liese didn't see Marissa again until after the final matinee ended. Even then, they didn't get a chance to talk. The cast kept her far too busy. The only time they stopped for a break was to scarf down a couple of slices of cold pizza before getting the performers back into makeup and costumes.

The next few hours passed in a blur of music, set changes, costume changes, makeup touch-ups, and a few minor freakouts. At the end, when the entire cast and crew went out for their customary bows, Liese found a reason to stay comfortably backstage as usual. But Blake had other plans for the final performance.

He beckoned her from her hiding place behind the curtain, and she reluctantly crossed the stage, her face turning the same red as the scarf she'd put on that morning. Blake grabbed Liese's hand and raised it in the air in a flourish, then bowed low, pulling her with him. Liese hated the feeling of so many eyes on her. This was why she'd chosen to be a librarian, buried behind stacks of books.

Knowing Ryder had to be out there somewhere, she worried about his reaction to Blake holding her hand, no matter how harmless it might be. Ryder wouldn't like what he deemed unnecessary physical contact. That made her smile. She looked out over the sea of faces to the back of the auditorium.

That's where she saw Sean. Standing in the very last row, he wore an expression that bordered on murderous. And he directed it right at her.

26

An Unparalleled Performance

HER HOLD ON Blake's hand tightened. She could see him wincing from the corner of her eye, but paralyzed by stage fright and a mounting fear of Sean, she couldn't release his hand.

It appeared her crazy ex-boyfriend extraordinaire had breached his restraining order and now sat in the very last row of the audience. Arms crossed over his chest, Sean shook his head in mock disappointment. Why would he show up at the school on a night like this? There hadn't been any recent calls to ignore, and she'd settled into the belief that he'd finally given up. Clearly, she'd been wrong. She met his accusatory glare and remained trapped there, unable to break eye contact.

The impulse to jump off the stage, kick him in the balls, punch him in the face, and Taser him—then vomit—was strong. Only she didn't own a Taser. And she couldn't force her body into action at all right now. Vomiting, however, wouldn't be a problem if her stomach kept up the acrobatics.

Blake's arm came around her shoulder, and he hugged her

to him, laughing jovially. He waved at the cheering, clapping audience and began to retreat from the front of the stage. Thankfully, her body obeyed his silent command and she followed his movement, her feet shuffling awkwardly across the stage.

"Are you okay?" he whispered through a smile. He looked surprisingly calm, although Liese supposed he had no idea why she'd broken into full freak-out mode.

"Sean's in the audience," she replied through clenched teeth, still unable to pry her eyes away from him. She plastered a toothy grin on her face to match Blake's in the hopes of masking her horror.

"What?" he asked.

They retreated further, allowing the cast to swallow them up and form a shield, hiding them from view. The cover also broke the spell of Sean's death stare.

"Sean's—"

"I heard you. Where? And stop smiling like that, you look insane."

"Last row on the left." Liese tried to make her grin a little less crazy.

The cast moved forward as one and bowed. As they bent at the waist, Sean came back into view. He still seethed at her from the back of the auditorium. She averted her eyes, searching the audience for a safer place to look—like at Ryder, but she couldn't find him. Liese tried to stay calm as she scanned the crowd, but Blake's incessant nudging made her doubt her success. Thankfully, no one but Sean and Blake seemed to be paying her any mind.

The students bowed again, and her heart lurched as Ryder appeared from behind the lighting box and headed directly for Sean. Ryder loomed over him, looking furious as he motioned to the exit. Sean stepped forward in challenge, his attempt at posturing rather abysmal considering Ryder was a full head taller. Still, his brazenness made Liese wonder if he might be carrying a weapon. He'd clearly moved into uncharted territory now.

Liese realized she'd been moving toward the front of the stage when Blake grabbed her arm and pulled her back to his side. "Don't. Whitehall will take care of it."

"He's dangerous. And what if Sean recognizes—" She bit her tongue.

Ryder pulled his walkie-talkie from his back pocket. Liese had no idea who he would page at this time in the evening. The office was empty, although she'd seen Harvey before the show began.

Sean said something to Ryder now, gesturing toward the stage, and Ryder's stance changed from calmly authoritative to aggressive. His lip curled into a sneer as his hand wrapped around Sean's bicep. Ryder yanked him firmly toward the back door and pushed it open, dragging him through.

The whole debacle had taken seconds, but it had been enough to draw the attention of a few people in the last rows. Liese felt Blake's hand tighten on her forearm, and then she was moving again, heading toward the wing and the glowing red exit sign beyond. Just before she and Blake exited backstage, Liese saw Marissa slip out the back door of the auditorium, followed by Harvey.

Liese hoped Ryder got the situation under control before something really bad happened. While part of her prayed Sean was too agitated to recognize him, she was far more concerned about the actions that same agitation might turn into if things escalated.

Once they were behind the cover of the curtains, Liese headed for the exit. Blake stopped her. "Do you think it's a good idea to go out there? That guy's a lunatic. You just said yourself that he's dangerous."

"Marissa's out there, and so is Ryder. I need to make sure they're okay." She pried at his fingers. "Please, Blake."

He hesitated before finally releasing her. "Be careful. I'll follow as soon as I can."

She stumbled forward and shouldered her way out into the hallway. Distress made her knees wobbly as she walked briskly to the front entrance, where she assumed they'd taken Sean.

She burst out the front doors and ran smack into Ryder's chest.

To her right, Sean lay sprawled out on the stone walkway, his hand over his mouth, swearing a blue streak.

"What the hell happened?" Liese shot Ryder a troubled glance, then surveyed Harvey and Marissa, trying to assess the damage. It looked like someone had just punched Sean, and she could only hope it hadn't been Ryder.

"You just hit Sean in the face with the door," Marissa supplied as she suppressed a laugh.

Under any other circumstances Liese might have found the situation funny. But Ryder didn't seem to share Marissa's amusement; he looked downright pissed. Harvey appeared confused more than anything else. And he was staring at Marissa's chest.

Liese stepped forward, keeping enough distance to prevent any contact with Sean. "What are you doing? You're not allowed to be here!"

He tried to speak, but it came out garbled. Blood seeped between his fingers. He pushed himself up to a sitting position, turned his head to the side and spat.

"Gross," Marissa said.

"You need to leave." Liese gestured to the stairs leading to the parking lot. "Now. Before parents see you bleeding all over the place."

"I fink you broke my nobe," Sean lisped as he struggled to his feet.

She moved away from him, scanning for places where he might conceal a weapon.

"And my front teef feel loof."

"It would serve you right." Anger replaced Liese's fear as she realized Sean hadn't come prepared for a showdown. He was his typical whiny self, looking for attention, nothing more. "I'm not sure how much clearer I need to be, Sean. I figured a restraining order would have made it obvious enough that I don't want anything to do with you, but apparently I was mistaken."

"I just wanted to see you."

"To leer at me from the back of a high school student performance?" she shrieked. "What the hell is wrong with you?"

"I think it's clear Annaliese does not want to see *you*," Ryder said.

Sean's head whipped around and he took a step toward Ryder, jabbing a bloody finger at him.

"No thanks to you, asshole. Don't think for a second I don't know what's going on here, you fucking thief."

Liese put her hand in front of Sean to stop him as she glimpsed a very befuddled Harvey. She worded her rebuke carefully. "Principal Whitehall has nothing to do with this. You need to leave, or I'm going to call the police and have them escort you from the property."

Ryder cleared his throat behind her. He pointed to the far end of the lot, where a cruiser idled. "They're already here. One of the officers has a nephew in the play." He inclined his head toward the school where the foyer was filling with parents. "I've asked them to be discreet, considering the circumstances."

While there were refreshments available, it wouldn't be long before the audience started to trickle out. Liese ignored Sean's muttering and looked to Ryder. "We need to get him away from the doors."

"I agree," Harvey piped up. He stopped ogling Marissa's chest to watch Sean stanch the flow of blood from his nose with his shirtsleeve.

"So glad everyone cares what I think," Sean complained.

"Shut up." Ryder's mask of composure dropped. "You lost your right to have an opinion when you stepped foot inside this school. I would like to know how the hell you managed to get in without being seen."

Sean shot him a menacing glare—its desired effect lost when he sniffled—but at least he kept his mouth shut. Ryder and Harvey flanked Sean, ushering him quickly down the stairs into the parking lot. Liese and Marissa followed close behind, hiding Sean from anyone leaving the building. The sooner they reached the waiting cruiser, the sooner they could remove him from the property. Liese reminded herself that winter break was two days away, and any rumors that might crop up would probably fade by the time they returned in the new year.

"Did Sean say anything incriminating?" Liese whispered to Marissa as they descended the stairs.

She shook her head, keeping her voice low as she filled Liese in. "He didn't have a chance. Ryder got all up in his face and started spouting a bunch of stuff about breaking the law and Sean's impact on your safety and the stress he was causing you.

Then you knocked Sean on his ass with the door before he could open his big mouth."

"Thank God." Liese relaxed a little. Until Sean was in the cruiser he could still cause damage. "What about Harvey? Do you think he suspects something?"

"Honestly, he was more interested in my chest than the situation. I think he might actually be drunk . . ." Marissa trailed off as she glanced at Harvey. Now that she'd said it, Liese could see a slight tremor in his hand and a weave in his gait.

They were almost at the cruiser when the officers stepped toward them. At the same time, Sean leaned toward Ryder and said something. Ryder stiffened visibly, his fists clenching, but he said nothing—even as Sean looked back at Liese and continued to goad him. To Sean's left, Harvey lumbered along obliviously, breathing heavily from the exertion as he hiked his pants up under his oversized belly.

Suddenly, Sean lunged at Ryder and shoved him from the side. Ryder stumbled and threw out his hands to prevent himself from face-planting into the ground as Sean took off at a dead run. He hurdled the flower garden and crashed through the bushes in a ridiculous attempt to escape. Harvey lurched forward, but didn't have the coordination or stamina to give chase. Ryder was already picking himself up off the ground. It was clear he had every intention of pursuing Sean, and Liese knew if he caught him, the result could be detrimental to his career.

"Sean is such an idiot," Marissa sighed.

"I can't let Ryder catch him," Liese said, tearing after the man before Ryder found his footing.

Her heels hit the barely frozen earth as she bore down on him, but the weighty thud of boot-clad feet came from her left. She didn't waver from her course, determined to reach Sean before Ryder could. Officer Tanner bounded past her, cutting her off and tackling Sean to the ground in three easy strides. Liese skidded to a halt, and someone slammed into her from behind. She nearly went down, but an arm snapped around her waist and kept her from falling.

"Are you okay?" Ryder asked, releasing his hold once she regained her footing, but keeping his hand on her back to steady her.

"I'm fine." She drew in labored breaths, watching as the officer wrangled Sean into cuffs and hoisted him off the ground.

Once Sean had been deposited safely in the car, Liese turned to Ryder. "Are you . . . oh, God, you're bleeding. Here let me—" She pulled a tissue from her pocket and reached out to inspect Ryder's skinned palms.

Ryder gave a quick shake of his head and looked toward Harvey, who regarded the two of them intently. "I'm fine, it's nothing." He brushed bits of debris from his shirt, maintaining an aura of calm.

During the altercation, parents and students had begun filtering into the parking lot. She prayed no one had witnessed Sean's failed escape attempt. This whole situation was mortifying on so many levels.

Ryder briefed the officers as Sean shouted muffled obscenities from the backseat of the cruiser. "Can we move this to the station?" Ryder looked around the parking lot, where cars were beginning to exit, which meant passing by the cruiser.

"Of course. We'll meet you there," Officer Tanner said.

Officer Cooke, his partner, leaned casually against the driver's side door, picking at his fingernails, as Sean continued to rail from the backseat. Tanner tapped the roof of the car and slid into the passenger seat. "Let's get this one out of here."

Ryder urged Liese toward his car. "I'll drive."

"But my purse . . ." Liese protested, feeling a little dazed.

"It's fine. I'll get it from your office and bring it home," Marissa offered.

In the mayhem, Liese had completely forgotten Marissa would be staying with her, but she was quite thankful. "Right, good plan." She hugged herself and rubbed her arms, finally noticing the cold. "And my jacket? Can you bring my jacket home, too?"

"Of course, anything you need."

"Harvey, would you let Marissa into the library?" Ryder asked. "I'll brief you in the morning."

"Right. Sure." Harvey looked at them for what seemed a beat longer than necessary.

Liese stepped away from Ryder as she realized their arms had been touching.

Just as they turned to leave, Blake barreled down the sidewalk toward them, panting from exertion. He skidded to a halt, gaping at Ryder, whose clothes were rumpled after the debacle. Blake examined the scene for a long moment before he turned to Liese. "Everything okay? I tried to get here as quickly as I could but I kept getting stopped."

"I'll fill you in." Marissa took his arm and guided him back toward the school with Harvey following behind. "I'll see you at home," she called over her shoulder to Liese.

"What happened?" Liese heard Blake ask. He glanced over his shoulder one last time, just as Ryder shed his suit jacket and draped it over Liese's shoulders. Unaware of their current audience, he tucked a stray lock of hair behind her ear, his fingertips grazing her cheek. Blake took it all in, his suspicion evident. She had the distinct feeling things were about to go from bad to worse.

27

Unfortunate Revelations

THE DRIVE TO the police station felt endless, though it only took a few minutes. Every so often Liese glanced at Ryder, but he kept his eyes on the road, white-knuckling the steering wheel. She'd never seen him so incensed, not even when he'd discovered her folder of photoshopped pictures. Silence and tension filled the small space, the energy oppressive. Liese picked at a hangnail until the loose skin tore away, a bubble of blood welling at the spot. She hissed at the pain and brought her finger to her lips.

Ryder made a sudden right turn, which Liese figured was a short cut until he slowed the car. He pulled over and stopped at the curb, then shifted the car into park.

"Are you okay?" His voice came out rough. He cleared his throat and shook his head. "No, of course you're not."

She wouldn't contradict him; she definitely didn't feel okay. He unbuckled his seatbelt and repositioned himself to face her. With an unexpected tenderness he stroked her cheek, catching a falling tear. He flipped open the glove compartment and pulled out a packet of tissues. Freeing one, he dabbed beneath her eyes. On the verge of breaking down entirely, she covered his hand to stop him, but ended up pressing her cheek into his palm, the comfort too enticing to resist.

"I think Blake might suspect something," Liese whispered, taking the tissue from him. She smoothed it in her lap, folding it over and over until it became a tight square. "Don't worry about Blake; I can deal with him." She recoiled at the spite in his voice.

"Sorry, I didn't mean for that to sound so severe," he added. "Even if he is suspicious, it doesn't matter."

"How can you say that?"

"Do you really think he would do anything to damage your career?"

Ryder had a point. As much as Blake hated him, he wouldn't expose him if it meant hurting her. "What about Harvey?"

"Harvey is oblivious at the best of times."

"But he might . . ."

Ryder shook his head. "He won't. And if he does . . . well, let's just say he has bigger issues to deal with than my personal life. He's treading a fine line right now, and it wouldn't be in his best interest to rock the boat."

Liese looked at her lap. "Marissa said she thought he was drunk tonight."

"That wouldn't be much of a surprise."

"Oh." There was a lot more going on at FAHL than Liese had realized.

Ryder took her hand and stroked the center of her palm. "We'll work it out, okay?"

"Okay," Liese said, but she wasn't convinced. She still worried there was no way it could be okay.

"Shall we file the report and get it over with?" Ryder asked.

At her nod, he leaned over, kissing her cheek before he put the car in gear. A short time later they pulled into the station. Liese checked her reflection in the visor mirror and cringed at her blotchy, tear-stained face.

Officers Tanner and Cooke met them inside. She reluctantly left Ryder in the waiting room and followed Officer Tanner to his office to give her statement, which reiterated much of the same information she'd provided when she filed the original restraining order. Then she filed a report regarding Sean's breech of that order.

Liese had just finished reviewing her statement when Officer Tanner cleared his throat. "Have you ever had any concerns about Sean's mental health?" He flipped a pen between his fingers as he assessed her reaction.

Her immediate impulse was to say no, but she paused to think about his erratic behavior over the last few months. She remembered once when she'd been rooting through his medicine cabinet for an aspirin back when they were still dating. She'd found several prescription pill bottles, almost all completely empty. She'd written it off at the time—lots of people took medication for various conditions. Now she wasn't so sure she should have.

"I hadn't really entertained the idea," she said. "But maybe I should."

Officer Tanner offered a short explanation about the markers of individuals with obsessive personalities. She understood the warning for what it was: Sean wasn't stable, and she needed to be careful. She knew that; she just hadn't been aware of *how* unstable.

Liese began to fit the pieces together. His highs and lows had always had a pendulum effect. After they broke up, he left her alone for a while, only to resurface with a vengeance. Ceaseless phone calls and texts would last a few days before he disappeared again. His absences never went on for long, though. Then he'd changed tactics, leaving strange and sometimes disturbing gifts for her at home and at work. Her anger at Sean ebbed to be replaced by a tingle of fear again. She'd written off his actions tonight as a pathetic attempt to gain her attention, but after the conversation with the officer, she realized it wasn't that simple. Thank God the evening hadn't been any more disturbing or dangerous than it was.

Report filed, Liese emerged from Officer Tanner's office to find Ryder waiting in the lobby. The receptionist kept up a steady stream of conversation, and Ryder indulged her while periodically checking his phone for messages. A pang of jealousy stung her as the woman mooned over him. Suzy, as her nameplate indicated, batted her eyelashes and twirled her processed hair around her finger every time he glanced her way. Liese wanted to punch her in the face. And maybe cry. Emotionally spent, she was overly sensitive and too strung out to deal.

As though he sensed her presence, Ryder looked her way and smiled, but his cheer faded as quickly as it had appeared. He moved toward her, leaving the receptionist mid-sentence, and without pause he cupped her cheek and searched her face, heedless of the people around them. "Are you okay? Did something happen during the interview?"

His touch calmed her, until she remembered they were in a public place. "Yes . . . no," Liese replied, taking a deep breath to gather herself. "Yes, I'm okay. No, nothing happened. I just gave my statement. Can we go? There are people staring."

Ryder dropped his hand and gave the station a covert scan. "The only person paying any attention is the desk clerk." Still, he led her outside.

Liese shivered, in spite of Ryder's suit jacket draped over her shoulders, yet he seemed unaffected by the cold, even in just a long-sleeved shirt. Once seated in the car, she made sure to activate both their heated seats.

On the drive home, Ryder held her hand, his gentle affection soothing. The interrogation by the police had drained her, and though Ryder asked if she wanted to talk, she didn't feel much like recapping the conversation. Only as they pulled into her driveway did Liese find her voice.

"I'm sorry," she said.

"For what?"

"For this mess: Sean, Blake. I know people must have seen. People are going to know—"

Ryder put the Lexus in park behind Marissa's car and sighed, giving her hand a squeeze. "Please stop apologizing. You aren't responsible for what others do and say, including Sean—or me for that matter. We managed the situation just fine at the school, and you don't need to worry. If anything, I should be apologizing for getting involved with you when I knew what a precarious position it would put us in."

Liese withdrew her hand. This reinforced the fear she'd harbored all along. She reached for the door handle as the locks clicked into place. "Don't," she warned.

"Don't what? Try to keep you from leaving? Allow you to avoid an important and necessary conversation?" Ryder replied, the sharp edge of frustration in his voice tempered by his pleading tone. "Liese, what's going on? What happened at the police station? *Talk* to me."

"What do you want me to say? Look at how complicated this thing has become."

"This thing?"

"Us. This relationship. You just apologized for getting involved with me. And I bring so much baggage to the school. It's not professional. Maybe it's just too hard." Liese wrapped her arms around herself to protect her aching heart.

Ryder appeared dumbfounded. "Everyone has a personal life, Liese. FAHL is lucky to have you, and I wouldn't want you to deal with Sean on your own. Are you saying you want our relationship to end?"

"No."

"You're sure?" He smoothed his tie, picking at the end before he looked at her again. "I thought we had this all sorted, but I would understand if you were having second thoughts."

"I'm sure," she said, her mind a whirl of emotions. "Are you?"

"Positively certain."

She jumped at the zip of his seatbelt retracting.

"Sorry," he murmured. "I didn't mean to scare you." His fingers slid into her hair, his palm resting against the side of her neck as he kissed her.

Her lips parted on a sigh when the warmth of his tongue met hers. Liese gripped his shirt, drawing him closer. She struggled against the restraint that kept her bound to her seat. All rational thought was obliterated in the face of so much anxiety. With her judgment clearly skewed, maybe it was best just to forget for now. Ryder's mouth and hands had a way of making that happen. She unbuckled her seatbelt and launched herself at him. Once they'd locked together in a frantic kiss, she climbed over and tried to straddle his lap. Ryder reclined his seat, providing more room to maneuver, and then she sat on the horn. The sound surprised them both, and Liese smacked her head on the roof of the SUV. Talk about a mood killer.

"Fuck," Ryder grumbled as the porch light came on and Marissa's silhouette appeared in the window.

"Not anymore." Liese struggled to get back over the console and into her seat before Marissa found her humping Ryder like a horny teenager.

He rubbed his fingers over his mouth in frustration and adjusted himself. "As wonderful a friend as Marissa might be, she certainly has horrible timing."

"Well, I did honk the horn," Liese offered.

With his hard-on adequately rearranged, he pinned her with a hot stare. "We'll talk tomorrow."

"Yes, sir."

His eyes blazed with promise. She knew the next time they were together it would be just as intense as the last. She didn't mind the prospect one bit; she just wasn't sure when the alone time might occur. They had yet to make plans for the Christmas holiday, but Liese's parents had recently returned from their trip abroad and had already informed her they were coming to Fullerton. Though they hadn't settled on the arrival date, Liese anticipated it would be soon, as they'd decided to make yet another road trip out of it.

Ryder came around to open her door, and lacing their fingers together, they walked across the driveway and up the steps to the front porch. Marissa hadn't come out, and Liese assumed she'd recognized Ryder's vehicle and was giving them privacy. She doubted the courtesy would last long, as Marissa would be dying to know what had happened at the police station.

"Come see me first thing in the morning?" he asked, his tone gentle. "I want to know how your night goes."

"I will. I wish you could stay." She picked up his tie, letting it slip through her fingers.

"Me too." Ryder hummed his agreement. "However, I don't want to ruin Marissa's current impression of me. I doubt she'd be amused by my spanking fetish in the same way you are. Besides, you only have one bedroom."

"Good point. The couch is a pullout, though."

"Tempting. But you have difficulty being quiet." "I—what?" Liese tried to sound incredulous.

Ryder grinned. "It's forgivable. I know it's a challenge to hold all your praise for my phenomenal skills until the end."

"You're so full of yourself."

"I prefer it when *you're* full of me."

Liese rolled her eyes, but smiled. Their banter lightened her dark mood.

"That's better." He skimmed her bottom lip with his knuckle, then replaced it with his mouth.

At first, the creak of the door didn't register. However, Blake's stunned expletive managed to break through the haze of lust.

If there was any doubt whether Blake suspected something going on between them, it was gone now.

28

Another Showdown

"SHIT! SORRY." MARISSA tried to act as a human shield, but she was about five inches too short to accomplish the mission. "Goddamn it, Blake. Didn't I tell you to stay in the living room?"

Blake put his hands on Marissa's shoulders to keep her from bouncing so he could see around her. "Are you two . . . is he? I fucking knew it!" He pointed an accusing finger at Liese. He turned to Ryder, then back to her before his angry glare settled on Marissa. "Did you know about this?"

Marissa was unapologetic. "Of course. She's my best friend."

Blake wrinkled his nose. To Ryder's credit, his only reaction was to move closer to Liese, draping his arm over her shoulder to draw her tight against him.

"I hope you aren't going to make this an issue." His tone made it sound more like a threat than the appeal it might have been had Liese been the one to speak first.

"Issue?" Blake scowled and rubbed the back of his neck as

he focused on his feet. "I don't even—" He stopped and took a deep breath. He looked more hurt than angry as he met Liese's terrified gaze. "Why didn't you just tell me?"

"I think the answer to that question is rather obvious," Ryder replied.

"I'm not talking to you, so you can just shut it, Whitehall." Blake raised a hand in Ryder's direction but didn't look away from Liese as he continued. "I wouldn't have judged you." Liese quirked a brow.

"Okay, fine, maybe I would have judged you a little, but only because it's Whitehall."

"What's that supposed to mean?" Ryder asked.

"You need to get over what happened in high school," Blake said. "It's been twenty years. Every damn person in the building knows you hate me." When Ryder went to cut him off, Blake shut him down. "I don't have the warm fuzzies for you either, but I'm not about to cause Liese more problems than she already has. If she wants to be with you, that's her prerogative." "Blake—" Liese interrupted.

He pointed a finger at her. "Oh, no. No way. I'm not done yet, and I'm pretty sure I'm not going to get another chance like this ever again." He took a breath before he continued his tirade. "And just so you know, *Principal* Whitehall, *I've* noticed the way you are with her. And I doubt I'm alone. If you decide to screw her over or hurt her in any way, I won't have any qualms about dragging your name through the dirt."

"Don't make empty threats, Stone. It's beneath you."

"Oh, it's not a threat, it's a promise," Blake sneered. "You think it won't reflect poorly on you if your relationship goes public? Hard not to question someone's ethics if they're taking advantage of a new, young staff member, isn't it?"

"And you'd drag Liese down along with me? How caring of you. Liese's well-being is my top priority right now, unlike yours." He gestured between Blake and Marissa.

Liese noticed Marissa wasn't wearing any lipstick—which never happened—and Blake's mouth was a more pronounced shade of pink than usual. Marissa's top was also a wrinkled mess. Clearly, they'd been a tad preoccupied.

Ryder hugged Liese to him and stroked her hair. "Liese has had an inordinately difficult evening. The last thing she needs is to be held hostage on her front porch, listening to you spew your hypocritical bullshit at me. If you'd like to continue this conversation tomorrow, please feel free to stop by my office. Otherwise, get the fuck out of the way so Liese can get inside her own house. If you weren't so busy shooting off your mouth, you'd notice she's damn well freezing."

Liese had curled into Ryder, as much to protect herself from the verbal sparring as to keep warm. But her teeth chattered as the wind blew through her skirt.

"Shit. I'm an asshole."

"Well, that's one thing we agree on," Ryder shot back as he moved past Blake and Marissa. They pasted themselves against the wall to give Liese and Ryder room to pass.

Once inside, Ryder led her to the living room and settled her on the couch. He wrapped her in the nearest blanket, kneeling on the floor to tuck the flannel beneath her feet. Marissa and Blake crammed in the doorway.

"Can we get a minute of privacy, please?" Ryder snapped.

"Right. Sure, sorry." Marissa tugged on Blake's sleeve. They bumped into each other as they backed away, shuffling down the hall toward the kitchen.

"This isn't good." Liese huddled deeper into the couch. The

chill of the wind seemed to have settled in her bones. Even co-cooned in the blanket she was cold.

"Everything will be fine. It's been a difficult night, and Stone's an insensitive bastard." Ryder fiddled with the blanket as he spoke. Liese couldn't tell if he was trying to placate her or if he truly believed what he said.

"But what if what Blake says is true? What if other people have noticed how we are when we're around each other? What if someone knows? Maybe I need to transfer schools—" Panic spiraled, and the dread she kept tamped down surfaced in the face of so much stress.

"Stop." Ryder placed a finger gently against her lips. "He was trying to wind me up, and he didn't take into consideration the effect it might have on you. We are very careful, are we not?"

"I'm not so sure about that." Liese dropped her voice until it was barely above a whisper. "Think about it, Ryder. We had sex in *your office* in the middle of the day with Betty sitting right outside. What if I was too loud? What if she heard me and told someone else—like Harvey? And what about the rehearsal? A student could have seen us together. What if people are just waiting for us to make one more stupid mistake so they can expose us?"

Ryder sighed and ran a hand through his hair. "Liese, I promise you, no one heard a thing. Betty listens to talk radio all day long, and she's more absorbed in her nails than what happens in my office. And you were very responsible during the rehearsal. More so than me, I'm afraid. I shall take future cues from you. But no students saw us that day, I can promise you that." He lowered his voice and leaned in close, his lips at her ear. "Besides, you certainly can be quiet when it's necessary."

"Don't," Liese said, pushing him away. "It's not funny, and

you're trying to distract me."

"You need a distraction." He rested his palm over her hand, which pressed against his chest, holding him at bay.

"Not this kind. This is why we have problems right now. We can't even have a normal relationship, Ryder. I can't tell any of my friends about you, except the one who lives out of town.

How long can we keep doing this?"

"Have you changed your mind about making this work?"

"No." Her voice caught. The thought of losing him scared her, but the thought of damaging her career frightened her as well.

"You're certain?"

"No. Yes. I don't know. I want to be with you, but it's complicated." Liese closed her eyes, pausing before she voiced the concern weighing heavily on her. "We'll end up resenting each other if our careers are put in jeopardy because of this."

Ryder swallowed audibly, and Liese looked up from her lap to find his head bowed. He wrapped her hand in his. "You've had a very stressful evening. I know you have a lot on your mind, and I'm asking you not to make any rash decisions, at least not tonight. You need to focus on you. This Sean thing is finally under control. It's going to be okay."

"I'm just overwhelmed." Liese ran her fingers through his hair. She wanted him to stay, but she needed him to go. An emotional battle waged inside her, and she didn't think she could hold it together much longer. Once the first soldier fell, the rest would follow in domino effect. Tears threatened to break her composure. "We'll talk about it tomorrow."

"Liese." He touched her chin, lifting her head gently. "I wanted to wait, but in light of recent events—"

Liese's stomach dropped. He looked serious—too serious.

"Ryder . . ."

"There's a superintendent position at the public school board in Montgomery County." He stopped and waited for a reaction. When she remained silent, he continued, "If I applied and got the job, it could make things easier."

"I'm sorry, what?"

"It would be a good thing. We wouldn't be working in the same building anymore."

"But wouldn't you have to move?" Montgomery was farther south. The prospect of a long-distance relationship did not ease the choked feeling that overtook her.

Ryder shook his head. "It would be reasonable to commute." He smoothed her cheek. "We would be free to pursue this relationship without fear of backlash."

"Which would be a good thing." Liese echoed his earlier statement.

"It's definitely an option to consider." Ryder gave her a tentative smile and kissed her cheek. "We can talk about this later. You've had enough thrown at you tonight without tossing this into the mix."

"It's a lot to digest." Her head swam with the new information. Piled on top of everything else, she didn't feel capable of processing it.

"I can only imagine." Ryder opened his arms, and she went into them.

This was the kind of physical contact she needed right now: benign and comforting. She felt him bury his nose in her hair and inhale deeply. They stayed like that for a few minutes before she extracted herself. He searched her face. After a long moment, he rubbed his hands over her shoulders and kissed her chastely.

"I should go. You need rest, and I'm sure Marissa would like to spend some time with you. I know she's been concerned." Liese snorted.

"At least Blake's no longer an issue."

"That's one way to look at it." Liese sighed.

Fatigue came over her like a leaden shroud as she walked Ryder to the door. He erased some of the cold she couldn't seem to shake with his goodbye kisses. She sensed desperation in the way he held her almost too tightly, his body taut and rigid as his lips pressed against hers.

"Call if you need me," he whispered.

"I'll be fine. I'll talk to you in the morning." She touched the side of his neck and felt his pulse pounding against her fingers.

"Liese, I—" He paused, meeting her gaze with one so intense her breath faltered. A range of emotions passed through his eyes before settling on agonized regret. "Get some rest."

She closed the door and watched him leave through the sheer curtain. Long after his taillights had disappeared, she focused on the darkness beyond, trying to figure out what he had wanted to say.

Eventually she made her way to the kitchen, where Blake and Marissa sat at the table, inches apart with their bodies turned into each other, holding mugs of tea. She wondered if their knees were touching under the table, and a stab of envy pierced her. They could have a normal relationship. They could be together, and no one would pass judgment on them.

"Can I get you something?" Marissa offered, her fingernails tapping the side of her mug.

Liese declined. "I'm going to bed. I'm exhausted." "I'll be up in a few minutes," Marissa promised.

"Don't rush. Sorry about tonight, Blake. I didn't mean to ruin the final performance." Liese gave him a pained smile.

"You didn't ruin anything."

But Liese didn't want to be mollified; she wanted to wallow. "G'night," she mumbled.

The blissful solitude of her bedroom offered the privacy she needed. She threw herself on the mattress and buried her face in her pillow. The tears came fast and hard, her body shaking with the weight of her sobs. She let the waves of uncertainty wash over her, and her tears carried her away.

Sometime later, Marissa's hand settled on her back. "Liese?"

With her face still buried in her pillow, she took a couple of deep breaths. The hiccups had started, but at least she'd stopped sobbing. When her breathing calmed, Liese rolled over and sat up, hugging the pillow she'd been snotting into.

"Did something happen with you and Ryder?"

"No, not really." Liese shook her head. "We haven't broken up, if that's what you're asking."

"But something happened?"

Liese sighed. "He's talking about applying for a job in another county."

"Which means?" Marissa prompted.

Liese explained what could happen.

"Then why don't you sound very happy about it?" Marissa asked.

Liese rubbed her face. "I don't know. Even if he did get the job—if he decides to apply—people will still talk when they find out we're together. And they'll already be talking about this mess tonight."

"So? Who gives a shit if people talk?" When Liese didn't reply Marissa was the one who sighed. "Look, I know it's been a hell of a day for you. I don't think now is the time to have a philosophical conversation about the losers who are going to gossip no matter what the deal is with you and Ryder. He cares about you, and you care about him. Right now that's all that matters. We'll figure out the rest when the time comes." "Sometimes I wonder if it's worth it," Liese replied.

"Can I ask you something?" Marissa said.

"Sure."

"Do you love him?"

"What?" Liese's voice rose two octaves too many.

"It's a simple question. Do you love him?"

Liese didn't answer for a long moment. Caught up in all the other crap surrounding their relationship, she'd avoided looking too closcly at her true feelings for Ryder.

But now she whispered a quiet *yes*.

"Then it's worth it."

29

Every Garbage Can Needs a Lid

LIESE EXUDED CRANKINESS the next morning. While she'd resolved that she wanted to be with Ryder, she still didn't know what that would look like, or how to manage her feelings. She planned to see him and then hide out in the library until the holidays arrived. Her cheeks flamed with heat every time she imagined having to answer questions about her crazy ex and what had happened at the play.

When she entered the office, Betty sat behind her desk, examining her nails. Her eyes lit up with the kind of gleam Liese associated with gossipy teenagers when she tried to sneak past. Obviously word had gotten out. Betty beckoned her over; peeking around to ensure their conversation was not overheard.

"I'm surprised you're here today, what with last night and all . . ."

"I'm sorry?" Liese decided to play dumb. What better way to find out what the rumor mill had churned out.

"Well, I—" Betty looked around again, seeming more uncertain this time. "I heard the police were here."

"To see the play?" Liese continued to feign confusion. "One of the officers had a nephew in the performance, and you know how supportive this community is."

Betty frowned. She clearly didn't like the thought of doling out inaccurate gossip. "Harvey mentioned they made an arrest." "Oh. That." Liese's voice cracked. So much for the ruse.

The sound of movement came from inside Ryder's office. Harvey opened the door and stepped out, saving Liese from further interrogation. He looked a bit worse for wear as he grunted a greeting at her chest and trudged past. But his slothlike appearance didn't mean he'd lost his smarmy touch. He paused at Betty's desk to make a comment that set her all atwitter. Liese barely suppressed a gag.

"Liese, come on in." Ryder smiled warmly at her, but he radiated tension.

Once inside, he motioned for her to close the door. She didn't know how to act and felt surprisingly ambivalent about being shut in his office with him alone. Every cell in her body begged her to move toward him and let him pull her into his arms. Yet she was determined to remain professional. As if he could sense her conflict, he rose from his chair, his hand passing over his tie.

"Did you sleep well?" he asked, voice gravelly. He cleared his throat and fidgeted with the cufflink at his wrist.

"Not really," she admitted.

"Me neither." He rearranged the pens on his desk.

Silence unfolded and stretched between them as she waited. When it became obvious she wasn't moving from her position in front of the door, Ryder stepped around his desk. He raised a tentative hand and pushed her hair back over her shoulders.

Gentle fingers skimmed the length of her arms until he

reached her hands. He held them in his own and gave a soft squeeze. "What's going on in that head of yours?"

Liese sighed, her brain fritzing out at the physical contact. Nothing and no one else existed when they were alone like this. She was fooling herself if she thought it would be easy to get over him if things didn't work out. "A whole lot of nothing at the moment."

"I call you on that lie." His sad smile eclipsed the humor in his tone.

"I'm just tired, and I'm nervous about dealing with everyone today. Betty's already grilled me about the police being here, and you know what that means." Liese focused on their twined fingers. If she kept looking at him, she'd get caught up in his intensity. After her conversation with Marissa last night, there was so much more to say, but his office wasn't the place to do that.

"She's fishing for details. She's already done that with me," Ryder said.

"Well, she's out there flirting with Harvey now, so who knows what she'll get out of him." Liese shuddered. "I feel like my personal life is on a billboard after last night."

"Do you want to take the day off?"

"And postpone the inevitable?" Liese shook her head. "I'd rather deal with the Sean crap before the holidays than spend the entire break stewing about the ridiculous stories people will concoct."

Ryder nodded as if he understood, but his experience differed greatly from hers. He'd played the hero, calling in the police again. She was the one with the whack-a-doo ex-boyfriend.

"And how are you feeling about the rest of last night?" he asked. "Managed to process that at all?"

"Still overwhelmed." Liese squeezed his hands, hoping it

came across as reassuring. Her heart began to race all over again just thinking about the possibility of him switching jobs.

"When can I see you?" he asked abruptly.

"Marissa leaves tomorrow."

"Shall I come to you?"

"Okay." She immediately began counting the hours until they could sort things through.

"May I kiss you?" He leaned in, stopping a few inches shy of her mouth and waited for permission.

Liese lifted her chin in agreement. Ryder slipped an arm around her waist, and dipping his head, he covered her mouth with his. The innocence of the kiss evaporated as his tongue swept out to meet hers, the pent-up desire and desperation she carried mirrored as he claimed her mouth. Liese was far too aware of their environment, though, and after a moment, she broke the searing kiss, though her body demanded more.

She pushed on his chest, but he didn't budge. "We need to stop," she panted against his mouth. "We can't afford this kind of indiscretion."

Ryder closed his eyes and took a deep breath, releasing her. "Just so you're aware, I plan to spend the holidays recreating every deviant fantasy I've had about you since you first spent the night in my bed."

"That sounds like fun." As she spoke, Liese retreated, afraid his proximity would cloud her sensibilities. She could settle for spending the next two weeks confined to his bedroom, but she needed to get out of his office before she did something stupid—like ask about those fantasies.

A knock at the door startled them both.

Without waiting for a response, Harvey turned the knob and poked his head inside. "Sorry to interrupt, but the director is here."

"We'll finish up later." Ryder looked vaguely ill. If things had escalated further, they could've been caught, and by Harvey of all people.

"Of course." Liese slipped past Harvey, who took up most of the doorway, and went straight to the library, where students checking out books for the holidays kept her busy all morning. An out and out brawl almost started over *The Catcher in the Rye*, until Liese pointed out there were six copies available for loan. At lunch she squirreled away in her office to finish up paperwork and hide from her colleagues.

This allowed her to successfully dodge Blake, but she'd planned to help take down the remains of the set and clean up the prep rooms behind the stage at the end of the day. He would inevitably be there.

After school, anxiety settled in her stomach as she opened the door to the auditorium. A handful of students carted the remaining set pieces off stage. She envied them, untainted by adulthood and its many complications. She almost yearned for the simplicity of high school, when her most pressing issues had been whether she'd aced her English essay and whether the boy she had a crush on liked her back.

She stood at the back of the theater, and the memory of Sean in the same spot, looking at her with scorn, made her skin crawl. Determined to stop thinking about such unpleasant things, she squared her shoulders and walked down the aisle. Blake knelt at the base of the stage, engrossed in a tangle of cables.

"Ms. Harper!" One of the cast members charged at her. The girl flung her arms around Liese. "Oh my God, you're here!

Someone said you were arrested last night, but I said no way; Ms. Harper would never do anything illegal."

Liese choked on a laugh. The girl cast a suspicious glance behind her before she lowered her voice to a whisper. "You know what those cheerleader types are like—all gossip, gossip, gossip. I didn't believe a word of it, not for a second. But then someone else said you had a stalker, and I thought, well, maybe, because you're so pretty, and all the boys in the play are in love with you. Except for a couple, but they're in love with Mr. Stone." The girl paused to take a breath, her eyes lighting up. "Are you in love with Mr. Stone?"

"I . . . uh . . ." Liese struggled to put words together for a moment, and thankfully, Blake saved her.

"Can you check the back room and make sure it's tidied?" he asked the chatty young lady. "Then we're done for the day." He fought an amused smile.

"Sure, Mr. Stone! See you later, Ms. Harper." She flitted away.

Blake came up the stairs, dusting his hands on his pants. "She's got a lot of energy."

"You don't say."

"She's a sweet kid."

"Not sure that's how I would describe her, but her concern is endearing." Liese paused to take a breath. "The rumors aren't, though."

Blake stuffed his hands in his pockets. "They saw a police car, so they make up stories."

"One of those stories included a stalker."

Blake shrugged. "Sean's been here a couple of times; maybe they noticed him before? Our kids are pretty perceptive, and they like you." He tilted his head. "They asked questions when you weren't here after the play last night. I tried to run interference, but there was only so much I could do. Even without the flashing lights, the police car gave them something to hypothesize about." He spoke with an air of apology.

Liese sighed. "It's just so embarrassing."

"Why, because you're ex is a psycho? At least he's your ex. What did the police do, anyway?"

"I'm not sure. I just gave them another statement. I think they'll give him some kind of probation and a caution, but I worry he needs serious help. I hope they make it some kind of stipulation." Liese picked an imaginary piece of lint off her blouse.

Blake dropped into one of the theater chairs and patted the seat beside him. They sat in silence for a long while, waving to the last of the stage crew as they departed. Liese wanted to address the elephant in the room, but she had no idea how. Blake, being the good friend he was, did it for her.

"Whitehall, huh?" He nudged her arm.

"Don't judge me."

Blake raised his hands. "I'm done with that. Every garbage can needs a lid."

"Hey!" She smacked his arm. "That's a horrible analogy for a relationship."

"It's just a figure of speech."

"No, it's not."

"Yes, it is," Blake argued with a smile.

"A figure of speech is a common phrase or saying. That is not a common phrase."

They lapsed into silence again.

"In all seriousness though, what's going on between the two of you? Is it a relationship?" he asked. "Must be pretty challenging to keep it hidden."

Liese stayed quiet, unwilling to voice her insecurities.

When she didn't respond, he pressed her. "How long has this

been going on?”

“Long enough,” she said.

“Liese.”

“We’ve been seeing each other for a couple of months.”

“Wow. I don’t know what to say to that.”

“Which is why I didn’t tell you. I don’t want people to think I’m trying to sleep my way up the ladder. I’m terrified of the impact this could have on my career—or Ryder’s, for that matter. Remember our conversation at orientation about the teacher who had an affair with her principal? I’m sure you can see why I wanted to hide it.”

“Well, yeah, I can see why you wouldn’t want *everyone* to know.” Blake peeled a sticker that read “Super!” from the armrest of his chair. “I mean, that would be awkward, and teachers are generally a bunch of gossipmongers. But this is me we’re talking about.”

“I couldn’t risk it.”

Blake looked at her with disapproval.

“Don’t try to make me feel bad; I already do. There was just too much to lose: my relationship with Ryder, my career, your respect. It’s not like I planned to get involved with him. It just happened. And I didn’t want to be judged—not like that couple all the teachers have been talking about since I got here.”

“I think you’re missing a crucial detail,” he said. “They got caught going at it under the bleachers during a school dance— by a student.”

“What?”

“Yeah. It was crazy. The kid videoed it and posted it on You-Tube. It went viral.” Blake looked like he might have seen the clip.

“Oh.” That put a whole new spin on her colleagues’ morbid

fascination with the situation.

"Look, I get why you would want to keep your relationship under wraps, because yeah, people make assumptions and judgments. But I'm not most people. I'm me, and I'm your friend before I'm your colleague." Blake made a fist and double tapped his chest, right over his heart, bringing their conversation to a whole new level of cheese. "You can date who you want, and I won't give a shit—unless it's that ex of yours. Then I'll have to intervene. Or that new guy in the science department who looks like a troll. He's off limits too; that would just be wrong."

"Are you serious?"

"Sorry, I got carried away. Truthfully though, if you'd told me about Whitehall at the beginning I could have gotten over the shock of you being with that anal prick."

"He's not an anal prick, and no, you wouldn't have. You would've tried to get me to break it off because you hate him," Liese countered, fending off a grin.

"Probably." Blake agreed.

"You're an ass."

"Sometimes. But just so we're clear, I'm not judging your actions. Although I'm still flabbergasted that it's Whitehall. Is he as wound up in bed as he is at work?"

"I'm not answering that question." Liese bent to pick up a ticket stub from the floor to hide her flaming cheeks.

"Huh. Not so sure I want to know why you've turned the color of a tomato."

"Can we please change the subject?" Liese gripped the armrests and pushed out of her seat.

"Sure thing." Blake also stood and offered her a sly grin. "So, in case you didn't know, I'm really digging your friend Marissa."

30

Unexpected Interruptions

IN THE WAKE of his disclosure, Blake asked Marissa out on a date for that very evening. Liese ignored her twinge of jealousy as she helped Marissa prepare for her night out. In public.

Once she ushered Marissa out the door, she sent Ryder a message. His response was immediate, but he had work he needed to finish if they were to keep their date for the following evening. Crestfallen, she uncorked a bottle of wine and plunked herself down on the couch to watch reality TV.

Her cell rang halfway through a depressing teen pregnancy fiasco. She checked the number, fingers crossed that Ryder had somehow managed to plow through his paperwork. It wasn't him, though, and she didn't recognize the number. Dread made her hands shake as she answered the call, afraid once again that the message hadn't penetrated Sean's titanium skull. That prospect scared the ever-loving crap right out of her.

"Hello?"

"Lee-lee? Is that you?" The static on the line made it difficult to hear, but she knew that voice better than anyone's. "Mom? What's up? Whose phone is this?"

"I got a cellular phone!" Static interfered with the rest of her mother's excited ranting, but from what she could tell, her parents had left California and were on the road, heading for Fullerton. Her last communication with them had been email a couple of days ago, just prior to their return to the States. Her mother had mentioned a plan to come for a holiday visit, but hadn't provided any details.

"What? The connection's bad. When will you be here?"

"I really hate these stupid things." Of course that came through loud and clear, but the shoddy connection cut out the important detail of when they expected to arrive.

Now that Liese had her mother on the phone, she wanted desperately to fill her in on everything that had happened over the last several months—some censored version of the events, anyway. She hadn't wanted to have a Ryder-related heart-toheart with her mother over email or Skype, but her opportunity for other methods of communication were limited.

"I'll try to call . . ." More static filtered through the line, followed by, ". . . Saturday, may—"

The call cut out, and Liese tried the number again, but ended up with voicemail. She settled on sending a text, hoping to get clarification on their arrival date, but all she got back was a bunch of gibberish and a frowny face. She'd have to give her mother a lesson in texting when she arrived. Technology was definitely not her thing.

Her parents' impending arrival had not been at the top of her priority list the last few days. She looked around the living room at the magazines and random papers lying on every available surface and decided to clean house.

A text came as she disinfected the bathroom, and she dove

for the phone. But her excitement was largely squashed when Marissa's name flashed across her screen. She wasn't coming home, the message reported, which meant she was probably going to find out what kind of weapon of mass destruction Blake carried below the belt.

Liese sighed and tossed the phone on her bed. At least someone was getting some action tonight. The more she thought about it, the more logical it seemed for either she or Ryder to apply for a position elsewhere. If she had to watch two of her closest friends have a public relationship while she struggled to keep her own covert, she might go ballistic.

Liese finished cleaning up, disappointed that scrubbing her toilet was the highlight of her evening, and went to bed early. But tomorrow night would prove much more exciting.

Marissa came in as Liese was walking out the door the following morning.

"Have fun?" Liese tried to keep a lid on the snark.

"No, he's so boring." Marissa unzipped her coat to display a man's shirt and too-big jogging pants. "And his penis is too small."

"What? Yuck! Why would you tell me that?" Liese covered her eyes, as if that could prevent the image that sprang to mind.

"Oh, relax. I'm kidding, on both fronts. That man is amazingly cool, and his piece is fantastic." She held up her hands and demonstrated his approximate size. "I wanted to ride it all night long." She added an obscene thrusting motion with her hips.

"Great, thanks. That was more than I needed."

"Oh, really? Kind of like I needed to know you're into bondage?"

"I'm not into—"

"Whatever, Miss Spanks-a-lot."

Liese sputtered an attempted denial, but Marissa waved her off. "I'm joking. Well, not really, but I don't care if you're into the kinky shit. I love you just the way you are." She pulled Liese into a hug. "Blake said he'd drive you to work; he's waiting out there for you."

"Oh, wow, that's uh . . . kind of weird." She peered out her front door at Blake parked in her driveway.

"You think?" Marissa asked. "You were friends before I started boning him, and you still are, right? So why wouldn't he give you a ride to work?"

"Did you just use the word *boning*?"

"Yeah."

"What are you? A sixteen-year-old boy?"

"Not sophisticated enough for you since you're being plundered by your principal?"

"Plundered? Okay, I need to go before this conversation degrades further." Liese gave Marissa a quick kiss on the cheek. "Call me when you get home?"

"Of course, and thanks for the good times." Marissa punctuated the statement with an eyebrow wag.

"I'm not taking the bait."

"I love you. I'll see you soon."

"I'll see you on Christmas day for dinner?" Liese asked as Marissa helped her into her coat.

"I wouldn't miss it," she replied and sent Liese out into the cold December morning.

Once settled in the car, Liese realized there were two distinct advantages to catching a ride to work with Blake: the vehicle was already toasty warm, and he stopped to buy her coffee. Surprisingly, the conversation between them flowed, even though he'd been *boning* her best friend the night before. Liese tried not to think about that.

They strolled into the building, neither in a particular hurry as half the school population had already left for the holidays. At FAHL, affluence was the norm, which meant students went on luxury vacations to beautiful destinations she could never hope to afford.

Liese occupied her time by organizing her already organized office and searching for gifts online, trying not to watch the clock. Before she left for home, Blake caught up to her and suggested they join the usual crew for a holiday drink at the local bar. Ryder wasn't expected to arrive until five, so Liese decided it would be the perfect way to kill a couple of hours. Two glasses of wine later, Blake dropped her off at home, and she had just enough time to freshen up before the doorbell rang.

She sprinted down the stairs and threw open the door to find a very sexy Ryder standing on her front porch. The warm, languid feeling incited by the wine fueled her longing for him. Now that they were alone, she had no reason not to give in.

She grabbed his tie and yanked him inside, slamming the door behind him. "Hi."

"Hi, yourself." He embraced her and dropped his head into the crook of her neck, his lips pressed against her skin. "I missed you."

Liese made a noise that came out sounding more like a moan than a word.

"Is that right?" Ryder teased as his lips moved across the edge of her jaw to her mouth. She nipped at him, hunger winning out over slow and sensual.

"Someone's impatient." He chuckled.

Liese took the opportunity to unbutton his thick wool coat.

"We have all night," he pointed out. "All week, in fact, and the one after that. So what's the rush?" He remained passive as she continued on her quest to rid him of clothing.

She pushed his coat over his shoulders. "Well, we have all night. But I believe my parents will be arriving sometime tomorrow. So why not get started now?"

"I thought it might be a good idea to talk first, before we get too carried away. As you've mentioned, there are important details to discuss—such as your parents coming to visit."

"I'm already carried away." Liese fisted his tie and pulled his mouth down to hers. She kissed him fiercely, parting his lips with her tongue. He met her stroke for stroke, taking control of the kiss until she was limp in his arms. She had no idea how he managed to turn things around so he was always the one holding the power.

Ryder forced her backward until she met the wall behind her. She used it to her advantage, holding him close and dragging her foot up his calf. Liese felt his erection, hard and straining beneath his dress pants. She helped him out of his suit jacket, letting it drop to the floor. She had no intention of doing anything that resembled talking, unless it included dirty words. Before Ryder could protest, she unclasped his belt buckle and pulled the leather through the loops. He snatched the belt from her hand, and it snapped out and hit her thigh with a heavy smack.

She sucked in a shocked breath. They both paused, eyes meeting as they gasped for air. Liese looked at the belt and filtered through the possibilities of what he might do with it. She looked up at Ryder, and he laughed.

With an arm around her waist, he spun her to face the wall. She splayed her hands, bracing herself as he pressed into her; she needed his hands on her, his body against hers. If he wanted to use the belt as foreplay, she could live with that. She might even like it. Just as long as he ended up naked.

Ryder's palm moved down her side and came to rest on her hip. With his free hand, he twisted her hair up, exposing her neck. She felt the warmth of his breath on her skin, then the soft press of his lips as his tongue swept out to taste her. She arched into him, and he pressed back, his erection hard against the small of her back.

Suddenly she felt the sharp sting of his teeth as he bit down hard enough to make her gasp. With quiet suction he released her skin and stepped away.

Rough hands found the hem of her skirt, hiking up the fabric until it bunched around her waist. Ryder popped her hips out, much like he had the first time they'd been together, except there was no desk for her to lean on.

"Is this what you were waiting for?" Ryder asked. A seductive taunt.

"It sure is." Liese craned her neck to get a glimpse of him.

A loud smack ricocheted around the hallway as his hand connected with her ass. Ryder followed the spank with the press of his palm. He repeated the action several times, until she was trembling. She heard the rustle of his shirt, followed by the clink of buttons as it hit the floor. All her senses felt magnified, her breath loud in her ears.

She jumped at the sound of leather snapping against leather, but before she could voice her uncertainty, it bit her skin. A pleasurable sting remained in its wake, particularly as Ryder pressed his hand against the tender flesh, the hot burn tempered by his touch. He issued several more quick flicks across her ass, each one eliciting a quiet moan from her.

"Fuck it," Ryder ground out, his voice thick with want.

He turned her to face him and fumbled with her skirt, cursing under his breath as he tore the button free. The zipper snagged on the way down, and in his impatience Ryder ripped it from the seam, leaving a gaping hole behind.

He issued a not-so-sincere apology as he dragged the fabric over the swell of her hips. It fell to the floor and pooled around her ankles. His palms flattened on the back of her thighs, below the curve of her ass. Liese braced her hands on his shoulders and jumped as he lifted her, wrapping her legs around his waist.

She remained sandwiched between Ryder and the wall, the thick length of his erection hidden in his pants, but their current position did not make further clothing removal easy. Liese looked to her right, and Ryder followed to see the side table a mere three feet away.

Understanding lit his features, and he tightened his grip on her thighs. Liese took the silent directive and hooked her feet at the ankles, squeezing her legs more firmly together. A few steps over and her bottom met the table. She leaned to the side and shoved her keys and mail out from under her, sending them clattering to the floor. The table creaked with her weight.

"I'll buy a new one if we break it," Ryder said as he shoved his pants and boxers down his thighs.

"I'll hold you to that; I like this table." Liese ran her hands down his chest, her eyes following the path until they rested on the erection jutting toward her.

Ryder braced one hand on either side of her, kicking his foot until his pant leg came free. He stepped on it, pulling his other foot loose.

Liese traced a line down the length of his shaft. "Is someone a little impatient?" she teased. She closed her fist around his cock and gave it a long, slow stroke.

"And it's entirely your fault."

His hands went to her thighs, inching inward to graze the juncture with his thumbs. Liese bit her lip, eyes fluttering closed as he swept a knuckle over her. It wasn't enough, though. With more aggression than she'd intended, Liese slapped his hand away. "Fuck your fingers, I want you." She stroked roughly, drawing him closer.

Ryder groaned and watched as she pressed the tip of his cock against her clit in firm, deliberate circles. He covered her hand with his own and guided his erection lower. He hooked his arms under her knees, setting Liese off balance so her head and shoulders thudded softly against the wall, then pushed inside.

The tension in his body and the dark expression on his face guaranteed she was in for one hell of a ride. She laced her fingers around the back of his neck. Ryder had her spread and opened for him, his eyes trained on where they were joined. He reared back, leaving her empty for a suspended moment only to surge forward again.

He pulled Liese closer, her ass perched at the edge of the small table. Buried deep inside her, he stilled, his breath leaving him in heavy, measured bursts, as if he were trying to regain control. On the next retreat he released one of her legs to wrap an arm around her waist, leaning into her until they were chest to chest.

He kissed her jaw and nuzzled into her throat. "God, I love you."

Liese froze as Ryder's head jerked up, his panic trumping her shock.

"I—I didn't..." he stammered, his arm tightening around her waist. "Damn it. This wasn't the way I had envisioned that particular revelation."

"You mean you didn't anticipate dropping the L-bomb while we have sex in my hallway?"

"Sort of sucks the romance out of the sentiment."

Liese shifted her hips, a reminder he was still inside her. "I think it's perfectly romantic."

"I should point out that I believe your idea of romanticism is likely skewed."

Liese squeezed her thighs around his waist. "I would've thought that was evident when you discovered my folder of porn."

Ryder's lips parted, eyes glazing, and in a particularly volatile burst of lust, he retreated only to push back into her with such force that the table knocked against the wall. She held onto his shoulders, fingernails digging into his skin as he fucked her senseless.

Soon the onslaught of an orgasm threatened, and she gasped his name in warning.

He grunted out an acknowledgement but didn't slow his quest to reach his own end, his focus singular and driven by a need she knew well.

"I love—" Liese didn't have a chance to finish her own admission. The wave of sensation overtook her, erasing all thought as she succumbed to it. She heard a loud crack and felt herself being lifted up as the legs of the table finally gave out. In one swift motion, Ryder had her braced against the wall.

She looked at him, his eyes brimming with emotion so intense she thought she might drown. With trembling fingers she touched his face. "Ryder, I l—"

The sound of the front door opening stopped her midsentence. "Lee-lee, we're here early!"

31

Celebrate, Revelate

A BLAST OF frigid air blew through the front door. Ryder had her trapped against the wall with his body, his cock still firmly seated inside her, but all the fire between them had snuffed out.

His eyes bugged wide. Liese would have laughed if she wasn't so horrified.

She unhooked one leg from around Ryder's waist and kicked at the door with her foot. "Oh my God! Don't you guys ever knock?" Her attempt to seek cover was futile; from where her mother stood, she had a stellar view of Ryder's ass.

Her mother processed the scene with a clinical eye and backed out onto the porch. "I think we should grab our bags from the car. Lee-lee's not quite ready for company."

"I thought I heard a crash. Is everything okay?" Liese heard her father ask, his voice overly loud. His fingers curled around the edge of the door to prevent her mother from closing it fully.

"Everything's fine, Marshall. She just needs a minute," her mother replied evenly, humor replaced with a subtle warning.

"Are you sure, Sandy—"

"She has *company*."

The emphasis did not go unnoticed. "Oh. Oh!" The door closed, muffling the rest of his response.

"You can put me down now," Liese said, trying to remain calm despite the bubble of panic-stricken laughter threatening to break free.

Ryder lowered her to the floor. She found her footing but held onto his shoulders to steady herself.

He used the wall as support, barring her in with his arms.

"Please tell me those aren't your parents."

"Those aren't my parents," Liese responded automatically.

"Those are your parents." He groaned.

"Yes, they are. I thought they weren't going to be here until tomorrow."

"Sweet Christ. Your mother just saw my ass." Ryder grabbed his discarded boxers from the floor and yanked them on.

"Don't worry, you have a great ass."

Ryder glared at her. "I don't see how this is funny. What the hell kind of impression am I going to make now? We were having sex in your front hallway," he said as he hastily buttoned his shirt. "I broke your damn table."

Liese looked at the decimated furniture. The calmer she remained, the less likely she would be to succumb to hysteria. "They'll get over it, and you promised to buy me a new one, so it's not really an issue, now, is it?"

Ryder looked at her as if she'd gone crazy. "That's—it's—that's not the point! The table is not the point. Fathers don't want to know their daughters have sex with their boyfriends." He cringed in disgust. "Even if they know it's happening, they sure as hell don't want to witness it firsthand, and your parents just walked in on some damn unconventional sex." Ryder jabbed his leg into his pants and nearly toppled over in his rush to re-dress.

"My mother's a sex therapist," Liese reminded him. "Wall sex is nothing compared to some of the whack-jobs she deals with." She pulled her blouse on and shimmied her way back into her ruined skirt. "At least they didn't come in when you were spanking me with your belt." Ryder blinked at her.

"What? It's true; it could've been worse."

"And what about your father? How am I supposed to introduce myself after this?"

"Meh. He'll get over it. It's not like *he* caught an eyeful of your ass."

"Why are you being so, so lackadaisical about this?" he whisper-shouted, hands flailing. He seemed on the verge of a full-blown panic attack.

"Ryder," Liese took his face in her hands. "Please calm the fuck down. I love you. You love me. My parents caught us having sex. Is it unfortunate? Sure. Is it embarrassing as hell? Definitely. Is it the end of the world?" She waited for a reply. When she didn't get one, she moved his head from side to side. "The answer to that is no, if you were wondering."

Ryder's hand covered one of hers, and he kept his eyes on her as he kissed her palm. "I would have preferred to meet them on better, more dignified terms."

"You mean fully clothed, not smelling of sex, and no broken furniture in sight?"

"You're not helping my anxiety level."

"I'm sorry. They're going to love you. I do."

He kissed her. "I'd like to hear you say that again."

"I'm sorry."

"No, the other part."

"My parents are going to love you?" Liese smiled at his put-out expression. "Oh. I love you."

"Me too." He kissed her again before he pulled away. "I have one more question."

"Shoot."

"Do your parents know about me?"

Liese hesitated, uncertain whether the truth would hurt his feelings. "No. I didn't think it would be a good idea. Do yours?"

"I don't tell Giselle and Donovan anything. They're assholes, remember?"

"Right, of course. How could I forget?" Liese smoothed her rumpled blouse, somewhat relieved they'd both been cautious.

"I suppose we should avoid telling them I'm your subordinate." "That might be prudent for the time being."

The sound of footfalls on the porch steps prevented further discussion. "Are you decent now?" Her father's voice carried through the door, and he knocked harder than necessary.

Liese took in Ryder's disheveled appearance and barely suppressed a cringe. "One second," she called as she adjusted Ryder's shirt and tried to tame his hair with little success. She could hear her dad grumbling on the other side. "You ready?" she asked Ryder as she prepared to open the door.

Ryder stepped forward silently to stand beside her, his face a shade of red appropriate for the Christmas season. They were a united front of embarrassment as he twined his fingers with hers.

Liese opened the door. Her parents stood on the porch: her father laden with bags and suitcases while her mother carried her purse and a magnum of wine. Her father looked annoyed; her mother looked ecstatic.

"Lee-lee!"

Liese found herself folded into her mother's embrace. Her

father sighed and stayed put. Releasing her, her mother inspected Ryder with curiosity. "And you must be Lee-lee's boyfriend. It's so very lovely to meet you. I'm Sandy, and this is Marshall." She motioned to Liese's father, who still hadn't moved. Ryder extended his hand but Sandy ignored it and hugged him.

When her mother finished gushing over Ryder, she moved out of the way to allow Liese's father to come inside. He had to turn sideways to get through the door. He dropped the bags with a grunt and lifted Liese off the ground in a bear hug. He thumped her on the back as he kissed the top of her head. "Good to see you, Liesie." Keeping one arm around her shoulder, he turned to Ryder and extended a meaty palm.

Ryder cleared his throat and took the offered hand. "Ryder Whitehall, sir."

Her father raised one bushy eyebrow and scoffed. "It's Marshall, son, not sir."

"Yes, sir, I mean Marshall. It's nice to meet you, sir."

Marshall laughed and dropped his arm from Liese's shoulder only to put it around Ryder's. While they were the same height, Liese's father was almost twice as broad. "I think I like this one." He directed the comment over his shoulder to Liese, as he was already propelling Ryder down the hallway. "I think you need a beer, son. Or maybe you're more of a scotch man."

"Scotch sounds good," Ryder agreed, leaving Liese and her mother in the foyer with the suitcases, presents, and broken table.

The embarrassment dissipated as drinks were poured and then refilled. Once Ryder relaxed, he was himself: charismatic, charming, and articulate. And her parents seemed to love him after they got past their initial introduction. When her mother invariably asked how they'd met, Ryder told them he also worked at FAHL, neglecting to mention he was the principal. Liese would drop that bomb later, when there were several states separating them.

Her dad looked suspicious. He was a snooper by nature. Considering his past profession, she wouldn't have put it past him to have done a search on her school. Ryder's name was uncommon and definitely memorable, but if her dad put two and two together, he didn't mention it.

The days that followed were a whirlwind of entertaining her parents, which meant she didn't have much time to spend with Ryder. Liese pushed aside her disappointment and tried to enjoy the time with her family. This time next year, things would be different. She and Ryder wouldn't be hiding their relationship, and she'd have the pleasure of meeting his whacked-out family just as he'd met hers. Well, hopefully not exactly the way he'd met hers.

Ryder stopped by early on Christmas Eve, unable to make dinner the following evening as he had his own family gathering to attend. She took solace in his lack of enthusiasm at spending time away from her. He assured her he would try to duck out early so he could make it back for dessert.

Later that same evening, Liese walked a reluctant Ryder to the door. "When do I get to be alone with you?" he asked.

"My mom gave me the impression they're leaving in two days. But you never know with my parents. I see them so rarely, I don't want to push them out the door."

Ryder groaned. "That's too long. Couldn't you sneak out one night? Come to my house? You must be tired of sleeping on that pullout couch."

Liese slipped her hands under his coat and ran them up his back. "It's not that bad. In a couple of days you'll have me all to yourself for the rest of the holidays."

"I plan to capitalize on that time, you know."

"I'm banking on it. I already have my bag packed." Three-equarters of her suitcase contained lingerie. She couldn't wait to model it all for him, and have him remove it piece by piece.

"Why bother packing a bag? I plan to have you naked and chained to my bed."

"Promises, promises—" Standing in the front hallway, she was reminded of the last time they'd been together, and what he had done to her before they were interrupted.

"I should go," Ryder said when she pressed her body tighter to his. She could feel his growing problem against her stomach. "You should," Liese said as they separated, staring at his crotch with longing.

He planted a chaste kiss on her cheek and made a swift departure.

Marissa called the following day, all Christmas cheer, to announce she would be in Fullerton later in the afternoon for dinner. Liese had extended the invitation to Blake as well, who had obviously been part of Marissa's travel plan.

A text came in from Ryder as the five of them were sitting down to eat, but the message was an autocorrected jumble of words she couldn't decipher. Ten minutes later she found out exactly what he'd been trying to tell her when he showed up at her door with Tiffany in tow. His strained smile and Tiffany's mascara-runny eyes told her Christmas dinner at the Whitehall residence had not been a joyous occasion.

"Tiffany! I'm so glad Ryder brought you!" Liese exclaimed as she put an arm around the girl's shoulder and ushered her inside, as if she'd expected them all along. She threw Ryder a questioning look, but he shook his head.

"Thanks." Tiffany gave her a halfhearted smile and sniffed. "Can I use your bathroom?"

"Sure thing. It's just there." Liese pointed down the hall. "What happened?" she asked Ryder once Tiffany was out of ear-shot.

"Our parents."

"Care to elaborate?" Liese eyed him skeptically.

"We were discussing potential colleges for Tiffany, and there were some issues with her choices. My own were cited in my parents' arguments. Tiffany came to my defense. It didn't go over well for her."

"Oh, Ryder, I'm so sorry." Liese opened her arms, and he embraced her.

"It's fine. I can deal with their ridiculous expectations, but Tiff shouldn't have to." She could feel his nose skim her neck and then his lips. Ryder released her as Tiffany emerged from the bathroom. He held out a hand to his sister and pulled her into his side, giving her an affectionate squeeze. "Feel better?" he asked.

She threw her arms around him, nodding into his chest. She looked more at ease than she had when she'd first arrived.

"Ready to meet my family?" Liese asked.

Tiffany's eyes lit up. "Ryder says they're nice. Is Marissa here? I really like her."

"She sure is. Come on." Liese threaded her arm through Tiffany's and led her in the direction of the noise. "Hey, everyone," Liese said brightly as they entered the cramped dining room. "Look who made it."

Blake choked on his wine, and Marissa patted him on the back. Liese's mother let out an excited shriek as she jumped up from her seat, and her father, who'd been on the verge of a smile, froze as his gaze settled on Tiffany.

"And he brought his sister," Marissa chimed in, with a look toward Liese's dad. She waved the hand that wasn't busy patting Blake's back. "Hey, Tiff, glad you and Ryder could make it."

Marshall relaxed back into his chair. Evidently brother and sister hadn't been the first blood tie that occurred to him.

"Oh, his *sister*," Sandy exclaimed. "Aren't you just the loveliest little thing? Come sit next to me. Liese, be a dear and grab two more place settings." Her mom guided Tiffany to the table and pulled up an extra chair. "Ryder, why don't we just slide a chair in right next to Blake? He was telling me he works at FAHL, too. Isn't that funny? The acronym for the school you teach at sounds like *fail*."

Blake coughed. "Teach? Whitehall isn't a teacher; he's the principal."

And so began the most awkward Christmas dinner in the history of the world.

32

Still Life & Resolutions

NO ONE MOVED. It was as though the entire table had become a still life painting, faces immobilized by shock. Then between one blink and the next, the scene came to life.

"Pardon me?" Marshall swiped at his mouth with his napkin, crushing it as he set it beside his plate, his eyes on Ryder. He looked calm, but Liese knew better.

"Ah, shit," Blake said sheepishly.

Ryder cleared his throat. His eyes darted around the table and paused at his sister before locking on Liese's dad. "Blake is correct. I'm the principal at FAHL, not a teacher."

"So you're saying my daughter works under you?"

Liese could see her dad fighting to remain composed. His eye did that weird twitching thing she'd grown accustomed to in her late teens, back when she spent her days stepping over the proverbial line. The buffer of company forced her dad to remain on his side of the table. Ryder, however, had a prime seat beside his would-be Christmas destroyer. Liese didn't want a full-on boxing match at Christmas dinner, but she was pissed enough at Blake to hope Ryder might dump the gravy in his lap. When the opportunity arose, she would be first in line to tear a strip off him for being so thoughtless.

"It's not what you—" Liese stopped short, unable to finish because it was exactly what her father thought.

A muffled giggle came from Liese's right. Every head turned to Tiffany, who had her hand clamped over her mouth, shoulders shaking.

"I don't see the humor here," Marshall said.

Tiffany didn't seem the least bit intimidated. "You said work under. Like, work *under*."

"Tiffany!" Ryder exclaimed.

"What? It's true, and it's funny." She giggled, unapologetic.

Marissa snickered, and Liese's mom covered a grin with her napkin. "It is funny," she said. "And rather ironic considering the circumstances under which we met Ryder."

"What circumstances?" Tiffany and Blake asked at the same time.

"Never mind. Marshall, can you please pass the gravy? Dinner's getting cold." Sandy busied herself with scooping stuffing onto her plate.

"It's a good thing I like you, son. Otherwise I'd put a bullet in your ass."

"You know the rules, Marshall. No threats at the dinner table," Liese's mother said sweetly.

"It was simply a statement of fact, dear," Marshall replied as he passed the gravy boat.

Liese and her mom shared a look. Crisis averted, at least for the time being.

Three days later, Liese lay on the couch, her feet in Ryder's lap. The Christmas Dinner Crisis—as Ryder had aptly named it— was over. Blake had called her the next day to apologize, then followed with a call to Ryder. They'd talked about more than just Christmas dinner, it seemed, and Liese thought the tension between them might have eased some. Her parents had left for California two days ago, and she'd been at Ryder's place ever since. Despite the shock of the impromptu revelation, Liese's parents eventually took the news in stride. They made it clear that their reaction had come from a place of concern, not judgment, and they trusted her to make informed decisions.

Ryder commandeered the remote control from its perch on her knee and flipped stations. "Has Sandy called yet?"

"No, but she's texted me three times to let me know which state they're in. An hour ago they were passing through Oklahoma. How's Tiffany?"

"She's a teenager: angsty, moody, and generally irritable."

"Ha ha." Liese nudged his thigh with her foot. "You know what I mean."

Ryder sighed. "She's as okay as she can be, considering. She has one more semester before she's off to college and out of that house."

"They're really that bad, aren't they?"

"Yes."

"I'll have to meet them one day." The idea both intrigued and terrified her. If Ryder's job wasn't good enough, she couldn't imagine how they would respond to hers.

Ryder sighed. "I know. I'm trying to hold off as long as possible. I need you to be so blinded by your love for me that you can look past their myriad of flaws."

"You met my parents. They're hardly conventional, and you still want to be with me," she pointed out.

"True, but Sandy and Marshall are personable and pleasant. My parents have the warmth of an iceberg."

"I'm just saying it's inevitable."

"Not if they die in a freak accident."

"Ryder!"

He grabbed her ankles, uncrossed them and slid smoothly between her legs. "I don't want to talk about my family. I've had enough of them over the past week and not enough of you." He braced his weight on his forearms as his lips met hers, ceasing conversation.

Ryder made good on his promise to keep her naked and in his bed for the remainder of the holidays. Liese spent little time in anything other than the vast array of lingerie she'd packed. When she bothered to put on real clothes, she found herself laid out on the closest surface available and promptly undressed. Ryder was insatiable, and Liese was happy to be the antidote for his appetite.

Marissa called a few times, mostly to complain about work. But Liese didn't feel too badly for her. Blake had driven to the city yesterday for a visit and stayed the night. So when Marissa invited Liese and Ryder to bring in the new year with them, she jumped to persuade Ryder to go. No one knew them in New York, and they could be together without running into colleagues or friends.

"You really want to go, don't you?" Ryder seemed less than thrilled about the idea.

"Not if you're not there." Liese followed the seam of his jeans with her fingernail.

"You want me to spend New Year's with Stone?"

"No, I want you to spend New Year's with me."

"But he'll be there." Ryder picked up her hand and brought it to his lips. He kissed his way along her wrist and up her forearm into the crook of her elbow. "Wouldn't you rather stay here, where we can celebrate in private?"

"As much as I enjoy an evening of bodily worship, I want to do something normal with you. We can't go anywhere together here, but we can in the city." When he looked like he was going to argue, she straddled his lap. "Please? He apologized for Christmas dinner, and didn't you talk things through? Marissa is my closest friend, and they're dating. It may be uncomfortable at first, but please, can't we just try?" Liese looked at him imploringly.

"Besides—" Liese traced the shell of his ear with her fingertip. "If all goes well, maybe you two can reconcile your differences." Hopefully without duking it out, she added silently.

Ryder looked doubtful. But if she could catch him at a moment of weakness, he might relent. Liese shifted, nestling his erection snugly at the apex of her thighs. "You were teenagers, Ryder. Teenagers do stupid things, like fight over girls. What if you'd ended up with her? Then you wouldn't have me, would you?"

"There is that." Ryder's grip tightened on her hips.

Liese ran her fingers through his hair. "Please? I can get dressed up, wear sexy lingerie underneath. You could peel it off later with your teeth. We could get a hotel room," she added, running her hands down his chest. "We could have sex in the Jacuzzi."

"We're getting a hotel room with a Jacuzzi?"

"So we're going? Her palms slid under his shirt, connecting with bare skin.

"Don't think I don't see what you're trying to do." Ryder's hand slipped under her shirt as well.

"Is it working?"

"Yes."

They didn't make it from the living room couch to the bedroom.

Ryder agreed to New Year's in New York, but voiced his concern about Sean's presence in the city. To put his mind at ease, Marissa made a point of avoiding their usual haunts as she made plans. Since the arrest Sean hadn't tried to make contact. A stalking charge had been issued, with a warning that a subsequent offense would result in third-degree felony charges. Liese hoped the potential for jail time would be the deterrent Sean needed.

In the end, the occasion went better than Liese or Ryder had expected, with no appearances from Sean, and Ryder and Blake finally putting to rest their tumultuous history. A bottle of Grey Goose could go a long way in loosening people up, even Ryder.

Ryder did manage to book a hotel room with a Jacuzzi, which they put to good use, and a four-poster king bed. He took Liese up on her offer to allow him to remove her lingerie with his teeth after he'd secured her to the bed with the fur-lined handcuffs she'd purchased for the special occasion.

But once the holidays came to a close, Liese and Ryder went back to struggling to find adequate time to spend together. Spoiled by the uninterrupted span of time over Christmas, Liese had forgotten how challenging it could be to work around his busy schedule with their need for discretion. When she did stay the night at his place, they tended to capitalize on the alone time, which meant she was tired the next day. But the days she dragged herself around from lack of sleep were regrettably few.

Today it was the beginning of the week, a rare Monday evening when Ryder didn't have a meeting to attend. They sat at his kitchen island, sipping wine and comparing calendars, trying to fit in another sleepover. But all of Ryder's meetings conflicted with hers.

"We'll have all weekend," he promised.

"What about the art show at Tiffany's school? Isn't that this Friday? You can't miss that."

"I thought that was next week." Ryder double-checked the dates and discovered Liese was right.

She didn't bother to express her disappointment over not being able to come along. There was always a chance they could be seen together by someone they knew. Besides, his parents would be there, and this occasion didn't seem the best for an introduction. According to Ryder, they weren't supportive of Tiffany's artistic pursuits. It was ludicrous that they didn't see her talent. Liese had learned the painting in Ryder's living room was indeed a portrait of a younger him, which Tiffany had painted from an old photograph. Liese didn't think she could hold her tongue if they referred to it as a "silly hobby" in front of her.

"It shouldn't run too late. I can call you on the way home . . ." he trailed off, apologetic.

Liese didn't want to be upset, but it was hard not to feel jilted. "What if something happens with your parents and Tiffany wants to stay with you?"

"I doubt that will happen—"Ryder hedged. His phone rang and he checked the number. "I'm sorry; I have to get this."

Liese sighed, drained the rest of her wine, and grabbed the bottle to replenish her glass. She shoved down the annoyance at being interrupted. Their conversation had seemed headed toward an argument anyway. Although, those were typically followed by hot sex. Ryder stood and paced the room, giving one-word answers to the other end of the line.

"I'd love to accept the offer," he finally said, looking over at her with an excited grin. "Thank you. Yes, tomorrow would be perfect. I'll speak with you then." Ryder ended the call and tossed the phone on the counter.

Liese regarded him curiously. Ryder rarely looked as thrilled as he did now, unless she was naked and offering her ass up for a spanking.

He scooped her into his arms, his smile widening. "I got it."

"Pardon?" She had no idea what the hell he was talking about.

"Remember that position I told you about before the holidays? The one in Montgomery County?" Excitement blended his words together.

"The superintendency?" Liese remembered the conversation: the one they'd had after Sean came to the school's holiday play. Ryder had never brought up the job again.

"That's the one. I interviewed for it, and I've been offered the position, effective at the end of this semester."

Liese's eyes widened as she processed the information. "But that's only a few weeks away! Why didn't you tell me?"

"Because I didn't want to get your hopes up. I thought I could just surprise you with good news." He set her down on the island. "Surprise!"

The granite countertop seemed as good a place as any to celebrate their newfound freedom and Ryder's new job.

33

Drop the Bomb

WHEN THE SEMESTER ended, Ryder left FAHL for the superintendency position, and a new female principal took over his administrative role. She was a take-charge woman who didn't put up with any crap, especially Harvey's. Ryder had set the wheels in motion prior to his departure, and by the end of the month, the assistant principal had been cited for workplace harassment by three staff members and offered early retirement.

Despite Ryder's departure, he and Liese had agreed it would be best to keep things low key until the end of the school year, when speculation and rumors would have less impact on her. It took time to find a balance with all the changes, but they made it work.

In the meantime, she'd managed to secure a librarian position at a school in Berks County, which was also close enough to commute without a move. Though she would miss the friends she'd made at FAHL, she knew it was best to move on. A fresh start would clear her head and remove any question about the beginnings of her relationship with Ryder. Now that the school year was hours away from being over, Liese could almost feel herself breathing more freely.

"I'm picking you up at the end of the day," Ryder said as he adjusted his tie in the mirror.

Liese stopped mid mascara-swipe. "Can you repeat that, please?"

"And I'm going to drop you off at FAHL this morning on my way to work," he said matter-of-factly.

Liese slid the mascara wand home, giving it a twist to secure it. "Are you crazy?"

"No. I'm slightly compulsive and overbearing, but otherwise I'm mentally fit." This time his eyes met hers.

Liese crossed her arms over her chest. "I'm not sure that's a good idea."

Ignoring her rigid stance, Ryder embraced her.

"It's the last day of school," she argued.

"Yes."

"You don't think its a little in-your-face to drop me off and pick me up?"

"Hardly. I've been gone for five months, and you'll be starting your new position in the fall. Why does it matter if the people we used to work with know we're together?"

"You can pick me up, but you can't drop me off."

"That doesn't make sense. How will you get to work?" Ryder reasoned.

She recognized his persuasive tone. It was the same one he used when he wanted to try something new in the bedroom. The man loved to role play. It kept things interesting, especially on the rare occasions when she got to be the principal.

Liese frowned. She hadn't thought that far ahead. She didn't want to fuel rumors. Lord knew there'd already been enough of them when he left. Thankfully, none of them had involved her. "You can drop me off at the coffee shop down the street."

She could feel him trying to will her into changing her mind, but she held firm. She didn't want her last day tainted by people running their mouths and asking overly personal questions.

Ryder sighed, defeated. "Fine, but I'm picking you up at the front doors."

Later that afternoon, Liese exchanged contact information and made promises to keep in touch with colleagues as she left the building. Blake carried her box of parting gifts from staff and students alike. She would miss FAHL.

Janet and Emily had followed her out and were now debating whether they wanted to go straight home or out for an end-of-year celebratory drink. Liese wavered as she scanned the parking lot for Ryder's Lexus. She didn't have to search hard; he'd parked as close to the building as he could get without driving up the front steps. As soon as she hit the bottom of the stairs he stepped out of the car and started toward her. Liese wished they'd discussed how forthcoming he planned to be. She braced for her colleagues' reactions.

Blake stepped over to greet Ryder, shuffling the box to one side so they could engage in some kind of ritualistic man handshake. Over the past several months she and Ryder had spent a lot of time with Marissa and Blake, and the two men had become friends. They bumped shoulders and patted each other on the back.

"Hey Ry, what's going on?" Blake asked. "You leave something behind?"

Ryder pursed his lips. "In a manner of speaking."

Emily and Janet looked surprised, but they greeted their former principal and made polite conversation while Liese hung back and tried to decipher his plan of attack. As if sensing her discomfort, Ryder pointed to the box under Blake's arm.

"Starting a pink coffee mug collection?"

"Hardly, the box of crap belongs to this one." Blake inclined his head at Liese.

"Oh?" He looked to Liese, and when she nodded, he took the box. Popping his trunk, he sauntered casually to the rear of his vehicle and deposited the box inside.

The silence that ensued reminded Liese of Christmas dinner. Emily and Janet looked utterly baffled as he closed the trunk.

"Well, it was nice to see you." Ryder addressed them cordially.

He slipped an arm around Liese's waist and tucked her into his side, his hand dropping low on her hip. She looked up at him, shocked by his overt display of physical affection. That was until he upped the ante and bent to kiss her. His lips met hers, lingering longer than necessary. Emily gasped, Janet made a strange noise, and Blake just stood there with his hands in his pockets. The ladies' bewildered looks turned to shock as they finally figured out why Ryder had stopped by the school.

"Are you ready to go?" he asked.

"Sure." Liese fought to hold a strained smile. "Have a great summer, guys."

She couldn't make eye contact as she rounded the car and waited for Ryder to open the passenger door. She slipped into the seat, palms sweaty and knees shaking. With one hand on the door and the other on the hood Ryder ducked his head. "That wasn't too bad, was it?" He brought his mouth to hers. And if that wasn't bold enough, he sucked on her bottom lip, if only for a second, before releasing it. At her outraged gasp he whispered, "Be thankful I didn't smack your ass in public. Imagine the response that would have gleaned."

A burst of laughter slipped out, and she slapped her palm over her mouth as Ryder closed the door. He crossed the front of the car, smiling at her dumbstruck colleagues.

Ryder slid into the driver's seat and started the engine. They waved in tandem at her gawking friends, and Liese watched them shrink into the background through the rearview mirror as they left FAHL behind.

"I've been thinking," Ryder said later as he sipped a glass of wine, idly running his fingers up and down her arm.

Dusk crept in, casting long shadows on the deck as evening turned to night. The sun threw off a pink glow as it made its way toward the horizon, turning the clouds the color of cotton candy. "That's new," Liese taunted, rolling her head toward him. She was on her third glass of wine, celebrating the end of the school year on the privacy of her back deck.

Ryder shifted in his chair as he ran his free hand down the front of his shirt, right where his tie should be. That put her on alert.

"Is everything okay?"

"Everything's fine." His tense smile told a different story. "Come here, please." He tugged gently on her hand.

Picking up her wine, Liese moved from her seat to his. "What's going on up here?" She tapped his temple. "You look way too serious for summer vacation." She settled in his lap, drawing her legs up so she could sling them over the arm of his chair. His palm traveled along her bare calf.

"Sorry," he said. "I've been thinking about my current living situation and what that will look like in the long term."

"And what conclusion have you drawn?" Liese fought off a wave of apprehension.

Ryder had already mentioned moving closer to his job, but he'd only said it in passing. Liese's commute to her new school, while relatively short, took her in the opposite direction. If either of them moved closer to their job, it would put more distance between them, not less. Liese had grown accustomed to staying at his house most nights of the week, or having him at her place. She didn't want to lose that.

"Well, I was wondering about your thoughts on the issue," Ryder said as he continued to focus on their linked hands.

"On the issue of commuting?" Liese asked.

"I know you've talked about buying a house. I'm curious as to whether this is still something you're considering."

"Oh, right." Liese inhaled deeply. "For now I guess I like this place well enough. I'd like to get a feel for my new school before

I make any life-altering decisions." "I see." Ryder's throat bobbed.

"What's going on? Why are you being so . . . sketchy?"

"Sketchy?"

"Yes. You're all shifty-eyed and vague, asking these questions that aren't going anywhere. You're stressing me out."

"I'm sorry; it's not intentional." Ryder shifted under her and took her glass, setting it on the table between their chairs. "I was wondering whether you might be interested in moving in with me."

"Come again?"

"I haven't even come a first time."

"Smartass. Are you serious?"

"Completely."

Liese could hardly believe it. Ryder made rational decisions, based on carefully thought-out plans. As alluring as the idea might be, it certainly didn't speak to logic. "We've spent all this time being careful and keeping things low key just to blow our cover by moving in together as soon as we start dating public-ly?"

Ryder laughed. "I think I managed to do that when I picked you up this afternoon. It's not exactly a stealth mission, Liese. Neither of us works there anymore; it's a non-issue."

After months of being cautious, of only going out in public together when they were at least an hour outside of Fullerton, they no longer needed to hide. It was strange.

"Besides, I want you to be the first person I see at the beginning and end of my day."

Her heart fluttered. "Are you sure it's a good idea?"

"Is that a yes?"

Liese mulled the prospect over. Of course it was a yes. Preoccupied with what would happen if they moved farther apart, she hadn't considered he would solve the problem by asking her to live with him.

"I can see the allure," she said thoughtfully. She ran her fingers through his hair and shifted to straddle him. The soles of her feet settled on the deck, and she leaned into his solid warmth.

"I'm greedy," he said, as though he still needed to persuade her. "I want more time with you—more mornings and evenings and weekends. I suppose now that we're at the point where we can be open, I want to push the boundaries. And just so we're clear, I'm not referring to sexual boundaries. I believe we've been pushing those from the beginning."

"Thanks for the clarification." Liese smiled.

"People will always talk. We're beyond that. I want you with me. The question is, do you want the same thing?" "Very much so." Liese kissed him softly.

"You'll move in with me?"

"Yes, I'll move in with you. I'm already halfway there."

"This is true. You know, I thought I'd have to work much harder to persuade you," Ryder admitted.

"Aren't you fortunate I'm easy?" Liese teased. She smoothed her palms over his arms, up his biceps to his shoulders.

"I'm quite fortunate, actually." Ryder nuzzled her neck, his lips against her collarbone. "I'm also fortunate you're intelligent and sexy and loud in bed—"

"I am not!" Liese exclaimed.

Ryder's hands grazed the underside of her breasts. She swiveled her hips. His erection lay snug between her thighs, and though it was still constricted by clothing, it provided the friction she wanted.

"You're not what? Intelligent?" "No." She tugged on his hair.

"Sexy?"

"Ryder!"

"Oh, you don't think you're loud in bed?" He grinned, his hands moving lower.

"I can be quiet when I need to be," Liese whispered.

"That's true. You were very, very quiet that one time in my office," he replied, his mouth against her ear.

"No so much that time in your car, though."

"But that time on your back deck? That was amazing." Ryder's hands found their way under her shirt, his fingertips whispering over the swell of her breasts.

"We haven't . . ." Liese stopped when she realized he was referring to their current situation.

Ryder nipped gently at her neck before he kissed her. His hands moved slowly, unrushed and deliberate, as he skimmed over her nipples through the satin of her bra. Liese ground herself against him, moaning quietly at the sensation.

"Shhh . . . you don't want to disturb the neighbors," Ryder goaded.

She ignored him and moaned again, louder this time, and was quietly thankful for the thick barrier of trees surrounding her property. No one could hear her unless she called his name at the top of her lungs.

She slid her hands down his chest and found his belt buckle, pulling on the clasp. She popped the button on his pants and dipped her hand inside to find warm, smooth skin, hard and ready for her.

"Did you want to go inside?" Ryder teased, hands tightening on her hips.

"I'm good here," Liese whispered, standing as she pulled her dress over her head and discarded it on the deck.

His gaze lingered on her pale satin underwear as he leaned forward and kissed just below her navel.

Soft light came from the window behind them, and Liese could see shadows on her skin. She reached behind her and unclasped her bra, letting it drop to the deck. He hooked his thumbs into the waistband of her panties and dragged them down her thighs. She steadied herself, one hand on each of his shoulders as she lifted one foot and then the other. Ryder discarded the scrap of fabric and pulled her forward to straddle him once again. The hard length of him pressed against her. Liese rose, and Ryder gripped his erection. When she sank down slowly, they groaned in tandem.

"Shh, you wouldn't want the neighbors to hear you." Liese

provoked him as she rocked her hips, keeping their bodies flush, her movements gentle and controlled. She grabbed the tail of his shirt and pulled it over his head, tossing it aside.

"You're such an exhibitionist," Ryder said through clenched teeth.

Liese's mouth moved along his shoulder toward his chin. "Don't pretend you don't like it." She nipped at his bottom lip.

"I wouldn't dream of it." He lifted his hips, his hands grabbed her ass, moving her faster over him.

Liese braced herself, lacing her fingers behind his neck as she allowed him to set the pace, going harder only when the sensation began to overwhelm her. She succumbed to the current that ignited in the pit of her stomach, shooting through her like lightning.

Ryder's head dropped against the back of the chair, the tendons in his neck straining as his eyes closed and his lips parted. Liese watched, entranced, as he shuddered. He pulled her tight against him, then bowed forward to bury his face in her hair. She hummed into his shoulder and waited for his ragged breathing to calm.

"I suppose we could have gone inside to do that," Ryder said, his head lolling on the back of the chair, eyes half-closed.

"We can always go inside and do it again."

Ryder's eyes opened. "You're insatiable."

"Only where you're concerned."

"I suppose it's a good thing you'll be moving in with me then, isn't it?" He stroked her cheek.

"It's a very good thing," Liese agreed. She rose to her feet, extending a hand. He linked his fingers with hers and followed her inside, leaving their clothing strewn across the deck.

EPILOGUE

Two Years Later

"LIESE? SWEETHEART, I'M home!"

The sound of Ryder's voice coming from downstairs roused her. Their bedroom was dark, which disoriented her. She'd only intended to lie down for a minute or two before she started dinner. Liese rolled over to look at the clock on the nightstand. It was six-thirty. She'd been out for two hours. And dinner was still in the fridge, rather than ready to eat.

She pushed herself up to sitting, but it took an ungodly amount of energy to accomplish the feat. She had to be sick. That was the only logical explanation. The mild roll of her stomach confirmed it. "I'm coming!"

"Not without me, I hope." Ryder stood in the doorway with his jacket open, his tie loosened. His cocky smirk fell away as he processed Liese's rather disheveled state. "Are you unwell?"

Liese pushed her hair back, trying to smooth it into some semblance of order. She doubted her success and didn't have the energy to care. "It's probably the flu. It's been going around.

Yesterday one of the students threw up in the middle of the library."

"We've had a few people at the office out lately for the same sort of thing."

He shrugged out of his suit jacket and pulled his tie over his head, messing up his hair in the process. Liese confirmed illness as a likely possibility when no tingles of desire followed the unfastening of his cufflinks.

"I should make dinner." The words came out, but she didn't move from her spot on the bed. In fact, gravity seemed to want to pull her back to a prone position.

Ryder folded his jacket and placed it neatly on the dresser before coming over to sit on the mattress beside her. Leaning in, he pressed his lips to her forehead. "You're not warm, but maybe you should stay in bed. We have chicken soup in the freezer?"

Liese nodded, grateful that Ryder knew his way around a kitchen as well as he did the bedroom. Not that chicken noodle soup was difficult, but the only thing her father knew how to prepare was meat over an open flame. Ryder was an amazing cook. Unfortunately, he was rarely home before Liese, so he only had an opportunity to showcase that particular set of talents on the weekend.

Liese must have fallen back asleep, because she woke up in the middle of the night, her stomach howling up a storm. Ryder had obviously changed her, as she was dressed in a satiny sheath, rather than her usual nighttime nothing. He lay on his side next to her, arm tucked under the pillow, as close to her as he could get without actually touching. She closed her eyes, unmotivated to get up, but her stomach growled again, the discomfort too pervasive to ignore. Slipping carefully out of bed so as not to disturb Ryder, she pulled her robe over her shoulders and padded down to the kitchen.

She blinked against the harsh light of the fridge and looked longingly at the pot of soup on the middle shelf. It would take too much time and effort to heat up something like that. Liese settled on a piece of buttered bread and a banana, both easy on her stomach and simple to throw together.

It was after three in the morning by the time she returned to bed. She hadn't had much hope of falling back to sleep, having already clocked more than eight hours, but the next time she opened her eyes, it was to the sound of her alarm clock in the morning.

"You should stay in bed today," Ryder said as he stepped out from his closet, suit in hand. He wore only boxer briefs, and Liese stared unabashedly at his mostly naked form.

"I feel much better than I did last night. My stomach is settled."

Instead of answering, Ryder passed her the phone.

"I'm fine. Really. It's too much of a hassle to stay home."

Ryder lifted a belt from the hook on the inside of the closet door and ran it across his palm suggestively. "Before you decide to go in, I think you should consider whether you feel well enough to be bent over my desk."

"Um . . ." Usually she'd jump at the chance, but today she questioned whether she'd enjoy herself at all. Despite all the sleep she'd gotten, she was dragging.

"That you would even hesitate tells me you need to call in." Ryder took her phone back and dialed the number for her.

So Liese did as Ryder demanded: stayed in bed all day. She only went downstairs for food and drinks. She didn't do anything remotely house-chorish, aware that Ryder would be able to tell. She just read a book, napping on and off. Mild nausea came in waves, and while she hated to admit it, Ryder had been right about her not going into work. However, by midafternoon the sick feeling had abated, and though she was still tired, she felt much better.

Ryder came home early—or earlier than usual—and Liese was in the kitchen, preparing dinner when he slipped his arms around her waist and kissed her neck. "Feeling better?"

She leaned back into his embrace. "Much. It must have been one of those twenty-four-hour bugs."

He skimmed the tip of his nose along the side of her neck. "You smell phenomenal."

"It's dessert."

He smiled against her skin. "You *must* be feeling better if you're offering yourself."

Liese laughed and turned around in his arms, fingering the collar of his shirt. "There's apple crisp in the oven."

"Hmmm . . . while lovely, that's not nearly as enticing as you served with ice cream."

"Why don't you get changed? Dinner's almost ready. We can talk about dessert later. Maybe we can even have that conversation in your office, on your desk."

Ryder placed a lingering kiss on her lips, a promise of things to come.

Forty-five minutes later, the apple crisp sat cooling on the counter and Liese was spread out on the sheets in nothing but her bra and panties. Ryder—fully naked, sat on his knees between her parted thighs. He hadn't been keen on the desk, thinking her fragile after having been ill. It didn't matter much; all she wanted was him, the location irrelevant.

"Is this new?" He traced the satin edge of her bra.

"No. I've had it forever." It was plain and something she typically saved for work or nights when she knew Ryder wouldn't be up for naked loving.

He cupped her breasts, squeezing them together, creating deeper cleavage. "You should wear it more often."

"It's plain."

"It fabulous." He bent down and kissed the swell. "You always look stunning, but this is unbelievable."

He loved her in lingerie. Some weekends he'd crank the heat and have her parade around in garters and a bra, panties be damned. They'd have marathon sex for hours, on all manner of surfaces. Ryder's favorite location tended to be the desk in his office. Liese's favorite was in front of the fireplace in his office on a bed of pillows.

"And this is extraordinarily convenient," he popped the front clasp, freeing her breasts from the satin.

When he brought his lips to her tight nipples, she gasped, the sensations seeming more heightened than usual. Ryder was gentle as he loved her, taking special care to go slow, seeing as she was just getting over a bout of the flu, or whatever it had been. She came twice before he'd even entered her.

Two days later, Liese was back in bed, having thrown up at work in the middle of the day. She'd scheduled a doctor's appointment, worried she had one of those horrible viruses running rampant through the schools that lasted for weeks, and her physician could see her the following morning. She hated taking the time off work, but it was necessary. She couldn't risk passing the flu to students or colleagues.

She was too tired to concentrate on reading, but if she napped now, Ryder might let her sleep through dinner, and she'd be up in the middle of the night again. Needing a distraction from the allure of her pillow, she called Marissa.

"Are you playing hooky today?" she asked by way of greeting.

"I'm sick and home in bed. And I'm bored."

"So you called me? How thoughtful. This better not mean you're going to cancel plans this weekend. Blake has really been looking forward to bromancing with Ryder, and you know how much I love making Ride-Me squirm with inappropriate sexual references."

"Last time you almost had him convinced we'd dated for a while."

"I know, right? I should consider a second career in acting. But seriously, you're not calling to cancel, are you?"

Blake had moved to NYC last year to be closer to Marissa and now worked at a fabulous art school in the city. It was the perfect place for him; the students at his school were prime candidates for some of the most renowned arts colleges in the state. The downside of his moving all the way to NYC was that Marissa didn't have a reason to come visit as often, and with Ryder's job, they didn't have as many free weekends to get away as they'd like.

"We're not canceling plans—unless I'm still puking on Friday."

"If it's the flu, you should be fine by then."

"I don't know. I've felt like crap for the past week."

"A whole week? That's not like you. Usually you bounce right back."

"Maybe it's an age thing."

"Because you're so ancient," Marissa joked. Then after a short pause she added, "Maybe you're preggers."

Liese snorted. "Yeah, right. Don't think that's even a remote possibility. No martinis for nine months? No thanks!"

They chatted for a while longer, making tentative plans for the weekend, until Liese heard Ryder downstairs and said good-bye.

That night, she had some seriously strange dreams. In the morning she was exhausted and relieved to be able to sleep in until her doctor's appointment. Ryder was already gone by the time she dragged herself out of bed and got into the shower.

Less than an hour later, she sat in a waiting room with a bunch of sniffling, whiny children. She closed her eyes in an attempt to tune out the unhappy kids and their equally unimpressed moth-ers, waiting for her name to be called. Ryder had gotten her the referral to Dr. Glass, one of the few female family doctors in the area, which was her preference. After having been with the same doctor for the past four years in NYC, Liese had been reluctant to make the change, but driving three hours for a yearly checkup wasn't reasonable. Fortunately, Dr. Glass was lovely and had turned out to be a fabulous physician.

Finally, it was her turn. After they'd covered the basic ques-tions, Dr. Glass asked, "When was your last period?"

"I've been getting the shot for a long time. I only spot once in a while, so no real periods for me for years."

"And your last shot was scheduled ten weeks ago, but it looks like you had to cancel."

Liese felt her eyes go wide as she rewound to two and a half months ago, searching her mind for something that would've made her cancel such an important appointment. It took a min-ute, but she finally remembered. Tiffany had been home from college for spring break. Her parents put ridiculous restrictions on her when she came home, so Ryder had brought her back to stay with them. Liese had canceled the appointment so she and Tiffany could spend the afternoon getting mani-pedis.

"Oh, shit."

"I'm taking it you forgot to reschedule?"

"I definitely forgot to reschedule." Panic bottomed out her stomach. She had no idea how Ryder would feel about something like this. Or how she felt about it. She was only twenty-nine. She'd never been in a rush to start a family; she'd always assumed as long as she jumped on the train before she turned thirty-five, she'd be fine. It wasn't like it was an issue. She and Ryder were focused on their respective careers, and they had plenty of time to figure out those details in the future.

Dr. Glass gave her a reassuring smile. "It's very unlikely you're pregnant, Liese. It can take months before your hormones regulate enough for you to start ovulating again. However, in light of your recent complaints and your missed shot, I think it would be a good idea to run some blood tests just to rule out the possibility."

Less than thirty minutes later, Liese had confirmation that however unlikely, she was indeed pregnant. She wasn't very far along, maybe only seven weeks, but the hormones didn't lie, nor did the stick she'd peed on in the doctor's office bathroom.

This explained the fatigue and periodic nausea. The term *morning sickness* was a farce, according to Dr. Glass. It usually didn't set in until around the eight-week mark, but lucky Liese had gotten to experience it early—and it could occur at any time of day. Some women felt ill all the time, throughout their entire pregnancy. Liese couldn't imagine nine months of feeling hungover.

She went to work in a daze. Ryder sent her messages to see how she was feeling, but she kept her responses brief. The last thing she wanted was to tell Ryder he'd be a daddy via text.

Liese was sitting at the kitchen island when Ryder came home. She waited for the water to boil so she could make pasta, which was about as much as she could handle right now where food was concerned.

He dropped his briefcase in the doorway, brows pulled low.

"Hey. I didn't hear you come in," Liese said, looking up.

"I called for you. Twice."

"Oh. I must have been daydreaming."

"Evidently." He crossed over to the stove and turned off the burner. Steam came out from under the rattling lid as he moved it aside. "Are you okay?"

Liese patted the chair beside her. "We need to talk."

Ryder froze, unease clouding his features. "Liese?" He rounded the island, taking her face in his hands. His thumbs brushed across her cheeks, spreading wetness. She hadn't even realized she was crying.

"Has something happened? Are Sandy and Marshall okay?"

Her parents had left on another of their many retirement adventures a few weeks ago. They were somewhere in Europe again, visiting tourist attractions. The last she'd heard from her mom, they were heading to Paris. She had a Skype date scheduled with them later in the week, provided they had service.

"They're fine." She sniffed.

"Then what is it? Liese, talk to me. You're scaring me right now. All I can come up with are worst-case scenarios."

She took a deep breath. There was no sugar coating it, so she blurted out the news. "I'm pregnant."

He blinked. And blinked again. "I'm sorry. Pardon?"

"I'm pregnant," she repeated, struggling to maintain eye contact.

"But you get the shot."

"I missed one."

He wasn't freaking out, so that was a plus. However, he wasn't doing much of anything, so Liese couldn't be sure how to gauge him. Ryder had a pretty good poker face, and while they'd been together the better part of two and a half years, sometimes he could be difficult to read. Especially through her tears.

He turned her chair sideways and dropped into the one beside her. He dragged her closer, chair legs screeching across the floor. He didn't so much as flinch at the sound, his focus solely on her. "How do you feel about this?"

"I don't know. I think I'm still in shock."

"Beyond shock are you happy? Is this what you want?"

"We haven't really talked about children, or what the future would look like." All discussions pertaining to their life plans had revolved around their careers.

"But you would want this? To have a child with me?" His hands slid up the outside of her thighs and back down to rest on her knees.

"I thought eventually, maybe . . ."

He seemed to understand her need for reassurance. "Planned or not, Liese, I want this with you."

"You do?"

"Of course. Why do you seem so surprised?" He knees pressed against the outside of her thighs.

"It's so unexpected. I'll have to take time off from my job, and you work such long hours."

"I will make amendments to be here with you more, as much as you need me to be. I want to make a life with you, Liese, and if that includes children, it's even better."

"Really?"

"Really." He smiled softly. "I'll be forty this year. It's about time I got you knocked up."

Liese smacked his arm. "Oh, God. What are your parents going to say?"

"Giselle will probably have a coronary. Wouldn't that be perfect?"

"Ryder!"

"It would solve so many problems."

"She's going to have a conniption," Liese said. "Remember how upset she was when she found out you'd moved me in here?"

Ryder rolled his eyes. "I think we're well beyond that mattering. She'll get over it if she has any desire to spend time with her grandchild—under careful supervision."

Liese bit the inside of her lip to stop her smile. Lord help them if it was a girl. "Still, I'm sure she'll be upset that we're going about this backward."

"Hold that thought." Ryder pushed his chair back and rushed from the kitchen.

Aside from his sudden and unexplained departure, the revelation had gone over much better than she'd anticipated. Ryder seemed genuinely excited.

He returned a minute later. Instead of sitting back down, he pushed his chair out of the way and rearranged hers.

"What are you—" Celebratory sex would be welcome.

However, Liese wasn't so sure she wanted to do it in a chair.

Ryder dropped to one knee. "I planned out a much more romantic venture for this, but in light of recent disclosures—" He produced a small velvet box from his pocket. Flipping the top open, he displayed a gorgeous white-gold ring inset with a ridiculously large diamond.

"Oh my God. Ryder! This is stunning, but you don't need to—" She had to wonder how long he'd had it, and when he'd been planning to ask.

"You will be my wife before you're the mother of my child— if that's what you want, of course."

"Are you asking or ordering?" Liese couldn't contain her grin.

"Asking. Mostly."

"In that case, I would love to be your wife. Mostly."

"I haven't even asked you officially yet, but that helps take the pressure off. Thanks." His expression turned serious, and he cleared his throat. "Annaliese Harper, I adore you. Will you be my wife?"

"Yes. Please. I would love to."

Ryder's smile was heart-stopping as he slipped the ring on her finger.

"I think I like the way that looks on you, Mrs. Whitehall." He brought her hand to his lips and kissed her finger just above the ring.

"Who said I was taking your last name?"

"Hyphenate?" Rising to his feet, he traced the contour of her jaw, the touch reverent. He stepped between her parted legs.

"We'll talk about it." Liese slipped his tie around her fist and pulled his mouth down to hers. "Later."

"Bedroom?" Ryder asked against her parted lips.

"Are you asking or telling again, Mr. Whitehall?"

"Both." Ryder dipped down. Slipping his hands under her ass, he encouraged Liese to wrap her legs around his waist. "Be aware, Mrs. Harper-Whitehall, being my wife isn't going to make you exempt from spankings."

"I'd hope not. Otherwise you can have the ring back." The dark look in his eyes made her smile wider. "And I think I prefer Mrs. Whitehall."

His smile widened, and then he grew wholly serious. "You can take whatever last name you want, just as long I get the most important part of you."

Emotion overwhelmed her as she watched her future unfold in Ryder's eyes. "And what part is that?"

He pressed a warm palm against her sternum and brushed his lips over hers. "Your heart."

NYT and USA Today bestselling author of PUCKED, Helena Hunting lives on the outskirts of Toronto with her incredibly tolerant family and two moderately intolerant cats. She writes contemporary romance ranging from new adult angst to romantic sports comedy.

Find more books by Helena Hunting

by visiting helenahunting.com